MANOEUVRES

MANOEUVRES

By Fredric Neuman

LONDON
VICTOR GOLLANCZ LTD · 1984

Copyright © 1983 by Fredric Neuman

British Library Cataloguing in Publication Data
Neuman, Fredric
  Manoeuvres.
  I. Title
  813'.54[F]   PS3564.E846

  ISBN 0-575-03358-4

Printed in Great Britain by
St Edmundsbury Press, Bury St Edmunds, Suffolk

Author's Note

LIKE ABE REDDEN, the protagonist of this story, I am a psychiatrist. I served, as he did, in the United States Army during the Cuban missile crisis and was posted, as he was, to the 20th Station Hospital in Nuremberg, Germany. I hope, therefore, I have drawn certain details of place and time and circumstance accurately. In all other respects, however, this book is fiction. None of the characters is based on anyone I have ever known. During my tour of duty, the United States came to a new status of forces agreement with the German republic. Under its terms the local German authorities could try American soldiers for crimes committed against German citizens. Since it is a matter of public record that I testified as an expert witness in the first such trial, I should add explicitly that there is no similarity between that notorious murder case and any events that take place in this book.

MANOEUVRES

Prologue

MY FATHER joined the army immediately after the bombing of Pearl Harbor and served throughout World War Two, mostly in Europe. I was seven years old when he enlisted and close to twelve when he came home. He was gone almost the whole time. I don't think I missed him very much, but naturally I looked forward to his return, which took place some months after the end of the war. My first conversation with him was delayed an additional few days because he needed to unpack, he said, and unwind. My father wound down very slowly, like a defective clock, in fits and starts and never altogether. We met that occasion in the library, alone, except for our ancestors, who stared down at us out of paintings hung at intervals about the room. Each portrait was underlined by an antique ceremonial sword drawn from my father's collection of antique ceremonial swords, dueling pistols, and cannon.

"Well, son, how have you been?" he said, addressing me from the other end of the couch.

"Fine."

"Have you been a good boy? Getting along with your cousins?"

"Well, sort of."

"I hope you've been listening to your mother. A wonderful woman, your mother, sensible most of the time and reliable. She works very hard. I hope you've been working hard too, in school. You practice the piano every day, I know. Do you enjoy that?"

"No."

"That's nice," he said. He drank a little out of a highball glass and looked here and there about the room. "It's very important to practice hard and work hard. Life is a struggle. In order to succeed, you have to give it everything you've got. You have to commit yourself. Do you play team sports?"

"No."

"It's very important to play team sports. You can't accomplish anything in life all by yourself. No one can. You have to get along with people. You have to be part of a team. That's the way it is in business. That's the way it is in the army. Most powerful army in the world. And how do you think we got that way?"

"Because everyone in the army played team sports."

"No, of course not. But everyone in the army is part of the same team. I was in the quartermaster corps. A major. Running a supply depot is like . . . it's like being a quarterback on a football team, making sure the ball goes where it's supposed to. Supplies. The army runs on its stomach."

"I play chess."

"And the other soldiers . . . just as important. And the navy and the air force. Everyone has his own part to play. Teamwork." He held his glass out in front of him, toasting the team. He went on to say something I didn't understand about Notre Dame drawing their linemen from all walks of life; then he fell silent.

"So, how was the war?" I asked finally.

"War is hell, son. Chasing back and forth all over Europe. Paris, Frankfurt, Berlin. Burning things down. Blowing them up. Destroying everything. Tanks. Airplanes. Blasting the damn Germans out of their holes. Hunting them down like animals, which is what they are. I went up to the front a few times myself."

"Sounds awful."

"Well, somebody had to do it."

"I want to be a doctor."

"The Germans need to be slapped down every fifteen or twenty years. You'll be in the army someday, hunting them down, blowing them up all over again."

"I don't want to go into the army. I don't like all that stuff."

My father stared at me soberly, swizzling his drink around
with a finger.

"Maybe the Germans learned their lesson this time," I said.
"Besides, they can't all be bad. Maybe you killed all the bad
ones. Blew them up or burned them down."

"Come over here for a second, would you?" my father said,
after a moment's pause.

"What for?"

"I want to take a good look at you."

I went over and stood in front of him. He put his glass down
on the arm of the couch and took up my head between both his
hands, turning it to one side then to the other. For some time,
intently, he stared at me.

"You know," he said thoughtfully, finally, "you look a little
Jewish."

"What?" I said, pulling back. "Jewish? I'm not Jewish! I'm
Methodist! We're all . . . aren't you Methodist?" Actually I
wasn't sure what we were. We never went to church.

"Yes, I am, son. But, you know, your grandfather, your
mother's father, he was Jewish. He died before you were born.
You were named after him. Abraham." He said my name slowly,
as if it felt strange on his tongue.

"So what? That doesn't mean I'm Jewish."

"It would if you were in Germany."

"Oh, yeah? Well, I'm not in Germany, and I don't have to be
Jewish or anything else I don't want to."

"Listen, don't be so sensitive. Your mother tells me you're too
sensitive about everything. That's no good. You can't go through
life being sensitive, you know."

"Yeah, I'm sensitive. And wool makes me itchy, so let me go."
My father had an arm around my neck and was rubbing the
sleeve of his uniform against my ear. Separated from the army
three days before, he was still wearing his uniform. "And you
smell from whiskey," I added, squirming around.

"You know," he responded, picking up his glass with his free
hand, "you're turning into a fresh kid. Besides being sensitive.
You better get used to this uniform. It's standard U.S. Army
issue, and someday you'll be wearing it."

"Like hell I will. I'm not joining any army," I said, wrenching myself away, spilling my father's drink all over his lap.

"Clumsy too," he commented.

I was drafted eleven years later toward the end of the 1961 Berlin crisis, in fact, after the end of it. The news reached me at the hospital where I was working as a resident.

"I can't believe it!" I cried out to my supervisor, putting down the telephone. "It's a mistake! Some kind of awful mistake! The crisis is over. They told me they weren't drafting any more psychiatrists. I've been going down to Washington every couple of weeks just to check. They don't need any more psychiatrists, they said. Jesus Christ! I don't believe it. This can't be happening. If I thought this could have happened, I would have joined the Public Health Service. I could have been a psychiatrist in Leavenworth for a couple of years. Convicts. I could have been curing convicts. Anything but the army. Shit. Hell, if worse came to worst, I could have joined that reserve unit downtown. A psychiatric unit. Forty guys training in Greenwich Village every Tuesday just in case there's a worldwide psychiatric crisis or something. All the latest equipment. Except no psychiatrist. Of course. What psychiatrist in his right mind wants to kill Tuesdays for the next seven years hanging out with the U.S. Army? Not to mention summer vacations. But I would have done it. Jesus, they were dying to have me. A fully trained psychiatrist. Well, almost fully trained. That would've been better than wasting all of my time for two whole years. Dammit, they told me they had enough psychiatrists!"

I got up and started pacing around the room, waving my arms and crying out from time to time. My supervisor, a blond, heavyset fellow, watched me thoughtfully, closing his eyes every once in a while in order to concentrate more fiercely. Up until the moment the telephone rang, he had been listening to me present my treatment of a schizophrenic, a woman who was convinced the world was coming to an end and who, it seemed to me suddenly, might have known what she was talking about.

"Do you know what this means?" I exclaimed. "I'm going to be gone in a couple of weeks. They won't even let me finish the residency. That research project I'm doing, forget that. Studying dying patients. By the time I get back, they'll all be dead. Goddamn it, I think it matters to those people that I come around every day. Now I'm going to be in the army for two years! Jesus Christ!" I said again, getting mad all over again. "They can make me an obstetrician if they want to. If they want to, they can send me to Korea or Alabama, or someplace like that. They can . . . Huh? What?"

I thought my supervisor had said something under his breath, one of those pithy but usually inaudible remarks he was wont to make about the vicissitudes of the superego or whatever. His eyes were closed again, his brows knit. It was an especially grave expression. Suddenly he snorted derisively, summing up, I thought, his feelings about the army, or about me, or maybe about the case I had been presenting. But it turned out he was snoring.

Because of the large number of doctors who had been inducted that year, basic training was shortened to two and a half weeks, distilled into an "especially intense and demanding experience," according to the master sergeant who welcomed us. We would be expected in this brief time to learn the use of firearms, survival techniques, map-reading, and a number of other subjects equally important to the practice of military medicine in peacetime. We would be challenged intellectually, physically, and socially. As a consequence we would grow as men so that we could take our honored places in the halls of the medical corps. The halls of the medical corps were somewhere near the halls of Montezuma, I supposed, this side of the shores of Tripoli.

As it turned out, the days resembled each other remarkably despite the diversity of our training and its varied challenge. The weather in San Antonio was uniformly hot. The temperature went over 100 degrees Fahrenheit every single day. "Very hot, but very dry," everyone kept saying, as if that made it all right. After a while I felt like I was shriveling into a new and unfamiliar shape, all wrinkled.

The landscape was also unchanging: army barracks, the parade ground, the desert. The classroom. Most of every day was spent in the classroom learning, for instance, how to salute. To make the subject come alive for us, the instructors staged a small entertainment in which soldiers of different rank walked back and forth across the lecture stage greeting each other. Intermittently throughout this demonstration and all the others, we were ordered to stand at attention so that no one would miss anything important by falling asleep. After the first week I found I had learned something interesting: It was possible to sleep standing up, a facility I had previously thought peculiar to ruminants such as cows or giraffes.

At the end of this intensive experience, the day before we were due to graduate, I was told to report to the office of the colonel in charge of our training program. When I walked in, he was speaking crisply into a telephone, at the same time fiddling absently with a pile of charts on his desk. He looked up at me from time to time, frowned, then went on talking. I waited patiently. He was discussing his bowling scores—not the sort of subject that could sustain anyone's interest for very long, it seemed to me; and so it turned out. Shortly he hung up and began leafing through one of the charts in front of him. Finally, he looked up at me, still frowning.

"Are you standing at attention, Doctor?" he asked.

"Sure. Can't you tell?" I replied. I had my thumbs along the sides of my pants legs. That's where they were supposed to be. Heels together. Shoulders back.

He stared at me. "Your shirt is unbuttoned."

"It popped a button. The shirt shrank. Everything seems to shrink in this climate. I think I shrank a little myself." I offered him an ingratiating little smile.

"You seem to have stained your pants."

"Right. Coffee."

He inspected me another moment or two, seemed about to say something else, then changed his mind. Instead he turned back to the chart. "You've been in trouble, one thing after another, the whole time you've been here."

"What? What do you mean?" I asked.

"Sir," he said.

"What?"

"Sir. Address me as sir. I am your superior officer."

"Yes, sir, but—"

"Just keep quiet until I ask you a question."

" 'This man has systematically flouted army regulations,' " the colonel read aloud from the chart, " 'and in general showed a lack of respect. He has failed to appear to company exercises on time. Despite repeated admonitions, he has failed to keep his bunk and his possessions presentable. Contrary to direct orders, he has persisted in eating in class. He has discharged his firearm into the air at the firing range, whooping as if he were an Indian and creating a hazard . . .'"

"Wait a second—"

"'. . . in an attempt to be humorous, he captured a scorpion and placed it in the women's latrine, creating a hazard. On two occasions he was found urinating on the company flagpole . . .' Do you think that's funny, Doctor?" he said, looking up at me. "Pissing on a flagpole?"

"No, sir, as a matter of fact I don't, but—"

"Do you think this is some kind of boy scout camp?" he asked in a rising voice.

"Now, wait a second . . ." I said, coming closer and craning my neck to look around at the chart he was reading.

"Just stand over there, please," the colonel said irritably, pointing at the place I had just vacated. I retreated, and he went on reading. "'Repeatedly this officer has engaged in brawls, the most serious incident occurring when in the company of two other officers he threw a chair through a window of a brothel in Ciudad Acuña, causing an altercation with the Mexican police, and also creating a hazard.' All right," the colonel said, tilting back in his chair, "you can talk now."

"Sir, it wasn't me."

"Well, I don't care if you threw the chair or not. You were there, weren't you?"

"I haven't been anywhere near Ciudad Acuña. I've been spending all my free time in the library. Or in the Alamo. Very historical, I'll always remember the Alamo."

"Don't give me that," said the colonel, picking up the chart again. "Your name is Robert Schulz, isn't it?"

"No. My name is Abe Redden."

"What? Redden?" He looked at my chest. "Where the hell is your name tag?"

"I forgot to put it on . . . sir."

The colonel made a few guttural sounds. Then he began shuffling through the charts on his desk. He seized one near the bottom of the pile, mine evidently, and began to read through it.

"Another troublemaker," he commented shortly, looking at me with renewed distaste. "'This officer has failed to enter whole-heartedly into the spirit of the training program,'" he quoted. "'At times he has allowed his mind to wander, marching off during parade exercises at a different angle from the rest of his unit. . . .' Does that sound more like you, Doctor?" he asked, glancing up at me.

"Well, I'm afraid it does. The heat, I guess."

"'Further, this officer has failed to keep his clothing up to the minimal standards required of a United States Army officer. He refuses to spit polish his shoes, claiming the climate is too dry to spit. His hair is not kept in a state of good grooming. As to his behavior, he has been a laggard. He is always the last officer to come to meals and the last to finish.'"

"I'm a slow eater."

"If you're such a slow eater, you should be the first one to meals," the colonel pointed out tellingly.

"'. . . Similarly, he was the last officer to finish rifle practice, obtaining a zero score. He was last to traverse the desert course during compass maneuvers, delaying the entire company. . . .'"

"I came across this family of armadillos. I never saw an armadillo before. They walk in a line."

"'. . . he was the last officer to finish the infiltration course, last to complete his mandatory series of vaccinations and shots, and last to hand in his insurance forms. In addition, he may be suffering some sort of physical impairment, repeatedly falling down while standing at attention in class. . . .'"

I could sleep while standing up, I had discovered, but not without leaning severely.

"'. . . Throughout, this officer has communicated in his remarks and in his manner a lack of respect for army customs and a lack of understanding of the army's mission.' Is that a fair assessment of your attitude, Doctor?"

I hesitated for a moment. "Well, I suppose so. I don't mean to be difficult," I said, speaking confidentially, "but the fact is, I think I could be spending my time more usefully doing something else."

"Is that so?" the colonel snapped back. "The hell you could. You're protecting your country. Let me tell you, fella, we're in a war. It's a cold war, but it's a real war. The Communist menace hasn't just disappeared in the couple of months since the Berlin crisis. The Russians got a couple of million men under arms. They got one of the biggest navies in the world, and they're turning out atomic weapons faster than you can spit—assuming it's not too dry for you to spit. They're mobilizing. You know why?"

"No. I suppose because they think we're a menace."

"Is that right?" The colonel sat forward on the edge of his chair. "All right, you don't know why, I'll tell you why. Because they want to take over the whole freaking world. That's why. They want to destroy civilization as you and I know it. And our mission—your mission—is to stop them. The U.S. Army is all that's keeping those bastards at bay. Them and the rest of the Goddamn Commies. The Chinese. You know how many Chinese there are?"

"Billions."

"Hey, listen. If you're going to be some kind of wiseass, you can forget about that cushy assignment in Nuremberg. You'll be figuring out how to spend your time usefully in some mobile army station hospital. A bunch of tents in the middle of a swamp in Korea where you freeze part of the time and fry part of the time, and sit around all the rest of the time shooting the breeze with a bunch of gooks and a few horny enlisted men. Am I getting through to you, Doctor?"

"Yes, sir. Very clearly, sir."

"Good." The colonel grunted by way of emphasis. "On the other side of the ledger, I have taken note of your academic credentials. It seems you are a competent psychiatrist. Dedicated even, according to these letters. It would be a shame to waste those skills. Psychiatry has its place in a modern fighting force. Mental casualties. But keep in mind that we also need doctors to treat ringworm and frostbite in Korea; so any more farting around and that's where you're going to end up."

The colonel went on in this vein a while longer while I sniveled a little and tried to appear contrite. He gibbered, and I nodded humbly. He waggled his finger at me, and I cast down my eyes. At the end of our interview I saluted smartly. Even so, he stared at me suspiciously as I turned to go. I could tell what he was thinking. He expected me to urinate on the flagpole as soon as I got out of his office.

I

"HEY, WHERE ARE WE GOING?" I asked, staring into the dark.

"He's around here someplace."

"Who? Major . . . uh, the major? He's out here in the grass? In the middle of the night?"

"Major Wormley. Yeah. He likes to . . . hang out here, you could say," the corporal replied, hurrying on ahead of me. The night was foggy and moonless, almost opaque. Corporal Vigliotti —that was his name—was only a few steps away, but no more than a furtive shadow. "Mostly in the evening, when there isn't so much traffic," he went on. "Besides, all day long The Chief is pretty busy, you know. Psychiatry and psychiatry research."

"Traffic?" I repeated after him vaguely. We were off to one side of the hospital, walking through an overgrown field. There were no roads. Not even a path. We had just driven out of the Nuremberg traffic, and I could hear it still faintly, but off in the distance.

"Listen, why don't we do this tomorrow," I suggested. "It's late. I've been traveling for the last day and a half, and I'd sort of like to get some sleep."

"Sorry, Captain, I got orders. This is very urgent, according to Major Wormley. He wants to see you first thing, he said, day or night, as soon as you get in. He's got something big on his mind, I'm afraid. Watch it."

This warning came too late. I had walked into a pipe laid out horizontally at eye level, like a piece of misplaced plumbing. It was only one small part, I could see when my vision cleared, of a peculiar system of intertwining and intersecting pipes stretching out seemingly without limit into the darkness above me.

"At ease, men," came a deep voice from somewhere within this structure.

"Yes, sir," replied Vigliotti, snapping to attention. "Major Wormley, sir, this is Captain Redden. Captain Redden, sir, this is Major Wormley, chief of the neuropsychiatric unit, 20th Station Hospital."

A low chuckle. "No need to be so formal, I think," said Major Wormley, who I could see now was hanging out—literally—above me on what seemed to be parallel bars. "After all, we're . . . going to serve together for . . . two years," he went on, stopping to take a breath every few words. "We're both professionals . . . right, Captain? Colleagues . . . like to think we could be . . . friends. You can call me . . . Chief."

"Uh . . . hello," I said.

With a grunt Wormley threw a leg up and clambered onto some kind of platform. He lay there, looking down at me, a heaving silhouette against the lesser blackness of the sky. Suddenly before my horrified gaze he grew tentacles and a beak. He was a spider, entangled in a web made out of plumbing, twitching nervously and waiting to pounce. Hissing. Do spiders hiss? It must have been the blow to my head. I rubbed my forehead and tried to gather my wits.

"I know just what you're thinking," Wormley said. "You're ambivalent. You have misgivings about being here. You don't have to tell me. I know because I felt the same way. All of a sudden you're an officer in the United States Army stationed a million miles from home. You've been looking forward to this chance forever, it seems. The opportunity to fulfill yourself. You're committed to doing whatever you can to help your country, and, who knows, maybe do something along the way to achieve a stable peace here in Europe. At the same time you're uneasy, unsure of yourself, worried about your ability to perform under stress. What if war should break out? You don't know how you would react. How could you? In school or in training all your life. Then one day the government comes along and tells you you're a man. It's a sobering thought."

"What?" I asked, still dazed.

"What 'what'?" queried Major Wormley.

"What . . . what are you talking about?"

"Your self-doubts. I just wanted to let you know I've been there myself, wondered whether I could hack it. But when the chips were down, I was there."

Wormley fell silent. A nearby cricket commented at length in a soft staccato, then farther away, a bird.

"Where?" I asked, feeling some sort of response was expected of me.

Wormley grunted. His silhouette was rising and sinking rhythmically. He was doing push-ups, I figured out.

"You'll make it too," he reassured me, stopping after the third push-up. "The army can be everything you expected it to be, a chance to make new friends and learn new skills, a chance to see a little bit of the world. And a chance to keep in top physical condition. You'll have the opportunity to play sports. But it's not all fun and games. Europe is a tinder keg, ready to blow up at the drop of a match. Berlin is still festering. Italy is full of revolutionaries. In England itself there are right-wingers and left-wingers and God knows what. This city is teeming with spies. Communists and neo-Nazis. Latvians even. Nuremberg is crossroads of a thousand dreams. And I hear from my sources that something particularly important is threatening. Something . . . *particularly* important," he said again for emphasis. "When I say 'sources,' I don't mean to imply intelligence sources, of course, or secret sources of any sort, or indeed any sources other than those sources readily available—and a few additional sources, I might say."

"What was that?" I called out. Although I could hear Wormley clearly, I had the strangest feeling I couldn't hear him clearly.

"There's likely to be a war," Wormley replied in a loud voice, "an historic confrontation between East and West right here in Europe and right now. Our mission, our purpose—our raison d'être—is to respond to that challenge. As psychiatrists we will have to set an example because esprit de corps is essentially psychological."

"What?" I cried.

"What I mean specifically is, number one, you can drink, but no lying around in a drunken stupor. Number two, you can have sexual intercourse, of course, but not in such a manner as to cast disrepute on our unit. Number three, absolutely no criminal behavior of any sort. I'm speaking as your chief now, but also as someone interested in your best interests. I have some special plans that I don't want to disclose just yet—very special plans—and you're going to play an important part. But, I know this is a lot for you to absorb your very first night here in Germany. Don't worry. I'm not talking about a time scale of days. It may take weeks, maybe months. But three months from now, at the latest, you watch. There's going to be a hell of an excitement around here." Abruptly, Wormley flipped himself off the platform and onto an adjacent pipe, from which he hung, his legs curled over the pipe, upside down, unmoving, like a bat.

After a moment or two, I realized our interview had come to an end.

"Is that guy a psychiatrist?" I asked the corporal as we withdrew across the field.

"That's what they tell me," he replied.

THREE MONTHS LATER

It was drizzling as usual. I sat with my feet up on a desk watching the rain on the windowpane flow into rivulets, each stream emptying abruptly to make way for another. Interesting that drops all of the same size striking the same surface still manage each time to trace a different path. Well, not terribly interesting. I turned my attention to the ceiling, which had a sort of interesting pattern of cracks radiating from the corner. Long-legged spiders, they looked like, chasing each other over to the light fixture, a not at all interesting cluster of three naked bulbs. One of the bulbs was flickering, and then, as I watched it, went out, as if my scrutiny were too much for it to bear. I slid my chair forward, and trying to disturb my position as little as possible, removed from a drawer that day's copy of *Stars and Stripes* in case there was a particle of news that had escaped me the first four or five times I had read the newspaper. But there wasn't. Carefully, I pulled the sheets of the paper apart, balled them, and set out to determine just how many I could propel directly into the wastebasket at the other end of the room under the sink. The sink made the shot tricky, and I ended up missing most of the time. I did better with a few pages torn from an army manual. Then, adroitly I thought, I flipped a couple of paper clips into a coffee cup that stood on a shelf. Finally I ran out of things to throw into things. In the United States Army, when you had nothing to do, you really had nothing to do.

There was also no one to talk to. The emergency room was empty of patients, and the nurse had wandered off to do other things. The sergeant on duty had retired for a few beers to the NCO club, off limits to me since I was a captain. It seemed to me at that moment I was not so much stationed in Nuremberg, Germany, as indicated on my orders, but in an empty cave far underground. But it was my fault, I knew, if I was bored. Whatever the army was doing, or not doing, I should have been able to find some useful way of spending my time. Still, I wished something would happen. I remember thinking that.

About midnight a young lieutenant walked into the emergency room carrying his eleven-month-old child, a fat little kid who looked at me suspiciously when I came at him with a tongue depressor. The baby had an acute tonsillitis. I had the nurse give him a shot of penicillin, which set him to screaming, a really huge sound for such a little kid. No amount of chucking him under the chin could pacify him, although he did finally accept a lollipop from me once he was safely on his father's shoulder and halfway out the door. Tonsillitis, luckily, was a condition still within the narrowing boundaries of my ability to practice pediatrics. Two years had passed since my internship, and my knowledge of general medicine was no longer what it should be. On that account I had suggested to the executive officer that the health of the community might be better served by leaving me off the medical duty roster, but he laughed derisively. Days, I was employed as a psychiatrist, so I didn't object to taking occasional night call. I was competent enough, I suppose, to handle most routine medical problems. Unfortunately, the problem of the woman who was suddenly brought into my office was not routine.

She was sitting in a hospital wheelchair, hunched over to one side, holding on to an arm of the chair with shaking and white-knuckled hands as if she thought she might otherwise fall to the floor. She was young, seventeen or eighteen, very thin, and pretty. For just a moment she smiled, which made her seem prettier still. Then she turned away, curling into the corner of the chair. She looked very small and insubstantial. The cotton dress she wore was soaked through. Strands of pale blond hair hung down before her face, which was also pale. She was shivering.

"Local polizei found her in the middle of the woods," said the orderly who wheeled her in. "They were searching for a lost dog. Just stumbled over her by accident. She was sitting against a tree."

"In the rain?"

"Yeah. All by herself, looking kind of sick. They took her here because she's American. You're American, right, kid?"

No response from the girl. She stared at the window or through the window at the rain.

"Yeah," the orderly went on. "I checked her ID. You know, maybe it's a good thing you're on tonight, Doc," he added, tapping his finger against his head and nodding in the girl's direction. "She looks upset."

She looked frightened, I thought. "Hello," I said, leaning forward and touching her on the knee. "What's your name?" No answer, although she did turn to face me. "What's your name?" I said again, a little louder.

"Sandra," she replied softly. "Sandra Collins."

"Good. My name is Redden. I'm a doctor. Now, can you tell me what happened to you? Are you sick?"

"What?" She frowned slowly, as if I had asked a terribly difficult question.

"I want to know if you are feeling sick," I said, still more loudly.

"I can't hear," she replied. "My ears are ringing. And my . . . my stomach hurts."

I reached out to her. She was holding a half-crushed box of candy and resisted for a moment my taking it from her. Her hands were cold. "Did you swallow any pills?" I asked, taking her pulse, which was very fast. Her breathing also was rapid and shallow. She looked at me strangely—suspiciously. Then suddenly her eyes lit up. "Oh, you're Dr. Redden. You're the psychiatrist."

"Yes. Do you know me?" I waited for her to say something,

but she looked past me. Her eyes began to close. "Listen," I said, grabbing hold of her shoulders, "did you take aspirin? Were you trying to . . . did you take a lot of aspirin?"

She shook her head no.

Tinnitus—ringing in the ears—and deafness are signs of aspirin poisoning. So is rapid respiration. And stomach pains. Aspirin is an acid, very irritating to the stomach, in large doses causing pain and vomiting, sometimes bloody vomiting. I could see there was blood on the front of the young woman's dress, almost washed away by the rain. Could she have tried to kill herself with aspirin? It was a method frequently successful.

"Get the nurse, would you," I said to the orderly, "and a stretcher." My patient, whatever was the matter with her, was plainly very sick. I thought she might be going into shock. Her blood pressure was low, 80 over 50.

The nurse and the orderly returned almost at once with the stretcher cart, and the three of us lifted the young woman onto it. She squinted at me as if she had trouble seeing in addition to hearing. That was not a symptom of aspirin overdose.

"I hear ringing and . . . people talking sometimes," she went on in a whisper, grabbing hold of my wrist. "Coming after me. Spying. Not real people. I don't know. I feel mixed up. I can't . . . I don't know what's real anymore. No one cares anyway. Doctors," she said, looking at me. "Even doctors. . . . They don't care, do they?"

"I'm going to try to help you," I said, trying to calm her down. She was writhing on the stretcher. "Are you in pain?" I asked. "Does it . . . where does it hurt?"

But she made no reply except . . . she said something about her father. She didn't want her father to know . . . something, but I couldn't make it out. She was becoming incoherent. Also her pressure was dropping, according to the orderly. She was probably going to need a transfusion. With that in mind, I managed quicky to draw a sample of blood for type and cross matching. At the same time I started an infusion, adding Adrenalin to it. The nurse draped her with a sheet and tried to slip off her dress. Only then, at that late moment, did I notice that the bloodstain on her dress was spreading.

"She's bleeding!" I cried out stupidly. I unbuttoned her dress, tore it a little. There was blood all over her abdomen and groin.

Jesus Christ. I'd been thinking about a drug overdose, not likely to be fatal, not right away anyway; now it turned out she was injured. I should have thought of that first.

"What happened to you?" I said, shaking the girl's shoulders, but she lay limply in my hands.

"Get the gynecologist on call, will you," I told the orderly. "Hurry, this woman's bleeding from her vagina."

"Cold. I'm very cold," the girl murmured.

The blood was welling out of her vagina. Her pressure was down to 55 now, not high enough to make it spurt. She was probably bleeding from an artery, though. Not that there was any way of knowing. I didn't have any GYN instruments, and I probably wouldn't have known how to use them anyway. I inserted some sterile packing into her vagina, although I knew she must be bleeding from farther up, her uterus probably.

"She's going to have to go to the OR," I told the nurse. "I'll take her. You alert the surgical team." I covered her with a blanket, hooked the IV bottle to the side of the trolley, and tried to pull the damn thing out of the office. I bounced a wheel against the doorjamb a few times, then finally maneuvered the stretcher into the hallway. With a shove I propelled it in the direction of the elevators. By the time we got there, a minute later, she looked still worse. I was running the infusion as fast as possible, but the Adrenalin didn't seem to have any effect. Her pulse was thready, barely palpable. Her hands were icy. I jabbed the elevator button again and again. Meanwhile, she lay in front of me, gasping weakly for breath, pale—as pale, literally, as the sheet that covered her.

She didn't actually die until two hours later. I was waiting outside the operating suite when the surgeon came out. I knew she was dead as soon as I saw him. He had that sort of twisted expression, irritable and disgusted.

I asked anyway.

"Yeah, she's dead. Very dead," he told me, sitting down heavily on the bench in the locker room. He pulled off his operating mask and cap, then lit a cigarette. "She had a puncture wound in the posterior vagina. Caught a small vessel. We tied it off, I think, but she must have been bleeding somewhere else. Poured five units of blood into her altogether, but she never got out of shock. Adrenalin didn't do a damn thing. We were going to go in through the abdomen to see if she had torn a hole in her gut, but there was no time."

"I know. No time. It's my fault, I guess. I didn't even realize she was bleeding."

He shrugged. "She must have been bleeding for quite a while. She had a hemoglobin of six."

"Still, you would have had a few minutes more. Who knows, maybe with those few extra minutes . . ."

"Yeah, who knows." The guy sounded bored. He got up and started climbing out of his scrub suit.

"Was she pregnant?" I asked.

"Sure she was. About two, three months. How do you think she got that hole in her vagina?"

"I figured she might have had an abortion."

"Yeah? Well, that's right. An abortion. I never saw such a messed up job. She was bleeding from the cervical os too, so whoever did it probably stuck her a couple of times."

"Could she have done it herself?"

"Not unless she was awfully good with mirrors." He threw the clothes into a locker and kicked the door shut.

"You know," I said, "there's something odd about all this. For one thing, the girl was found sitting in the middle of the woods. What the hell was she doing there? In the middle of the woods, in the rain. When she was brought in, she wouldn't say a thing. She must have had an idea she was bleeding to death; you'd think she'd say something . . . unless she had some special reason. What she did say was all mixed up. Something about spies. She was in a delirium. Hallucinating. Maybe a drug effect. What I really thought was that she had an aspirin overdose. Is that possible, you think? I mean, besides the abortion."

"Listen," the surgeon said, tying his tie and staring at me in the mirror. "She bled to death. From a Goddamn abortion. She made the mistake of getting pregnant in this Goddamn country. She couldn't get a legal abortion, so she went to some Goddamn idiot who stuck a clothes hanger into her up to the level of the umbilicus and killed her. That's all." He buttoned his jacket and slapped his officer's cap on his head. Halfway out the door, he turned back to me. "You did what you could," he said in a quieter voice. "So did the rest of us. It didn't matter. It was just too late, so forget it."

But some things are hard to forget.

I passed the remaining hours of the night sleeping, or trying to sleep, in the on-call room. Emergency was quiet, so no one came for me, but I kept waking up anyway under the impression that the telephone had just rung or that someone was calling my name. Once the sensation was so real I went to the door and looked out into the hallway, but there was no one there.

I was back in my office (the following morning) in time to watch the flag being raised. Each morning, around eight thirty, a group of enlisted men and an officer marched out of the hospital from an exit below my window onto a large field that served usually as an arrival point for ambulances and medevac helicopters, and occasionally as an exercise ground, and also, I was told, as a place for the enlisted men to fornicate, there being bushes. The detachment of soldiers who marched smartly to the flagpole each morning were apparently of a serious turn of mind, unsmiling, very military. They performed their ritual with verve but a certain lack of precision, raising the flag each time—the first time upside down. The second time around they usually got it right. Because this flawed routine was reproduced unfailingly every day, I began to suspect something beyond incompetence, some ulterior purpose. What that purpose could be, though, escaped me. I brought the matter to the attention of the executive officer, Colonel Beasely, who pronounced their performance "overall exemplary," missing the point, perhaps. "Superior training," he explained.

Training was considered very important at the 20th Station Hospital. Our unit had to be in a high state of readiness, for we lay directly in the path of a possible Soviet armored strike across Europe, an "inevitable" attack according to Colonel Beasely, a man whose knowledge of military tactics was picked up over the course of twenty years of practicing obstetrics at various army bases. "The Russian hordth are gonna come thcreaming out of Chec-o-thlo-vakia into Ba-varia, and they're gonna climb all over uth," he liked to say, lisping because of the toothpick he kept wedged in his teeth. We were going to be invaded by a noisy but affectionate band of prostitutes, I thought, the first time I heard this indistinct remark.

The rest of our small psychiatric unit arrived at our suite of offices that morning in the usual order: Corporal Vigliotti first, but already twenty minutes late. He was a chubby, scragglyhaired kid of about nineteen who had been drafted after making the mistake of dropping out of college temporarily to open a fast-food business. Because he was a pretty good cook, the army in its wisdom made him a secretary. I liked having him around to talk to, but his not being able to type was an inconvenience.

Herr Bromberg, who did most of the typing and most of everything else, came punctually at nine. He greeted me in his invariable good humor.

"*Guten Morgen,*" I replied, exhausting my German.

Herr Bromberg was a very neat man, about forty-five, one of the German nationals employed by the 20th Station Hospital in order to free army personnel for combat assignments, of which at the moment there were none. Like all the Germans I had met so far, he had fought on the Eastern Front during the war. He had no totalitarian sympathies, he assured me, Nazi or Communist. I liked to think he was telling the truth since he seemed to be a nice guy.

There hurried into the reception area finally The Chief, Major Edward Wormley, hunched over, jaw thrust forward. A quick hello, then into his office, not to emerge, hopefully, for the rest of the morning.

"Only ten minutes to go until coffee break," observed Vigliotti, sitting behind his desk and looking at his watch. "That's six hundred seconds. Five hundred and ninety-nine, five hundred and ninety-eight . . ." Since coming to Germany, the corporal had become adept at converting any unit of time into seconds, practicing most of the day, as he did, figuring the number of seconds left in his tour of duty, then about thirty-seven million.

I looked over his shoulder at my schedule for that morning. As usual I was doing most of the work. Wormley had no patients. The mentally ill made him feel uneasy, he once confided in me. Usually I didn't mind. What the hell, there wasn't anything else to do. But that day I would have preferred having fewer patients. I kept seeing that young girl bleeding to death in front of me, and I knew I was going to have trouble thinking about anything else.

The only person in the waiting room was, surprisingly, a full colonel. Usually if a bird colonel wanted a psychiatrist for some reason, the psychiatrist visited him rather than the other way around. I thought he had come to see Wormley about some administrative matter, determining why there was disaffection in the canine unit, or something similar. That very problem, in fact, had been brought to my superior's attention six months before. He pointed out that the low morale was probably due to the high frequency of getting bitten, an observation for which, unbelievably, he was awarded a medal. The experience had left a considerable mark on him. He thought of himself now, he confided in me one afternoon, as having a special insight into the nature of human affairs that went beyond mere training but was in its essence intuitive. On this occasion, however, the colonel was waiting to see me.

"Colonel James Collins, sir," Vigliotti announced, standing up rather stiffly behind his desk, managing a degree of formality I had thought beyond him.

But there was something about the man who came up to me that seemed to call forth a certain amount of respect. Even I felt it. Not because he was a senior officer; I had seen enough of them to be unimpressed. Nor was there anything obvious that set him apart from those others. His uniform was ornamented by the same obscure insignia. His chest bore perhaps somewhat more than the usual number of ribbons, most of which meant nothing to me except the striped red of the Silver Star and the badge of the expert marksman, an indicator of a real skill, however irrelevant to the pursuits of civilized men. What distinguished him was something in his expression, a silent, unmoving cast to his eyes, although he smiled at me politely. I brought him into my office and we sat down to stare at each other.

"What can I do for you, Colonel?" I asked finally.

"I understand you took care of my daughter last night, Dr. Redden."

For a moment I couldn't think whom he was talking about; then I sat up quickly. "Oh, I'm sorry," I said. "I thought . . . I didn't realize who you were."

"Yes. I understand. No reason why you should." He sat quietly with both hands on his knees, looking around the room, at my cluttered desk, at the spittoon I kept within throwing distance, and at me. "You didn't even know Sandra, did you?" he said. "You never saw her before last night?"

"No. I didn't know her. That's right. Although I thought for a moment she might have known who I was. I'm terribly sorry about what happened."

"Thank you. She was a nice girl. A good daughter."

"I'm sure she was."

"You say she knew who you were?"

"I'm not sure. She seemed to recognize my name, but she was obtunded. I mean . . . her mind wasn't clear. Drugs, maybe. Or . . . she was losing so much blood."

"Did you have the opportunity to speak to her?"

"Not for long. She needed emergency surgery. I guess you know that. At first I thought it was something else. I thought she was emotionally disturbed . . . but I only spoke to her for a few minutes," I said again, lamely.

"Probably you were right, Doctor," he replied, turning to look out the window. His gray eyes were red-rimmed. He must have been up all night, I thought. Still, he was clean-shaven. "My daughter and I aren't . . . we weren't very close, but for some time she seemed to be worried. Something must have been troubling her. It's funny, you live with someone, all alone practically, and yet you don't know what the other person is thinking."

"Your wife . . . ?"

"I'm divorced. I have a son, too, who lives with me. Almost two years old. But he's not . . . normal. Sandra used to take care of him. I don't know what I'm going to do now."

"She must have been a very special person."

"Yes."

"Colonel," I said after a moment's thought, "did you know your daughter was pregnant?"

"They told me. If she had confided in me, I would have found some way to help her."

"I'm really very sorry," I said.

The colonel studied me for a moment. "Not your fault, Doctor," he said abruptly. "I came to see you this morning just in case. . . . I thought Sandra might have said something to you before she died."

"She was rambling. Not making much sense. She said I shouldn't tell you *something*, but I don't know what she was referring to. Probably she didn't want you to know she was pregnant."

"Probably. There was . . . nothing else?"

"No. Why? Were you wondering . . . did you know who the
. . . the father was, or . . ."

"No, I don't care about that. What difference would that make
now?"

"Of course you're right," I said.

Collins got up and, smiling at me mechanically, came over to
shake my hand. "Thank you, Doctor."

"Colonel," I said, walking with him to the door, "there were a
couple of things I was wondering about your daughter's death,
if you don't mind my asking."

"What do you want to know?"

"Sandra was acting very strange in the emergency room, confused. And paranoid, I think. I suppose she could have been de-
lirious, or simply reacting to the trauma of the abortion, but I
was wondering . . . had she been showing signs recently of
being especially upset? Not just worried, but—"

"No, Doctor," he replied. "Sandra was not psychotic and she
didn't use drugs. I didn't spend as much time with my daughter
as I should have, but I would have noticed if there was something serious the matter with her. She was lonely, impres-
sionable. She didn't always behave sensibly, but she wasn't
crazy. She was just an ordinary kid."

"Was she all right physically? She didn't seem to be able to
hear me very well. She wasn't . . . deaf, was she?"

"Deaf?" He looked at me critically. "Certainly not."

I felt like I had asked a foolish question, and perhaps I had. A
man whose daughter has just been killed shouldn't have to satisfy someone's medical curiosity. The colonel turned to leave.

"Just one more question," I said, hesitating, but not for very
long. "Sandra was found in the middle of the woods. Do you
have any idea what she might have been doing there?"

"I'm not sure, Doctor," he said, his voice quiet. "I imagine the
people who did this thing wanted to get rid of her, so they took
her there and left her. In the rain." He looked out the window as
if that awful place in the woods was within view. The weather
was clear for a change, but I could see the rain coming down
still, reflected in his eyes.

The empty, silent space he left behind was filled a moment
later by Vigliotti, who leaned into my office to tell me I was

wanted urgently by Major Wormley for a departmental meeting. The department of psychiatry consisted of Major Wormley and me, and the departmental meetings were conversations between the two of us, with the major doing most of the talking. Corporal Vigliotti usually sat in to answer the telephone. Herr Bromberg took verbatim notes, which were compiled as a monthly newsletter and distributed to Major Wormley and me. These urgent meetings were held every day.

"Look, Ed," I said, standing in the doorway to his office, "how about holding today's meeting without me. I have an important phone call."

"No can do," Wormley replied brusquely, holding up a sheaf of papers. "It's urgent."

"Listen, this awful thing happened last night. This young girl . . ."

"Later, Abe. Later. I just now got back from Frankfurt, and there are urgent matters I have to take up with the whole department."

I was going to argue with him but thought better of it. I sat down heavily and propped my feet up on a coffee table since Wormley was inevitably propelled into a bad mood if I put my feet up on his desk. Even so, he frowned at me.

Wormley had a round face and a reddish complexion, studded with freckles. A frizz of red hair surrounded his head like a halo, making him seem fuzzy and indistinct, a sunset on a hazy day. Any strong feeling brought him to a still ruddier hue. He was this striking color now.

"All right, Ed. I'm here," I said, trying to pacify him. "I'm paying attention."

"As I was saying, we just returned from this extraordinary meeting in Frankfurt," he began, averting his eyes from my general direction. I noticed that I had put on striped socks. That was probably what was annoying him.

"I had the opportunity there of exchanging ideas with all the senior psychiatric staff in the European theater, division level on up. Two or three hundred years' cumulative experience, going back to the Second World War, some of them. All different points of view. Eclectic. It was quite a sight, all those brains in the same room. If someone had set off a bomb during happy hour, he would have wiped out mental illness from London all the way down to Munich." Wormley chuckled a few times over this obscure remark, then cleared his throat. "Seriously, these were the best minds in military psychiatry, and they're privy to information not usually available to us ordinary mortals. That isn't the way it should be, of course. We're here in the front lines, expected to handle anything that comes our way, from homesickness to senile dementia, perverts, criminals, your garden variety psychotic. Adolescents who suck their thumbs. In between times, we're supposed to weed out the bad apples, oversee the stockade, and God knows what else. But, of course, nobody ever lets us in on the big picture, unless there's a war on. Are you getting all this?" he said to Herr Bromberg, who had been holding a pad in his lap, ready to mark down something as soon as somebody said something. The fellow sat up with a start and began scribbling.

Wormley cleared his throat again. "Well, things are going to change now," he said, nodding his head with satisfaction. "Now we're going to be on top of the action."

"Why?" I asked, smiling tolerantly. "Is war about to break out?"

"So, you've read this morning's paper," he replied.

"What do you mean? No, I haven't read the paper."

"They found missiles in Cuba."

And so I learned about the Cuban missile crisis from Major Edward Wormley. As he explained it to me, the Russians, with the connivance of Fidel Castro, had surreptitiously emplaced ballistic missiles on Cuban soil and were in a position now to bomb all of the continental United States with nuclear weapons and poison gas. There was also the possibility the Russians might invade Haiti and take over the Caribbean. An invasion of the United States itself was not impossible. I was somewhat taken aback.

"The Russians are going to invade the United States?" I repeated after him. "The Cubans? That's a little hard to believe."

"Then again, you're not inclined to believe anything, are you?" Wormley replied sharply.

This was a familiar complaint, made most recently after he informed me of the "well-known" homosexual liaison between Freud and Jung.

"It's all front-page news," he said, tossing a newspaper from his desk into my lap, "if you put any credence in the Associated Press."

Sure enough, banner headlines proclaimed the discovery by overflight camera of missile emplacements on the island of Cuba, sixty miles off the Florida coast, bases of a type known to be built by the Russians. In a number of places on the island Russian support troops had been observed. The only Communist country in the western hemisphere not only was arming but was arming to the teeth, with nuclear weapons. President Kennedy was to address the American people that night on television.

"Read about it later, would you, Abe?" Wormley went on impatiently. "The point is, this Cuban thing, whatever is going on, is sending chills up and down everyone's spine. Command is worried. Before you know it the troops will get edgy. The fact is"—he lowered his voice—"we're not really prepared for a military confrontation. Not here in Europe, anyway. *Psychiatrically,* I mean."

"What do you have in mind," I asked, "issuing Thorazine to the troops?"

"No, of course not. Drugs like that can't be handed out indiscriminately. Besides, there's no problem with the availability of drugs or other equipment, for that matter. We have a half-dozen straitjackets in the supply room. That should be enough for anything short of a full-scale war, I should imagine. What I meant is, we're unprepared *psychologically* for war."

"It's true," remarked Vigliotti. "I'm not ready."

"We've been so busy with administrative matters, we've lost sight of our primary mission."

"Which is?" I asked. I had been wondering.

"To provide psychiatric support for the United States Army," Wormley replied emphatically, making it all clear. "I don't mean just in combat, although God knows that's important. Warfare is emotionally upsetting to everyone. If there's going to be a shooting war, we're going to have to treat shell shock and battle fatigue, which, I think, is a little different from shell shock; although, as I'm sure you know, battle fatigue may not occur solely in the heat of battle, but also from tiredness and strain. In the event of an all-out nuclear war, I imagine there will be great numbers of people who will be depressed. They may not require the attention of senior medical personnel, but there should be an elite cadre of medical corpsmen trained to give them supportive psychotherapy, tending to their immediate needs, listening to them, providing emotional support. It's a matter of getting them to look on the bright side. Without, of course, being unrealistic.

"But, you know, we have a larger mission. Because of our special expertise in psychodynamics and group process, we're in a position to facilitate the operation of the army as a whole, expediting command functions, providing liaison, boosting morale—that sort of thing. The army psychiatrist with his special insight into interpersonal relationships provides not just one more medical service; in a way he's the linchpin of the combat team. Well, I think I've explained my ideas on this subject to you before, haven't I, Abe?"

"Yes. A number of times." I looked at my watch. Four and a half minutes. It was getting so Wormley only took about four minutes to irritate me, down from sixteen or seventeen when I first met him.

"The problem is, of course, we still know so little, really, of the human mind." The major paused and swiveled his chair slightly so his eyes came to rest on a plastic model of the brain, which sat on his desk. The answer would be found there some day, he seemed to be saying. "Research," he said out loud. "Research is crucial to the advance of psychiatry and to military psychiatry in particular. Well," he said, tilting his chair forward, "I'm pleased to tell you that now at last, with the threat of war hanging over us, we have the go-ahead, finally, to set up whatever training and research programs we need here in Nuremberg to meet the current crisis."

"Look, Ed," I said, spilling over, "a young girl came into the ER last night. She bled to death, right in front of me practically. From an abortion. She just bled to death. Someone dumped her out in the woods. Do you know what that means when someone dies like that? The hole it leaves in other people's lives—"

"What was that?" said Wormley. Wormley was such a compelling speaker, he had trouble listening to anyone else. I started to explain again, but he interrupted again. "Does this have anything to do with the current military crisis?" he asked, frowning slowly.

"No. I'm telling you this because . . . Aren't you interested? A teen-age girl died here just a few hours ago. Right downstairs. She was killed."

"Killed? With a bazooka?"

"With a bazooka?" I repeated, dumbfounded. "Are you crazy? Of course not with a bazooka! She had an abortion!"

"Oh. I thought you were talking about that corporal. The one who shot his grandmother with a bazooka. Well, it doesn't matter. If someone got killed, I'm sorry; but if war breaks out, you know, there's going to be a hell of a lot of people killed."

"What war? There isn't any war!"

"You're right. And if we keep ourselves strong militarily, there isn't going to be any war. The Russians are no match for us, even with the Cubans. Wait a second!" he said in a louder voice as I started to get up. "I haven't told you the plan."

"I'm sorry, I have to make an important phone call. You'll have to excuse me."

"Listen," Wormley said, speaking quickly. "The plan's already been cleared by the CO. This is the plan. You're going to be in charge of combat training and supportive psychotherapy."

"Me?" I exclaimed. "Why me?"

Wormley smiled. "Don't be so modest. You're a damn good clinician. You've got a lot of innovative ideas. Very independent. Sometimes too independent." A friendly chuckle.

"And you? What are you going to be doing while I'm getting everyone set for World War Three?"

"Research. It's my forte."

Talking to Wormley was like having an itch in one place and getting scratched in another.

The telephone call I had in mind was to the senior pathologist in Frankfurt. The first time I tried calling him I was connected to the office of the judge advocate in Munich, then to a medical corpsman on a naval vessel somewhere in the Mediterranean. Finally, with the help of a local operator in Frankfurt, I was put through to a Major Stanley Sedgewick, the assistant chief pathologist for VII Corps.

"Yeah, I have a superior," he said in response to my question, "one Colonel Benjamin Cochran, but you can't talk to him. Even I don't get to talk to him. He's in with the senior brass trying to figure a cut-rate way of shipping bodies home. Shallow coffins or something. Or he's playing golf. Kind of rainy for golf, though. Raining where you are?"

We made small talk for a while about the weather and about a cholera epidemic he thought was in the offing; then I told him about Sandra Collins.

"Don't think I can help you, fella," he said. "Not our job. She's a civilian, so the postmortem will be done by the Germans."

"Can't you kind of . . . sit in?"

"Sorry."

"Listen, the Germans get kind of sloppy when Americans are involved. And the army's got a legitimate interest in this kid. She died here in a station hospital. And her father's a colonel. He's going to want to know what happened to her."

"You just told me what happened to her, didn't you? She had a botched abortion and she bled to death, right?"

"Right, that's right, but she was acting funny. I thought she might have taken something."

"Would that make a difference?"

"I don't know."

"Well, I'm sorry. I still can't help. First off, I'm here in Frankfurt and the post'll be done in Nuremberg. Besides, it's against the rules."

I should have guessed that. If there's one thing the army had enough of, besides straitjackets, it was rules. "All right, could you run some tests for me, at least? I drew her blood for a type and cross match. I have some left I could send to you."

I held the test tubes up in front of me. Three small vials, stoppered brightly in purple and red, a thin distillate of all that Sandra Collins had been.

"Sure. Glad to." Sedgewick's voice crackled over the line. "What do you got in mind? We're running a special on lead poisoning. You want to rule out lead poisoning?"

"Hey, I'm not in the mood for joking. The girl practically died in my arms."

"Yeah, right. I'm sorry. Listen, send the stuff along. I'll do what I can. The usual toxicology. Unless you want something special."

"I don't know what I want. Uh . . . aspirin. Can you do an aspirin level?"

"Aspirin? You think she had a headache, too? Oops. Forget it. Forget that remark. I don't know what I'm saying anymore. I spent the morning cutting up a week-old corpse, all bloated and smelly, and it's put me in a nervous mood."

When I hung up, it was almost noon. I could hear the sounds of people walking along the corridor outside my office, talking among themselves, and there was music being played somewhere. I was struck again, as I often was, by how noisy a hospital was. For a moment I held the three small tubes of blood in my hand. In the dimness of the room the liquid looked black and opaque, inert, not the sort of stuff for the want of which someone might die. I wrapped the tubes carefully in a couple of lab sheets and a mailing wrapper and put them to one side on my desk. Next to them I put the crumpled box of candy I had taken from Sandra Collins, jujubes, they were, a kind I used to like when I was a kid because they made my teeth stick together. A last forlorn memento.

Then I began glancing idly through the week's accumulation of memoranda: a list of the movies showing on base, all of which I had seen six months before; new guidelines for the use of intravenous corticosteroids in cases of poison ivy, not relevant to my work; changing hours for the nursery school, even less relevant; a variety of administrative requests from the sergeant major including some insurance forms he wanted me to fill out. I had filled out the Goddamn forms eight or nine times already, it seemed to me. I opened a week-old invitation to a cocktail party at the home of the commanding officer. The party had been held two days ago. There were various other messages from various people. Then, toward the bottom of the pile, I found a note dated the day before yesterday, to call one Sandra Collins. She had left a number. So, she had known me after all, known who I was, at least. She wasn't a patient, even a prospective patient; otherwise her message would have been handed to me. Why had she called, I wondered. What did she want to say to me?

II

PFC PHILLIP MINTON was referred to me for evaluation because of having been found "lying dead drunk on a park bench, his pants open with an erection," which struck me right off as unlikely based on my knowledge of physiology. Because this particular bench was known to be visited by homosexuals, I was asked to determine if an incident of a homosexual nature might have occurred and if so to recommend a suitable punishment, dismemberment, perhaps.

"Maybe you were urinating," I suggested to the private, hoping to find a simple solution; but he denied any such thing. If his penis was outside his pants, he declared primly, it was not done by his hand.

"The work of a masked man?" I enquired.

"All I know is I didn't do it," he insisted. He added parenthetically that he only got an erection in the early hours of the morning, a remark which I took to be whimsy.

A half hour's conversation made plain that I was not going to find out anything about Private Minton's sexual orientation or about his behavior on that particular night. Since he was drunk at the time, he didn't remember anything. Maybe he was smart enough not to remember anything. I sent him away finally with the admonition to be more careful in the future, what with the cold weather coming on. I informed his commanding officer in my report that I couldn't discover why the private's privates were on view. A stern talking-to might be in order, I suggested, but I would not sanction a bad discharge from the service, or mutilation.

I hurried through the paper work, then waited patiently for the second soldier I was scheduled to see that day for administrative action. "Hurry up and wait" was the army motto, after all. But he never arrived. "Hurry up and do nothing" was more like it. How the hell was I going to cope with the army for two whole years, I wondered. I wasn't up to counting off a billion seconds one at a time.

Other people managed better, I couldn't help noticing as I walked through the hospital corridors to the medical library. Various enlisted men, part of the medical detachment, were climbing cheerfully up and down the stairs carrying their belongings from the second floor, where they had been billeted previously, to their new residence on the third floor, where they had just been assigned by our new commanding officer. Each time a new CO was appointed, he put his stamp on the organization by moving the detachment around, usually back and forth between the second and third floors. This migration had been undertaken perhaps ten times during the previous seventeen years. Obviously—obvious to the troops involved as well as to everyone else—one place was no better than the other. But knowing they were wasting their time didn't seem to prevent them, as far as I could tell, from having a good time. One fellow was singing in a quavery but unabashed voice, and snapping his fingers. A coupe of others were tossing a beer can back and forth. I went down another corridor and came across a medical officer and a male nurse pitching pennies outside the obstetrical suite, the officer exclaiming gleefully at a particularly good shot. At the chart rack just inside the ward a few soldiers were hovering about an attractive nurse, telling stories and laughing. Of course, there were some who could not amuse themselves simply by tossing around a beer can or pitching pennies or playing tiddleywinks. (I had discovered a high-stakes tiddleywink game on the dental unit.) For those few, happily, there were the Monkeybar races.

The Monkeybars were a set of intersecting construction pipes that extended like scaffolding from the ground to the third floor just outside the whole west wing of the hospital. It was this structure that I had banged up against the night of my arrival and from which Wormley was dangling, as was his wont, in the name of exercise. The construction had been put up originally to facilitate the removal of the last vestiges of that period when the hospital served the soldiers of the Third Reich—a row of stone swastikas set at intervals into the wall. Unappealing though they were, these symbols had been ignored successfully by a generation of American soldiers until the previous commanding officer, who was a dermatologist, chose to find them offensive, "like a pox, a scab on the face of the edifice." On his own initiative, without the help of the corps of engineers or whoever usually did such things, but with plenty of advice from the orthopedic department, he put up Edifice II, as it was called by the troops, a huge Tinkertoy, assembled in part from cast supports and old bed railings and here and there an occasional fracture pin, joined together with the usual nuts and bolts, and for added strength some plaster of paris and, for those hard-to-reach places, poured cement. It was a good training exercise for the medical detachment, he explained later to the board of enquiry, toning the troops physically, bringing them to a high state of combat readiness. Whatever the benefit to them, unfortunately the structure itself, now called "The Tinkertoy," was out of plumb and so immediately tilted three feet away from the wall, putting the swastikas out of reach. It could not be said, however, to be a fragile device. On the contrary, when the engineers were called in finally to tear the thing down, they found it necessary to use explosives. Even so, half remained standing, judged too dangerous to remove entirely without damaging the hospital itself against which it abutted, at least at ground level. So it was left for the time being, a gigantic skeleton waving its hands frantically in all directions. It was rechristened "The Skeleton" by the troops.

Naturally, there was scarcely a soldier anywhere nearby, brought as they all were to a high state of combat readiness, but with no war to fight, who did not feel impelled to test himself by climbing this tower. Although a straightforward ascent was not easy, there being little to hold on to at this point except jagged metal rods bent at strange angles, the climb was nevertheless soon mastered and other more difficult routes were mapped out, not all in an upward direction. People jumped across from the laboratory on the third floor to a platform made up of a steel stretcher and a filing cabinet bolted together, then climbed down. The filing cabinet seemed to me to detract from the medical motif that made The Skeleton so distinctive; but no one else seemed to mind. The structure was climbed also from side to side, from inside out, diagonally, and so on. The favored route was from the base next to the blood bank up past gynecology and pediatrics to the summit and then by a not inconsiderable leap to the roof of the hospital, from where you could see into the nurses' residence. Although all this climbing seemed dangerous to me, so far only one person had fallen, breaking his leg; and he claimed he had been distracted by a low-flying airplane. Soon there were races and, inevitably, wagering. Tag-team matches were popular, and races against the clock. Seats were rented out in the OR close to the finish line. The record was set finally by a man called "the Monkey," more for reasons of appearance than agility. He beat everyone's time by three full minutes. And henceforth The Skeleton was known as "The Monkeybars."

But after the first week or so even the Monkeybar races, dramatic though they were, lost their appeal for me. I just didn't know how to enjoy myself, my father used to point out to me, holding his whiskey up to the light.

I sat by myself in the medical library, trying to find Sandra Collins in the pages of a medical textbook. There was something unexplained about her death, something I had failed to understand, but whatever it was eluded me still. I closed the book slowly and put it to one side.

The telephone rang distantly, three, then four, times, then stopped. After a time I looked up to see the librarian walking over to me. I was wanted, she said, at my office. An emergency. Sandra Collins was dead, I reminded myself, coming to my feet, but there were other people still alive and not beyond help.

There were two men waiting for me, a Lieutenant Sidney Konigsberg, a young man, unremarkable in appearance, and a sergeant, evidently his escort, who didn't bother to introduce himself. Vigliotti handed me a chart he had made up, which indicated that the lieutenant reported himself as depressed and suicidal. "Upset," the corporal had indicated in parentheses, either by way of summary, or as a preliminary diagnosis. Certainly the fellow looked upset. He was standing uneasily, shifting his weight from one foot to the other, at the same time restlessly rolling and squeezing a cylinder of paper, tearing it without seeming to notice. His jaws were clenched, and he was frowning. He stared at me intently. He started to say something, but then looked at the others and stopped.

"Why don't you go inside, Lieutenant," I said, smiling at him and pointing at my office.

He turned and preceded me into the office, sitting down where I indicated on the couch. I sat opposite. The sergeant, whose name was Kraven, according to his name tag, came in also and sat down inconspicuously next to the window.

"You can wait outside, Sergeant," I said.

"I'm afraid not, sir. I've been ordered to remain with the lieutenant."

"In here? Why?"

"The lieutenant hasn't been debriefed. You know . . ." he said, looking at me expectantly, "debriefed. I think you know about this, sir. Lieutenant Konigsberg was supposed to have an appointment to see somebody here in psychiatry later this week. Our CO sent you a preliminary report."

I looked over to the pile of papers on my desk. I thought I had gone through everything that morning. I moved a couple of papers here and there dispiritedly.

The sergeant glanced at the lieutenant, who remained silent; then he went on. "He . . . uh, the commanding officer thought that under the circumstances it would be better if Lieutenant Konigsberg came today, as . . . well, as an emergency. That's right, isn't it, Lieutenant?"

"I don't understand," I said, interrupting. "What's all this stuff about debriefing?"

"Sir," replied the sergeant, sitting up straight. "As you can see from the records on your desk, the lieutenant—"

"What? What records? I don't see any records."

The sergeant came over and retrieved a manila envelope from under my checker set. He handed it to me. For some reason Major Wormley's name was written across the front. No one could be expected to keep track of all the stuff that came across my desk, I told myself, even if it was addressed to the right person. Most of it had nothing to do with patients at all. This particular record, as it happened, was a good example. No past medical history. No referral form. There was nothing at all to indicate why the lieutenant had to see a psychiatrist. Just a lot of stuff about his military career, much of it obliterated by the notation SECRET OR TOP SECRET.

"What does this have to do with anything, Sarge?" I asked. "Obviously I can't examine a patient with someone else present in the room."

"Sir," he snapped back, "as you can see from that file, the lieutenant's MOS is in security. It's secret work, sir," he went on, speaking slowly and distinctly. He was a top sergeant, which meant he was used to talking to dumb officers. "He has to be debriefed . . . uh, interviewed by a senior security officer before he can talk to you or to anyone else. He may have certain information which he will be instructed not to refer to. Secret information. Just a matter of proper procedure. Until then, I have to remain with him. Of course, no one expects him to betray any secrets, or you either for that matter."

"Oh, good," I said.

"But you don't even have a security clearance. Not that that would be good enough. We operate strictly on a 'need to know.'"

"I don't need to know why the lieutenant is coming to see me?"

"Lieutenant Konigsberg's work is sensitive, sir. Even so, maybe since it's an emergency he would have been allowed to see a psychiatrist alone; but certainly not under these circumstances."

"What circumstances?"

"Well, you know." He glanced quickly at the lieutenant, who seemed to be getting angry in addition to being depressed, suicidal, and upset. "The lieutenant made such a point of it. He asked to see a psychiatrist *alone*," said the sergeant.

"Wait a second," I said, a little confused, "the reason he can't see a psychiatrist alone is because he asked to see a psychiatrist alone?"

"Well, you know. It suggests he might . . . well, might have something to hide."

"All right," I said, anxious not to prolong a discussion, the object of which was sitting uncomfortably a few feet away. "What do you say, Lieutenant? Do you think . . . can I help you in any way?"

"I want to talk to you about something . . . personal, sir," he replied slowly. "That's why I asked to see you alone."

We both looked over to the sergeant, who had taken out a clipboard and was preparing to take *notes*, for Christ's sake.

"Get your commanding officer on the phone," I told Kraven finally.

"It won't do any good," the sergeant replied, coming over to my desk.

"This telephone isn't working," I said. "Use the one next door."

He smiled wanly at me, then went into the waiting room, leaving the connecting door open. I listened to him speak into Vigliotti's telephone, and I watched the lieutenant, whose mood had not been improved so far by having visited a psychiatrist.

But an idea had occurred to me. Very quietly now I got up and, catching Konigsberg's eye, signaled him to follow me. He hesitated but then came after me through the door, a second door to my office, that led directly into the hallway. I pulled him along past the entrance to the waiting room, where I could see Kraven, with his back to me, talking on the telephone. Vigliotti stood next to him, chewing a candy apple and looking out the window. A moment later the lieutenant and I were seated in Wormley's office. Wormley, I knew, was at the local PTA, where he was lecturing on the subject of "Children Who Spit," taking, he had led me to believe, a generally adverse position.

"I don't think this is a good idea," Lieutenant Konigsberg said. "We're breaking all kinds of rules."

"My responsibility," I replied grandly.

Then, having opportunity at last to talk openly, the lieutenant had nothing to say. Frowning still, he stared at the floor, absent-mindedly folding and unfolding the same torn piece of paper. A few moments later the sounds of raised voices, muffled but plainly arguing, penetrated from the next room, then doors slamming, then someone hurrying down the hall. Then, at last, silence.

In that encouraging quiet, finally Konigsberg began telling me why he had come. He spoke in such a low voice, though, and so obliquely, I thought he was trying still not to be overheard. I

wondered why. Nothing he said would have been interesting to
a foreign power. He was feeling awful, he told me, and had
been for weeks. That was no lie, he said, as if I were inclined
not to believe him. He couldn't eat. His sleeping was bad, interrupted by nightmares of people dying or being killed. He felt
discouraged. No matter how much he tried, things went wrong.
No matter how much depended on him, he was a failure. Now,
when success mattered more than ever. A matter of trust. A matter of honor. When the chips were down, no one could count on
him. He couldn't count on himself. When I asked in what way
that was so, he only repeated again that he was a failure. "I feel
terrible," he said again a moment later, absentmindedly pulling
things from his pocket, some loose tissues, a pencil.

"You feel so bad you're thinking of killing yourself?" I asked
when he fell silent.

"No. I just said that because . . . I had to see you right away.
Later this week would have been too late."

"Why?"

"You don't know what that place is like," Konigsberg said,
leaning forward intently. "First of all, it's a secret base. That
means the only people we get to talk to are each other. The married officers live on the economy, in a little rinky-dink German
village in the middle of nowhere, and the rest of us in the BOQ.
Tight discipline. You can't turn around without first getting the
CO's permission in writing. There's no way of getting out of military channels without going to see a psychiatrist or something.
Not that that wouldn't be a good idea for half the people there.
You wouldn't believe what's going on. One guy's out-and-out
crazy. He talks into his headset all day, quotes Deuteronomy,
and no one even notices. Anyway, that's not why I'm here. I'm
depressed, God knows; but I didn't come for that reason either.
Not really. I need your help. Before it's too late. I—"

At this juncture Vigliotti poked his head into the room. "Hey,
so there you are, Captain. You know, everybody's looking for
you. Colonel Beasely is . . ."

"Vito, just close the door, would you, please," I said quickly.

But it was too late. Sergeant Kraven shoved the door open all
the way and charged in. He was pale and breathing hard and
plainly vexed. While Vigliotti went on amiably about how they
searched through all the bathrooms and even that little closet

where they keep the mops and the beer, the sergeant made now familiar noises about regulations and security.

Suddenly there came a brief pounding on the hallway door, followed by the appearance of Lieutenant Colonel Beasely, his face, at least: coal-black eyes focused narrowly along a wide, whiskey-stained nose, rosy lips encompassing the inevitable toothpick. It was a robust face, animated by an expression of surprise. "Why, there he ish!" he said, coming all the way in and pointing at me. "What do you mean, he'sh hiding, Shergeant? Why, he'sh not hiding at all."

I looked over at Konigsberg, who had become very still.

Almost at once our little group was enlarged by Major Wormley, who smiled politely to Beasely, then squeezed by him into his office, now crowded not only by people but by something more abstract, a kind of military presence, musty and discolored, an irritating miasma made up of words like *command responsibility, primary mission,* and *insubordination,* and a certain amount of saluting. The colonel and the sergeant entered into a dispute of sorts that seemed to center on whether or not I was present. Vigliotti went on talking to himself. Meanwhile, Wormley strode over to the desk and stared searchingly at Lieutenant Konigsberg, who appeared in considerably more distress now than when I first saw him.

"This man is sitting in my chair," Wormley said, after a moment's thought.

"You're home early, Ed," I remarked. "Spit problem under control?"

"Why is he sitting in my chair?" Wormley said.

"Because it's the only comfortable chair in the Goddamn office."

"Well, why is he . . . why are you all in my office, anyway? What's going on?"

The sergeant interrupted. "Captain, I'm going to have to report this incident to my superiors. You don't realize . . . you don't know what's at stake here. I think Lieutenant Konigsberg will agree," he went on, speaking quietly again and carefully, "this interview should stop now. I can tell you one thing. You're certainly not going to get rid of me again."

I looked over at the lieutenant, who got up to go. "All right," I said, accepting the inevitable, something I don't like to do. "Get

him debriefed, whatever the hell that is, and I'll see him as soon
as possible. Tomorrow." At least I knew he wasn't going to kill
himself in the meantime. I had learned that much at least. So I
thought.

A little while later, after being scolded properly, which was
also inevitable, I suppose, I was back in my own office, looking
out the window and listening to Wormley, who had pursued me.
He had finished reading to me from the military code, which
looked very severely on soldiers who disobeyed orders, even
doctors; and he was now bringing me up-to-date on the missile
crisis. Russia and the United States were set on a collision
course. Missiles were being reprogrammed to point at population centers. Every hour brought closer the real possibility of a
nuclear holocaust. He asked me if I had come up with any ideas
yet for getting the troops ready.

"You know, training them," he said when I turned to stare at
him. "Like we talked about."

"Uh . . . right," I said, trying to think quickly. "First off . . .
first of all, we'll run a series of lectures."

"Good. That's good."

"Get them used to thinking the unthinkable. Can't help anyone unless they know what they're getting into. Blast effects, radiation sickness."

"Good. I like that."

"We'll teach them triage. How to separate those who are
maimed—torn apart or crushed, let's say—from those who are
really bad off. You know, if someone's vomiting right after the
blast, that means he's going to die sooner or later from radiation
poisoning. Can't waste time treating him. He could be routed to
. . . let's say, the storage depot. I think if you have a soldier
who's not trained—I mean, psychiatrically trained—he might
have trouble with that situation, storing kids, for instance, when
he knows they're going to die anyway. Could be emotionally trying."

"I think you're right," Wormley said, nodding.

"Soldiers have to know their mission," I went on enthusiastically. "The secret of good morale. If they can come to understand the usefulness of what they're doing, they'll communicate
that attitude to others. So they can look on the bright side."

"I was thinking the same thing myself."

"Group therapy in the management of Doomsday!" I said, waving my arms about insanely. "And what about the psychodynamics, the phallic imagery of the missile, the fireball, and the primal scene, the breast, etc., etc."

"I think you're on to something, Abe. There's the makings of a paper there. One of the analytic journals. But I don't like the word *Doomsday*. Has bad connotations. If you're going to lecture to the troops, you've got to stay away from words like *Doomsday*. And don't get carried away with the theoretical stuff. Practical advice. That's what we need. Also, don't focus exclusively on nuclear war. There's a good chance of all-out conventional war, which we should prepare for. Maybe you can work up a series of lectures for that. Don't forget training exercises. We can't do it all in the classroom. And remember, we may not have much time left." He smiled at me bravely.

"One thing more, Abe," he went on in suddenly grim tones, "you'll be talking to those lads about matters of life and death. If there's a war, some of them aren't going to make it. How well they do is going to depend in large part on what they've learned. That's going to be your responsibility, Abe, to teach these lads. But they're not going to pay any attention to you, they're not going to respect you, Abe, if you address them with your shirt unbuttoned. A word to the wise."

I stood silently, stupefied.

"Now for the big news," he said, after taking advantage of the dramatic pause. "Colonel Poole has given the go-ahead for my research project. I didn't want to tell you until it was all set; but that's why I came back early this afternoon. What with this crisis and everything, the individual commanders have more leeway setting up what sort of response they want to make. Well, Abe, you want to guess?"

"Guess?" I mumbled, coming back to life a little. "Guess what?"

"Name the single most troublesome symptom of an emotional nature to strike at the armed forces. Year after year. From time immemorial."

"Uh . . . I don't know."

"Guys getting kicked out of the service," he said, helping me along. "Loss of morale. Trouble in the barracks."

"Schizophrenia," I said, taking a wild guess.

He shook his head no. "Nah, the schizophrenics show up right away, most of the time. They don't get drafted in the first place. It's the guys you spend all that time and money training, ship them overseas, then find out you can't use them. Those are the ones who cost you. Every guy separated from the army costs the U.S. government twenty grand."

"I give up."

"Enuresis."

"Enuresis?" I repeated after him. "Bed-wetting?"

"That's right," he said, tilting his chair back and smirking.

"This is going to be our response to the missile crisis?" I asked in a rising voice. "An attack on bed-wetting?"

"Hey, listen. This crisis is going to be over one way or the other. If there's going to be a war, that's going to come to an end too; but there's still going to be bed-wetting. We might as well take this opportunity to learn something useful. Accomplish something. Think what it could mean if we could wipe out bed-wetting. The embarrassment. The human suffering. And the financial loss."

I was staring at Wormley, trying to figure out as usual if he was serious, and concluding, as usual, that he was, when Sergeant Kraven burst into the room.

"Where is he?" he asked, breathing heavily. "Is he here?" The sergeant walked over to me, then turned to look suspiciously at Wormley.

"What the hell you doing, soldier," Wormley said, "charging in here without knocking? I'm running a departmental meeting in here."

Kraven didn't answer at once. He went over to my *Schrank,* an oversize wardrobe used by the Germans in place of a closet, and peered in. "I'm looking for Lieutenant Konigsberg," he explained finally. "He's missing."

"You want to check the wastebasket?" I enquired. "It's under the desk."

"There's no one here, Sergeant. Now get out," said Wormley, who had little patience with other people's nonsense.

Kraven apologized and left promptly, although not without glancing about the room a second time. It was too late though. Wormley's mood was spoiled. He got up to leave, mentioning that he had already set his research program into motion. A command had been sent that morning to all the units in the area, ordering into the hospital all enlisted men known to have wet their beds in the previous month. Officers evidently were not considered to be subject to such a wanton loss of control. "I have some original, I think, ideas about treating enuresis," Wormley said, "that I want to bounce off your head, but I think it would be better to hold up until the patients start coming in. If you don't mind waiting."

I was prepared to wait, I told him quickly.

As he left, my telephone rang—actually my telephone was working as well as it ever did, which was minimally—and I heard someone's gravelly voice, sounding like it came from the moon, telling me that I was hereby ordered by Colonel Poole to remain in my office, alone, until further notice. I was not permitted, the voice said, to talk to anyone. Colonel Poole, our current commanding officer, was an anesthesiologist, a retread. Having served during World War Two, he entered into the larger arena of civilian life, only to retreat once again for some reason into the army. He had only been in command of the hospital for a week or two, but he seemed decent enough, although given to mumbling. I hoped he wasn't angry at me for sneaking off with Lieutenant Konigsberg. They still needed doctors in Korea to treat frostbite.

I was playing solitaire and listening to Armed Forces Radio, a blend of country western music and apocalyptic bulletins about Cuba, when I was informed by Corporal Vigliotti that one Henry Fitch was waiting to see me, sent by Colonel Poole.

A civilian, by God, I thought, reaching up to shake his hand. He was dressed in an ordinary and inconspicuous gray suit, blue tie, striped delicately. His hair was light brown, graying a little at the temples. His features were unremarkable: tired blue eyes, bunched up little mouth, almost petulant. He was sort of middle-sized, in fact, very middle-sized. In fact, he was so unexceptional in appearance, I immediately assumed he was a spy, which turned out to be not very far from the truth.

"You are Captain Redden, aren't you?" he said, looking for my name tag, which had fallen to the floor.

I wrote out a message to the effect that I was indeed, and that I had been ordered not to talk to anyone.

Fitch read this note, crumpled it, and tossed it into my lap.

Then he sat down unceremoniously on my desk and on my card game. "Listen," he said, carefully unwrapping a cigar, "don't act like an asshole, huh?" He inspected me through eyes narrowed against the smoke as he lit up.

I collected myself. "Excuse me," I said finally, "am I to understand by your manner of address that you are in the military after all?"

"CID," he said, handing me a plastic card with his picture on it.

"Ah, a CID," I echoed. I examined the card very closely under the desk lamp. The photograph made Fitch look like Edward G. Robinson, actually a sleeping or dead Edward G. Robinson, since he had been caught blinking. Also there were a lot of numbers and small writing. I turned the card sideways, then upside down. I picked up the king of clubs and studied them both up against each other.

"A policeman, Captain. I'm a policeman," Fitch said, taking the card from my hand and giving me a sour look. "I'm here to investigate the disappearance of Lieutenant Konigsberg."

"You're kidding. He really disappeared? Aw, hell." I began wondering immediately if Konigsberg might have been worse off than I realized. Maybe I should have had him admitted to the hospital.

"I take it that means you don't know where he is."

"That's right. I haven't seen him since he went off with his sergeant, a guy named Kraven, three or four hours ago. In the middle of a big fuss, by the way."

"I heard."

"The sergeant came back about twenty minutes later, looking for him. I suppose that's when he disappeared?"

It was a question, but Fitch didn't bother to answer. He had removed himself from my desk and was looking out the window. It had begun to drizzle again.

"Captain," he said, turning back to me finally. "You went out of your way to get Lieutenant Konigsberg alone. Why?"

"Because I'm a psychiatrist, for Christ's sake," I said, losing my temper. This was the third time I was explaining something that didn't need any explanation in the first place. "Because he said he was suicidal. Because he was coming to me in order to confide in me—and he wasn't able to do that with someone else

sitting in the room taking notes. That's not so hard to understand, is it?"

"Was he? Suicidal, I mean."

"Mr. Fitch, I think you understand that what passes between
psychiatrist and patient is confidential."

"What do you mean? You're a captain in the United States
Army."

"So what?"

Fitch looked at me, then turned and spit a piece of cigar onto
the carpet. "Look, Doctor," he said, "let me explain to you what's
going on. There's this business in Cuba. You've heard all about it
today, I'm sure. It's no joke. The Russians have put up a bunch
of missiles with nuclear capability. That much you can read on
the front page of your newspaper. Now I'm going to tell you
something you can't find in the newspaper. There are nuclear
warheads on their way to Cuba. We know where they are. Some
are in Eastern Europe. Some are already on the high seas. There
are four, for example, currently being loaded onto the freighter
Novgorod setting sail today out of Riga. This is all very important information. The source of much of this information is Lieutenant Konigsberg." Time to blow a cloud of acrid smoke in my
direction.

"As you may know," he went on, "Konigsberg is stationed in
Waldheim, a couple of miles from the Czech border. His work,
which is secret—but which I am going to tell you about now—is
listening. He listens into a special set of earphones attached to a
special electronic device which has the very special capability of
picking up telephone conversations from hundreds of miles
away. In fact, farther away. Because he speaks three or four languages, including Russian, he knows a hell of a lot about what's
going on behind the Wall, and, it turns out, in Cuba too. More
important, maybe, he knows the limits of American intelligence,
what we know and what we don't know."

"So?" Fitch was frowning at me as if he expected some sort of
response.

"So, he's been acting funny recently. Depressed and suspicious. Wants to see a psychiatrist right away. Then right after he
sees one, he disappears. Where the hell is he? What the hell is
he feeling bad about? Some moral crisis? Maybe he's decided
eavesdropping isn't the kind of thing a gentleman would do. Is

he feeling so guilty he's decided to join the Russians? Not too hard to do. The border is only a few miles away. Did he get kidnapped? It's happened before. Either way, if the Russians, or East Germans, or whatever, get ahold of Konigsberg somehow, they're going to realize we know more than we'd like to let on—about their communications, about their codes. More important, this Cuban thing is building to some kind of crisis, and we don't want these bombs suddenly disappearing from view. Of course, Konigsberg could have just snuck off someplace to kill himself. That would be okay, but so far no corpse."

"Well, what do you want from me?" I remarked irritably.

"I recognize that since you're an asshole," Fitch went on in a bland voice, "you're not going to cooperate with me just because I happen to outrank you or because somebody orders you to. That would be expecting too much. So I'm telling you all this very sensitive information in order to enlist your support." He smiled at me, sort of. The teeth in his mouth were too crowded, so that both canines were overlapping his incisors, like fangs. He looked like a snake.

"You certainly have a way of winning a fellow over," I commented.

Five minutes later Fitch and I were alone in the sergeant major's office on the ground floor. He was explaining to me how Lieutenant Konigsberg had disappeared—through the door, it turned out.

"Well, maybe he went through the door, maybe he went through the window, which was open. That isn't the point," said Fitch. "He was here with Kraven waiting for transportation back to their unit. The sergeant was called into the next room for a telephone call, and when he came back Konigsberg was gone. Nobody saw him leave. As far as we know, he never left the hospital. He didn't have a car. I checked with the taxi services; nobody came to pick him up. Besides, his leaving like that, without any explanation, is out of character. He's supposed to be a serious, responsible guy. That's why I'm talking to you. He hasn't been behaving normally. In a lot of different ways. Now, I want you to tell me why." He stuffed the cigar into the middle of his face; and he stared at me.

"I don't know why," I said after thinking about it for a minute. "I only saw Konigsberg briefly, and during that time he didn't say very much to me, practically nothing, now that I think about it. Just the usual things people say when they're depressed. He had failed, he said. He was no good. He talked about how bad he was feeling. Guilty. Which doesn't mean he actually did anything wrong, of course. Anyone who feels depressed, feels guilty. He told me he had trouble sleeping and a loss of appetite. Those are cardinal symptoms of depression. Otherwise, he said nothing. Nothing about what was actually going on in his life. He did say he had to see me right away because later on in the week would have been too late. I don't know what that meant. He said . . . He also said he needed help."

"That's it?" said Fitch.

I nodded.

"Maybe he said something else you don't remember right now," Fitch remarked.

"I got a bad memory for everything except conversations, which I remember exactly. My job, I guess."

Fitch didn't seem pleased by this information, or lack of it. He assumed an expression of distaste, and stared at his cigar, rolling it between his fingers. Maybe it was the cigar he found unpleasant.

"But you didn't think he was suicidal?" he asked me again.

"No. That was the most important thing, the first thing I tried to find out. I can't be sure, but I don't think so."

"Well, maybe he'll turn up," Fitch commented, not very hopefully. "There are a lot of people out looking for him besides the CID. Military police. The polizei."

"You called in the German police?" I was surprised. The Americans made it a policy to avoid local authorities whenever possible. "Hey, are you sure you're telling me everything? This seems like a lot of trouble to go to over one more security officer, who's been missing for all of maybe three and a half hours. There are a half-dozen so-called secret bases around here that everybody knows about; and I bet ten or twenty guys are doing just what he's doing. What makes him so special?"

Fitch looked up at me sharply. "Some secrets are special," he said. "Important enough to keep secret. Important enough, maybe, to kidnap somebody or even, maybe, to kill somebody. Matter of fact, maybe it would have been better if you hadn't seen the lieutenant alone. Somebody might get the idea he told you all his secrets." He smiled a fangy smile at me.

"I hear a lot of secrets," I told him, "like maybe somebody enjoys making love with his socks on, but so far nobody's tried to kill me."

By the time we had finished talking, it was evening. Instead of returning straight to the BOQ, though, I drove into Nuremberg, partly for practice. I had ordered a Volkswagen in New York City fully five months before, and it had arrived only a couple of days ago, although it was manufactured about twenty miles away. Learning to drive a shift car turned out to take longer than I had expected. I had spent Saturday lurching from one block to the next, a source of amusement to the populace, who tended to look benignly on their conquerors as naive and clumsy children, probably not far off the mark in my case. But now I was finally getting the hang of it. I drove past Fürth, a Communist town before the war, the scene of a number of pitched battles with the predominantly Nazi Nurembergers. Fürth was a suburb of Nuremberg now, but there were still Communists around, no doubt. Refugees from East Germany, only a few hundred miles away, had settled in the area. Probably among them were a few spies. And, of course, there were still Nazis. If Konigsberg was anxious to reveal military secrets to somebody, to anybody, he wouldn't have to go very far.

I turned in to the circle of streets that surrounded the city. At intervals I could see church spires silhouetted against the dark blue sky. Standing out from this shadow was the castle on my right, lit up magically by floodlights, colored pennants flying. The walls of the old city were visible also, narrowly separating the old section of town from the very old, although the jumble of houses on both sides were similar—fairy-tale houses, all of them two or three stories high, gabled and shingled the color of rust, centuries old; but people still lived behind their stuccoed walls. A warm glow issued from windows that were graced, every one, by a flower box filled with red flowers, always in bloom, it seemed. One row of houses, trimmed in wood the color of gingerbread, sat on arches across a river. The water gleamed and sparkled, reflecting back another set of quavery arches and the lights of the city. I looked away from the river just in time to avoid driving into it.

I was sort of hungry, so I turned in to one of the streets that led into the center of town, and looked for someplace to eat. The problem was, I knew, if I went into a restaurant, I was likely to be seated in the midst of a German family busy talking among themselves; and I would feel like an interloper. The beer halls were worse. Usually, just when I was bringing a bratwurst to my lips and beginning to feel safe, the band would play a drinking song. My neighbors would wind their arms through mine and tilt me vigorously from side to side, meanwhile singing raucously and cheerfully. All I could do was grin idiotically and pretend to sing along. I was never very good at parties; but without being able to talk to people, I was terrible. When I first arrived in Nuremberg, I took a two-week crash course in German, but all I remembered was the phrase, *"Ich bin ein blauer Zwerg,"* which means, "I am a blue dwarf," a remark that I had not yet been able to work successfully into a conversation.

I drove around a little while longer looking for a hot dog stand, but, of course, there were no hot dog stands in Germany. Finally I went home.

I spent the rest of the evening by myself watching television. Not listening, just watching. The programs were American for the most part, but dubbed into German. It was kind of amusing for a while hearing American Indians exclaim in guttural German, but John Wayne had a high-pitched, squeaky voice that I found unsettling. I turned down the sound and read lips. Worse was Mr. Ed, the talking German horse, who lost in translation what little credibility he had originally, and who was very hard to lip read. I shut the damn thing off and went to bed.

I was awakened in the middle of the night by a loud noise, the sound of splintering glass, much of which landed on me. Something had been thrown through my window, which was closed at the time. I'm not sure I know exactly what I thought, peering sleepily at my watch, which read four o'clock, something about the damn kids who were always playing ball outside. I am not at my most incisive at four o'clock in the morning. The thought of rocks passed through my mind. Possibly the women in the neighborhood were throwing rocks at the BOQ. They had reason, I knew, to feel pique at one or two of the officers. I wondered briefly if World War Three had broken out. In any case, I brushed a couple of pointed shards of glass from my pillow, rolled over, and went back to sleep.

III

I WAS AWAKENED finally by fragments of the sun shining through the broken pieces of glass still remaining in my window, and by the sound of a woman laughing in the next room. Or did I imagine the laughter? I had been dreaming about a woman, it seemed to me, but all I could remember was a small and distant figure waving to me; and as I lay there quietly, even that image faded away. There was no one occupying the next room, I remembered finally. Besides, I was living in bachelor's quarters; and, after all, it was six thirty in the morning.

I got out of bed and kicked the loose pieces of glass over into a corner, not a sensible thing to do in bare feet. I put my socks and shoes on after bandaging myself, and went over to the window. There was a large courtyard immediately outside, edged by tall bushes. Beyond was a heavily trafficked road and a hill terraced by long, angular brick buildings—American-style housing with central heating and a shower in every apartment, made by and for Americans of course, home to members of the United States Army and to the larger army of their wives and children. No ball field, though, closer than a block away. No bomb craters. No line of women protesting cavalier treatment at the hands of my fellow officers. Nothing, in short, to explain whatever had been propelled through my window. Nor was the thing itself anywhere in evidence. Having found myself in the company of spies, I looked around my room for a rock with a message tied around it; but there was no rock. There was nothing. Just a lot of broken glass and a cool wind blowing in.

I gathered up some soap and a toothbrush and went across

the hallway to our communal bathroom, where I was discovered
a few minutes later in the act of urinating by a couple of adolescent girls, who stood in the doorway pointing at me and
giggling. This sort of thing always disconcerts me. I stood there,
not moving, not even urinating, while the girls chatted in German and laughed. Even the laugh sounded German, a low-
pitched, gargly sound. They left after a while, and I went back
to what I was doing.

I was shaving a few minutes later when the doorway was
filled by another figure. A tall, thin man, clothed in an elaborate
dressing gown and leather slippers, was lighting a pipe and looking at me with a bemused expression. He took a couple of puffs,
leaned gracefully against the doorjamb, and smiled.

"Hey, you don't look so funny," he said.

"Thank you," I replied gravely. My face was half lathered,
and I thought he was giving me the benefit of the doubt.

He laughed. "The girls," he said by way of explanation. "Sorry
if they bothered you. I didn't think anybody would be in here
this early. They came back to my room claiming they had been
frightened by a funny-looking man in baggy underwear."

"They didn't look frightened. Still, I'm glad to know it was
only my underwear they thought was funny-looking. Are they
. . . uh, both those girls staying with you?"

"Yeah," he said matter-of-factly. He came over to a sink and,
after rolling up his sleeves and borrowing my soap, began
washing. I watched him in the mirror. He was good-looking, I
suppose. Regular features, almost chiseled, wavy brown hair,
brown mustache, both long by the standards of the army. He
looked like the sort of man women might be attracted to two or
three at a time.

"Kind of cute, the girls," I commented. "They look like cheerleaders. High school cheerleaders."

"You think so? I'm not a connoisseur of women. More an ed-
ucated consumer. They are definitely not cheerleaders, though.
When I ran into them, they were coming out of a hotel room
with a guy who was about sixty-three."

"Oh, I see. How come you brought them here?" I asked, turning back to my own face. "I thought no women were allowed on
the premises."

"Rules, rules," he replied with a sigh. "The United States

Army has too many rules. You wouldn't report me, would you, buddy?"

"No," I said, scraping my chin.

"I'm glad to hear it. We're going to be neighbors, I think. I wouldn't want to offend my neighbor's moral sensibilities by screwing a girl, let's say, on army property."

"You're safe on my account. I may have the occasion to do the same someday." Like maybe around the turn of the century, the way things were going.

"From time to time I like to get high too. Have a little fun. I hope that won't bother you."

"Judge not, lest ye be judged. That's my motto," I told him.

"Terrific. The name's Bob Schulz, by the way," he said, extending a wet hand in my direction. "Just got transferred in last night from 3rd Division, out in the middle of nowhere."

"Schulz, Bob Schulz," I repeated to myself, trying to remember. "*Robert* Schulz! Say, aren't you the guy who likes to piss on flagpoles?"

A startled look, then a modest lowering of the eyes. "How did you know?" he asked.

I explained how near I came at Fort Sam to being punished for his sins.

"Yeah, the army gets annoyed at the stupidest Goddamn things," he said, using some toilet paper for a towel. "And that punishment stuff is no joke. I wish it did happen to you. That's how I ended up in the boondocks for the last three months. Ridiculous. I'm a board-certified surgeon, and they had me treating athlete's foot. The only reason I'm here now is because one of the surgeons at the hospital rotated back to the States. Christ, I don't know how I'm going to put up with this Mickey Mouse crap for two years."

"You know, I'm glad to hear you say that. I thought I was the only one having a hard time."

"Hey, look, buddy," he said, "what do you say we get together and enjoy ourselves despite these bastards? I'm not going to let anyone run my life, army or no army."

"That would be great." He sounded so definite, he made it seem possible. "Uh . . . wait a second," I said, catching him before he left. "I remember you also liked throwing things through windows. Like chairs. Right? A whorehouse in Ciudad Acuña, was it?"

"They refused to give me my change."

"Yeah . . . well, did you, or maybe one of your girl friends, throw something through my window last night?"

"No, not that I remember," he replied thoughtfully. "Are you missing a chair?"

"Never mind."

Probably spontaneous combustion. Something like that, I decided, washing my face clean. I once parked a car in the sun, and when I came back the windshield had shattered into a thousand pieces. That must have been it, a change in the weather.

It was still early when I left the BOQ, but I had a long way to go, it turned out, before beginning work that morning. My trouble started in the driveway. Slowly and carefully, I backed my new car into a Cyclone fence at just the precise angle that made possible hooking the metal end pole between my rear bumper and fender. In fact, when I got out to look at what I had done, it didn't seem possible. On the assumption that what can be got into can be got out of by going backward, a theory I developed when I was playing potsy as an eight-year-old, and which didn't work then either, I started inching backward, then forward, then backward again. As a result, I stamped a very peculiar pattern of grooves in the fender, a series of parallel lines, like a grid. The small crowd of German citizens that had gathered around seemed also to be impressed, murmuring to each other in hushed voices. After inspecting my fender carefully, I got back into the car again and indented it a few more times until I had wedged the pole in far enough to prevent any movement at all. Similarly, I was wedged into the driving seat in a hunched-over position, gripping the wheel tightly, jaws clenched tightly, trying to control myself, when I could feel myself tilting forward into the air. Three or four burly onlookers, including one lady, had picked up the rear of the car with me in it. Someone leaned against the pole, and a moment later I was pulled free and set back on the ground. Carefully, as always, I backed into the roadway, thanked everyone, and drove away. At least to the stop sign at the end of the street. I was sitting there, looking into my side mirror at the small crowd I had left behind, all of whom were looking back at me, when all of a sudden the mirror made a loud noise and fell off, not at the socket, I discovered when I picked it off the ground, but in the middle of the steel shank connecting it to the car. I felt the jagged edge. The damn thing had blown up. Weird. The only other trouble I had en route was on Otto Strasse, where I drove into a fruit stand.

When I arrived at the hospital, I was called to attention by Colonel Beasely, who had been standing on the front steps talking to a couple of guys and twirling his toothpick.

"Cut it out, Bease. I don't have time for this today."

"Aw, come on, Abe. Shtand at attention. I want to show you off to the boysh here."

"What are you talking about?"

What he was talking about was the change of seasons and my uniform. By proclamation of the Commander of the United States Army in Europe, it was now officially winter, and I was still wearing cotton khaki while everyone else was wearing itchy green wool. This was very amusing to Colonel Beasely.

Back to the BOQ to change uniforms. Rather than drive myself, I asked Herr Bromberg to give me a lift in his Messerschmitt. The Messerschmitt—this Messerschmitt—was not a fighter plane with a cross on the wings; it was a three-wheeled, two-passenger car, really a motorcycle with a canopy, although it looked more like an oversize grasshopper. It had very good gas mileage, I was told. On the way out of the hospital grounds, we passed my Volkswagen. Herr Bromberg looked at the car thoughtfully for a moment, then asked why I had chosen to buy a secondhand vehicle. Usually he was more tactful.

On the way back to the hospital he handed me a box of candy and a very creased piece of paper, which he said he had found in Major Wormley's office that morning. "It has your name on it," he pointed out, "but I think it belonged to Lieutenant Konigsberg."

The candy was the jujubes I had taken from Sandra Collins. The paper, however, I recognized at once as that which Konigsberg had been fiddling with all during the time we spoke. It was a German timetable, for a local bus line, according to Herr Bromberg. I recognized the names of some nearby towns. Someone had written on it: my name, some numbers, and some other letters I couldn't make out easily. No destinations were underlined as far as I could make out. Too bad, for it seemed Lieutenant Konigsberg had been planning to go somewhere after all.

The missile crisis was worsening, according to *Stars and Stripes*. The Communist buildup in the Caribbean was continuing. President Kennedy had responded by announcing a blockade of Cuba. The scenario now envisaged by Colonel Beasely and the other senior officers of the hospital to whom I spoke, or rather listened, over coffee that morning went as follows: The Russians, who hadn't been slapped down really during the Berlin crisis, or in Korea (Korea?) or in Latvia (*Latvia?*) were now too cocky to back down in the face of a simple threat by the President of the United States. So, first off, they were going to move those six or seven nuclear subs they had on station in the mid-Atlantic in a little closer to shore in order to make themselves obvious. To keep them company, that small fleet of nuclear armed cruisers currently showing the red flag off the Costa del Sol was going to turn around and head west. They were going to park right in the middle of the shipping lanes and thumb their noses at us. The U.S. couldn't afford to stand still for that, of course, so Kennedy was going to put SAC on the alert from Maine to Frankfurt to Alaska, rev up the motors, and pop in a couple hundred H-bombs. Then to make sure the bastards knew we were really serious, that carrier fleet we had posted in the Indian Ocean to keep the Indians in line was going to move into the Atlantic. The Russians, too dumb to take a hint, would respond by moving a couple hundred thousand tanks up to the German border, packed so close together you wouldn't even be able to walk between them. Meanwhile, the Chinese, who do what they're told, were going to mass troops all along their border with Korea and Turkey (*TURKEY?*). In case that didn't frighten us enough, the Russians were going to put all their rinky-dink bombers—what's its name, can only carry two H-bombs—in the air. Naturally, the U.S. couldn't fold under this kind of pressure. Before those Russian freighters started unloading nuclear weapons on Cuba, Kennedy was going to march the Marines up from Guantanamo. Round about then, the Russians, who didn't give a shit about world peace, were going to land on the north end of the island. Then: Boom. Boom coming in installments: a land battle on Cuba between the forces of Good and Evil, the mining of the Port of New Orleans, the invasion of Japan by China, and, of course, in the end, nuclear war. This gloomy assessment was offered cheerily, for some reason.

All of this contrasted somewhat with my own view. My theory of life states simply that nothing ever happens—or, more precisely, nothing you ever anticipate happens. Sure, there are earthquakes, occasional muggings, stuff like that; but the things you really worry about, like flunking out of school, or developing cancer—they never happen. I had done a lot of unnecessary worrying about those things, and none of them had ever happened. Nuclear war between Russia and the United States was another good example. During the Berlin crisis, everyone was talking about the risk of all-out war; but except for my getting drafted, no such disaster took place. Still, listening to Armed Forces Radio that morning, it did seem possible to me that just this once a catastrophe was possible.

I left Beasely at the point where he began figuring the likely number of casualties, using a log table, and returned to my office. Fitch was there. He had the timetable spread out carefully on my desk and was examining it with a magnifying glass.

"Any clues?" I asked.

"Clues?" he repeated absently. "Yeah, right. Clues."

"Does it mean anything?"

"I don't know." He rolled a cigar from one side of his mouth to the other, then bent over the paper again, very close, so close a little dribble of ash settled on it intact.

"What are you looking for?"

"Usual stuff. Microdots."

"Microdots. Spy stuff, huh?"

"Right."

"Secret codes? Ciphers?"

"Never can tell."

"I guess that means the lieutenant hasn't shown up yet?"

"That's right."

"Didn't go back to his base?"

"Nope."

"Visiting his girl friend, maybe?"

"Did he say he had a girl friend?"

"No."

"Well, he probably didn't have a girl. Only been around a month and a half, two months."

"That's long enough to get a girl friend."

"Yeah? You've been here three months. You don't have a girl friend."

"How the hell do you know?"

He looked up at me thoughtfully. "Just guessing." Then he turned his attention back to the piece of paper in front of him.

I stood there for a moment watching him. "Did he . . . did Konigsberg have any friends, any family, around here?" I asked.

"Why? Why do you want to know?" Fitch said, looking up at me sharply. "Did he say anything about his family?"

"He didn't say anything about anything. I told you. But it's natural if you're depressed to want to be with someone who cares about you."

Fitch dusted his cigar off in my coffee cup. "Yeah, well, that's possible. I thought of that. Fact is, oddly enough, for a guy who comes from Muncie, Indiana, he does have a lot of family here. Did have, anyway.

"See," he said, pointing at one of the columns on the timetable. "*Koenigsberg*," he read off to me. "It's a small town about fifteen miles from the East German border."

"That's a place, not a person," I commented.

"So it is. But according to the police back at Muncie—I got onto them last night—both his parents came from somewhere around here. From Germany, anyway. Grandparents. Great-grandparents. Eight or nine generations. Back then people used to take their name from the town they came from."

"It's spelled differently."

"So it is." He held the document closer to the light in order to make sure. "Still, he was carrying this thing around for some reason. Going someplace, or thinking of going someplace."

"Are there a lot of people named Konigsberg in Koenigsberg?" I asked.

"Sure are. And not just in Koenigsberg. In all of Bavaria. Probably in all of Germany. But not many, I think, are going to be related to our lieutenant."

"How come?"

"He's Jewish. Most of his relatives got killed long ago. Those that didn't must have gone into hiding. First thing they would do is change their name."

"I don't think the lieutenant would have bothered to hunt up a distant cousin. Not because he's depressed, anyway."

"Probably you're right. Still, it's a place to start. Besides, he might have had a special reason to look them up. Maybe not so much emotional, maybe a political reason. German Jews as a group were politicized during the last war. A response to Hitler."

"No kidding?"

"Yeah. Some of them turned to Communism, unfortunately. Two or three are big wheels in the East German government. Maybe some of that rubbed off on the lieutenant. You know, he requested a security assignment. Dropped out of college to enlist. That should have alerted somebody. And he asked to come to this part of the world. He must have had something in mind. Shit," Fitch said perfunctorily, sliding his chair away from the desk. "Trouble is, there's no time."

"No time for what?"

He leaned forward again. "What I need to know to find this guy is . . . everything. Sure, I need to know if there's anybody around here, family or friends or anybody else, he might turn to if he's in trouble. So I got to know has he visited anyone since he was stationed at Waldheim? Has he gone anyplace? When he doesn't go anyplace, who does he hang around with? What does he talk about? Why the hell is he depressed? Did something happen? If I wanted to do the job right, I should start back in Muncie. Who is this guy? That's what I need to know." Fitch looked up at me as if he expected me to have the answer. "Speaking about codes," he said, "does the number one zero four five mean anything to you?"

"Sure. That was the year William the Conqueror became Duke of Normandy. He was three years old at the time."

"Konigsberg wrote this number here, next to your name. You think he was planning to talk to you about William the Conqueror?" Fitch looked at me with distaste.

"Come to think of it, no. I got the dates wrong. It must have been around 1037 or 1038 when William became duke. 1045. Let's see, that could be . . . Isn't that a short ton, in metric units or something?"

I was able to inform Fitch a moment later, after a brief conversation with Vigliotti, that 1045 was the time of my emergency appointment with Konigsberg the day before. He had arrived late, which required no special explanation. Everyone arrived late.

"And these letters—words—do you know what they are?" Fitch asked, pointing at the timetable.

"Sorry, I couldn't make them out either. The guy's got a bad handwriting. Could have been a doctor. Look," I said, trying to cut all of this short, "I sent you this thing because I figured you'd want it. I thought maybe Konigsberg took a bus ride somewhere. That's all. It was obvious from the way he was holding the timetable that it wasn't important. He wasn't paying any attention to it. He didn't leave it behind because of any secret message. He just forgot it."

Fitch grunted, a small, opaque sound. The expression he wore was similarly vague. It was hard to know what he was thinking. Or if he was thinking. Shortly he drew forth from an inside pocket a glassine envelope from which he extracted another piece of paper. It was colored bright yellow.

"Take a look at that," he suggested, pushing it over to me.

It was a laundry ticket.

"This is a laundry ticket," I said.

"That's really terrific," he replied. "You have a mind like a steel trap. I was talking about what's written on it. The same illegible handwriting, you'll notice."

"Oh, yeah. I see. You mean these letters here, right under HERMAN'S CHINESE LAUNDRY. Looks like, uh . . . P . . . PLMS. Four letters."

"Are you sure? Look carefully. Could that L be an E, maybe?"

"I suppose," I said, looking at the damn thing up close. "It could be an E or an H. The way this guy writes, it could be an X. What the hell is this all about, Fitch?" I said, losing patience finally. "I have work to do. I don't have time to sit around playing word games."

"Well, you know I'm sort of busy myself," he replied irritably, at the same time chewing on his cigar, which made it bob up and down. He seemed to be using it to draw punctuation in the air, an exclamation mark here, a question mark there. "And I'm asking you these questions for a reason. Konigsberg may not have left that timetable here for any particular reason, but he left that laundry ticket in plain sight, where it would be sure to be found—on the floor right outside the sergeant major's office."

"On the floor? You think he purposely left a message on the floor? Why? Why a laundry ticket? Maybe he just dropped it accidentally. I guess you don't really think he defected. Defectors don't leave messages behind, do they? Besides, it wasn't in plain sight. I didn't see it."

"I found it earlier. There wasn't any reason then to show it to you; but I want to know if you recognize that word."

"PLMS?" I said, trying to read it off as if it had a vowel somewhere.

"Take a closer look. Could it be . . . PENK?"

"Penk? Penk? That isn't much of a word either."

Fitch had stopped puffing for a moment and was staring at me intently.

"It looks like PLMS to me," I went on. "Well, maybe not PLMS, maybe PEMS. Not PENK, I think. I don't know. Jesus Christ. Maybe it's PENK. Who cares?"

"Doesn't mean anything to you? PENK?" he said again. He wiggled his cigar at me one more time, suggestively.

"Fitch, get the hell out of my office. This is a hospital. There are a lot of sick people around here, and somebody's got to take care of them. Wormley's off waging the war against bed-wetting, so that leaves me. I wish I knew what happened to Lieutenant Konigsberg, but I don't know; and you obviously don't know. Obviously, Konigsberg wouldn't have chosen to inform us where he went by scribbling a message on a laundry ticket and throwing it on the floor where we would be sure to find it—not sure to find it, it seems to me. Furthermore, I don't believe there is any such place as Herman's Chinese Laundry."

Fitch departed. Vigliotti came in immediately to remind me that my first patient was waiting and had been for about two or three thousand seconds. That was only about half an hour, but bad enough. Psychiatrists should not be late. Their patients get upset. I had kept this particular patient, Sergeant Lingeman, waiting once before when I was called away for an urgent pistol practice. I was excused early, but not early enough, after demonstrating that I was capable of shooting a small cup off a nearby table while seeming to aim at a target down range. Lingeman had particular difficulty waiting. He was phobic, which means fearful in certain situations, in closed-in places, for example, such as elevators, buses, or trains; crowded places, such as theaters or shopping centers; or places far away from home. Really the fear such a person has is of his own feelings, that trapped in such circumstances he will lose control of himself, fall to the ground, scream, go crazy, or die. Waiting in such a situation, or even anticipating having to wait, is very painful.

Lingeman had all these fears to some extent, except perhaps the fear of being closed in—he worked routinely in cellars—but he was bothered especially by heights. He couldn't go above the third floor, even in a windowless room, without feeling anxious. Any height at all made him uneasy, but once he had risen above a certain critical point, his heart began to race, he had to struggle to catch his breath, his fingers and lips would begin tingling, and other strange, undefinable sensations would wash over him in waves until he became convinced that this time . . . this time he was really going to die. In that panic, he would run away, sometimes literally running down the stairs. These symptoms had ruled his life for years, preventing him, for example, from going to college, since inevitably that would have meant attending class, at least occasionally, on the fourth or fifth floors. Yet no one could sensibly describe him as easily frightened, certainly not as cowardly. He was a demolitions expert. He learned the business from his father and uncle, who made a living tearing down old buildings. In the course of that work he went readily into very dangerous places—dark basements, for instance, often flooded, supported by rotten beams, or girders bent out of shape by a boiler explosion. Often he set charges in buildings that were already falling down around him—but he would not, if he had to, go above the third floor.

Drafted into the army, Lingeman was assigned, oddly enough, to the kind of work for which he was trained. He went through basic training, did well for the most part, and was ordered to a unit in Germany, to which he traveled by ship, then by rail. Upon arrival he was attached to an artillery battalion; but he worked also in a bomb disposal unit, disassembling bombs and artillery shells left over from the previous war and uncovered from time to time as the Germans pulled down the old Germany and put up the new—mostly high-rise apartment and office buildings. All this went on at ground level, or, more often, below ground level. So far, so good.

Too good. A demand grew up for the services of this particular bomb squad. Their help was requested in a number of different geographic areas, including the British zone, for instance. The commander of the unit, one Buckley Turner, had reason to feel pride, and satisfaction with the performance of his men, particularly that of Lingeman, who, besides being knowledgeable in this specialized field, was reliable and eager, a "good guy." There came a time, though, inevitably—Lingeman had known it would come—when those virtues were not enough, when he was asked not just to walk up a few flights of stairs, which he might have been able to manage for a while, although terrified, but rather to step into a helicopter. The squad was needed urgently fifty miles away, and no other transport was available. A helicopter was too much. It would have been as if he himself were taking wing and flying up into the sky. He remained behind to explain to Turner, haltingly, painfully, about his fear of heights, about all those years of running away, those years of failure, which was how he understood them. However skilled he was, or responsible or eager, he was a failure in his own eyes.

Turner was a man of some experience in the army. He was not someone who saw men simply in terms of their being "good guys" or "bad guys." They also divided neatly into "rough, tough guys" and "weaklings," into "go-getters" and "slackers," and into "heroes" and "cowards." Lingeman was pronounced a "weakling," a "slacker," and a "coward." To say no one could sensibly describe him as a coward is not to say the army could not. In addition, according to Turner, there were those who were "schlumps," a vague term of disapprobation which he considered personified in the person of Lingeman. "You're a perfect schlump," he told him, indicating also that the sergeant was no longer to consider himself a "good guy."

The United States Army was not going to tolerate in its midst any such undesirable type. Lingeman was court-martialed for disobeying orders and sent to Wormley with a recommendation for an administrative discharge. The Chief concurred after thinking about it for a minute or two. That would have been that, except that Vigliotti, who could be very inefficient when he

wanted to, immediately lost the paper work; so all that work had
to be done again.

I found Lingeman in my office the following day. Vigliotti explained his error to me and asked me to evaluate the sergeant
rather than bothering Wormley a second time, in fact, without
letting him know, if possible. Vito thought Lingeman seemed
upset, emotionally disturbed would not be putting it too
strongly; and as Wormley had indicated on numerous occasions,
people who were emotionally ill or "flaky" made him uneasy.

"The treatment of phobia is simple," I explained to Lingeman
after listening to his almost despairing account of himself. "Not
easy, but simple. You're going to have to learn from your own
experience that you're not going to die, or scream or go crazy.
You're not going to lose control of yourself, even in a helicopter.
But in order to really know that that's true, you're going to have
to go just where you've been avoiding going all these years—up
above the third floor."

"Don't you think I've tried that?" Lingeman said, his voice
breaking.

"There's a way of doing it," I told him. "I'll show you. We'll
do it together. Just a few months of hard work, that's all it takes
usually."

"There isn't . . . I don't have time. Captain Turner wants me
out right away. He says I'm not a stand-up guy."

I picked up the telephone and called Turner. He was unavail-
able except in the event of an emergency, his aide informed
me; but when I explained about the bomb in my office, I was
given a number where he could be reached. It turned out he
was in his quarters. We had a bad connection as usual. I could
hear girlish sounds in the background.

I launched into what I hoped was an effective defense of Lingeman. He was, I pointed out, one hell of a soldier, a "man's
man," an "up-front, right-on, no-nonsense, straight-shooter." Also,
basically a "good guy"—but with a little problem. He was afraid
of heights.

"Sounds like a weak sister to me," Turner replied dubiously. I
heard someone giggle; in fact, there was a lot of giggling, high-
pitched and gay, also low and sexy. Either we were hooked into
a party line, or I had interrupted Turner at a bad time.

"Hell, no," I said. "This guy would bite the nipple off an M-1, chew the ass off a bear. He walks around with nitro in his back pocket." Not much of an exaggeration, I thought. "Just a matter of getting him over this height business. It'll take a couple of months maybe."

"That's cute, but we don't got time for that now, honey."

"Excuse me?"

"Not you. I wasn't talking to you. But I don't got time for that either. This is a hot dog, quick-strike helicopter squad I'm developing here, and I don't feel like waiting around a couple of months for you to teach someone to walk up a couple of flights of stairs."

"Lingeman is a valuable man, Captain. You can use him. Besides, you don't want him walking around with a bad discharge just because he's got a problem, do you?"

"Yeah. That's just the way I like it. You got it now."

"Why?"

"I wasn't talking to you. And I don't give a damn what he's walking around with. All I care about is this crack helicopter squad. Mobile. Swoop down out of the skies . . ."

"You know, with a bad discharge he's going to have trouble getting work. He doesn't deserve that."

"In and out. In and out real quick. That's the way."

"Uh . . . Captain, are you talking to me now?"

"Of course I'm talking to you. I was explaining about this helicopter bomb squad. You know, one of these days, just maybe, there's going to be a war. Bombs all over. These guys are going to be moving in and out real quick. There's not going to be time to coax Lingeman on board. And I can't wait around a couple of months until you cure him."

"One month, Captain. Give me one month."

"Tell you what, Doc, a week."

"A week? It can't be done. This man has had this problem all his life. I can't make it go away in a week. Listen, Captain, Lingeman is one hell of a hotshot, a hotshot . . . uh, fireballbuster. Give us just a few weeks, and he'll be a credit to you."

"A fireballbuster?"

"Right. Just give me three weeks, that's all, and you'll have a real fireballbuster."

"Hey, I like that."

"Terrific," I said, hanging up without bothering to find out who he was talking to.

That wasn't going to be enough time, I thought, looking up at Lingeman, who was staring at me disconsolately and running a hand through his hair, over and over. Probably three months wouldn't be enough time.

But we tried, Lingeman and I. Each day we practiced together, climbing a little higher, first in the hospital itself, from the third floor slowly to the fourth and then beyond, stopping to talk when he became very panicky, to take notes, to do anything at all that would distract him from his feelings. Some time later, he literally crawled the last few steps up to the roof, shaking, stopping to rest frequently, but then crawling up another step. Then we went to other, taller buildings, among them the visiting BOQ in downtown Nuremberg, then to the castle. Encouraging him, cajoling, arguing with him to some extent, I was able to get him finally to the edge of the wall, which looked down a couple of hundred feet onto a sloping hill.

Once upon a time there had been a knight on horseback who breached the castle's defenses to rescue a fair damsel. He pulled her from a parapet and, holding her in one arm, jumped, still on horseback, from the castle wall to the hill below, and rode off into glory. This unlikely story, told to us in graphic detail by a guide, was enough to upset Lingeman, who had a very vivid imagination, whose problem was precisely that he had a very vivid imagination. He saw himself, *felt* himself, flying from those ramparts out into space.

Then, to the Stadium. We walked together through that great empty arena where Nazi luminaries had once addressed thousands of *Schutzstaffel,* thirty to forty thousands of troops at one time, all standing in precise formation, helmets agleam, rifles all pitched to the same angle, all vanished now. We scrambled up the cement steps to the forum where Hitler himself had stood. Then, slowly, and for Lingeman, painfully, we went higher still, to the very top, where we paused at the base of a row of columns. I sat while shakily he grabbed hold of a column. We remained there for perhaps half an hour, until he was able to stand by himself. From that lofty, windy perch, we could see past the Stadium walls, past all of Nuremberg, into the surrounding countryside. Farms and villages, all neatly tended, were set off by stands of very tall trees, leafy only at the top. Their lower branches had fallen or were cut away, making them look groomed. Patches of sunlight moved across this green landscape. Whatever awful things had happened in Germany—were happening still in parts of Germany, so I was told—it was a beautiful country.

Two weeks had passed since Lingeman and I had begun these excursions, and he had improved much faster than I had expected, probably because he practiced for hours at a time by himself. He could go now more or less comfortably to any ordinary place, up escalators or narrow stairways. He could look out of windows, even stand on terraces or ledges. And he had been up and down almost every tall building in town. What he hadn't done yet—couldn't do, he said—was get into a helicopter. Just looking at a helicopter made him feel sick. Today's session, delayed by the events of the last few days, and now by an additional couple of thousand seconds, was supposed to be a tour of a medevac helicopter.

"I'm never getting into one of those things," Lingeman said. "Suppose he takes off. It's not safe, the way those guys fly."

"Come on, you know better than that. They're the best in the world."

"Well, I still can't do it. I just can't. And I don't know why I should have to. It doesn't matter back home if I can't get into a helicopter."

But it did, I explained. If he avoided any place at all just because he was afraid of getting panicky, he would end up getting panicky again in other places. "This is the last step. It won't be bad at all if you can just . . . do it."

"I can't."

"We only have three days left!"

"I can't help it."

More practice. Since the helicopter was out, I took Lingeman up to the roof to watch the lunchtime Monkeybar races. That was the closest thing I could imagine to a trip in a helicopter. The races were limited strictly to lunch hour and "Happy Time," 1630 to 1800 hours. Poole would have banned them altogether, but when he tried, the effect was something like prohibition, people sneaking out in the middle of the night to do some illicit and really dangerous climbing. Like many other vices, climbing had proved easier to regulate than to ban altogether.

Lingeman walked out on the roof readily, showing no obvious trace of the panic that had paralyzed him only a couple of weeks before and for so many years before that. We walked to the edge of the roof and, to my surprise, he climbed over the edge onto a platform, which looked awfully rickety to me and which swayed a little when he sat down on it.

"Jesus, it really isn't necessary to go this far," I advised him nervously, sitting down beside him.

He made no reply. He held tight to a metal pole and stared down through the maze of intersecting pipes to the base of The Monkeybars. Someone leaned down from the roof and offered us some beer, which we drank slowly while a crowd gathered below us. The weather was still warm enough to picnic on the grass; and someone at the bottom of The Monkeybars was playing music on a record player. I could hear other people laughing. The roof door clanged behind us repeatedly and a second crowd of spectators appeared shortly, leaning up against the ledge of the roof. The remaining seats on the platform were taken by a couple of attractive nurses. I wondered why an attractive girl would want to join the army, or why anyone would want to join the army. The young woman next to me seemed to be having a good time, though. She smiled at me and began swinging her legs back and forth.

The featured race that day had attracted considerable advance notice. According to the mimeographed program handed to me, it was "a grueling test of the indomitable spirit of the individual United States Army Fighting Man" and starred the Monkey, himself. (I could see him far below me, doing his Monkey imitation, walking bowlegged, scratching himself.) He was single-handedly going to race against a team of three orderlies. In such high regard was he held, the odds were still 5 to 3 in his favor—although to some extent that support was sentimental. He had a vivid personality that some people found appealing.

Suddenly the marshal called everyone to attention by banging a couple of bedpans together; and in a moment the race had begun. Making chattering noises, the Monkey swung arm over arm from pole to pole and from one crosspiece to another. He skittered quickly up an inclined plank, hopping once or twice. Then, seemingly without even stopping to measure the distance, he leaped into space to grab hold of a broken pipe that surely could have been no closer than two feet above his outstretched arm. With just one hand he seized it and hung there, twisting slowly from side to side, scratching his ribs with his free hand, showing off, of course; but it was an impressive performance. I wouldn't have been surprised had he wrapped a tail around the pipe and begun swinging from it. All of this frightened the woman next to me. She wove her arm through mine and covered her eyes with her other hand. But Lingeman was holding up pretty well, just a little pale; and he was talking very fast to the people around him, or to himself. Talking was a device he used to control his anxiety. I felt a little queasy myself, watching the Monkey pull himself up hand over hand, his feet dangling over a sheer drop. He grabbed hold of a chain that was hanging loose like a vine and used it to swing up onto an orthopedic bed. It was two minutes later when the first orderly, a muscular and now red-faced young man, having taken a safer, more circuitous route, collapsed on the same bed. Immediately the second orderly sprang out of a window at that height and continued the pursuit of the Monkey, who, by that time, was much higher. A few minutes later the third orderly took over; but it was no contest. Amidst cheering from the spectators, the Monkey leaped from a set of exercise bars onto our platform, shaking it so hard I thought we were going to fall. From there to the roof. Victorious, he began beating his chest with his fists and bellowing jungle fashion.

I disentangled myself from the nurse, who had grabbed me around the neck, and I congratulated Lingeman. "If you can sit on that platform, you don't have to retreat from anything. Tomorrow we go on the helicopter."

"I'm not ready. I don't think I'm ready for that," he said quickly.

If he said he wasn't ready, he probably wasn't, I realized. But there wasn't going to be time for him to get ready. I was going to have to push him somehow.

I walked over to the edge of the roof to retrieve my beer where I had left it, on the ledge. As I reached out for the bottle, though, it shattered, spilling beer over my sleeve. I just stood there, shaking my head from side to side, and dripping. Something like that had happened to me once before. I was toasting a good friend at a wedding when the glass I was holding aloft, just holding, not squeezing, broke in my hand. It was considered a bad omen and, indeed, the marriage was annulled some months later. But this time I hadn't even touched the damn thing.

I left Lingeman talking to the nurses, and returned to my office, where Vigliotti was waiting phone in hand. Major Sedgewick, my contact in the pathologist's office in Frankfurt, was on the other line.

"The postmortem was done this morning on your lady friend, what's her name . . . Collins," Sedgewick said. "Her abortion was botched, all right. Lacerations, like you said, fore and aft, three centimeters in the fornix. Snipped the bowel actually. Bled like a stuck pig. Couple of liters of blood in the pelvis. Too much blood almost."

"What do you mean?"

"Well, she had a lot of different holes punched into her, all right, but . . . no artery. Just a small vessel that got tied off in surgery anyway. So they said. This stuff I'm giving you, by the way, I got from the German ME, in German, that is, which I don't *shprecht* too good. So I'm not exactly sure of everything. You can't trust these Germans anyway. Very precise, you know, but they lose sight of the big picture. Like when they invaded Russia. Know what I mean?"

"No."

"Well . . . *you* know," he said with emphasis, as if I were purposely being obtuse. "They'll measure all the blood down to the last millimeter, but if she happened to have a bleeding disorder, they'd never pick it up. Not that this little lady had a bleeding problem. The only problem she had probably was screwing around a little too carelessly. Young kids today. You know what I mean, it's a problem with the schools. Sex education. No one teaches them right from wrong anymore. Whatever happened to coitus interruptus? Anyway, she had a perforation in the uterus too. What's kind of interesting is with all this chopping her up she never passed the fetus. Hey, are you there?"

There was a lot of static on the telephone. Also clicking and clacking sounds. "I'm here," I said, my voice coming out hoarse.

"According to the Germans she was okay otherwise. A healthy

kid. Toxicology negative so far, but I don't think they would have bothered to do much under these circumstances. Any tests they didn't run, I'll do. If you sent the blood off yesterday, I'll probably get it tomorrow or the next day. Let you know as soon as I can. Oh, one other thing. The fetus had a number of malformations, chest deformity, spine. Probably other stuff. A little difficult to tell in a twelve-week fetus. Just as well the kid wasn't born, although it's a shame it happened this way."

"Any reason . . . I mean, for the malformations."

"Well, you know, it's hard to say. Certain drugs, illnesses. Sometimes no reason. God moves in His little old mysterious ways."

"Uh, one other thing," I asked in a voice loud enough to be heard over the various other voices muttering in my ear, mostly in German. I wasn't surprised we had sophisticated equipment capable of picking up telephone conversations in Russia. I could pick up Poland on my office telephone. "I asked the guy who was operating on her whether he thought she could have done this thing to herself. He said no. What do you think?"

"Well . . . anything's possible, you know. Clothes hanger. Not too likely, I should imagine, in a seventeen-year-old kid. But possible. Anything's possible. You wouldn't believe the things I've seen. Heh. Which reminds me, would you believe a Coke bottle in a bladder? A *man's* bladder? I was doing a postmortem on this guy, and when I open up his bladder, there it is. A Coke bottle. Do you believe that?"

It was a moment or two before I could respond. "No, I don't. Listen, Sedgewick, you think I'm in the mood to listen to you make up some kind of funny story?"

"Well, maybe I was exaggerating a little. It wasn't a real Coke bottle. It was one of those little cigarette lighters in the shape of a Coke bottle. Not so little, come to think of it. He must have had trouble pushing it up past the prostate. The damn thing still worked when I got it out."

I sat there gripping the telephone and listening to Sedgewick chuckle. Suddenly I could hear a high-pitched voice singing about love. "Love and pain," it crooned mournfully, "on the banks of the Seine."

"I don't think so," Sedgewick went on, apparently getting serious. "Nobody pokes things into themselves that hard. No, somebody did it to her. They just waited too long, that was the problem. Twelve to thirteen weeks pregnant. Bad time to do an abortion. They poked her, and when nothing happened, they poked her again and again, and again."

I was notified a moment later as I sat staring into space that Colonel S. Poole wished to see me. In fact, he commanded my presence at once in his office without delay in connection with an urgent matter that he wanted to discuss with me immediately —right away, Vigliotti explained, in case I had trouble catching on. What it meant was I was going to have to keep other patients waiting. Why is it that everything important in life has to wait for everything else to come first?

On my way to see the colonel, I came across a number of strangely silent soldiers clogging the hallway outside the office of the administrative OD. Since they were carrying duffel bags, canteens, and the like, I naturally assumed they were heading off on maneuvers.

"Another alert?" I asked one of them, meanwhile trying to squeeze by. He was a very big man, about four inches taller than I and about twice as wide. He looked like he had been chipped off a mountain.

He made no reply. He didn't move, either.

"Off to Turkey to rescue more earthquake victims?" I went on, smiling a little. "Or is it the real thing this time, the big show— Cuba?"

The fellow was not amused. He stared at a crack on the wall. I smiled at the private standing next to him, who was also not amused. Boy, what a sullen bunch of guys, I thought. Maybe they were really going off to war.

But, of course, it turned out they were coming into the hospital, not leaving it. They were a contingent of Major Wormley's bed wetters, gathering in larger numbers than I would have expected. Judging from their expressions, which were remarkably the same, gray and threatening, eyes clouded over—overcast, in a word—they were not looking forward to being made well.

I ran into Schulz at the door to Poole's office. He was exiting. Having introduced himself as required to his new commanding officer, he was all tuckered out, he said, and was returning at once to the BOQ to rest up for the evening ahead, during which he expected me to show him the sights of Nuremberg, principally the red-light district, it seemed. I offered instead to show him the castle, which was unforgettable, like the Alamo. He laughed and patted me on the shoulder. We made arrangements in any case to meet for dinner.

Colonel S. Poole, our new commanding officer, was short and thin, delicate almost. He wore a thin mustache, daring by the standards of the U.S. Army, and a clue possibly, I thought, to hidden depths. When I entered, Poole was turned away from me and toward Mr. Henry Fitch. There were only the three of us in the room.

"Mr. Fitch has been telling me all about Lieutenant Konigsberg. About his disappearance," the colonel said, glancing over to me. "Actually, I understand he disappeared twice, the first time when he was with you."

"Sir, the man was very depressed. He had been talking about killing himself. I suppose I violated some regulation or other talking to him alone; but I don't see that I had any choice. Besides, we were only alone for a few minutes. He didn't disappear because of anything I said to him."

Poole stared at me critically for a moment. "Well," he said, "that's done now." He leaned forward abruptly and straightened a piece of paper that was fluttering on his desk. A window was open and a breeze was stirring, bringing with it the rotor sounds of a helicopter that was landing on the other side of the hospital.

"Captain Redden," he said, after settling back in his chair and studying me a while longer, "I've been getting a lot of funny communications in the last ten or fifteen hours, starting yesterday with the commander of Nuremberg post. The only time he talks to me usually is when he wants some cough medicine. Now he orders me, *orders me,* to cooperate fully with Mr. Fitch here. Mr. Fitch is a member, a senior member, of the CID."

We both turned to Fitch, who was sitting back to the window, his face in shadow. In that light he looked a little more like George Raft than Edward G. Robinson.

"This morning I got a call from Paris," the colonel went on, "from headquarters NATO Command, instructing me to assist the police authorities—Mr. Fitch, I think they were referring to —in every possible way. Top priority, they said, whatever that means. Something about the security of Europe. I can't tell you exactly how Lieutenant Konigsberg's disappearance is threatening the security of Europe, Captain Redden, because nobody has bothered to tell me. You see, my security clearance isn't high enough." At this point he began to mumble something about being good enough to fight his way across Europe, but not good enough for something or other. "Anyway," he said, clearing his throat, "this morning, perhaps to make sure all of this was crystal clear, I was called from medical rounds by the ambassador, the American ambassador to Germany, who told me, diplomatically, of course, that to some considerable, although still undefinable, extent, our relationship with Germany depended on the satisfactory resolution of this affair. Not just West Germany, but East Germany too. Now, this is beginning to sound like a lot of bullshit to me. You know these diplomats. The whole future of the world rests on whatever they happen to be worrying about that minute. He said something about the new status of forces agreement governing crimes against civilians. What the hell that has to do with . . . And Cuba! He mentioned the Cuban missile crisis. Well, hell"—Poole gestured with both hands—"no one has to hit me over the head. If they want me to cooperate, I'm going to cooperate." He looked over to me, as if he expected me to say something.

"Well, sir, if there is something I can do to further East-West relations, protect the peace, or whatever, you can count on me."

Poole went on staring at me from the depths of his chair.

"Yeah," said Fitch, stirring at last, "that's good. I asked the colonel to call you here so you'd understand . . . uh, how important this is. Because I'm going to need your help."

"Hey, I've been helping. You don't think I've been helping? I gave you that . . . that bus schedule, didn't I? And I've been telling you everything I know."

"Sure. You just haven't been what I'd call . . . enthusiastic."

"What do you want me to do, Fitch, wave a banner?"

"I'll tell you what I want," Fitch replied, taking out a cigar. He began to unwrap it, but then looked up at Poole, who had evidently already made known his aversion to people smoking in his presence. The man was, after all, a specialist in lung disorders. Fitch made a wry face and put the cigar away. "I want you to come to Waldheim with me."

"Waldheim? Why?"

"Listen, this guy Konigsberg is missing now twenty, twenty-one, hours, despite the fact a couple hundred military police and German police too are out looking for him all over. The barracks, the hotels. Those girlie places downtown. The Germans in particular can be very thorough, you know, when they want to be. If they didn't find him, I don't think he's here. Not in Nuremberg. Either that or he's holed up so good we'll never find him in time."

"In time for what?" I asked.

"Anyway, the logical place to start looking for this guy is Waldheim," Fitch went on, ignoring me, "where he's been for the last month and a half. Yesterday . . . well, I put off going there yesterday for reasons; but there's no way out of it now."

"So what do you need me for? I'm not a detective."

"All right. Let me lay this out for you in one package. Konigsberg had access to very secret, very dangerous, information. He disappears, either under his own steam, or somebody grabs him. It follows, naturally, his disappearance has something to do with this information."

"I don't see that," I said, interrupting. "He was depressed. Maybe he left . . . maybe he disappeared because of something in his personal life. I don't know many spies, but I guess they're affected by the same kinds of things that go on in everyone else's life. Maybe—"

"Jesus Christ!" Fitch waved his hand at me impatiently. "In the first place, he wasn't a spy. If he was spying for anybody, it wasn't for us. The guy had a job, turned out to be important, maybe, but all he was doing was sitting at a desk and listening into an earphone. Second, I'm not going to hang around here theorizing about his unconscious motivation, or whatever, on the basis of no information at all. He lived in Waldheim and worked there, and that's where we're going."

"Why me?" I said again.

"I'm trying to tell you," Fitch replied in a rising voice. "Two reasons. Three reasons, maybe. First, you met Konigsberg, talked to him. Maybe you know more about him than you think. If you see his stuff, talk to his friends. I don't know, maybe you'll get an idea. Second . . . uh, more important, I can't just . . . show up there to conduct an investigation. I need some kind of cover. The fact is, by coincidence, I've had some dealing with those guys before. On that base. Not personally, but they know who I am. Homosexuals. Got wind of them a couple of weeks ago. A whole nest of homosexuals."

I looked over to Poole, who was staring fixedly and silently at Fitch.

"A nest of homosexuals, did you say?" I repeated after him.

"That's the way we pick them up out here. In bunches. Homosexuals are a big problem out here. They seem to infiltrate everywhere. Especially security posts. Anyway, right now if I go out there and introduce myself as Henry Fitch, I'm not going to get any cooperation. That's where you come in. Turns out they got some kind of psycho out there, a guy praying a lot to Christ, only most of the time he's talking to the toilet seat. So instead of him coming out here to see you, which didn't work out so good last time, anyway, we go out there, except I'm going to be Captain Redden. It's a terrific cover. As a psychiatrist, I can ask any kind of question I want."

I probably stared at Fitch for a moment or two before starting to laugh. "I don't know, Fitch. You don't look much like me. George Raft, a little, maybe, but not me."

"Nobody out there has ever seen you except that sergeant, Kraven, and he's been told to keep his mouth shut. And the CO. You met him yesterday, I think. Colonel Collins. He knows what we're going to do. It's okay."

"Collins? The guy . . . the man whose daughter died here yesterday morning from an abortion? He's in charge of that post?"

"Yeah. He's not going to be around too much probably the next couple of days. His daughter is going to be buried. But he runs the place."

"That's a funny coincidence. So he's Konigsberg's commanding officer. You know," I said, thinking about it, "maybe it isn't a coincidence. A small post. Maybe they both knew each other. I mean, Sandra Collins and Konigsberg. She was saying something about secrets before she died."

"Yeah? What?" Fitch enquired. He put the cigar, still unwrapped, in his mouth.

"Look, Fitch," I said, suddenly remembering what was going on. "I spent thirty billion years learning to be a psychiatrist, and you're not going to be able to fake it."

"I don't know. I once lived across the hall from a psychiatrist. Besides, that's where you come in. In case I need coaching."

"And what about the poor bastard who's talking to the toilet seat? Are you going to undertake to treat him?"

"You'll be there to help. Look, we're not going to be doing this forever. A few days only. If we don't find Konigsberg by then, it'll be too late. Then you can psychoanalyze this looney all you want."

I looked over again at Poole, who had remained silent throughout this exchange. "You're not going to agree to this, are you?" I asked him. "This is one really stupid idea. In fact, I've been in the army four months and this is the stupidest idea I've heard so far."

"You don't think that's putting it a bit strongly?" Poole replied, smiling faintly.

"I'm not going to collaborate in any such scheme," I said flatly.

"Wait a second," Poole said quickly, tilting forward in his chair. "You'll do what you're told. I'm going to cooperate fully, and that means you're going to cooperate fully. This idea doesn't sound any better to me than it does to you. So what? We're just doctors, we don't have to figure strategy."

"Well, if you're supposed to be me," I said, turning back to Fitch, "who am I supposed to be?"

"I thought Vigliotti. He's a member of your staff. Nobody would question his coming along."

"Vigliotti? *Corporal* Vigliotti? Sir," I said, addressing myself again to Poole. "I don't think I can be legally ordered to impersonate an enlisted man."

"Listen to me, Redden," Poole said, speaking very distinctly to make sure I understood him, "you can be turned into a real corporal. That's right. Your medical degree doesn't guarantee you any particular rank. You disobey orders and you'll face court-martial. And if you get off—let's say you manage that—you're still going to be under my command for the next couple of years, and I can give you one hell of a lousy time."

It seemed to me suddenly that the room was expanding. Poole was getting larger too. I could see his shadow creeping up the wall. He took a couple of minutes to explain just how lousy a lousy time could be, then started muttering something about psychiatrists, bed-wetting, and the Goddamn Monkeybars. I couldn't exactly make out the connection. Then he shrank quickly back down to size with a few remarks about line of command and medical support responsibilities during a military emergency.

"The uniform," I said finally. "I have a captain's uniform. The pants have a stripe down the side."

"So you'll borrow someone else's pants," Fitch suggested, his voice taking on an edge.

"I can't. I can only wear my pants."

"Why?"

"My pants are lined. I'm allergic to wool."

This intelligence struck Fitch and Poole dumb. They looked at each other, then at me.

"It makes me itch," I said.

"Civilian clothes would probably be better anyway," Fitch said to Poole after a moment's thought. "Considering he doesn't salute."

"Oh, for Christ's sake, Fitch," I said, "what are you talking about?" All of this was beginning to annoy me.

"You don't salute. I've been watching you. Other people salute you, and you stare off into space."

"I do, too, salute!"

"No, he's right," Poole remarked wanly. "You don't salute. I think you mean to," he added, "but you don't. Not usually. Sometimes you do, but not usually."

"He's better off in civilian clothes," Fitch concluded, shaking his head. "A captain not saluting is one thing. A corporal is no good."

Poole nodded. Fitch nodded back.

"The third reason, Fitch," I said wearily. "You said there was another reason for my going with you to Waldheim. What is it?"

Fitch smiled. "Well, it's true you haven't been cooperating with me enthusiastically, waving a banner, so to speak; still, I would feel bad, a little bad anyway, if someone decided to eliminate you. You know, what with all those people telling you secrets—Konigsberg, Sandra Collins—you're going to tell me her secrets, I hope, when you get around to it. Anyway, with all this going on, I think you might not be too safe around here. You'll be better off in Waldheim with me." Fitch paused for a moment.

"Well, maybe that's not too important, come to think of it. So, all right, maybe you can count only two reasons," he said, getting to his feet. "In a situation like this, your safety is not much of a consideration."

When I took organic chemistry in college, the students were marked in laboratory on the basis of their yield, that is, the amount of substance they could produce by boiling other substances. If someone cooked up more of the stuff than his classmates, he was marked a plus. For an average amount, a zero. Below average, a minus. A double minus was awarded for conspicuous failure, blowing up the apparatus, stabbing someone with a pipette, hitting the teacher, and the like. I started the course with a zero and sank at once to a minus, then to a double minus. By applying myself from then on, I managed a final grade about halfway between double minus and minus, sort of a double-minus plus.

Walking restlessly across the grounds of the 20th Station Hospital, I found myself remembering this unsatisfactory episode in my life. I wondered if my military career would follow a similar course. Having begun as a captain not long ago, I was about to make corporal. Soon I would be a minus corporal, then a minus captain. The uniform of a minus captain would be all wool, including the underwear. Mohair pants and tweed socks. A twill shirt with a collar three sizes too small. With little spikes.

I was wandering around and dwelling on this cheerless prospect, in preference to attending the lecture Wormley was delivering at the same time to his newly admitted corps of bed wetters and to which I had been invited/ordered. Having failed to entertain myself, though, as usual, I turned back. Still, I found myself lingering a while longer in front of the doorway to the emergency room, where the real business of the hospital was going on. Sick people came one after another to be treated for conditions not much different from those treated in an ordinary municipal hospital. A woman who was coughing leaned up against the wall for a moment before entering. A man holding his wrist as if he had sprained it walked by.

An ambulance, its sirens whining, rushed through the gateway to the hospital grounds and yielded up a person on a stretcher, I couldn't tell which sex, wearing an oxygen mask and attached by way of intravenous tubing to a bottle of blood, reminding me of Sandra Collins, who was similarly encumbered when I saw her last. Finally, a taxicab drew up and disgorged an immensely pregnant woman. She was obviously at term. A man, probably her husband, had hold of her and was helping her across the threshold of the hospital. Soon he would have two people to hold on to instead of one. Someone dies, and in his place someone else is born. I was arrested for a moment by this stupendous truth, banal though it was. Then I walked after all the others into the hospital.

As I stepped into the doorway I heard a loud noise. A flower pot, which had been sitting on a windowsill above my head, *and which I wasn't even near,* had exploded spontaneously and fallen to the ground! One piece came off hard enough to cut me on the ear. Jesus Christ!

IV

WORMLEY had delayed his lecture so that I could be present.

"I wish you hadn't done that," I told him.

"That's all right," he said, grabbing my elbow and propelling me along the corridor to the classroom. "We're breaking new ground here. In a few minutes I'm going to be reaching out for the hearts and minds of these young men. I got what I think is a pretty terrific presentation, but . . . well, I want your honest reaction, I respect your judgment."

"Look, I can give you my reaction now. I don't think this project is a good idea. Enuresis . . . well, it's a problem, I suppose, but there are recognized treatments already in existence. We don't have to break new ground. Almost anything works. If you wait long enough, it goes away by itself. I mean, why don't we just forget about the whole thing."

"You asked me, Abe, I'm going to tell you. These guys are eighteen, nineteen years old. Not kids anymore. Marked already, some of them, by the emotional stigma of bed-wetting. Crippled, maybe. They've come out here, six thousand miles from home, to fight for their country if need be—it's not impossible, you know —and we owe it to them to give them the best in medical care, second to none."

"I think they'll be better off if we just let them alone—you know, unless someone wants to be treated, comes in on his own initiative."

"You can't always wait for that, Abe. People are frightened, ignorant. Sometimes they don't always know what's best for them. Do you know the trouble Jenner had introducing vaccination?"

"Hey . . . uh, I'm sorry, but I'm too busy to attend your lecture," I said, pulling away. "They asked me to see a patient up on Medicine."

"I know all about it. Don't worry. She's been here a month. She'll wait till tomorrow."

"Well, what about those lectures to the troops you want me to prepare? I got to work on them. And the training exercises."

"Abe, all that's important, but this is more important. Abe," he said again, investing my name with a kind of paternal reproach, "we have a chance here to make a real contribution."

"Listen, Ed," I said confidentially, after pulling him into a doorway and looking around to make sure we couldn't be overheard, "I don't know if I should be telling you this, but the fact is, I'm on a secret mission, very secret. Hush-hush, actually. I'm working for the CID. European security."

"I know," Wormley said, lowering his voice. "Poole told me. Not everything, of course. Just need to know. I'm not surprised," he added, beaming at me. "You have the makings of a front-line psychiatrist."

A front-line psychiatrist? What the hell was a front-line psychiatrist?

"You see," I went on, "I have to prepare for this very secret mission, which is going to start this very afternoon; so I won't be able to attend your presentation."

"Nonsense. According to Poole, you won't be detailed full-time to the CID. He expects you to assist them and do your work here in the hospital too. Or else, he said." This must have been a funny thought, because Wormley began to chuckle.

There were twenty-three soldiers in the classroom, among whom were the sullen young men I had encountered previously. Those whom I had not seen before seemed in no better mood. Everyone was silent, frowning, most of them, slouched in their chairs, staring at their hands or out the window. No one stood at attention, or so much as twitched, when Major Wormley and I entered the room. I was introduced to the troops and seated to one side, where I could observe "reactions." Wormley immediately entered into his address, to wit:

"Fellows, you've all been ordered into the hospital for observation and treatment. I think you know why. Because of enuresis, known by most people as bed-wetting, which is another name for it. All of you have been observed to wet the bed at least once over the last month or so. Now, this is nothing to be ashamed of. Bed-wetting is very common among the population at large, especially children under the age of three or four. Studies show that over fifty percent of firemen, for example, were bed wetters when they were children, although it is not known whether they became firemen as a result or whether some underlying psychodynamics underlies both their becoming firemen and bed wetters in the first place. Or in spite of. You can see the connection, I'm sure. Sort of amusing, this sort of thing, to psychiatrists. Enuresis runs in families sometimes. A genetic weakness, perhaps. Small-volume bladders. Primarily, however, enuresis, or bed-wetting, should not be regarded primarily as physiological, although there are physiological elements present, any more than psychological, although there are psychological roots, too, primarily. Or both. For example, there may be an outbreak of enuresis after the birth of a younger sibling, for instance, as there may be encopresis, which is children moving their bowels in their pants, for example. In other cases, like a man I know who wet his bed until the night he got married, then never again. Now, in a case like that, obviously this man had a psychological need not to urinate on or near his wife. Although, when . . . uh, before they were married . . . Anyway, the psychological roots can be overemphasized. The fact is, enuresis, or bed-wetting, is a habit disturbance, like thumb-sucking, or like other things, like trichotilomania. These habit disturbances are called masturbatory equivalents, which means . . . well, it doesn't mean anything. Forget that. Uh . . . trichotilomania. That's eating hair, by the way. Because enuresis is a habit, it can be treated like a habit. Remember that. Just a bad habit. Not the kind anybody should be ashamed of, naturally. If you were teased growing up, put that experience behind you. It's no sin wetting your bed, God knows. Now the army regulations . . . you all know the army takes a strong stand against enuresis. Enuretics can be discharged under article 209 as quote, unsuitable, unquote, for service, like what you get for going AWOL a few times or getting drunk repeatedly. Or homosexual. Not really a moral thing. Soldiers who are considered quote, undesirable, unquote, on the other hand—people who are court-martialed repeatedly for drugs or criminal activity or disobeying orders—those are a different kind of fish. Then, of course, for the real troublemakers there are bad-conduct discharges and dishonorable discharges. The point is, sure, the army regards bed wetters as quote, undesirable, unquote, because being the object of derision, they cause morale problems in the barracks and worse in the foxholes. In the event of war. But that's a practical issue. There's no reason to think of yourselves as unmanly or weaklings or anything like that.

"I know many of you have had disturbing experiences as the result of your bed-wetting. I think it would be useful to share those troubled times among ourselves. Help break the ice. Would someone like to get up and tell us about his most embarrassing experience wetting the bed. Anyone at all."

The uneasy silence in which we all sat became more uncomfortable and profound. I could hear someone breathing at the other end of the room. Perhaps he heard himself, for after a moment, even that sound stopped.

"Come on, fellows. We're all in this together," Wormley said, offering up an encouraging smile. "Shared, each man's burden becomes lighter."

Stubbornly, each man went on shouldering his own burden.

"You," said Wormley, pointing at a skinny kid in the front of the room, who jumped as if he had been prodded in the ribs.

"Sir," said the young man, standing up more or less at attention. His arms were at his side, but his shoulders were hunched. He looked like he was cringing from the neck up. "Sir," he said again in a loud voice.

"Yes," said Wormley. "Yes, go ahead."

"Sir," the young man repeated, "I don't think I should be here. I don't wet my bed, not really. It happens when . . . only, you know, when you have a dream. Sex and . . . uh, well, I haven't even seen a girl for a long time. I been here a couple months, and I just work on the cars. We're shorthanded in the motor pool. Nobody has time to go around with . . . Well, nobody has time to do anything. Eat lunch. I never get a chance to eat lunch, even, let alone have relations. Besides, there's my religion. I was brought up to respect girls a lot, so, when I . . . you see, I was having this dream. See? That's not the same thing, is it?"

"Sir," said another man, coming to his feet. It was a moment, though, before he was able to command Wormley's attention, which was focused still on the skinny young man. "Sir," the second soldier said again, plaintively. "I don't need treatment. It only happened just this one time. I was out on pass, drinking beer with Harry, who is a guy in the next bunk. Well, I had a little too much beer to drink. That can happen to anyone. Besides, Harry was sitting on my stomach. That's his idea of funny. I mean, if a guy is actually sitting on top of you . . ."

Someone at the other end of the room got up and started edging toward the door. "Excuse me," he said, after Wormley looked in his direction. "I got to go to the bathroom. I got a weak bladder."

"Me too! Me too!" I blurted out, holding my hand up. "I gotta go too. Can I be excused?"

"Wait a second!" Wormley called out abruptly, turning a slightly auburn color. "Wait just a second! This is a serious research project we're embarking on here, and I hope there's not going to be any horsing around." He thrust out his chin and glowered at the various soldiers who were standing, and, as they receded into their seats, at me. He looked angry and sort of nervous for a minute, then, in an obvious attempt to control himself, ventured a tentative, although slightly crooked, smile. He muttered something about the strain of the Cuban missile crisis taking its toll on everyone.

"Treatment," Wormley began again. "I'm sure you've all been subjected probably to a variety of treatments as you've been growing up. Psychoanalysis, bladder exercises, bells attached to the mattress. I know a guy who tried to treat himself with a rubber band. Very dangerous. If any of these remedies had worked, you wouldn't be here now. Proper treatment is based on a proper understanding of the process of sleep.

"The stages of sleep," he announced dramatically, unveiling in a sudden gesture a chart that hung behind him on the bulletin board, obscured until then by a sheet. Although plainly labeled "The Stages of Sleep," it seemed to show a cross section of skin. It was, I recognized with a start, a chart of the skin that had hung previously in the CO's office when the dermatologist held sway. Someone had drawn over it in colored crayon. The epidermis had become stage one, the dermis stage two, and so on, down to stage four. Dream sleep was drawn in next to a furuncle, which is a pimple. Wormley entered immediately into an exposition of the process of sleep and the habit of bed-wetting. It was an interesting, although not altogether accurate, account. He was under the impression that sleepwalking ("the other side of the bed-wetting coin") was an occasional early sign of syphilis. "This is where bed-wetting occurs," he said, pointing at a hair follicle, "during the transition from stage four to REM sleep, when there is generalized autonomic discharge, low-voltage beta waves, and considerable twitching. That's it, gentlemen," he said, turning back to his audience, but continuing to tap the chart with his finger, calling attention now to an abscess. "Treatment, real treatment begins here."

Slowly and silently Wormley began pacing back and forth at the front of the classroom. "I've been thinking about this problem for many years," he said finally. "Hard." He furrowed his brow as if to illustrate how hard he was thinking. Watching Wormley think was like watching someone try to loosen a rusted screw. He went on:

"Enuresis is, first of all, an unconscious habit that takes place, second of all, during a state of disturbed sleep. Treatment, therefore, is two-pronged. The patient will have to be trained through practice to urinate properly and to sleep properly . . ."

At this point I became agitated. Some people, I know, can sit in a classroom and listen to nonsense, *knowing* it is nonsense, and be comfortable nevertheless. Some listen for the fragment of truth that may or may not be hidden in all the nonsense. "Hmmm, practice urinating," they might think. That thought would set off a chain of associations, reminding them of cases of bed-wetting they had seen or articles they had read, enlarging their perspective on enuresis in some subtle way, perhaps. And perhaps not. Others, a greater number, I think, would simply sit there stupefied, thinking about what else they had to do that day, or where they were going that evening. But not me. God knows, I had plenty to worry about that afternoon. In just ten or fifteen minutes, whenever Fitch showed up, I was beginning my new career as spy, or was it counterspy? There was Konigsberg, in trouble of some sort. He was a real human being, whatever fanciful story they were telling about him. And the death of the Collins girl was still nagging at me. But there I was writhing uncomfortably in my seat, befuddled, enthralled by this idiotic lecture just because it was so idiotic, unable to think of anything else, feeling not very different, I imagine, from what Lingeman must have felt a few months before, if he had looked out a window, anxious and restless, and worse—panicky. I was afraid I was going to lose control of myself and punch Wormley right in the nose for picking on these guys and annoying the hell out of me.

I was saved from committing a court-martial offense by the appearance in the doorway of a beckoning cigar. Wormley was just getting into the meat of his address, I think, a description of sensation within the bladder itself and the role of the spinal cord, when I tiptoed by him. A moment later he was still scowling at me, I could see, as I closed the door carefully behind me.

Fitch handed me some clothes, a button-down shirt, a corduroy jacket, and a pair of pants rolled up into a ball. They were mine.

"How the hell did you get these?" I asked.

"I stopped in at your BOQ to save time. Your door was unlocked."

"Oh yeah? How'd you know my door was going to be unlocked? You went there to look around, didn't you? You'd have gotten in some way or other whether or not the door was unlocked. A chance to do a little spying, right? Fiddle around in my drawers?"

"Relax, will you. Nobody wants to fiddle around in your drawers. Which are empty for the most part, anyway. You got one very empty room. Some clothes and a toothbrush. Doesn't look like anybody lives there. Breezy, though."

I found one of my ties in a pants pocket, also rolled into a ball.

"Right. That's right. Breezy. Somebody broke my window, I think."

"Yeah? How come?"

"I don't know."

"Well, how did it happen?"

"I don't know. I was sleeping at the time."

"Oh. No kidding." Fitch leaned up against the bookcase in my office and watched me while I changed clothes. He was already dressed for our little charade in a captain's uniform borrowed, he said, from a friend of his. It fitted him better than my uniform fitted me, I couldn't help noticing.

"The broken window," Fitch went on, looking at me curiously, "it didn't sort of make you a little nervous?"

"Not at the time." I tossed Fitch the small metal caducei I wore on my lapels signifying to the world that I was a doctor and should be forgiven, therefore, if I forgot to salute. I found my name tag at the back of my desk drawer and gave him that also, not without a small pang. My identity had been eroding bit by bit since I joined the army, and I was hesitant to give up such tangible evidence of who I was.

"While I was in your room, I . . . uh, did sort of look around," Fitch said, pinning these insignia on his chest and putting my name tag in his pocket. "There was a hole in the headboard of your bed, about four inches long. You had a pillow over it. I found this embedded in the wall." He handed me a misshapen lump of metal. It didn't look much like a bullet, although I guessed that was what it was.

"From an M-1 probably," Fitch said, "judging from the angle and the fact that the bullet was almost spent. It was fired probably about a quarter mile up that hill outside the BOQ, somewhere in that housing complex. A good shot."

I nodded.

"You don't look very surprised," Fitch added, "considering just yesterday you thought it was ridiculous, the idea that somebody might want to get rid of you."

"I know. Well, it wasn't just the window. Every time I turn around, something breaks. A couple of hours ago I was standing under a windowsill when a flower pot that was sitting there blew up. I put the pieces back together and found a little round hole right in the middle of it."

"Is that right?" Fitch sounded interested, vaguely, although he kept looking at his watch. "Maybe now you thought about it again you remembered something the lieutenant said to you, something that would be reason for someone trying to kill you?"

"No."

"Too bad. Whoever's shooting at you must be making some kind of mistake. Hurry up, will you," Fitch said irritably. "We're late already, and I got to stop off first at the morgue."

Before the morgue, we stopped off at the police station, an adjoining building, in order to meet Herr Emil Fuchs, the Nuremberg police chief, who was in charge of the German end of the search for Lieutenant Konigsberg. He was a large, gruff man who smiled a lot and laughed readily, usually running his hands through his hair at the same time. His news was not cheering, though.

"Except from incident I told you, Fitch, dere is not much," he said, speaking English evidently out of deference to me, since Fitch had greeted him in German. I assumed it was a greeting, although the guttural sounds of German imbued with essence of Fitch made it sound like a growl. "No lieutenant hiding out somewhere. No body in da river. No trace of nothing. Strange, Fitch." He pronounced the name with a soft *sh* sound, which made it seem for a moment that he was calling my companion a strange fish, which he was. "A corporal," Chief Fuchs added. "We find AWOL corporal we return to you, but dat's it."

"You looked in all the cracks?" Fitch remarked, more a statement than a question. "That place around the corner from the church, you know, where you can get prophylactics with little pimples on it. And did you check the airport motel? The Lions Club? What about that clothing store where they're running a special on coke all the time, a couple of snorts for a mark?"

"Ho, ho. Not dat cheap, Fitch. Dat cheap, I buy some a dat stuff myself. Dat Fitch, vonderful sense of humor," the policeman commented in an aside to me.

Vonderful, maybe, but not irrepressible. Fitch was sitting eyes narrowed, lips turned down, looking as if the cigar he was chewing on was a pickle.

"No, Fitch. Believe it," Fuchs went on, "dis guy's novhere around."

"What about the border?" Fitch asked.

"Vot border? Czechoslovakia? Italy? Austria? Da other Germany? Sure, da army shipped a couple regiments more soldiers to border duty, but Germany got lots of borders. Besides, as far as I know, dere is notting at any border. Vell, maybe not notting. A couple crossovers at Berlin, but coming dis way, East to Vest. Like usual. So far, I didn't catch no spies yesterday or today. A slow couple days. Ha. Very much radio traffic from other side, more than usual. But you know about dat, Fitch.

"Fitch," Fuchs said again, slapping his hands decisively on the arms of his chair. "I think your lieutenant is gone. Verever he was going to go, he has gone. Vatever he vas going to do, he did it already. If he knew any secrets, it's not a secret anymore. It's too late, Fitch."

"Aaa, I don't know," Fitch replied. "Maybe not. I got some other indications. For one thing, somebody's been shooting at Captain Redden here just because he spent a couple of minutes alone with Konigsberg. Obviously, somebody thinks there's a secret that's still secret, that Konigsberg might have told Redden."

"He didn't tell me anything," I pointed out again.

"Either that," Fitch went on, ignoring me, "or you're right. Konigsberg already spilled what he knows, purposely maybe, and somebody thinks he might have let on to Redden ahead of time. So, in order to keep us from finding out, they shoot Redden. In a situation like this, that would be just as important. Or, who knows. Maybe they think Redden's in a position to find out something."

"Wait a second . . ." I said. This was going by a little too fast.

"Or maybe they're just playing it safe, biding time until they decide which way they're going to jump on the Cuba thing . . ."

"What are you talking about?" I said, sitting forward on my chair. "What is this about Cuba?"

". . . after all, Redden's life is worth nothing."

"I think you may be right," Fuchs said, looking at me thoughtfully. Then he laughed. "Of course," he said, addressing himself to me, "ve mean your life doesn't matter to da Communists. For dem, it's easier to kill somebody den argue about if dey need to kill someone or not. Yes," he said, scratching his chin audibly, and turning again to Fitch. "You're right. It's a good sign."

"Yeah," Fitch muttered, coming to his feet. "Well, keep at it, will you?"

"Sure," Fuchs replied, also standing, "but keep in mind, please, I got plenty of other business too. A big burglary just today. Smuggling. Last couple months not just people crossing borders; but gold, paintings, Dresden figurines." He smiled again. "Da Communists, dey having vot you call a garage sale."

"Yeah, I know," Fitch remarked sarcastically. "These international incidents are a big distraction. Well, just a few days more, and you can get back to policing your garage sale."

Before we left, I asked Fuchs whether he knew anything about an investigation into the death of Sandra Collins. It turned out he was in charge of that too.

"Terrible," he said, "but abortion is alvays terrible, don't you think? The taking of a human life."

"I don't feel that way."

"Oh."

"On the other hand, I don't approve of stabbing a woman with a scissors or whatever, then leaving her to bleed to death in the rain."

"Of course not. I understand. Also it's not da first time, I'm afraid. Another voman vas killed just da same two months ago. And another six months ago. But ve have some idea who is doing dese tings. She's not going to get avay."

"Enough of this crap," Fitch said, "we're late."

The morgue was remarkably bright and clean, considering its grisly purpose, much neater than similar facilities I had seen back home. Then again, the Germans had a reputation for being clean. Wormley gave the conventional explanation for their excessive cleanliness and orderliness: a too severe toilet training. This theory, he told me in an uncharacteristic moment of uncertainty, was not entirely satisfactory, failing to account for how the same nation that produced Adolf Hitler could also have produced Johann Mendelssohn and Edvard Grieg.

Just inside the door to the morgue we met a couple of men with whom Fitch was evidently acquainted.

"Looky here," one of them said expansively, "the boss finally made captain."

"Only thirty years in the service and you did it. Or are you working your way down again, Fitch," the other chimed in.

"What the fuck are you bastards doing here?" Fitch snarled. "Didn't I tell you this morning to make the rounds, that bus station, the railroad, that . . . that temple? All those places? You through already? I don't see the lieutenant standing here with you."

"Well, no, Fitch," the first man responded, blanching a little. "We . . . uh, we heard about this woman, and we thought we'd come over and . . ."

"I don't need you to think, Goddamn it!" Fitch was yelling now, loud enough for a number of people standing nearby to move away. "You just do what you're Goddamn well told to do! We're running out of time. Didn't I tell you that this morning? Now, get the hell out of here!"

One charming fellow was Mr. Henry Fitch.

The attendant opened a gleaming refrigerator door and slid out the body of a young woman—well, perhaps not so young. I couldn't be sure. Death blurs distinctions of age as it does all other differences between people. And she was naked. Without clothes I couldn't tell if she was American or German, rich or poor, sophisticated and fashionable, or ordinary. In the end, I suppose, everyone is ordinary.

"A whore," said Fitch, bending closely over the body, ignoring the cold that rose up from her. He dribbled cigar ash on her breast, then dusted her off. "This is the story," he said. "This lady was seen last night in the presence of a lieutenant in the United States Army. Of course, she was seen with a half-dozen other guys too. But still, she was seen with a lieutenant. No other description. Later on she turns up dead, strangled. See . . . uh, that's a blue strangle mark," he said, pointing out the blue strangle mark. "Made by a stocking probably, or a tie, looks like. Something thin. Bite marks here. And down here around the thighs.

"Well, what do you think?" he said, looking up at me.

"What do I think about what?"

"About this . . . this woman. What do you think I'm talking about?"

"I think it's awful."

"Jesus Christ! I'm not asking if you approve of sex crimes. I want to know if you think Konigsberg could have perpetrated an act like this."

"Konigsberg?" I repeated incredulously.

"Yeah. She was seen with a lieutenant, I told you. You said he was depressed and angry. Emotionally disturbed. Maybe he got a little frustrated trying to talk to you. He takes off from the hospital, begins to feel worse and worse, and then . . . this."

"Is that what you think happens with depressed people, Fitch?

They get a little frustrated, maybe, begin to feel worse and worse until after a while they go out and bite some lady on the thigh?"

"Goddamn it, Redden. I'm fed up with your wiseass remarks. I'm asking you a simple question. You're a psychiatrist. You met Konigsberg. I want to know if you think he's capable of this crime."

"Well, Mr. Fitch, I spoke to Lieutenant Konigsberg very briefly, as you know, but he didn't say anything during that time to suggest to me that he was planning on strangling anyone or biting anyone. Nor did he seem to me that sort of fellow."

Fitch grunted, then bent over the corpse again. "Come to think of it," he muttered, "I'm not so sure these are human bite marks." He made enquiry on this point to the attendant, speaking German, although not precisely enough evidently to make himself understood. He entered into a kind of pantomime, grimacing and pointing at his teeth, and working his jaws. The attendant smiled and nodded agreeably, but seemed to understand no more of this than I did.

"Could be pig bites," Fitch said, poking his finger at one of the marks. "There are some wild pigs around here. In Arkansas we used to see pig bites like this. Especially on the thighs. The acid discharge from the vagina," he explained.

I looked up to see if Fitch was giving evidence at last of his wonderful sense of humor, but he had turned and was walking away.

The Autobahn, the superhighway linking Nuremberg to Munich, and all the other German cities, was Hitler's saving grace, people said. As Mussolini had made the trains run on time, Hitler had built the widest, straightest road in the world, capable, one war and a generation later, of bearing traffic traveling at an average speed of eighty or eighty-five miles an hour. Fitch and I were traveling at ninety-five miles an hour, and still an occasional car passed us. We rode through the same landscape I had seen from the top of the Stadium, looking not much different from close up, a picture postcard enlarged to show details, a stand of trees, thirty or forty bunched together in the midst of a cultivated field, a thatched barn, a beer truck on a side road overtaking a horse-drawn wagon. There were eight or

nine houses jumbled together at an intersection, each one bordered inevitably by window boxes and the same red flowers.
Farther on I saw two lonely women bundled with sweaters and
skirts, bending from the waist into a furrow, harvesting something, I guessed, although they looked more like they were simply tidying up. At intervals of a few miles, there were placed by
the side of the road wooden statues—the arresting figure of
Christ. He hung there on the cross, briefly in view, then flew
away to our rear only to reappear in front of us a few minutes
later, watching us sadly trying to escape His presence. Were the
Germans really using the figure of Christ as a scarecrow, I wondered.

"Listen, I'd like to get something straight with you if I can," I
said to Fitch, breaking the silence in which we had been sitting
since we got into the car.

Fitch showed no sign of hearing me. He went on driving,
hunched over the wheel as if he were trying to get closer to the
road. He was always peering up close at something, it seemed to
me. Considering the speed we were traveling, I hoped he wasn't
nearsighted. Every once in a while he blew smoke at the windshield as if he thought there were cobwebs blocking his view.

"I'm worried about Konigsberg just as much as you are," I
said, "although maybe for different reasons. He came to me for
help. I don't like to think I let him walk out of my office and into
some kind of trouble. Also, since the matter seems to have come
up—security clearance, where do my loyalties lie, etc.—I think I
should tell you I'm rooting for our side in the cold war. I want
to be really clear about that. What the hell, I was born in the
United States, you know, lived there all my life. I like it. It's a
parochial view, I suppose, but that's the way I feel. I believe in
our political institutions. I'm proud of the United States of
America. The Supreme Court. Congress. Even Congress. Kennedy, I sort of like Kennedy. I would have preferred Adlai
Stevenson, it's true, but Kennedy's all right. He has a kind of appealing little-boy quality, and he might amount to something
one of these days. The Communists, on the other hand, strike me
as arbitrary, unfair, and mean-spirited, sort of like the U.S. Army,
except bigger, and you can't get out after serving two years.
Also, although I'm bad-tempered, I admit, I hope I don't have to
tell you I would not do anything, out of pique, for instance, to

jeopardize the peace. What I'm trying to tell you, Fitch, is I'm on your side. Now, it's not easy to be on your side. First of all, you have an unpleasant personality. You've probably been told that before, I imagine. Second of all, it's obvious to me you have not been telling me the truth, not all of it anyway, about Lieutenant Konigsberg. This PINK business, or PANK, or whatever it is, for instance. And the Cuban missile crisis. I'd like to know, naturally, what the lieutenant's disappearance has to do with the Cuban missile crisis and East-West relations in general. Well, that's all right. You have reasons, I suppose, for not telling me. It doesn't matter. I feel an obligation to help anyway. That's what I'm supposed to do. So, I want you to know that whatever feelings I have about this idiotic plan, I'm going to do my best . . . to work together with you."

"Terrific," said Fitch, turning off the Autobahn onto a smaller road. "I'm glad to hear it. This sort of business goes better when things are pleasant."

The afternoon sun moved to our rear and was enveloped slowly by a cloud, edging the green landscape with gray. It looked like rain again. There was also a cloud in the car; fumes issued from Fitch with every breath.

"Since we're going to be partners," I said pleasantly, "I wonder if you would mind not smoking for a little while. The smoke is making me cry."

Fitch took his cigar from his mouth, looked at it dispassionately for a moment, then put it back in. "That's tough shit," he said.

I opened my window and looked out. A flock of birds were wheeling far above, crying out to each other in an oddly human voice. The wind had a sharp edge, and I could feel a few cold drops of rain. I thought USAREUR command was probably right: winter had arrived in Europe.

V

WALDHEIM itself was a moderate-sized town squeezed between two hills and surrounded by forest. I looked down at its
narrow streets and carefully enclosed gardens from the distance
as we passed from one hill to the other. The road we were traveling sloped upward perceptibly, then narrowed and ultimately
divided in two, its largest branch bending sharply and disappearing around the curve of the hill. We went the other way.
This fork had a dirt surface, transformed into mud by the recent
rains. Untended bushes edged in from the sides. A mantle of
trees, colored by autumn some of them, but mostly evergreen,
obscured the sky. Boulders jutted into and out of the road at
such inconvenient places, I thought they might have been placed
there to discourage anyone curious enough to explore such an
obscure byway. Fitch steered around these rocks, going at about
twenty miles an hour, which was still too fast. We veered from
one side of the road to the other. Whichever side we were on, he
seemed to favor the other, cursing under his breath until we slid
back the other way. We were proceeding now at a very sharp
angle up the hill, and skidding backward as often as side to side.
Nevertheless, after a time we had climbed to a considerable
height. We reached a point finally where the trees seemed to be
growing out more than up. I looked down between the branches
at the tops of the nearby hills, but all I could see was haze. I
was considering asking Fitch if he was sure we were headed the
right way—after all, this was his first visit too—but just then, in
the midst of this thickly wooded area, we came upon a swinging
metal gate, rusted and dilapidated. There was a sign on the

fence, also in disrepair, that suggested in peeling letters and numbers that the 3rd, or 13th, Reconnaissance Squadron of undecipherable division and indistinguishable army corps was posted beyond. A similarly anonymous and also rundown-looking soldier—no name tag, no insignia, shirt out, tie askew—was lounging against a railing, sucking on a piece of straw. He ambled over to us casually, but snapped to attention as soon as Fitch identified himself.

"Captain Redden," Fitch said. "On an emergency mission," he added. Whereupon the soldier ran over to the fence and threw it open.

Emergency mission. I liked the sound of that. The mention of my name by itself didn't usually excite such prompt attention.

We drove past the gate, bumped along for a while, and suddenly came upon a much higher fence, barbed along the top and electrified, according to a large and legible sign. On the other side was a narrow but well-tended gravel road and in the distance a row of angular cement buildings, blank on all sides.

"By God, Fitch," I exclaimed. "This isn't the 13th Reconnaissance Squadron of who knows which division and who cares what army corps. That's just cover, right? This place is actually supersecret, scientific Army Base Number Forty-three. Of course! Smart touch, that straw the soldier was chewing on. Had me fooled completely. You spies," I said, giving Fitch a little punch on the shoulder. "You're so clever."

We were checked through by a helmeted guard and directed to one of the larger cement cubes, or rather to an unobtrusive cabin that lay just behind it. This was HEADQUARTERS, the address of Colonel Collins, according to a sign posted next to a large mushroom. It was of a more traditional style, having windows, for example. We went not to the colonel's office but next door, to that of the sergeant, my old friend Kraven.

He came to his feet smartly, then looked at us and hesitated. Fitch had put on my name tag. I was not entirely visible, wearing civilian clothes. Kraven was evidently forewarned of our imposture, however, for he collected himself quickly and went to the door, shutting the three of us in together, alone.

"I know Captain Redden, you must be Fitch," he said, extending his hand to Fitch, who was leafing through a small notebook and seemed not to notice. "The lieutenant hasn't shown up yet, I guess, huh?" Kraven went on. "Jesus Christ."

He walked around the desk and sat down again. "Sir, I hope we find him. Forgetting about whatever the hell he knows, I mean, whatever he may have heard on the Big Ear, he's a decent guy. I'd hate to lose him. A post like this, everyone thrown together all the time, doesn't always bring out the best in people. But Konigsberg's okay. You had the feeling . . . well, he was a decent guy, like I said. I feel responsible in a way for what happened. First, getting faked out by Captain Redden here. I don't suppose that mattered very much; but after that I should never have left the guy alone, even for a minute. . . ."

"Hey . . . uh, there was some information I asked you guys to get for me," Fitch remarked impatiently. "And why am I talking to you? I understand the colonel is off somewhere with his dead daughter, the funeral or something, but don't you have an executive officer on this post? Somebody?"

"Sir, Colonel Collins felt the fewer people to know about your investigation, the better. Nobody even knows Konigsberg is missing except me and the colonel. Everyone thinks he's in the hospital, sick."

"Why did you?" I asked Kraven, who looked at me. "I mean, why did you leave him alone, seeing you were so worried about him? Fitch said you made a phone call. How come? Couldn't it wait until you got back to base?"

"I didn't make any telephone call. There was a call waiting for me. When we left your office. Downstairs. They told me an urgent call had just come through from Colonel Collins and I was supposed to take it in private."

"So private the lieutenant couldn't hear?"

The sergeant looked at me somberly. The room itself had a melancholy air, part the quiet gray miasma of late afternoon in the woods, which seeped in, it seemed, through the windows, and part the room itself, a typical army office, sterile and drab. "Things are very private around here, Doctor," he said. "Nobody knows, nobody wants to know, any more than they have to."

"Listen," Fitch interjected again. "I want you guys to understand something. We got to find Konigsberg, if we're going to find him at all, *now*. . . . Not next week. Next week is too late.

Right? Now, I got a lot of ground to cover, and I want to proceed expeditiously, without going over the same old shit a couple of extra times. Right? Okay?" Fitch tendered us both a tiny smile, showing his bad teeth. Then, having commanded our attention, he turned back to his notebook.

"This is new ground for me, Fitch," I pointed out mildly.

"The lieutenant reported in September fifth, is that right?" Fitch enquired of Kraven, who reached into a drawer and pulled out a folder before replying.

"That's right," he said, having found the appropriate document.

"And that was the first time he ever set foot in Germany, despite the fact he was fluent in the language?"

"Well, as far as we know," Kraven said. "You know what these security checks are like. That information probably came from the local branch of the FBI in Muncie, and I guess they thought they had more important things to do at the time."

"Anyway, so he's been here on base less than two months. He's signed in and out, what, a half-dozen times? We should be able to trace every move he made. I mean, if someone got to him, it had to be outside, right? No one's allowed on post without a security clearance, right? No visitors, certainly."

"That's right, sir. Nobody. Doesn't matter who. Not anybody gets on board here without a security clearance. That is . . . uh, except Captain Redden here. But this is the first time in the three years I been here. But I'm not so sure about that tracing-every-move business. You know, it doesn't matter what kind of secret equipment we got here, we got just ordinary soldiers using it, and they do what soldiers do everywhere. Sign in for each other. That kind of thing. Besides . . . something happened. It's not usual policy for a guy who just transfers in, but Lieutenant Konigsberg told us he had some family around, and somebody was sick or dying; so the colonel gave him a three-day pass. Not only that, the lieutenant probably could have slipped off base at night if he knew the guy standing guard, for a couple hours, anyway. This isn't a prison, after all. We don't expect somebody to run off and marry a Russian."

Kraven sounded a little put out. Konigsberg's disappearance seemed to have set everyone's teeth on edge. Either that or Fitch's charm was having its usual effect.

"Matter of fact," Kraven went on, "I know for a fact Konigsberg was taking off in the evenings. He has a girl in town. Had a girl. I heard they were planning on getting married maybe."

"Is that right?" Fitch said, looking up.

"Well, who knows?" Kraven replied. "You know the way these kids are. They're off in a foreign country, get lonely, and fall in love with the first girl they meet sometimes. A couple of weeks later they think they're in love with someone else. Anyway, this girl used to pick him up down the hill in a nice little BMW sports car. We don't let anyone use company transportation. That's one thing we do keep close track of. Besides, he doesn't drive."

"What? He's twenty-one years old, grew up in Indiana, and he doesn't know how to drive?"

"Well, he's not yet twenty-one, and he promised his mother not to drive until then. That's what he says. His older brother was killed at the age of seventeen in a car accident. One of the guys here, a sergeant, is teaching him now. Was teaching him."

Fitch began questioning Kraven about exact times and places. Where did Konigsberg go, when, and with whom. No *why*, I noticed. *Why* didn't seem interesting to Fitch. He also wanted to know how much. How much interest did Konigsberg have in his job, in other people's jobs, in politics. How much time did he spend talking on the telephone, how much money did he have in the bank, how many people did he know. And was he a homosexual.

Kraven knew more of the answers than I would have expected. Evidently considerable effort had already been spent tracing the lieutenant, tracing his recent past, anyway, up until the time he disappeared, diagramming it literally on a large piece of paper which Kraven read from, then handed to Fitch.

"So, this is what we got," Fitch said a few minutes later, after spitting out a piece of cigar. "Three things: First, this guy's been covering an awful lot of ground. Munich and Berlin, besides Nuremberg, according to a couple of train receipts off his dresser, right? And that's just places we know about already. Second, a hell of a lot of money is going through his bank account considering he's only a second lieutenant. Three thousand dollars. Another time, five thousand dollars. In one day, out the next. And that's just American Express. He might have opened accounts in any of the local banks. Third, just the opposite. Instead of too much, too little. No phone calls. No outgoing phone calls, anyway. Except to his girl friend. And a couple to his mother. Even guys who don't travel around a lot, who don't have sick family in the neighborhood, make phone calls sometimes. But not this guy. Now, are you sure about this, Kraven? All outgoing calls go through the switchboard, right?"

Kraven nodded assent. "Incoming too; but no one keeps track of them. The only reason we keep a record, you know, is for billing purposes. We're not looking to catch any spies by bugging the BOQ. There was one incoming call the operator remembered, though, three or four days ago, a guy with a German accent. That narrows it down to forty or fifty million people. He called three times before reaching the lieutenant. Later we traced the call back to Berlin. Narrowed it maybe to a couple of million people."

"I don't like the way this adds up," said Fitch, leaning back in his chair. "Looks like Konigsberg had something special in mind before he even came to Germany. First chance he gets here, he finds an excuse to get off base, obviously to make contact with somebody. No one goes off to sight-see in Berlin and Munich, both on the same three-day pass. I don't buy this bullshit about sick family he's got to visit. If he's so worried, why doesn't he call them up sometimes? Whoever he has to make contact with, he doesn't want anyone here to know about it. And there's the money. For services rendered. He's doing something for the money."

"You think he's selling military secrets?" I asked, trying to wade through all this. "I thought you were under the impression he was kidnapped. You know, PLINK. He was leaving us a message, right?"

"I don't know what happened. I'm trying to find out. Maybe he was being blackmailed and paid off at the same time. The Cuban thing comes along. Maybe that was too much for him. He balks, they take him away. I told you, I don't know," he said again, waving me away with the cigar.

"Are you sure he's not homosexual?" he said to Kraven.

Kraven shifted nervously in his chair before answering. "Sir," he said, his voice taking on an edge. "We've talked about this before, you and me, over the phone. I told you then that I got no special way of knowing what people do to each other sexually. I don't look through their windows. I don't follow them around. I don't see anybody dressed up in a dress. As far as I know, everybody around here is straight."

"Oh yeah?" said Fitch, suddenly in a rage. "What about Johnson? You remember him? It wasn't so long ago. Last month this time he was the head of security on this post. Unbelievable. The head of security. We caught him in bed with a fifty-year-old man. An *ugly* fifty-year-old man. Disgusting. You can't tell me he was the only one here doing things like that. Homosexuals. What do . . . what do you think?" Fitch said, turning to me. "They hang out together, don't they? Not likely he was doing it here by himself, was it?"

I considered this for a moment. "I think it is by definition possible to commit a homosexual act by oneself," I said finally, "in the privacy of one's room, often the bathroom. But I agree, except for logicians and others very literal-minded, those who speak of homosexual acts usually have in mind an act of love— no, let us not say love, for who can speak of what is in someone's heart—rather, an act of passion among a number of people all of the same sex, that number being at least two. Usually two," I added, to make myself entirely clear, an effort I could not consider altogether successful, judging by the look on Fitch's face.

"He had these . . . these pictures," Fitch said, fumbling inside his jacket, which looked like my jacket, since it had my name tag on it, except that my jacket never had my name tag on it. "Look at these," he said to Kraven, spilling a couple of photographs on the desk. "I know for a fact he got a hold of this stuff here. On the post."

Kraven didn't seem interested, but I leaned forward and picked one up. It was a photograph of a pencil drawing. A muscular young man was depicted legs apart, arms resting languidly on his knees, staring thoughtfully off to one side. Although underwear was drawn in for purposes of modesty, it was plain he was in a state of sexual excitement.

"Wow," I said, turning the picture from side to side. "My God, you can see the man's . . . the man's *sexual organ*. Look at that, Fitch." I waved the photo in front of him. "In outline, see? Under the underwear. There it is. There. That's it, all right."

"What's the matter with you?" said Fitch, looking at me as if I had suddenly developed an exfoliative rash.

"He's good-looking too, Fitch," I said, taking another look. "Handsome. A man like that could turn anyone's head. A real cutie." I held the photograph an inch in front of my nose. "Yum, yum," I said.

"You're a . . . a doctor," Fitch spluttered indignantly. "You think laughing at this filth . . . Is that your idea of—"

"Yum, yum, yum, yum."

Kraven interrupted. "Why do we have to go through this again? I don't know anything about homosexuals on this base, I told you. And like I told you before, offering a reward was a bad idea. Now you got everyone pissed off. Nobody's going to help you if they find out you're the same Henry Fitch that's been sending those wanted posters around."

"You posted a reward for homosexuals?" I asked Fitch, studying him closely. Here, I realized, was a truly unconventional mind. I wondered to what lengths he was likely to go to find Konigsberg. A query in the lost and found?

Fitch didn't think I merited any more attention. After assuring himself there was someone absolutely trustworthy manning the switchboard, he took Kraven's seat and in quick succession made a series of telephone calls. As a further precaution he "scrambled" most of them, a scrambler being a coding device, Kraven explained to me, evidenced only by a modest yellow button on the telephone, but with the capacity to make speech unintelligible to anyone listening in, "including sometimes the guy on the other end," he added glumly. These calls were, in order:

To the offices of the CID in Berlin and Munich. Konigsberg had asked about the names of hotels in each city, and Fitch wanted them checked. Also, the lieutenant had purchased traveler's checks prior to his pass, and it was just possible he was foolish enough to have used them for expense money, foolish, that is, if he was engaging in any secret or illicit activity. They could be traced readily.

To Fitch's office in Nuremberg. More checking. Konigsberg had asked someone casually about the nearest synagogue, which turned out to be in Nuremberg. The CID had already begun questioning members of the congregation, but so far no one they had spoken to had seen him, or was willing to say they had seen him. It was a small congregation, fifteen or twenty families, all that Hitler had left of a thriving Jewish community, and it seemed likely that if Konigsberg had ever attended services, his presence would have been noticed. On the other hand, German Jews got a little nervous still if they were questioned by the authorities, and they might have decided not to notice anything. As to where the lieutenant was currently, still no news. Fitch read off a further list of places to check. Also, he wanted enquiries made with army intelligence. Was there really increased traffic of refugees from East to West? And why? Intelligence from the CIA was being channeled to Fitch through the diplomatic mission, but they had nothing new. As far as Cuba went, everyone was getting his information from Armed Forces Radio. Russia and the U.S. were heading for a showdown in the mid-Atlantic.

Briefly, to Chief Fuchs. He had news, but not about Lieutenant Konigsberg. In the short time since we had sat in his office, the murderer of the woman whose body we had seen had been apprehended. He was a known sex criminal and, luckily, not an American soldier. Under the new status of forces agreement, such an offense would have been tried in German courts and would certainly have been an embarrassment to the United States, coming at a time when the Eastern European press was trying to depict us as the oppressors rather than as the allies of the German people.

Finally, to the police chief in Muncie, where it was still early morning. The preliminary screening of Konigsberg done by the FBI six months ago was inadequate, Fitch told him. The police would have to undertake a new investigation. It was necessary to know everything about Konigsberg in detail, especially any unusual or uncharacteristic behavior prior to his entering the service. Fitch had a list of names—friends in Konigsberg's college fraternity, members of his temple—people who were to be interrogated. It was important especially to learn about the lieutenant's financial status, and, in particular, any recent bank transactions he may have made. Fitch had to know all of this immediately, he said. A matter of the utmost urgency.

I sat there listening and began to think Fitch might be pretty good at his job after all. Certainly someone thought so. He had been given, and was acting with, wide authority. Konigsberg had disappeared less than twenty-four hours ago, and Fitch was already reaching out for him across a distance of hundreds, even thousands, of miles with hundreds, perhaps thousands, of men. He was a little paranoid, I thought, but for all I knew, being a little paranoid might be an advantage for a detective. He wasn't buggy just on the subject of homosexuality, he was suspicious of everyone. Right now, while he was talking on the telephone, he was staring at me suspiciously, an Oscar Homolka kind of stare. But maybe that was sensible under the circumstances. Maybe. Then again, maybe not.

"I want to see Konigsberg's room now," Fitch announced, putting away the telephone and getting up from the desk.

"What about Lieutenant Baker?" Kraven asked. "He was the guy you . . . uh, Redden here was supposed to see. You're going to have to examine him or it's going to look funny. He's in a bad way. Off the wall."

"Yeah, I heard. Talks to toilet seats. A nut case," Fitch commented.

"Hey, Fitch," I complained, "why don't you take care of the detective work and let me handle the practice of psychiatry?"

"Oh yeah? I'm not so sure I need you at all. You act like an asshole half the time. I think I'm better off on my own, faking it. You can go home and get your head shot off as far as I'm concerned."

"This guy Baker, I don't know," Kraven said, shaking his head. "He needs a real psychiatrist. Besides talking to himself, he's hearing voices. God's voice, or General MacArthur—somebody like that. Yesterday he started crying for no reason. And he hasn't slept or eaten in a couple of days."

"Sounds like your garden variety psycho to me," said Fitch.

I cleared my throat. "If you're going to represent yourself as a psychiatrist, Fitch," I told him, "I think you should be aware that we in the trade do not ordinarily refer to our patients as 'psychos' or 'nut cases.' These terms are imprecise and have little diagnostic significance. More important, they suggest to some people a certain lack of warmth, an inability, as it were, to identify strongly with the patient's point of view. The same objections apply to 'fruitcake.'"

"I don't think you'll want to spend an awful lot of time talking to him today," Kraven commented. "He's passed out or something."

"What do you mean?" I asked, getting serious quickly.

"No, he's okay. I think he's okay, anyway. We called up the medical officer from 3rd Division—you know, we don't even let doctors on the base unless they got a security clearance—anyway, he ordered some medicine over the phone. I guess we gave too much. Baker's been asleep since noon."

"Well, do you think maybe we can go look at him," I asked. "Since that's what we came here for."

Kraven looked over at Fitch, who nodded.

"This is *not* exactly what we came for," Fitch confided in me as we went to the door. "We came to find out what the hell happened to Konigsberg, that's what we came for. So let's just do this quickly, whatever you're going to do. I still want to look at Konigsberg's room. If this guy Baker's real sick, you can fix him up a little. I don't want to have to transport him to a hospital. But . . . uh, you don't have to exactly cure him. We can use him as an excuse to come back here the next couple of days."

"You know, Fitch, you're beginning to annoy me."

Fitch and I were escorted to the infirmary by a corpsman, to whom we had been introduced respectively as Captain Redden and Corporal Vigliotti. The corpsman was also a corporal, a round, harried-looking fellow who looked like a teen-ager, and probably was. He mentioned his name, Randy Biddle, speaking in a clear, high-pitched voice, and staring at Fitch with great intensity. I recognized the look of adulation that I think is proper in someone meeting a psychiatrist, and that in my experience lasts about a minute and a half. But then again, that was only in my experience. Fitch responded effusively, for him, with a grunt.

Along the way I enquired about the various cement buildings that loomed up suddenly and peculiarly out of the woods.

"Wow," Biddle replied, breathlessly, "that's all secret, very secret. Those buildings, they got some of the most secret stuff you ever heard of. Electronics equipment, we're not supposed to tell *anyone*. That one . . . that one over there behind that big bush. You see that big bush? I think it's a juniper bush. That building alone, you should see the machines they got in there. Radio receivers. Microwave. So sensitive they can pick up television from the Balkans, and they don't hardly *have* no television in the Balkans. See that aerial sticking way up there past the trees? You wouldn't believe if I told you how powerful that aerial is. That aerial is powerful enough to pick up conversations from Russian tank forces out in the field. Of course, you got to understand Russian. When stuff is beamed out straight to us, we can pick up *Moscow*! Diplomatic stuff, sometimes. And over there, computers. Monsters. In that little building. Big as a room. What the computers do is deciphering, unscrambling, and filtering out television from the secret stuff. Otherwise, all of a sudden in the middle of tank maneuvers, you get Marshal Dillon. Nobody would think we got the latest computers in a place like this. That's because they're not supposed to think anything like that. Deception.

"We broadcast out too, you know. Nobody is supposed to know that. That's *really* secret. Those radar-looking dishes just looks like radar. Isn't really. We control agents in Germany, Poland, Czechoslovakia. You know, when there's something top-drawer secret, too secret for slipping in Radio Free Europe. Like this Russian colonel Penkovsky, the guy who's giving us all this dope on the missile business in Cuba . . ."

"For Chrishaksh!" Fitch exclaimed, trying to get his cigar out of his mouth. "I thought this stuff was supposed to be secret!"

"You bet it is, sir. I hate to think what would happen if any of this got out. If the Russians knew we know what they're going to do in Cuba, the whole thing might turn out different. If it's one thing we understand around here, it's the need for strict security." Biddle had heard, he went on to tell Fitch, who was making guttural sounds, that during the Second World War, loose lips had sunk ships.

I pulled Fitch to one side. "I take it this PENK you've been worried about stands for Penkovsky?"

"None of your fucking-A business!" he yelled at me.

Baker was lying flat on his back, arms at his sides. No pillow. Except for undershorts, he was naked. His skin was glistening, and his breathing was slow and deep. He looked as if he were sunbathing. But no sun penetrated that room. Night had come finally, blacking out the window. There was scarcely any light at all, only a feeble yellow glow issuing from a reading lamp off in a corner. The infirmary was just that one room, a hospital bed, a few shelves holding medicines, and a couple of filing cabinets.

"It's more like a first-aid station than an infirmary," Biddle said apologetically, echoing my thought, "but most guys here are pretty healthy. Comes from selecting only very healthy people. Someone has an accident, we take him over to 3rd Division, or transport him to Nuremberg. No nurse or anybody here. Just me. I don't do much treatment myself, which I don't know how to do really. Most of the time I do typing. Which I don't do so good either."

While Biddle was rambling, I was examining Baker. He had passed out, all right, but was rousable. I shook him a couple of times, and he was able to tell me his name and age, and the day of the week. He started to fall asleep again when I asked him what post he was on, but judging from the sign out front, that may have been a tricky question. His blood pressure and other vital signs were normal. A quick neurological examination was also within normal limits.

Fitch was also examining Baker, impelled either by the wish to convince Biddle, who was watching, that he was in fact a psychiatrist, or by some obscure curiosity. First he grabbed hold of Baker's wrist, putting his thumb against a bony process, and looked at his watch, as if he wanted to know if his patient's pulse was strong enough to palpate through bone. Then he took a stethoscope from the wall and listened to Baker's sternum. Then, very carefully, very close up, he looked at Baker's arm, then his legs, then his neck, both sides, finally he carefully picked up the elastic of Baker's undershorts and peeked underneath.

"Do you mind . . . sir," I whispered to him, "telling me what you're doing?"

He leaned over Baker, who had started to snore faintly, and whispered back, scarcely moving his lips, a facility I attributed to his having a cigar clenched permanently between his jaws. "You know what I'm doing," he said, nodding his head imperceptibly in the direction of Biddle, who was staring wide-eyed at us from the foot of the bed. "I'm examining the patient."

"This guy's problem is hallucinations," I whispered back. "Why are you looking in his underwear?"

"Marks," he whispered, a little louder. "I was looking for marks."

"What sort of marks?"

"Jesus Christ." More a growl than a whisper. "What difference does it make what sort of mark? I was looking for drug marks. Tracks or something."

"Tracks?" I said in a loud voice. "On his . . . on his . . ."

"Hey, it's been done, you know. Maybe I know more about this than you do."

"Listen," I said back in a whisper. "What makes you think this guy was shooting up?"

"I didn't say he was shooting up. I didn't say anything. It doesn't hurt to check, does it? You want me to stand here with my tongue hanging out?" He stared at me defiantly, eyes narrowed, his cigar hanging out.

I turned to Biddle. "Can you tell me what medication this man has been given? He's stuporous, semicomatose almost."

"Seconal. The doctor said he was afraid to prescribe anything else without seeing the patient."

"How much?"

"A lot, I think. Two hundred milligrams IM every hour until he fell asleep. He got three doses."

"Holy smoke."

"Boy, he was really agitated. Screaming. The first couple of shots didn't touch him at all."

"How long was that going on?"

"Well, he was sick probably for some time, talking to himself; but until yesterday, nobody paid attention. That's the way things are around here. As long as someone does his job, it doesn't matter what else he does. Colonel Collins isn't around much to keep an eye out. He's in charge of a string of these bases. Not just here. Anyway, a couple of days ago, Baker, instead of talking quietly to himself, starts talking loud. All about Jesus hanging out in the canteen. He's sort of religious. Then he starts laughing for no reason. Getting all excited. Then crying. Also, he says he hasn't been eating or sleeping. And the way he talks is funny. Kind of disconnected."

Biddle was giving a good account of a typical acute paranoid schizophrenia. I started to explain to him that his patient was going to be pretty sick for a while. "The disruption of his thinking you're referring to is called 'loosening of associations.' It's one of the primary signs of schizophrenia. Another is inappropriateness of affect. When someone starts laughing like that, it means . . ."

"Corporal Vigliotti, this man needs our help," Fitch said, tapping Baker on the nipple. "We got no time to give a lecture now. Biddle, I wonder if you'd leave us alone with the patient for a minute or two. You understand, psychiatric conversations with the patient are confidential."

Baker snored loudly as if to register a concurring view.

Biddle left promptly.

"What are you trying to do, Redden," Fitch asked me as soon as we were alone, "embarrass me? You're making it look as if I don't know birdshit. You better cut it out, if you know what's good for you. Now prescribe whatever you want for this guy—mark it down here—and let's get going."

A few minutes later Fitch handed my prescription to Biddle, for Thorazine instead of Seconal, enough to calm Baker down, hopefully, without knocking him out altogether. We were coming back the next day, Fitch added, to interview him properly. Then, abruptly, he disappeared in the direction of Konigsberg's room, into the woods.

I lingered behind long enough to give more detailed instructions; and I left my telephone number, suggesting that Captain Redden would appreciate being called if Baker's condition got worse.

"Did you see which way he went," I asked, heading off after Fitch.

"This way, I heard him tell Kraven he was going to the BOQ. That's this way."

We stepped over a couple of logs.

"He's really sharp, isn't he?" Biddle commented. "And dedicated."

"Huh? Yeah, dedicated."

"That's what I heard from the grapevine. He's not into this Mickey Mouse army stuff. All he cares about is whether somebody is a human being, you know, how he feels."

"What? That prick? Are you kidding?"

"Prick? Hey, that's not a very loyal way to talk. The guy treats you decent, listens to what you have to say. I noticed that. I can see he taught you something too. That's a terrific job you got there, working for him. It's been two years I been around this base, and people treat me like shit. Just 'cause I can't speak Russian."

"Are you sure we're going the right way? This looks like jungle."

"Camouflage."

He was right, I walked into a tangle of camouflage netting.

"How did you get it?" Biddle asked me.

"What? Get what?"

"Your job."

"This job? You wouldn't believe it if I told you."

"You type good, right?"

Biddle left me at the BOQ. I told him Fitch's cover story, that we were going to pick up some stuff Konigsberg left in his room and needed in the hospital.

"I hope the lieutenant feels better soon," Biddle said, shaking his head. "A nice guy. Tell him we're keeping a lookout for him."

Yeah. Sure. So were a lot of other people.

Konigsberg's bachelors' quarters were two rooms and a bathroom, large by the standards of the Nuremberg BOQ, maybe to compensate for being stuck out in the middle of nowhere. The army was pretty good that way. Troops posted away from access to women, for instance, were entitled to a Ping-Pong table.

"Shut the door behind you, and don't move anything around," Fitch told me as soon as I walked through the door. "Goddamn it," he added softly, looking about the room. "This is some place. Some contrast to yours. I was in your room a minute and a half, and I knew everything I needed, or wanted, to know about you. God knows how long this is going to take."

Fitch was standing in front of a long slab of wood, which served apparently as a desk. Papers, books, travel folders, different-sized notebooks, and loose pieces of shirt cardboard were strewn across the surface. On one corner was an uneven pile of magazines. On top of the pile was a box of typing paper, and on top of that, loose sheets of memorandum paper imprinted with the slogan "Things to do soonest!"—"soonest" being army talk for right away. These, and everything else I could see, were written on, including a small bright-yellow ticket that lay alongside a calendar and that I recognized as the emblem of Herman's Chinese Laundry.

"Lots of clues here, I bet," I said enthusiastically.

Fitch said nothing. He must have agreed, though, for he sat down and began going through this stuff page by page.

The rest of the room was similarly cluttered. A chair and couch were piled with cushions and loose articles of clothing. A shirt was sitting up in the chair, one arm resting quietly in its lap, the other draped casually over an adjacent lamp table, as if the person who had been wearing it had evaporated suddenly, as in a sense he had. The invisible man had abandoned his shoes in front of a television set. His socks were nearby. Other socks led away like footprints into the bedroom. There was opposite me a small and obviously unused fireplace, an indication that the building was put up originally by someone other than the Americans, who were great believers in central heating. There were radiators, too, to mark the coming of their reign. Above the fireplace was a mantel laden with utensils, a pepper pot, and a hot plate. In odd juxtaposition to these domestic articles was an elaborate porcelain tableau. A tall Diana, her bow drawn, was set to impale a buck arching majestically behind the boughs of an elm tree. These figures were posed before a small and partly cracked mirror. My reflection, the little I could see of it, startled me. Just for a moment I looked like a civilian. Other knick-knacks were placed here and there on shelves in peculiar arrangement, a clock running, I noticed, three hours slow, another calendar, a dead potted plant, not even recently dead, judging by the color of its leaves, a rock with eyes and a smile painted on it. A jelly donut. Dominating the room, however, in every corner, on shelves, in piles, laid out on a lamp table, propping up the lamp table, there were books.

"This guy's got more books than the hospital library," I said to Fitch, who wasn't listening.

I walked into the bedroom, where I found more scattered about, including a novel printed in Russian, lying open on the unmade bed, but open only to page 5. Konigsberg, plainly in the habit of reading, may have become too depressed to read. This room too was in disarray. A *Schrank* standing in the corner was ajar, revealing a few crumpled uniforms squeezed together by a half-dozen civilian suits and jackets. Underneath, but reaching

up to knee level, was an immense pile of dirty laundry, which
spilled out onto the floor. The bureau drawers, on the other
hand, which were also open, were almost empty of clothes.
There was some underwear, but no shirts. On the top of the bureau was another collection of odds and ends, a brush and comb,
of course, but also paper cups, a jar of mustard, and a bag of
pretzels, a couple of which had spilled from the bureau to the
floor. Having made home visits to people who were depressed, I
wasn't surprised to see such a mess. Someone who has lost interest in life, finds little reason to tidy up. But this place was especially messy. Either Konigsberg had been depressed longer than
I thought, or he was just naturally messy. A messy guy who
liked books. I hated to see guys like that get into trouble.

I went into the bathroom. The medicine cabinet was standing
open, like everything else. I could see, besides the usual para-
phernalia of shaving, a few vials of pills. I reached for them, but
was arrested momentarily by Fitch, who was evidently staring at
me through a wall.

"I told you not to touch anything," he reminded me.

They were only cold tablets, I discovered—antihistamines,
systemic decongestants, over-the-counter pain medication, no
drugs that could produce depression or be subject to abuse.
Konigsberg wasn't feeling low by virtue of getting high. Nor was
there any medicine that would suggest he was suffering from
any of the wide variety of physical illnesses that sometimes
cause depression.

I meandered back into the bedroom and was about to rejoin
Fitch when my attention was caught by one of the jackets hanging in the *Schrank*. Most of the clothes squeezed in next to it
were conservative: jeans, a blazer, a couple of wool suits, a corduroy jacket, all in gray or dark brown, and all threadbare. By
contrast, this jacket was new and a glowing green, the color of
grass; and in the vest pocket was folded a pink handkerchief, the
color and shape of a tulip. I noticed, taking a closer look, that
the sleeve length was just a little longer than the other jackets'.
Either Konigsberg had grown an inch or so since joining the
army, or it was someone else's jacket. I started going through the
pockets—experiencing a sudden interest that was almost embarrassing. This is why I became a psychiatrist, I thought, in
order to search into everyone's private places. Jesus Christ, I
thought to myself next, where do I get these stupid ideas?

The pockets were empty except for another bus schedule, and folded inside that, a train schedule. I took these to Fitch, explaining where I got them.

"It's another copy of the same bus schedule I gave you before," I pointed out, "except a couple of places are underlined. Not Koenigsberg. Nearby towns. The train schedule covers all of Bavaria, and Berlin. He must have used it on the three-day pass. He has particular trains marked back and forth to Berlin. And to Munich. Also there's an address written along the margin. And, see, he's written in a name, the Augustiner Keller. That's a beer hall in Munich, I think. Hitler made the place famous. Used to meet there with his buddies during the early days of the party."

I thought Fitch was going to reproach me for touching things, but he just sat quietly at the desk for a moment, staring at the two timetables. Then he commented mildly that he thought that information would be helpful.

"In case you're wondering what this stuff is," he added, shoving some papers around, "Konigsberg wrote. I mean he wrote letters to his mother. To his friends. He wrote—what is this—an essay. Something about man's place in the environment. It's missing pages fifteen to twenty-two. It looks like every spare moment he wrote something or other. That's terrific, isn't it? Konigsberg's missing, probably ran off somewhere to commune with nature, taking along pages fifteen to twenty-two; and I'm left here to wade through this crap. Also, he wrote half of it in abbreviations, shorthand maybe. Looks like code. Poetry. He writes poetry too."

I grabbed the piece of paper Fitch fluttered at me. It was a poem, all right, or parts of a poem at least, scribbled in pencil. It began:

> A raucous bird twists out of the sun
> To perch unafraid on a stranger land.
> Within his ken a man's life is begun,
> Mustered to service unsought, unplanned.
>
> The man and the bird live out the year.
> The man remembers to live for ten.
> He lives ten again 'ere his purpose is clear.
> Confirmed in the cause of his countrymen.

There was a space then with a few tentative rhymes written in the margin, and there were other entirely illegible notes. There was also a last verse, marked, as a matter of fact, *the last verse.*

> A towering spire cast fully enameled
> To weather smooth the wordly clime,
> His soul embossed if still untrammeled,
> Crumbles at last in the traffic of time.

It was the sort of thing I might expect a bright twenty-year-old to write: very grand, grandiloquent even, and very serious. He was writing about himself, of course, making himself the hero; but if the poem meant anything else, it wasn't apparent to me. What was beginning to become clear, however, was that Konigsberg was in a number of respects not just an ordinary bright twenty-year-old.

While Fitch went on muttering to himself and shuffling papers, I looked around the room again. It seemed inviting, comfortable somehow, despite the clutter. But that was probably a matter of point of view. Other people's rooms always looked more comfortable to me than my own.

I heard the creak of a door behind me and turned to find a very big man, tall and broad, a broad, pale face surrounded by a stubble of gray hair, looking at us suspiciously. He was dressed in fatigues.

"What are you guys doing here?" he asked.

"Uh . . . Corporal Vigliotti, I thought I told you to close the door," Fitch said, looking up.

"I thought I did."

"You guys better tell me who you are," our visitor said, moving into the room.

"I am Captain Redden, a psychiatrist," Fitch replied, smiling vapidly. He did not look natural smiling, perhaps because of his crooked teeth. He looked peculiar, his lips pulled and curled into a grimace. It was sort of a Lon Chaney look.

"Yeah?" said our visitor. "Yeah?"

"That's my assistant," Fitch said, pointing at me. "And who may I ask are you?" he added, taking a surprisingly arch and urbane tone.

"My name is Bell. I live next door," the man replied. "I'd still like to know what you're doing here."

"Oh yeah, Sergeant Bell," said Fitch. "You're the guy who's been teaching Konigsberg to drive. How come you live here in officers' quarters?"

"We're sort of relaxed about those things out here. Now I'm going to ask you one last time. What the fuck are you guys doing here?"

Fitch stared at Bell for a moment. "Listen, Sergeant," he said finally, "I may be sitting here smiling at you pleasantly, but that doesn't mean I want you coming on to me like I'm your God-damn nephew. I can see you're built like the rear end of an elephant, but I'm not impressed. Just watch your fucking mouth."

So much for the urbane Fitch.

Bell turned a mottled color. He leaned forward, resting a few fingers on the wood slab, which tilted perceptibly, and glowered. Fitch was not a small man, but I had the clear impression that were he not wearing a captain's uniform, he would be resting in a heap in the corner. But he himself didn't seem worried. He was smiling again and blowing smoke around.

"But since you're so nosy," Fitch offered up gracefully, after a moment or two of hard staring back and forth, "we came to run an errand for your friend Konigsberg. He's in the hospital, you know."

"Yeah, I heard," said Bell, backing off a little. "What's the matter with him? I been trying to call, but they tell me each time the hospital don't have a patient by that name."

"On my orders," said Fitch promptly. "The man is very depressed. I don't want him bothered by phone calls or visitors or anything."

"From his friends even? That's peculiar. Wouldn't that be a help? Cheer him up."

"You would think so, wouldn't you?" I interjected. "Just common sense. But you'd be surprised to know a lot of psychiatric hospitals have a policy of barring visits from friends or family, sometimes for weeks after a patient is admitted. No telephone calls, even, and—"

"Corporal Vigliotti . . . uh, just carry on, will you?" Fitch frowned at me and waved his arm vaguely, as if I were supposed to be engaged in some important task at the other end of the room.

"I'm pretty sure Konigsberg would want to talk to me," Bell said.

"Why?"

"Well, you know. We were . . . buddies."

"Nope. He didn't want to talk to anyone. I asked. He wants to rest and think about things. A sad guy like that has to come to terms with the meaning . . . the existential. Besides, he's got therapy all the time. Group. Occupational. Recreation therapy. He's busy."

"Paper-doll cutting and doodling," I explained. "It's very intensive. Helps with the existential."

Fitch was looking at me with what I took to be disapproval, although having, as he did, only a limited repertoire of expression, ranging from a sneer to a snarl, I couldn't be sure.

I went over to a bookcase and pretended to be looking for something. Konigsberg had very protean tastes in literature, I noticed, everything from science fiction to *War and Peace*. Next to Raymond Chandler's *The Big Sleep* was something called *The Zionist Idea* by Hertzberg.

"There's something funny about all of this," said Bell, taking a step back so he could look at both of us at the same time. "Your patient is supposed to be in the hospital, and you guys are here. Besides, Redden," he said to Fitch, "you don't sound like no psychiatrist to me. I know most of you guys are half nuts, but you look three-quarters nuts to me."

"I would like to take exception to that remark," I said, holding aloft a finger.

"Shut up," said Fitch.

"You expect me to stand by silently when he's fresh like that to you?"

"Also you're too old," Bell added, walking over to a table where there was a telephone. "I mean, to be a captain in the medical corps."

"Oh yeah?" said Fitch. "You look pretty old to be a staff sergeant. So what?"

Bell picked up the telephone. "Hello? . . . hello. Get me Colonel Farber."

Fitch began to look uncomfortable. "Listen," he said, "talk to Kraven. He knows we're here. Or Colonel Collins. Farber doesn't know."

Bell held the receiver to his ear and stared silently at Fitch, who went on, "We came to pick up some toilet articles, for Christ's sake."

"You lookin' for his toothbrush in all those papers?"

"And a book. Konigsberg wanted a book. Did you find it?" Fitch said to me, looking up suddenly.

"Well . . . uh, yeah. Here it is." I picked up the first book I saw. It was lying on an end table, as if someone had just put it down.

Bell looked startled. "Konigsberg wants to read . . . *that*? In the hospital?"

I looked at the book. It was Fodor's guide to Germany.

"Sure," I said. "He's not going to be in the hospital forever, you know."

Fitch tendered me a sour look, almost dead center between a snarl and a sneer.

"Kraven, is that you?" Bell said into the telephone. "I'm calling from . . . right, from Konigsberg's room. I thought I'd talk to . . . oh. Well, there are these guys here . . . You mean, it's true? This . . . He's a psychiatrist? . . . All right, listen. I'm hanging around anyway, just in case. You know, make sure they lock up . . ."

"You don't have to bother," Fitch said, getting up. "We're leaving. We got everything we need, for right now, anyway. You can tell Kraven we'll be back tomorrow to examine that case of . . . uh, that case of coma."

I went back to the bathroom and collected Konigsberg's razor and some other stuff. We were making up this stupid story as we were going along, but I didn't want to make that any more obvious than it already was. I put these things into a small laundry bag along with the Fodor's.

Fitch and Bell were waiting for me at the door. We made an elaborate show of exiting together, Fitch pulling the door shut then pushing on it to make sure it had locked, as if we were each afraid there was something valuable left inside that the others might steal at the first opportunity.

There were recriminations on the way home. Fitch explained to me again and in more than usual detail why I was a wiseass and an asshole, two kinds of ass, as it were. I complained in turn about his wasting time putting a sergeant in his place when there was no time to waste, when East-West relations, the future of the world, and God knows what else was hanging in the balance. In such a way we railed at each other, until after a time, finally, we ran out of things to say. Fitch drove on quickly and silently through the blackness. I was comforting myself, as I often do in moments of quiet, with the thought that whether or not I accomplished anything that day, it would all be the same a million years from now, when suddenly a car drawing up behind us backfired. Aware, as I was, that whoever was shooting at me had refrained during the previous few hours, and was perhaps, therefore, behind schedule, I slid in a rush to the floor of the car —stimulating the first genuine amusement I had seen Fitch display. He chuckled malignly, and continued to chuckle at intervals over the next half hour, as if the memory of my abasement was echoing down the narrow passages of his mind.

VI

"JUST MAKE DAMN SURE you're ready," Fitch told me before letting me off at the front gate to the Nuremberg BOQ. He was referring to our appointment the following day and our further collaboration, if such a fanciful term could be used to describe the ragged three-legged race we were running.

I was more concerned at the moment, though, with getting ready to dash from the gate to the front door of the building. My car had been standing only a few feet away that morning when someone shot off the mirror; and it seemed reasonable to think that whoever was looking for me then might still be around. Fitch was not so moved by my predicament that he was willing to get out of his car, open the gate, get back into his car, proceed a hundred feet up the driveway, and then have to turn all the way around again.

"I don't got time for this," he declared indignantly, as if I had suggested we slip away for a weekend excursion. "Besides, if they're going to shoot you, they're going to shoot you."

Having offered that consoling thought, he prodded me out of the car, immediately shifted into gear, and sped away, leaving me crouched in front of the gate, leaves swirling about my feet, my shadows, both of them, also shifting about nervously against the wire fence. I squinted up at the two streetlamps, bright moons, put so near to each other and to the driveway, I remembered, for purposes of "safety." Quickly, I threw myself against the gate and bounced off. My accident that morning had pulled the fence out of line and someone had wedged the gate closed. Still staying in a crouch, I put my shoulder to it again and bounced off hard enough to end up slipping off the curb into the street. I was almost hit by a panel truck, which screeched by close enough, however, to provide momentary cover. I came at the fence again, kicking the gate at the crosspiece and pronouncing a few magic words under my breath, but no opening appeared. Damn it, other people must have managed somehow to get in and out all day long. It was then that I noticed the latch was down. I pried it up—it was bent now, whatever condition it might have been in a moment ago—and threw the gate open. Hunching over, like they taught us during desert maneuvers at Fort Sam, I ran a zigzag course up the driveway, from a line of bushes over on one side across to the other side into a garden, back over to the bushes, then back the other way again. Finally I tumbled over a bush and landed on my ass; but by then I was in shadow. I limped the last few feet on the grass over to the doorway of the BOQ. There was a man standing there, holding a pipe in one hand and in the other a lighted match that had burned down most of the way. He was staring at me wide-eyed.

"The latch," I explained as I brushed by him. "They usually keep the latch open."

There was a note pinned on my door. "Greetings," it began, calling to mind unpleasant memories of my draft notice. "It is now 6:30. I am waiting. I am hungry. Come to my room. Schulz. P.S. Urgent matter to discuss." Below this message was an arrow penciled in, pointing off to my left.

I went next door, which was in that direction, knocked a couple of times, and when there was no answer, walked in. The room was dark. There was no one there.

"Hello? Schulz? Robert Schulz?" I cried, leaning out into the hallway again, in case he was in the bathroom or somebody else's room; but again, no reply. I flipped the light switch on. Schulz had very definitely moved in. There were Persian rugs on the floor and a leather recliner. Photographs of expensive-looking cars were hung neatly on the walls. The faint aroma of a pipe also hung about. Near the window was a desk and on top of it a desk lamp. Taped to the lamp shade was another note, which, it turned out, was also for me.

"Captain Redden, M.D.," Schulz had written in large block

letters. "It is now 6:35. I am hungrier. Too hungry to wait. Meet me at Der Turm (see below). Hurry." A tiny arrow pointing down was squeezed into the remaining space.

The rather formal address was an allusion to a book, *Captain Newman, M.D.*, which sat on Schulz's desk and which, as it happened, I had read. It was about a noble psychiatrist who is called to service in the United States Army and who tries to preserve his patients' well-being by opposing the army's single-minded attempt to return psychiatric casualties to active duty. My appreciation of the story was spoiled by knowing that the army was right and Newman wrong. In general, the faster patients return to their units, the better they do.

I looked "below," under the book, on the floor, under the desk, without finding anything; but then again, I didn't know what I was looking for. I snapped on the desk lamp. Off to one side of the desk, facing the wrong way, was a silver picture frame. Turning it around, I discovered it held a photograph of Schulz and a girl dressed in a mink coat; and tucked into one corner of the frame was a third note, folded over, my name inscribed on the outside in the same bold handwriting, but in a more relaxed style.

"Dear Abe, buddy," the note read. Underneath there was a sideways arrow sketched in to make sure I would understand that I was supposed to unfold the note and read further. For a moment I was inclined not to. I was annoyed by all these messages pointing me in different directions. I felt as if I had been drawn somehow, unwillingly, into a treasure hunt. Now if I went seven paces in a northwesterly direction I would find an arrow marked in the sand. This would direct me to another arrow, which would direct me to another arrow. I would find one arrow after another, but no treasure. Not the way things were going. My life had devolved more into a Monkeybar race than a treasure hunt, quick dashes from nowhere to no place, to no purpose.

The remainder of this final memorandum was given over to detailed directions to Der Turm restaurant, the text illustrated by more arrows. The guy definitely had a thing with arrows. Evidently the restaurant could be approached only from one direction, since the last arrow described three sides of a rectangle. None of this information proved helpful. I got into a taxi fifteen minutes later, carefully pronounced the name of the restaurant, and was delivered to its door ten minutes after that.

I was ushered through a crowded but quiet dining room into an alcove, where Schulz was sitting at a small table. He waved his pipe at me when he saw me approaching, then turned back to the women at the adjacent table to whom he had been speaking. He was animated, and they were both laughing. I was surprised he was willing to spare me a glance. The woman sitting across from him was thirty or forty pounds overweight; but the one on his right was beautiful. Long blond hair was pulled back sharply, framing an oval, almost angular face, pale eyes, a full mouth. Of course, there was something more, as there always has to be if someone is truly beautiful—a liveliness of expression, intelligence perhaps, some aspect of charm. She glowed.

I sat down opposite Schulz without distracting him from the story he was telling, an involved account of his participation in the recent war games along the course of the Danube: ". . . which is not the blue Danube, you must know," he pointed out, smiling a little, eyes sparkling. He had a glow of his own. "The Danube is shallow and muddy. The brown Danube, it should be called, judging at least from that grubby little spot where our forces came together—excuse me, converged—in one last brutal drive to destroy the imaginary enemy, Polish troops, I think they were supposed to have been, backed up by the Russians, of course, and possibly by certain confused elements of the Austrian army. At the time I was sitting around in a tent, like I had been doing the previous week, warming my hands over a pot-bellied stove and listening to the rain drumming on the canvas. I was considering running through the multiplication tables, just to keep my mind occupied, when suddenly, dramatically, there rose up, I thought, the distant noise of engines, a low-pitched noise, like gargling, and above that the faint sound of music.

"'Hark,' I said to a couple of corpsmen who were playing gin rummy their thirty-eighth straight hour by the dim light of a kerosene lamp, and who, maybe for that reason, hadn't noticed yet that the deck had only forty-nine cards. I addressed them again. It was hard to get their attention. They had served three or four years in the army, each of them; and their brains had liquefied. You could see the stuff running out of their ears.

" 'Hark,' I said to them still again, 'do you hear the gargling of engines and above that the faint sound of music?'

"They turned their heads slowly and blinked at me a couple of times—a sign, in them, of almost unbearable excitement.

"Yes, the sound was unmistakable now, engines—tank engines, I thought—and the melodic strains of 'Sukiyaki.' You know the song 'Sukiyaki,' ladies? Yes? Well, American soldiers have a tradition of singing whenever they enter into battle. It used to be 'Yankee Doodle,' but nowadays they sing 'Sukiyaki,' a song written to commemorate Admiral Dewey's destruction of the Japanese fleet in Tokyo bay.

"Stirred by that memory, I hurried to the front of the tent and threw open the flap. The day was foggy and misty and cloudy, an indistinct sort of day. Everything was the color of mud, especially the muddy, brown Danube. Even the red cross on the side of the ambulance was brown and almost invisible. Then, in the distance, through the mist, over the rise of a hill, there came hurrying in our direction, its loudspeaker playing loudly, a tank, the first tank I had seen in a week of tank maneuvers. And just then, by God, from the opposite direction, from starboard, or maybe larboard, a second tank appeared, quickly rolling over a bush and knocking down a tree. Both tanks were moving very quickly. A pincer movement, probably. An enveloping action. They were racing directly at each other. At about sixty miles an hour. In a straight line. Like two arrows.

"Yes, that's right, ladies. I was witness to a head-on collision between two M-60 tanks, the only moving objects anywhere in sight from one end of the horizon to the other. Calm though I usually am, I was taken aback. The sparks, the momentary flash of flames, the smell of burning rubber. The noise. Especially the noise, a grinding, crunching, metallic sound. And then the silence. No more music. No more growl of the engines. Just the brown Danube, making its little brown sounds. This is what they mean, I realized, when they say war games are hell.

"I went over and knocked on the side of one of the tanks. It was warm to the touch, which I took as a sign of life; and, sure enough, I could hear someone moving around inside and talking, a few curse words, subdued screaming. A moment later a hatch opened up and a man appeared bleeding from a three-inch laceration right across his forehead. At exactly the same time, as if they had it all rehearsed, another guy popped up out of the other tank, also bleeding, from the scalp someplace.

" 'You fellows came to the right spot,' I said, pointing out the aid station; but they wanted to talk to each other.

" 'What's your date of rank,' they both said.

"You see, ladies, if two soldiers meet up someplace, one of them has got to be in command; and if they're both the same rank, it's the guy who made rank first who's in charge. Well, it seemed by some Godawful coincidence, that these two gentlemen, who even looked alike, had been promoted to major on the same day. So, you see, that meant they had no way of telling who was right and who was wrong, who was the good driver and who had been driving carelessly at top speed across unfamiliar terrain. So, instead they argued. Each tank had a tech sergeant in it; and these guys squeezed out somehow and began arguing too. Went something like this: . . .' "

At this point Schulz affected a high-pitched Southern accent.

" 'JesusChristman,   yadrivindafuckintankoverdafuckingroundon'tgiveashitwheredafuckyagoinlikeamuddafucker . . .'

"Excuse me ladies, but that's the way tech sergeants talk. They're simple, down-to-earth folk.

" 'Youfuckinblinefuckinsonofabitch,' the other sergeant said, 'yagottawholeGoddamfuckinfieldtomovethatfuckintank, forsomefuckinreasonyagottaaimforme? Man, yawannafuckincommitsuicide, yagottafuckinGoddamriverrightdere, whyyagottarollyourfuckinass . . .'

"The sergeants went on this way while the majors went on in their own way. Everyone was angry and getting angrier. It was a first-degree uproar. In case you didn't know, ladies, an army uproar comes in three different sizes. What you get in a first-degree uproar is a lot of screaming and people sticking out their lower lips, and saying fuck. In a second-degree uproar, there is physical contact, like kicking somebody in the knee. A third-degree uproar is where there is actual loss of human life. World War Two is a good example of a third-degree uproar.

"Now, ladies, here comes the exciting part of the story. What we had here was a first-degree uproar threatening to worsen directly to third degree. These fellows—military types with military minds—well, they naturally opt for a military solution to their quarrel. One fellow grabs his turret machine gun, while the other fellow on the other tank grabs his port machine gun, or maybe it was the aft. Anyway, to prevent further bloodshed, in an act which, I think, can only be described as heroic, I step between the tanks, in the line of fire.

" 'Hold,' I say, raising up my hand. 'A man shall not war upon his brother.' I said that, I think, or something like that.

"One of the sergeants replies, 'GetyoGoddamfuckinassoutda- way, man, aforeIfuckinshootyafuckinballsoff.' And one of the majors snarls and swivels his gun around impatiently.

"I stare back at them all calmly; and I speak to them soothing words about brotherly love, the spirit of the game, and the difficulty of driving safely in Germany, where all the signs are written in the wrong language. And I point out also that they are bleeding and likely to die in the next few minutes if I don't sew them up right away. This thought gives them pause. They go on grinding their teeth and making faces for a minute or two; but finally they climb down and jostle their way over to my tent.

"It turned out they were all injured. One of the sergeants had a dislocated shoulder and kept crying out that he was in big pain. I would have offered him some codeine or Demerol, but I sort of used that stuff all up during the previous week in order to keep my spirits up. Besides, how was I to know there were going to be casualties? I tended to the majors first, of course. First things first. In fact, since they both wanted to be first, I set up two tables and sutured them both at the same time, using both hands, the sort of thing only a virtuoso surgeon would attempt. And even I had trouble. I stitched one guy's earlobe to his cheek.

"Now, here comes the really strange part. In walks a light colonel. That's a lieutenant colonel, ladies. No big deal. It seems he dropped in by helicopter to see what's been holding up our final push against this invisible enemy we've been fighting. Right away, both majors jump off the table, 4-0 silk hanging off their wounds. They stand at attention. Salute. The sergeant gets up and tries to salute with his dislocated arm. All of them listen for a couple of minutes while the colonel lectures about the importance of close liaison between infantry and mobile cavalry, and don't forget close air support. Also he has a few words to say about the two tanks outside propped up against each other at an acute angle. Then he says, 'Let's get out there, men, and beat team B across the river.'

"And, what do you know, all these guys, including the guy who's in this big pain, they rush out to conquer somebody. The Russians? The Poles? Team B? Who knows? Why? That's what I don't understand. Why is that? The majors, both of them, are so hot to go, they bang into each other on the way out and start bleeding all over again. There's something crazy there, right? A guy with a dislocated shoulder runs out in the rain, he's going to float a tank across a river for no reason I can see except somebody tells him to. Is that crazy? I don't know, I think that's crazy. What do you think?" Schulz said, turning to me abruptly.

It occurred to me this story might be true, some of it, Schulz was so riled up by the telling of it. His flip nonchalance had faded, along with his glow; and he was staring at me seriously, as if he expected me to explain the army to him.

"You got me," I said, looking for the tail in my oxtail soup.

"How come? You're a psychiatrist." Schulz turned back to the ladies. "This is Dr. Abraham Redden," he said, choosing to introduce me at last, "the famous psychiatrist. You've heard of him, perhaps. He doesn't look like much, but he was trained in America's finest institutions, and he's achieved national stature. A talented researcher. A super clinician. He represented the United States in an international symposium on the emotional problems of dwarfs. A short assignment, but he handled it well. Heh. And then there was his work with disadvantaged young sex perverts. And, would you believe, prior to all that, he was a starting quarterback at Michigan State University, a very large school."

"I don't know," replied the beautiful girl in barely accented English. "Is all of that true?" she asked, smiling at me.

"None of it," I told her. "Unless it's the part about my not looking like much."

Schulz made a wry face. "Well, you're a psychiatrist. That much is true. Psychiatrists know everything; so I want you to explain that tank crew to me. How come some guys—whenever somebody snaps his fingers—they jump. They don't even bother to ask themselves what's in their *own best interest*. That's crazy, right? . . . Well?" Schulz added impatiently.

"Maybe they believe in what they're doing," suggested the beautiful one.

The women, to whom Schulz had evidently been a stranger prior to dinner, were named Krista—that was the beautiful one, just now staring at me enigmatically—and Hilda, the overweight but otherwise not unattractive one on my left. They were teachers, they told us, Hilda in the local community school, Krista in the grade school the U.S. Army maintained for dependents, where she taught special education. In response to Schulz's pointed and, I thought, occasionally impertinent questions, Krista offered up fragments of her biography. She was an orphan, her father having died in combat early in the war, her mother at the very end, when the Russians came west. She spent most of her childhood in an orphanage outside of Karlsruhe, then lived for a while with an aunt, then for another while with another aunt. She went to school here and there, ending up at Heidelberg University, where she sat on the castle ramparts on warm days looking down at the town and drinking Rhine wine, and for the most part having a good time. Soon after, she married an American army captain. He helped her to get her current job, then ran off with the school librarian. She was divorced now but would not describe herself as "available," she informed us, in reply to Schulz's particularly blunt question.

He meant, of course, only to ask if she was available for a tour of Nuremberg, he explained. I wondered if this was the same tour I was supposed to be arranging. The way the invitation was put, I had the feeling Schulz was offering to show Krista around, rather than vice versa. She listened politely, which seemed to encourage him, although he didn't seem to need much encouragement. The thought of seeing Nuremberg reminded him of the Nazi war crimes tribunal held there so many years ago, and he launched into a gay and lurid story about Goering's last days. For the next half hour he told one funny story after another, mostly about the army and his recent tour of duty with 3rd Division. Meanwhile the girls had coffee and dessert; and I tried to catch up by ordering a sandwich.

"You're not very hungry?" Krista asked me abruptly, interrupting Schulz and annoying him possibly.

"Uh . . . well, sort of," I said. The young woman was staring at me intently through wide hazel eyes; and it seemed to me she wanted to know very precisely just how hungry I was. "I don't remember eating lunch," I said, stopping to think for a moment.

"Dr. Redden, brilliant though he is, is not too . . . uh, organized," commented Schulz, pleased at having found just the right word. "Like his driving. Sort of drives in a lot of different directions all at once. I was watching this morning, Abe, while you made a path through the fence. That's why I left you detailed instructions to get here. So you wouldn't have to think and drive at the same time. They worked out, I see."

"Listen, you were in 3rd Division," I said, anxious to change the subject. "They're spread out all over Bavaria, aren't they? Were you ever . . . did you ever hear of a town called Waldheim?"

Schulz lit his pipe.

"There are Waldheims all over Germany," said Krista. "Forest home, that's what the name means. There are two, I think, in Bavaria."

"This one's a small town near the Czech border."

"Yeah, I know the place," said Schulz. "We lost a soldier there, maneuvering around as usual. He fell off a tank and got run over. Died of his wounds before we could fly him back to a station hospital."

This remark set Hilda to giggling again, suggesting that her command of English wasn't all I had taken it to be.

"Why didn't you take him up the hill to that secret base?" Krista asked.

Just as I thought, everyone and his aunt knew about the secret base.

I didn't wait for Schulz to answer. Having contained myself as long as I could, I began explaining, and complaining about, my adventures over the last twenty-four hours, leaving out any reference to Penkovsky, just in case there were still some secret secrets, but telling all about Konigsberg and Fitch, and all the rest of it. I had trouble making Fitch sound real.

"Sounds a little nutty to be a senior CID officer," Schulz commented.

"I think so too," I told him, "but I'm not sure I can tell anymore who's nutty and who isn't. My boss—he's a psychiatrist, too, after all—he spends all day thinking very hard, which is very hard for him to do, about bed-wetting and the Cuban missile crisis. They're tied up somehow in his mind."

"Maybe it's the crisis atmosphere," said Krista. "On the German radio, all they talk about is war. Will there be war? How many missiles are aimed at the West? Will they close Berlin again? Troop movements. I heard so many troop movements, I don't know what. Everyone's very upset. But more important, someone is shooting at you," Krista said, leaning forward. "You might get hurt."

"It's surprising I haven't been hurt already," I said, looking around for the pickle that came with my sandwich and that, it turned out, Schulz had eaten. "They just barely missed me four separate times, I think."

"You might well have survived anyway in the hands of a competent surgeon," Schulz commented, spooning chocolate syrup over some ice cream. "Modern medicine has made great strides in the management of trauma."

"Yeah, right. Like that soldier who got run over. Also, we lost another citizen of Waldheim a couple of nights ago, from an illegal abortion. Modern medicine didn't stop her from bleeding to death."

"Bled to death? From an abortion?" Schulz repeated after me. "A couple of days ago? Oh. Yeah, I guess that still happens sometimes." He toyed idly with his ice cream.

"That's terrible," said Krista.

Hilda cackled, then, evidently sensing a change in everyone's mood, fell silent.

"Well, we all got to go sometime," said Schulz.

"Sure," I said sarcastically. "After all, she was seventeen years old. What more could life offer her?"

"Hey, buddy, relax."

"Listen, I don't feel like relaxing. Besides getting shot at, which I find very upsetting, everybody has been ordering me around and threatening me. I don't feel like sitting still anymore, just waiting for the next thing to happen. I'm going to start doing something . . . just as soon as I figure out what to do. Well, one thing," I said, making up my mind, "since I've been dragged into this mess, I'm going to find out what's going on— what happened to Konigsberg, and what happened to that girl too. Before the missile crisis explodes, before the Communists win the cold war, and before anyone shoots me. Besides," I added uncomfortably, "I feel kind of a responsibility."

"Uh . . . know what you mean, buddy; but don't you think you should leave all that detective work to the experts? If I were you, I'd sort of maintain a low profile, stick to the important things—analyzing people or whatever it is you guys do."

"What makes you think the army is any better at detective work than at tank maneuvers?"

"You are right to get involved," Krista said. "You can't trust the army with anybody's life. As a German, I can tell you. God knows, everyone is telling the Germans that all the time. If we had got involved, instead of leaving things to the army and to the party, there wouldn't have been any awful things happening. And we wouldn't have everybody else's troops living in our country and dividing it up. You know," she added a moment later, looking at me speculatively, "if you would like, maybe I could help in some way. One of those aunts I grew up with lived in Ansbach, which is not far from Waldheim; and I speak German well." She smiled at me.

"Why are you going to help *him*?" Schulz complained, loud enough to make a waiter a few tables away look up. "He doesn't need help getting killed. I'm the one who needs help. Even a virtuoso surgeon can't do it all by himself." Schulz went on about how important his own work was: the precise joining together of delicate tissues sundered by disease or by injury, the healing of the human body, and the like—meanwhile placing himself at the focus of Krista's attention by leaning far enough over the center of the table to upset a vase of flowers on the remains of my sandwich. He proceeded to describe an emergency gall bladder operation he'd performed once on a fat lady in the circus who had just finished a gallon of ice cream, the only funny account of a cholecystectomy I had ever heard. He made witty talk, smoked his pipe with élan, and, for a guy who frequented Mexican brothels, looked, in general, very much at home in this very sedate, very elegant restaurant on the other side of the world.

After dinner, Schulz invited the women out for a drink; but they demurred, Krista shaking her head at Hilda, who I had the feeling might otherwise have been willing to come along. Before getting into their car, Krista handed me her telephone number.

"I really mean it," she said softly, "if I can help you in some way."

"*Ja*," said Hilda, cheerfully handing her telephone number to Schulz, who held it gingerly between two fingers, as if the paper were soiled.

"That was a clever ploy," Schulz said to me later, walking through the parking lot, "coming on, you know, *dedicated*, like that. 'Responsible, da, dah, da, dah.' I should have known that bullshit would work, what with her being an orphan, I mean. Orphans got a lot of *angst*."

"You know, Bob, you're kind of a cynical guy."

"Old buddy," he said to me, driving smoothly through the narrow and slippery streets—it had begun raining again, and the ticking of the windshield wipers made an oddly musical cadence with the patter of the rain—"would you like to make some money?"

"No," I replied.

That was worth a laugh. "Like you said before," he went on, "I used to move around a lot with 3rd Division. Met a lot of people. All sorts. Well, I was playing poker one night with an American Indian, of all things. A tech sergeant. I didn't know they allowed Indians in the army. You know, split loyalties. Anyway, this guy is backing two low pair just as hard as he can—which tells you something about why there aren't a hell of a lot of Indians around anymore. Anyway, he tells me a crazy story about a band of gypsies who wander all around Eastern Europe and, whenever they feel like it, Western Europe too. American Indians got an in with the gypsies, he claims.

"Look, Abe," Schulz said, suddenly very serious. "This crazy story turns out to be true. More or less. Not only are there gypsies moving back and forth from East to West, across this supposedly impregnable border the Communists have built, but also maybe hundreds of other guys, chauffeurs and the like, laborers, diplomats, somebody's relatives, people with special passes for one reason or another. And, of course, soldiers. American soldiers. You and me, Abe. We're allowed to cross into East Berlin, if we like, into enemy territory, walk all around those empty streets, assuming we have nothing better to do. Have you been to Berlin yet?"

"Yes. It's terrible." I remembered that day when I stood for an hour on a wooden platform looking at the wall. The thing was stone and iron, topped by a fence of barbed wire, and supported farther back by a second wall. It was an act of violence made concrete, literally. I felt embarrassed, as if I were watching a parent strike his child publicly.

But it turned out Schulz was talking about the Eastern Sector itself. ". . . *bor* . . . ing," he said, "and drab. All those drab little people dressed in their drab little clothes hiding out in their drab little candy stores. Half the city is bombed out, the other half is one gigantic project. Drab and boring. But, Abe," he said, steering with one hand and with the other grabbing hold of my sleeve, "the spirit of capitalism has not faded entirely from the hearts of those drab little people. They're scurrying around, selling stamps, antique jewelry, little porcelain angels with fat faces. Anything they can get their drab little hands on. I don't know what they do with the money, probably buy more trinkets to sell. Anyway, this is where we come in. It's a buyers' market. Some of that stuff they're selling is valuable, and they're selling it cheap. American currency, you know. Now, some of this stuff isn't easy to fence . . . uh, *fence* isn't the right word. But still, you've got to sell it to make a profit. Buy it and sell it. You got to do both, and you need contacts to do both. That's where I come in. It's taken a couple of months of following people around like a spy, talking to people and convincing them; but I think I got it set up now."

"Sounds sort of illegal to me," I commented idly.

"Illegal?" Schulz repeated after me in a rising voice. "Of course it's illegal. It's smuggling. That's why there's so much money in it. There's nothing to worry, though. There's no risk. The more hard currency that goes East, the happier they are over there. And the police on this side got more important things to do. The whole setup is simple and safe. But we need money to get started. That's where you come in."

"Me? Why me?"

"Because the word is you're loaded. That's what I hear. You come from a rich and snotty family. Am I right? More money than you know what to do with."

"If I have so much money, what makes you think I want more?"

"Everyone always wants more. I'm not a psychiatrist, but I

know that much. Whatever it is—power, sex, and especially money—everyone always wants more. Besides, if you had *that* much money, you'd be driving a Mercedes, instead of a beat-up Volkswagen."

"I'd be driving a beat-up Mercedes, which would make me feel worse than driving a beat-up Volkswagen."

We screeched to a halt abruptly as a car hurtled out of a side street, just missing us. Schulz, seemingly out of reflex, immediately took after it, hunched over the wheel and cursing malignly under his breath. He was in a rage. A moment later he must have realized what he was doing. He slowed down and went back to explaining just how well we were going to do with my money and his brains. The fellow seemed to have a volatile personality; but then, I knew that much before I ever met him. A senior psychiatrist, an instructor of mine, claimed he could discern basic emotional conflicts in people by observing the way they behaved at intersections; but he talked nonsense most of the time, so I didn't see any reason to put credence in that particular idea.

After a while Schulz and I arrived back at the BOQ. I slouched down in my seat as he went about the business of getting us through the gate and up the driveway.

"I'm beginning to think you're not interested in this deal, Abe," he said, turning off the ignition, then turning around to look at me. "Is that what you're telling me? Are you sure?"

"Listen . . . uh, where did this poker game take place, with you and this Indian?"

"In Waldheim . . . as a matter of fact. Why?"

"I don't know. Tell you what, let me think about it."

"Now you're talking."

My sleep was interrupted again that night. I was lying on the floor in a dark corner of my room, away from the window and out of sight of anyone who might be aiming a gun at me through the window, although anyone so inclined could just as easily have leaned into the room and shot me. No one had replaced the shattered glass. A cold and noisy wind blew into the room along with leaves; and I thought I could hear the scratching sounds of a small animal at the other end of the room. I felt like I was camping out in the woods. The telephone was ringing.

I lay there wrapped up in blankets, my head propped against the wall; and I stared at it. The room was dark for the most part, but a glow from one of the streetlamps, or maybe the moon, made bright the covers at the head of my bed and the night-stand alongside. The telephone was sitting in this patch of light. I wondered if someone had in mind coaxing me from my burrow into the line of fire by calling me. The telephone rang a third time. I considered not answering it; but I was a doctor, after all. I thought of the psychotic lieutenant in Waldheim hovering be-tween coma and a paranoid excitement. He might need more medicine, or less. He might be convulsing, coming off all that Seconal. The telephone rang a fourth time. Dispiritedly, trying not to feel like a rabbit, I uncovered myself quietly with one paw and padded silently on all fours over to the edge of my closet, keeping below the level of the window. I crouched there, still in shadow, staring at the buildings across the way, mostly unlit this early hour of the morning. Except for the distant whir of traffic and the dry rasp of the wind moving through the trees, there was silence—interrupted again, suddenly, by the tele-phone. Carefully, imperceptibly, I hoped, I pulled the telephone toward me by its cord until it fell off the table with a clatter. I yanked the pieces over to me—the mouthpiece had fallen out—and tried screwing it back together. Meanwhile, indistinct but urgent sounds came from the other end.

"Hello? Hello?" I said finally.

"Captain Redden. I want to speak to Captain Abraham Red-den. Hello?"

"Hello. Yes, hello."

"It's important. I have to speak to Captain Redden."

"Yes. Yes. It's me. Emily, is that you?" Emily was my house-keeper. The last time I saw her, only a few months ago, al-though it seemed much longer, she was wringing her hands and crying out that the only son she had ever had, her little Abe, was leaving her. In less distress at the time was Long John, who stood nearby on his perch. He was the family parrot, a misera-ble creature who had survived and reciprocated the ill will of three generations of Reddens, and was vigorous still. "Fuck off," were his last words to me.

"Hello? Hello?" said Emily again.

"Hello. Yes, hello," I repeated idiotically.

"Abe, is that you?"

"Yes, Emily, it's me." I was shouting now. "How are you?"

"I'm fine, Abe. The family's fine. Everyone. But how are you?"

"Healthy," I replied.

"But are you all right?"

"Sure, I'm fine."

"You've been behaving yourself?"

"Yes, of course I've been behaving myself."

"You used to get into trouble all the time when you were growing up. I haven't forgotten that. How could anyone forget? Are you sure you're all right?"

"Emily . . ."

"All I had to do is look away for one minute, and you were getting into some kind of trouble. Fresh with your teachers. And all that fighting."

"Emily . . ."

"Even then I used to warn you, you can't go through life provoking people, telling them what to do—"

"Me? I never tell anyone what to do. Live and let live, that's my motto. . . ."

"Remember when you tried to hit that bully and fell into the lake?"

"Listen, Emily. That was ten years ago. You called me up now, in the middle of the night, to tell me to stay away from that bully?"

". . . almost drowned."

There was a noise—I was sure I could hear a noise—from the other end of the room. Suddenly a cold wind seemed to blow at me from all different directions, and I shivered.

"Emily, I'd love to talk to you, but now isn't a good time. It's very . . . it's very *cold* here. This time of year, I mean."

"I took care of you for twenty years, and it's too cold for you to talk to me? You probably aren't dressed warm. All those cotton clothes. Listen to me, Abe, all kinds of people, men with gray hats, felt hats, you know, have been coming around here today asking all kinds of questions about you. I thought you should know."

"Men with gray hats?"

"Like whether you had suspicious friends or belonged to something or other, parties or clubs."

"Parties?"

"Abe, you haven't been getting into any trouble with . . . boys?"

"With the boys? Emily, what are you talking about? I'm not a kid anymore."

"No, you don't understand. They wanted to know if you . . . if you made love to boys. Who would want to know such things?"

"Never mind, Emily. I just figured out who." Fitch. He wanted to know if I was in league with the Communists or the homosexuals.

"I told them you weren't that kind of person, Abe. A good-looking, healthy young man like you. I told them to talk to that girl, Suzanne. You remember . . ."

"Yes, yes."

". . . I thought after all that trouble that time, she ought to be able to tell them . . ."

"Terrific."

Having warned me against men with gray hats, Emily went on to remind me, as she always did, to dress warmly and to drink soup. She also asked if I was appreciating Europe. She had enjoyed the hot baths at Baden-Baden when she was much younger, she told me, and recommended them for all-around good health purposes. That was before World War One. Emily was almost as old as the parrot and just as lively. For a while I listened to her gossip about things back home; then finally, regretfully, I hung up the telephone.

I brushed away a few leaves, and lay there, pulling the blankets closer around me. I vaguely considered crawling back to the other corner of the room, but one corner seemed as good as the other. Instead, I blinked a couple of times and stared absently into the blackness. After a moment of emptiness, during which I thought nothing, felt nothing, I began to see something, I thought, an indistinct shape at the dark end of my bed, on top of the bed, it seemed. I remembered, then, a monster from my youth who used to live on a chair in my bedroom. Taking form out of my discarded clothing, he stood night after night, hunched over, peering at me evilly, waiting for me to move and give myself away. Waiting to pounce. This figure was smaller, possibly a pillow bent into an odd shape, I thought, half-asleep,

when suddenly I saw it move. These things always seem to
move, I reminded myself quickly, drawing farther back into my
corner. Your eye moves and then the thing moves. But then my
childhood specter became real; and the thing leaped at me. I
may have let out a cry. I know I covered my face with one hand
and flailed at it with the other as it clambered over my legs,
then jumped to the windowsill, where it remained a moment
chittering at me before disappearing out the window. It was
only a squirrel, of course, but in the nervous state of mind I was
in, it scared the hell out of me.

VII

I GOT UP NOT LONG AFTER, while it was still dark, dressed, and took a taxi to the hospital.

I was walking in the direction of my office, whistling, I think, when I heard a louder whistling and the sound of someone counting cadence.

"One . . . two . . . three . . . go. One . . . two . . . three . . . stop," went a singsong voice that I thought might belong to Corporal Vigliotti, although that hardly seemed possible. Put off, as he was, by the sight of blood, he didn't frequent the medical wards, certainly not at a quarter to seven in the morning. I followed this melody through the silent hallways and at its source came upon something that even looking at it seemed impossible: Private Vito Vigliotti was standing inside the men's bathroom on the third floor of the 20th Station Hospital in Nuremberg, Germany, holding a clipboard in one hand and a stopwatch in the other. He was chanting rhapsodically to a half-dozen men who were lined up in front of urinals. Of these, some were dressed in pajamas, others in full field packs. Still others, similarly dressed, or undressed, were leaning up against the wall or lying apparently passed out on the floor. When Vigliotti called out "go," the men in front of the urinals began to urinate, when he called out "stop," they stopped. While they were urinating, they also whistled. They did this over and over. I steadied myself against the doorjamb and watched. It came to me, after a little boggling of the mind, that I was observing Wormley's program for the treatment of bed-wetting. What I didn't understand was everything else.

"Time," Vigliotti cried out abruptly.

"Wait a second . . . I'm not through," one of the men mumbled. The fellow was speaking with difficulty, which was understandable, since he was wedged into the urinal, his head propped up against the wall.

"That's enough for today," Vigliotti replied. "C'mon, c'mon. Next bunch."

The four or five guys in front of the urinals zipped up, or whatever, and staggered off. Another group took their place.

"Ready, you guys? Here we go. One . . . two . . . three . . . go. One . . ."

"All right, Vito, I give up," I said, interrupting. "What the hell is all this?"

"Hey, Captain, what are you doing here? You want to take a piss?" he asked cheerily. "Hey, you, over there, make room for the captain . . ."

"Listen, Vito. I don't want to take a piss. I just want you to explain to me what's going on."

"Oh, God, Captain," Vigliotti replied, hitting himself in the head with his stopwatch. "You wouldn't believe it."

"I'm sure you're right, but tell me anyway."

"Exercises. That's what. A couple of hours at a time. Starting at *four* o'clock in the morning. What these guys need, according to Major Wormley, is practice urinating the *right* way. Wetting the bed is the *wrong* way. If they practice, they get control over their unconscious habit. Making the unconscious conscious, he calls it. In so many things in life, practice is what counts. That's what Major Wormley says. Habit disturbance. See, the starting and stopping over and over again, that's where all the practice comes in. And the exercise. Something about the neck of the bladder. The spinck . . . the spincter of the . . . pincter. Is that pincter? The part at the end of the bladder?"

"Sphincter."

"Right, it's the sphincter. The part that you exercise. What I don't understand is why it has to be at *four* in the morning." Vigliotti leaned forward in order to whisper to me. "These guys, they're not *used* to getting up at *four* in the morning. They're all pissed off. Uh . . . which is maybe not the best way of putting it. I'm not so happy being here myself. The hours between four and six are maybe my favorite hours for sleeping out of the whole day. But according to Major Wormley, all this on-and-off, stop-and-go urinating has to go on while it's still dark outside because that's when the bed-wetting is, usually. The association. He says it all follows logically; but I don't know, doesn't that sound kind of farfetched to you?"

"Yes. Farfetched."

"Hey, hold it in, for Christ's sake!" Vigliotti called out to a man who was urinating on the floor. "Now you're not going to have any to practice."

"Vito . . ."

"Jesus. There goes another one. You got to watch these guys every minute."

"Vito, I look around this room with my trained clinical eye, and I notice right away some of these men are a little under the weather. Obtunded. Ataxic too. What I mean is, they're falling out all over the place. Why is that?"

"Well, according to Major Wormley, bed-wetting takes place in, like, a sort of twilight state. Half dreamy. So, in order to practice, the guys got to be dreamy a little. Not too awake. So he ordered some sleeping medicine for them. It all follows logically. Of course, that stuff is hard to regulate or something. Either that or some guys are very sensitive to the stuff."

"Uh . . . the fellow lying facedown over there?"

"Right. That's either a very heavy twilight state, or he's asleep. Anyway, when you get in this state, this twilight . . . he calls it state-pacific . . . uh, specific learning. It only works, though, in this twilight zone because of—"

"Right, right. I got it. A twilight state. And . . . uh, the whistling, Vito? How come they're whistling?"

"That's a real innovation, according to Major Wormley. He bases it on the Lemoze method. You know, the Lomoze method?"

"Lemoze? Lomoze? The Lamaze method . . ."

"You got it."

". . . of natural childbirth?"

"You rub your belly and pant, and that's what makes the baby come out. Loosens the spincter. So while these guys are in a twilight, they distract themselves with whistling, and they learn to stop and go on an unconscious-conscious—"

"Right, right. I got it now. I should have guessed. It all follows logically, like night and day. Just one thing more, Vito, then it'll all be clear. Now, tell me very slowly, Vito, why are some of these guys wearing full field uniforms?"

"I don't understand this part so well."

"*This* is the part you don't understand?"

Vigliotti frowned and made a noise like sucking on a straw. "Captain, you know the way Major Wormley is," he said, hesitating every few words, "he likes to explain things . . . well, in depth. Well, he was taking an awful long time explaining about the twilight state and the spincter. About two and a half hours. When he got around to talking about guys doing it in battle dress, I just sort of nodded my head."

"So you don't know?"

"We can ask him later."

"That doesn't seem sporting, Vito. We should be able to figure it out. You know, put ourselves in his place. Suppose you're trained at Walter Reed Hospital three or four years, and privy to all the army records on bed-wetting, and at the same time you're off your fucking head—"

Just then a man fell into a urinal. He cried out so loudly, he woke up the man who had been lying facedown on the floor, who cried out in turn and began thrashing his arms. While the first fellow subsided into sleep, the second awoke. I thought he might be disoriented still, though, from the sleeping medication, for he launched immediately into a description of a movie he had seen recently.

I left Vigliotti to deal with all this, and I returned to my office.

The clutter on my desk was enlarged by a new pile of paper, which I was about to displace to one side when I discovered on top a detailed telephone message from the pathologist's office at Frankfurt. According to Major Sedgewick, the routine laboratory studies performed on Sandra Collins by the German authorities had been reported back and were all negative. Toxicology was negative. He himself had run blood tests on the specimens I had sent him, and these, too, were unrevealing. In particular, there was no evidence of aspirin poisoning. He was holding on to the vials in case I thought of some other test I wanted him to perform, but nothing too subtle, please, like looking for the unconscious in the globulin fraction—or trying to figure out why she got pregnant in the first place. As far as he could determine, the young woman had expired from extreme but uncomplicated blood loss. That was all he could tell. He sent his best regards.

I imagined Major Sedgewick turning from his telephone and from Sandra Collins's life, and death, to the more satisfying study of a spleen or a liver.

I understood the way he felt. Before I made up my mind once and for all to become a psychiatrist, I had considered pathology. People are more interesting than anything else in the world; but, as Sedgewick intimated, they are elusive. Their feelings and thoughts are complicated and mercurial, their motives impenetrable most of the time. The account they give of themselves is always incomplete; so it seems impossible to really understand them, let alone affect them in any substantial way. In contrast, physical disease has a nicely unequivocal aspect, or so it seemed to me at the time. You look at a slide, hold an organ tissue in your hand, examine any of the various effluvia of the body, urine or blood, in one of those humming and pulsating machines that tell you exactly what elements a person is made of, and exactly in what proportions. Facts, these are. Little fragments of Truth. If there is a difference of medical opinion between, let's say, an internist and a radiologist, or a surgeon, that debate is likely to be resolved once and for all by the pathologist, especially if the patient dies. He knows the name of the disease and its course. If pathologists have the last word, psychiatrists have scarcely any word at all. They have only a vague glimmering of what's going on, only a supposition about the past, and no knowledge at all of the future. Treatment, however long it lasts, is too short to learn what you would like to know. It's like opening a book in the middle, reading a few pages, then putting it down again, still in the middle. You never get to find out how it all turns out. Also, you begin inevitably to care about your patients, which is inconvenient, since in the end they disappear from your life. But I became a psychiatrist anyway. It was much later before I realized that pathologists don't know any more of the truth than anyone else. They disagree among themselves just like psychiatrists do—well, no, maybe not that much. But they're not infallible. Someone dies, and a good part of the time nobody can figure out why. Not with microscopes. Not with all the machines in the world. "If you're going to find out anything," a medical examiner once pointed out to me, "it's a good idea to know what you're looking for ahead of time." In the case of Sandra Collins, though, there was evidently nothing to find out, other than what was already in plain view. She was just one more young woman who died from a back-alley abortion.

While these thoughts ran through my mind, I signed the forty or fifty administrative action forms that made up most of the pile of papers on my desk. In order to separate an unsuitable person from the service, my signature was required ten times, one for each of ten copies of the same form. No one could ever explain to me why. One day I submitted only nine copies. This act of negligence, or sabotage, as my commanding officer would have it, set into motion a cloud of additional memoranda, copies of army regulations, admonitions, abjurations, and the like, all of which settled on my desk, arriving sometimes along with their own duplicates. The last such reprimand arrived directly from USAREUR in an official-looking envelope, which, as a matter of fact, was stamped OFFICIAL in two places. "Ten copies means precisely ten," the author pointed out precisely, "not eleven and especially not nine!" Although it was vital that I sign exactly ten copies, it didn't seem to matter exactly how I signed. My name, although not as long as some, was too long to write fifty or sixty times a day, so I wrote it any old way. The scribble I dashed off was not always recognizable to me as my signature; but no one complained. After a while even this abbreviated inscription began to shrink. I flattened out my b's and d's and squeezed together my m's and n's. When that deficiency went unnoticed, I started leaving out vowels. That too was satisfactory. After a brief, giddy period of leaving out consonants, or skipping the capitals, I settled on just writing an A and an R with a wavy line. Then I left out the A and the R. When I had reduced my signature to its essence, a short, straight line, there was again a reaction from the authorities, although muted. I walked into Colonel Beasely's office one day—that was where they kept the candy machine—and he called me over to his desk.

"Did you shign these forms?" he asked, holding up a piece of paper that had sped through my hands that morning.

"Sure," I replied.

"Thish?" he said, pointing at my mark.

"Sure. Abe . . . Redden," I read out to him, pointing at the beginning and the end of the line.

"Oh," he replied, nodding his head.

But I felt a little embarrassed. I was too old to engage in schoolboy protest, I decided. From then on I signed my name in a pattern of symmetrical loops, which looked, at least at first glance, like a proper signature, and which I could perform almost as quickly as the straight line anyway. And which had a sort of artistic flair, I thought.

The last form I signed that day turned out on closer examination not to be a form; it was a memorandum from Vigliotti informing me that a number of telephone calls had come in for Lieutenant Konigsberg over the last twenty-four hours and had been routed to my office, as per Fitch's orders. The corporal had been instructed by Fitch to get as much information about the caller as possible, and to report these conversations in detail, with Herr Bromberg listening in, if necessary, to take notes. Vigliotti knew, of course, that Konigsberg was not really in the hospital, that he was, in fact, missing; but that was as much of our little plot as he had been told. That was enough to satisfy him. He had been working in the department of psychiatry nigh onto thirty million seconds and had long since accustomed himself to irrational and inexplicable instructions, witness today's experiment in the men's room. Herr Bromberg, for his part, was a citizen of the New Germany. He didn't know anything and didn't want to know anything. The transcripts of yesterday's telephone calls had been sent downtown to Fitch's office. Copies addressed to me were appended to Vigliotti's memorandum. I glanced through these.

A man, an American, it seemed, had called twice in the morning, but had hung up each time without leaving his name. I figured that was probably Sergeant Bell. He did say, I remembered, that he had telephoned a couple of times, although calling anonymously seemed kind of circumspect, considering he and Konigsberg were supposed to be good friends. A second man, a German this time, called in the afternoon, around the time Fitch and I were meandering through Konigsberg's apartment. This brief conversation was reproduced with Herr Bromberg's usual and recognizable precision.

MAN: (*Mature voice, German accent, but not pronounced*) Yes. I was asking to speak to Lieutenant Sidney Konigsberg. Is that permitted?

VIGLIOTTI: Who is this I'm talking to?

MAN: I am a good friend of the lieutenant.

VIGLIOTTI: Yes? What's your name?

MAN: My name? My name is . . . Beck.

VIGLIOTTI: Your first name?

MAN: Sidney will know who it is, if he is permitted to come to the telephone.

VIGLIOTTI: Uh . . . wait just a second. (*Pause*) I'm sorry, he can't come to the phone now. If we can just have your full name and your telephone number where we can reach you, he can call you back later.

MAN: (*Speaking in German in a low voice to someone*) They won't . . . sick . . . (*Then in English again*) Thank you. I will perhaps call back again later. Good-bye.

VIGLIOTTI: Wait a—

The man hangs up.

According to a second note, made obviously without benefit of Herr Bromberg's shorthand, Randy Biddle also called, partly to ask about Lieutenant Konigsberg. The note:

This guy, who I never heard of before, starts off by saying a big hello, Vito, and asking me about how my typing is coming along, which struck me as a little weird, I thought.

I sort of smile at him over the phone to keep him talking.

He asks me if I got caught in any more camouflage netting, which, I think, is some kind of joke because he starts to laugh. So I ask him right back if he stepped on any more land mines, which apparently doesn't strike him as funny, because he stops laughing. There is a silence for a while. Finally he asks about Lieutenant Konigsberg, which is how come he got connected to me in the first place. So I go through my routine. He's better, but can't come to the phone, etc., etc. Who are you? What is your number? etc. He says what am I talking? I know where he is. And he tells me again his name, Randy Biddle, a couple of times. Very loud. I know who he is, he says, I met him yesterday. I ask where was that, and he doesn't say anything for a while. Finally he asks for Captain Abraham Redden, pronouncing the name very carefully. When I tell him you're not available, he says to tell you the lieutenant is awake and talking to God again, but no violence. (I figure now we're playing some kind of game. This is a reference to Konigsberg talking to the Russians, or something. The crack about violence refers to torture. Somehow.) So I just say, "No, no. He's here in the hospital resting, a little depressed." So he asks how come Captain Redden is depressed, so I explain I mean Konigsberg. There is another long silence, which I think at this point is very suspicious. Then he says, "What?" So I decide I'll draw him out by talking about Cuba and the blockade, but he doesn't say anything except "What? What?" a couple of times. Then, without saying good-bye or anything, he hangs up. Before I could trace the call. (By the way, the only call I could trace today was from Wiesbaden, from a girl I know who works there on a bus. For practice. But it didn't work, and they said she was calling from Italy, somewhere near the Brenner Pass.) By the way, the number this guy left is legitimate. I checked. An artillery post on the border near a town called Waldheim, which, as I remember now, is where Konigsberg was posted. And there really is a Randy Biddle attached, so maybe the whole thing is legitimate.

Herr Bromberg had recorded a final, very brief conversation:

MAN: I want to talk to Lieutenant Konigsberg. He is a patient there. (*This man, too, is German, but a different man. He speaks in a lower voice*)

VIGLIOTTI: I'm sorry, sir. He can't come to the phone just now. If you can give me your name and telephone number, I'll— (*The man hangs up*)

I was surprised that Konigsberg, living on a restricted army base, and only for a few weeks at that, should have come to know any Germans well—well enough, anyway, for them to call so quickly after his being admitted, supposedly, to a hospital. He knew the language, it's true, and some people make friends easily; but, still, he was an introvert, judging from all the books in his room, and depressed recently. He was not likely to have been very sociable. I was more surprised, come to think of it, by who hadn't called.

I walked into the waiting room. According to the appointment book on Vigliotti's desk, there were only two real patients I was supposed to see that day—not counting, that is, the three or four enlisted men ordered in for administrative action. Probably I wouldn't be able to see any of them, what with Fitch dangling me at the end of a string. One of the patients was a dentist, a compulsive gambler who also had sexual problems. The two sets of problems were related, as a matter of fact. He was simply more interested in gambling than sex. Missing an appointment wouldn't really matter very much to his treatment, which wasn't going so well anyway. We were thrown together adventitiously too often to maintain a working relationship. For example, I kept running into him in front of the slot machines at the officers' club. Each time he had a beautiful girl with him, a different beautiful girl. He felt embarrassed a lot, and I felt a number of things, all of which made it difficult for me to be objective. The second patient, however, was Sergeant Lingeman. His treatment couldn't be delayed by my missing still another appointment. By the end of the week, he had to be traveling in helicopters, or he would be traveling home. Then again, I thought, he was so close now to managing that, maybe someone else could provide the last push. Vigliotti, maybe. Right on cue the corporal walked through the door, looking worn a little and disgruntled.

"*C'est la vie*," he said to me for about the two-hundredth time, apropos of nothing in particular.

I explained to Vigliotti that I wanted him to work with Lingeman, which meant getting the sergeant to look at helicopters, learn about helicopters, and damn it, fly in a helicopter. There wasn't much time left. He would have to be patient, but firm. There was a lot at stake.

"Do I have to?" Vigliotti asked finally. "I was planning on taking a nap."

"Yes, you have to," I told him.

Herr Bromberg came in, said hello, and immediately began transcribing some notes. Then, a little earlier than usual, Major

Wormley, The Chief, entered. In person. Smiling. Rubbing his hands together at the prospect of a new day full of discovery. Or maybe he was just feeling chilly.

"Did you hear about what's going on around Cuba?" he asked. "Hah."

Having posed that tantalizing question, he went into his office and closed the door behind him. I looked over at Vigliotti, who shrugged; then I returned to my own office.

"Vito, get in here! Quickly," I cried out a moment later.

"Captain, are you calling me?" came back a lazy drawl from the other room.

"Hurry up!"

"What is it, Captain?" Vito said, strolling in finally. "Something the matter?"

"Look out the window. Do you see what they're doing?"

"Who?"

"What do you mean, 'who'? Those guys down there raising the flag. You see that?"

"What? Yeah, sure. They're raising the flag."

"Uh, uh. Right now they're lowering the flag. See? Now they're going to raise it again. The first time they raised it, it was upside down. Did you see that?"

"Really?"

"Come on, Vito. Didn't you notice that the flag was upside down?"

"Looks okay now."

"Sure it's okay now. But a minute ago, the first time they pulled it up, it was upside down. They do that *all the time*. They must have some reason for doing that. First they raise the flag upside down, then they lower it, then they raise it up again the right way."

"No kidding. Why do they do that?"

"Jesus. I don't know why. I was going to ask you. You've been here longer than I have. Look, they go through this routine every day practically. You must have noticed."

"No, I never did. I don't think they would do anything like that."

"Dammit! I'm telling you they do."

"Oh, I believe you. I believe you, Captain," Vigliotti said, putting his hand on my arm. "It's just that I don't know why anyone would do anything silly like that."

"Yeah. Well, neither do I. So, I want you to find out. I want you to try, anyway. I don't know if it's possible to find out anything about anything around here; but you know lots of guys. Enlisted men. You know, soldiers. Ask around. Use your initiative."

"I was planning on taking a nap."

"Forget the nap. Didn't anyone tell you there's a crisis on? Here—take these with you." I swept all the papers on my desk into a cardboard box—it was a pizza container that someone had left in my wastebasket—and handed it to Vigliotti, who left.

My desk had a nicely civilian look to it, I thought, without the usual clutter of military memoranda. It was, in fact, bare entirely except for the box of jujubes. For a minute I looked stupidly at the box of candy, then reached into my pocket, where I remembered putting it, and took out its twin. I had two boxes of jujubes. It took another moment before I realized the second box of candy must have belonged to Lieutenant Konigsberg—which is what Herr Bromberg told me in the first place. I emptied them both out on the desk, looking for . . . I didn't know what I was looking for. Certainly not secret messages, I told myself. And not little rubies and emeralds smuggled from East to West. There were, in any event, none of these. The little red candies were too soft to be rubies, and they tasted of cherry; the green ones tasted of lime, not my favorite. I liked the purple best, sort of a grape flavor, but not quite. Konigsberg and the Collins girl must have known each other, I decided. Two young people, stuck off together, more or less, in the middle of nowhere, with the same taste in candy. It was inevitable. It all followed logically, as Major Wormley would say. Then again, Konigsberg was engaged to some other girl; and Sandra Collins was pregnant—had been pregnant—by some other guy, a couple of months before Konigsberg ever showed up in Germany.

I was considering calling Fitch when Vigliotti leaned in to tell me that another departmental meeting was about to begin, and my presence was required. There was no point in protesting. I walked quickly over to Wormley's office, and sat down. I wasn't going to pay any attention, and I wasn't going to get upset. I wasn't even going to *look* at Wormley. But, as usual, he proved impossible to ignore.

He began the meeting silently, poking himself in the throat repeatedly, and sort of winking at me. He's invented some new kind of sign language, I thought. He grabbed himself finally around the Adam's apple, and made a small, clotted sound. Either that, or he's choking. He called a departmental meeting so he could choke to death in front of an audience.

"Your collar, Abe," he said to me, frowning.

Aha, that was it. My collar was unbuttoned. My shirt had shrunk at San Antonio, along with the rest of me, and was too tight to button. But I pulled up my tie as a concession, and the meeting proceeded. Herr Bromberg had already begun taking notes, and Vigliotti had settled into a position of great attentiveness, leaning forward with his chin propped on his hand. I would have thought he was listening, if his eyes hadn't been closed.

"First, a word about the missile crisis," Wormley said, making a tent out of his fingers. "As you have probably heard, Russia has announced to the world that the United States has no legal right to blockade Cuba. Kennedy, of course, is proceeding anyway. He's ordered the fleet to intercept the Russian ships, twenty-five of them, I think, on the high seas. The navy is expected to make contact within the next twenty-four hours. The Russians meantime are steaming other vessels into the area. Now, let me explain the significance of all this. First of all, from now on no medical officers will be permitted to absent themselves without leave from the hospital." Wormley paused for a moment to purse his lips and stare at me somberly. I stared back.

"Are you addressing yourself to me, Ed?" I asked finally.

"Not necessarily, no. This applies to all medical officers," he replied smoothly.

"Well, there are just the two of us here in the room. Vigliotti over there is only a corporal, even on his best days. Herr Bromberg is a German civilian."

"A word to the wise. I'm speaking now as your chief."

"Listen, I've been hanging around this hospital day and night, practically, ever since I got here. I get in here in the morning before you do, and I leave in the afternoon after you leave. And I don't go AWOL."

"Well, the hospital is in a state of alert now, and the colonel isn't going to tolerate any medical officer going AWOL. That's all I wanted to say. Now, if you don't mind, I'd like to go on to point two.

"Point two: a lot of the top brass will be heading out here into the front lines to take a look around; so I want this place neat. The charts are left out all day, sometimes. Candy wrappers. Last week I saw some Monopoly money lying on the floor. I don't want to say who is responsible. That doesn't matter. Let's just all watch it.

"Point number three, the hot plate . . ."

I really ought to be able to figure out why Wormley had those guys in the bathroom dressed up in full field pack, it occurred to me. His ideas were peculiar and unpredictable, but they were always founded on some premise, however outlandish. He didn't just have people hang from the chandeliers, for instance. Or if he did, it was because hot air was good for their sinuses, and hot air rises. Maybe the *symbolism* of the uniform. Wormley was very big on *symbolism*. For example, the swastika, the Symbol of the Dancing Man, Wormley called it, was central, in his opinion, to the Nazi's success in uniting the German people following the runaway inflation of the Weimar Republic. They had something to fight for, to look up to. The reverse swastika, the good luck symbol of the American Indian, had not served that more primitive people so well because the arms of the Dancing Man pointed counterclockwise—to the left. The left, itself, of course, is a symbol of wrongness or evil, *gauche,* in French, meaning "left" and also "in bad taste," as in the disreputable "left bank." In English, *sinister* comes from the Latin *sinestro,* meaning "left." On such subtle distinctions hinge the fate of nations, he assured me. A full field uniform could symbolize practically anything—courage, manliness, fortitude. The fortitude to remain dry all night long, perhaps. Maybe it was the physical aspect of the uniform, the full field pack pressing on the bladder, strengthening it. Except, of course, the pack was a back pack and the bladder was in front . . .

". . . your contribution will be important, Abe," Wormley said, still explaining the significance of the Cuban situation. "The training program you're designing. In case war breaks out. As your chief, I don't mind telling you that. How far along are you?"

"Up to *R*," I told him.

"*R*? You're up to *R*?"

"Yes. I'm going alphabetically."

"Oh . . . good." He looked at me thoughtfully for a moment, then turned with a smile to Vigliotti. "Vito . . . how's the research project coming? Vito? *Vito*? The project, how's it coming? A little too early to see results, but so far, so good?"

"Uh . . . yeah. I suppose so. Well, I don't know," Vigliotti responded blearily. "There's a lot of hard feeling, I have to say that; but everyone's cooperating. No one wet his bed last night."

"Hmmm," commented Wormley. "That was even before we started the program."

"That's right, sir."

"Good. Good."

"It's not all good. One fella got all upset or depressed or something. He took off without leave back to his unit. Beasely had the MP's pick him up. He's in jail now."

"Some guys are bound to crack up."

"And the sleeping medicine. We had some trouble, the captain'll tell you. We had some guys falling down. One guy, a real dark Negro, all of a sudden he turned to a light tan, and began to roll his eyes."

Wormley nodded his head thoughtfully, then frowned. "He turned into a light stand, you say?"

"Tan! Tan!" I exclaimed, starting to lose control of myself. "Brown! You know, like the color of this office."

"Oh, pale. The Negro turned pale. I understand. An effect of the drug. Well, we'll have to watch that. Anyone who passes out gets a lower dose from now on. We don't want to kill anyone, do we? Heh. Sort of like throwing out the baby with the bath water. By the way, Abe, this office is green, not brown."

"This whole thing sounds backward to me," I said. "People wet their beds about an hour after going to sleep, not in the early morning. And if you want them sleepy for some reason, why don't you just keep them up later?"

Wormley seemed to weigh these ideas carefully.

"And, by the way," I added, "for what it's worth, this office is brown."

"No, no, Abe," Wormley said finally, nodding his head gravely from side to side, "I'm sure, it's green."

"Vito, what color is this room?"

Vigliotti looked around. "Gee. Well, I don't know. Brown, maybe—but with a lot of green. I can see how somebody might think the room is green. Or brown. On the other hand . . ."

"Herr Bromberg," I said, "stop doing that for just a moment." He was writing very quickly, recording this screwball conversation in detail, evidently. Or pretending to. His expression was pained when he looked up. "Is this room painted green or brown," I asked him.

"Captain Redden," he said hesitantly, "if you don't mind, I would prefer not to express my opinion on controversial matters. I am not a political person. I . . ."

"Abe, don't you think it's a little ridiculous arguing over what color the walls are painted," Wormley said, looking put out. "All you have to do is look it up in army regulations. All hospital offices are painted green. A restful color. It says so very clearly in army regulations."

"Goddamn it, I don't care what it says in the regulations. This room is brown. Brown! Here, look for yourself," I said, turning on his desk lamp. Suddenly it seemed very important to me to prove to somebody, to myself, maybe, that the color of the paint on the walls was really brown, that I wasn't going blind, that Wormley wasn't really driving me crazy. There was a paint blister about a foot over the desk. I leaned up, broke off a piece and held it under the desk lamp.

"Look at that," I said. "It's brown, can't you see?"

"What did you do? What did you do?" Wormley said, getting up suddenly into a crouch.

"What?"

"What did you do to the wall? Look! Look at what you did. You made a big . . . a big hole in the paint. Right over there!"

"What are you talking about? I just peeled off a tiny little piece. Here, I'm sorry. Take it back." I threw it on the desk.

"What am I supposed to do with that?" Wormley said indignantly, his already dark-red complexion turning blotchy. "You want me to *tape* it back on the wall? Is that what you want? Here, *you* keep it. Have the paint analyzed for brown, if you're so smart."

"Jesus Christ!" I said, grabbing it up again and stomping my feet. "Jesus Cheerist! Jeee Sus *Christ!*"

"You know, Abe," Wormley commented, suddenly very cold. "Every time we have a departmental meeting, you have to go and spoil it."

Still fuming, I charged into my office, where I found Schulz, dressed in a scrub suit, waiting for me.

"Look, you got to see this," I said, holding out my tiny fragment of Wormley's office, which had grown tinier from being tossed back and forth.

"What is it?" he asked, looking into my hand, which was shaking.

"It's paint. What color is it, is the question."

He looked at it more closely. "Brown," he said.

"Brown. Are you sure? Look again. With a lot of green in it, maybe?"

"It's brown all through. No green."

"Thank God."

"How come?"

I explained to Schulz what Wormley was doing to me. "You don't know what it means to me to have someone around here who sees things—literally sees things—the way I do."

"Good. Does that mean, maybe, you've decided to accept my little proposal?"

"Schulz and Redden, Smugglers Inc.?"

"Right."

"First I'd like to talk to your connection, the Indian, or whatever."

"I don't think so," Schulz said, playing with the boxes of candy on my desk, then sitting on the desk. "This sort of business, the less everybody knows everybody else, the better. A gypsy, let's say, gets picked up smuggling a piano across the border, you don't want him knowing your name, do you? Besides, if I introduce you to my contact, what's to stop you from making the deal without me? You impress me as a really trustworthy guy, on the basis of my knowing you the last twenty-four hours, but I like to do business in a businesslike way. You understand."

"If I don't get to meet him, you don't get the money. By the way, how much money are we talking about?"

"Five thousand dollars."

"Five thousand dollars? Are you serious?"

He was. He expected me to hand over five thousand dollars on the basis of some second- or third-hand story about crooked Indians and gypsies.

"And what do I get for that?" I asked.

"Fifty percent. Look, I know that's a lot of money, but we're not going to be dealing in chewing gum. This is the big time. Besides, that's all you'll ever have to put up. We sell whatever we buy and use that money to buy more. It adds up to this: you lend me five grand for a couple of weeks, maybe less, and you get fifty percent of the profits from then on. Now, if you're really determined to meet this guy—well, okay. It's stupid, but that's your lookout. But first I get the money."

"Hey, why should I trust you on one day's acquaintance, when you won't trust me?"

"Look, Abe. No kidding. This guy I'm dealing with doesn't know you. For all he knows, you're working for the police. God knows, you hang out with the police. This way I hand him five thousand dollars, and he believes us. If for no other reason, he's got an entrapment defense. But if he's introduced to a stranger ahead of time, he's not going to want to do business."

"Why don't you borrow the money? That way you don't need me at all?"

"Because there isn't time. I need the money now, and I can't wait around while a bank checks my credit rating, which, by the way, isn't so hot."

"What about that girl in the picture? She looks like she has money."

"What?"

"You know, the picture on your desk. The girl in the mink coat."

"Doris? Yeah, she's loaded all right. But I'm not about to rock that boat by asking her for money. We're engaged. As it is, her parents don't trust me."

"You're engaged? To be married? Wow, no wonder her parents don't trust you."

"What do you mean?"

"What do you mean, what do I mean? What about those two chippies you were playing around with night before last?"

"Hey, listen, it's been three months since I saw Doris!"

"No kidding? Three whole months. I thought abstinence makes the heart grow fonder."

"I wouldn't know about that. I never tried it. Also, if this deal works out, maybe I don't have to marry her at all. Now, God-damn it," Schulz said, standing up, "do you want to do this or not? I got a bleeding ulcer to take out, and I don't want him dying on me while you and I go through the fine print."

Around about then, Fitch came through the door, unannounced. "We gotta go," the policeman said to me abruptly.

He was dressed again in a captain's uniform with medical insignia, but without name tag. He may have wished to spare the hospital staff the disturbing notion that there might be two Dr. Reddens.

Shulz looked annoyed, but smiled tentatively and held out his hand to Fitch, apparently under the impression he was meeting another doctor. "I'm Bob Schulz."

"Yeah," agreed Fitch, shaking hands perfunctorily. "You were supposed to be ready," he added, turning back to me. I was wearing a uniform. My civilian clothes, I indicated to him, were in a pile on the couch.

"Yeah," he said again. "Well, get dressed. We got to go now."

"I just came on staff," said Schulz, looking a little puzzled.

"That's nice," said Fitch.

I started to write out a check. "This is Captain *Fitch*," I said to Shulz. "I'll be with you in just a second, Fitch," I added, "soon as I pay Schulz here. I owe him for uh . . . a couple of pizzas." I made out the check to cash. Five thousand dollars. That would buy a lot of pizza.

Schulz chuckled nervously, realizing finally who Fitch was. "Not pizza, exactly," he said, feeling perhaps that one ordinarily didn't pay for pizza by check. "Uh . . . it's a wager. We bet on . . . we're betting on the Cuban missile crisis."

That story didn't seem to me much of an improvement over mine; but Fitch didn't seem interested, except to enquire mildly which side I was betting on.

"The Russians, but I gave him the point spread," Schulz replied giddily.

"Are you hurrying, or what?" Fitch asked me.

"Yes, I'm hurrying," I said, dashing off my signature.

I handed the check to Schulz, who raised his eyebrows just a little. I didn't know whether he was surprised that I kept five thousand dollars in my checking account, or disappointed that I wasn't carrying it around in cash. Having this certificate safely in hand, finally, he walked at a secure distance around Fitch, who wasn't paying much attention, and left the room.

Fitch leaned up against a wall and watched silently while I struggled out of my pants, trying not to rip the lining, and got into a pair of slacks. I kept on my black shoes, which had dulled to a properly civilian finish. I buttoned my shirt quickly, first the wrong way, then the right way. Fitch, making an obvious effort, said nothing. Also he refrained from rolling his eyes.

"So you're still alive," he commented idly.

"So far so good."

"Hmmm." A thoughtful murmur. He looked a little disappointed.

"I'm thinking of killing myself," I said to cheer him up.

This seemed to work. He began to chuckle, then cough. Apparently even he wasn't entirely resistant to his cigars. "By the way," he said, when he could talk again, "looks like things are coming to a head. In case you're interested."

"Yeah?"

"Yeah. The crisis is kind of developing a crisis. That's in the first place. We're getting indications from Russia that Khrushchev and his friends are meeting right about now trying to decide whether to run Kennedy's blockade, move into Turkey or Iran, which seems a possibility, or maybe just fold up their tent peacefully and go home. This Colonel Penkovsky, who is connected, sort of, with Konigsberg, like you guessed, is still on line, and this is what we're getting from him. We think he's on line, anyway; and we think the stuff he's telling us is accurate. Which means that Konigsberg hasn't gone over to the other side. It means he wasn't dragged over there, either. A couple of days already, by now he would have told them everything they wanted to know; and Penkovsky wouldn't be talking to us, to his colleagues in army intelligence, or to anybody else. Unless . . . there's always an 'unless.' Unless they're stringing us along. That's if Konigsberg is alive. If he's dead, we got another problem, of course, like who killed him. That's the way things figure now. Unless, of course, the Russians are better figurers than us."

"I don't know what you're talking about. And how come you're telling me all this stuff, anyway?"

"Because as of now, you got a security clearance. Congratulations. We used up half the FBI on the Eastern seaboard for about twenty-four hours, but at least we're pretty sure now you're not a spy."

"That's nice."

"No entanglements, no political commitments, no religious interests. It's like you haven't been around at all."

"No homosexuality?"

"Not unless you're one of those closet guys. By the way, your neighbors like you, you might be interested. Despite everything."

"What's that supposed to mean?"

"You used to run a home for stray cats or dogs, or something?"

"Animals tend to follow me around."

"Howled all night, according to the neighbors. You played the piano and the dogs howled."

"Our nearest neighbors were a half mile down the road. If a couple of barking dogs bothered them, they must have awful sensitive hearing."

"Also you blew up a shack with firecrackers, or burnt it down, or something."

"It was a chemistry set. And what the hell does that have to do with anything?"

My God, what was happening to me? I was standing there arguing with a paranoid cop about a fire I started when I was ten years old. A few minutes before, I was arguing about what color the walls were. Another couple of months of active duty, and I'd end up fighting about how many cracks there were in the linoleum.

"There's some stuff about Konigsberg," Fitch said, "but that'll wait until the flight out to Waldheim. You're expected to keep your mouth shut, you understand, about whatever you hear."

"What do you mean, 'flight'? We're not driving?"

"I keep trying to tell you, we're in a rush. Would you forget about the tie. You don't look convincing in a tie."

A few minutes later, we were standing in a patch of flowers, waiting for the helicopter to settle to earth. Immediately thereupon we ran hunched over below the spinning rotors and climbed in, Fitch leading the way. It was a bubble helicopter, and there were only two seats. One was occupied by the pilot, a man dressed very informally for a soldier, even by my standards. He had on a leather jacket, vintage World War Two, complete with arm patches and OH, YOU KID embroidered in dirty pink silk on a breast pocket. Wound around his earphones, like a turban, was a discolored but reddish scarf, raggedy and unraveling. Perched on top of all this was a brighter red Cincinnati Reds baseball cap, worn back to front. The man's complexion, too, was ruddy, and I thought he might have been drinking. He was either singing or talking to himself. I couldn't tell over the engine noise. Fitch took up most of the other seat, with a little left over for me.

"Close the door," Fitch yelled at me.

I reached around behind me and pulled the door shut.

"Up. Up," Fitch said to the pilot, who it turned out was singing and couldn't hear even with the cabin sealed, probably because of the headphones.

"Up," Fitch said again, indicating the proper direction with his thumb.

"Roger. Uu . . . up, up, up, uuuu . . . uuup we go," the pilot replied.

And so we did, tilting forward, then rising effortlessly. The pilot began singing louder.

"This guy used to be terrific up until the Korean War," Fitch informed me in a smelly whisper. "Saw too much combat."

"Faster," Fitch yelled to the pilot, who didn't seem to be listening. "We're in a *rush*," he added, prying one of the pilot's earphones away from his head.

"Ro—*ger*," said the pilot, eyes aglow. Suddenly we tilted forward at about a ninety-degree angle. Then we tilted sharply to the side. "Wheeee . . ." went the pilot, which was the last sound I heard before falling out of the helicopter.

VIII

"QUIT THE HORSING AROUND, would you?" Fitch said, pulling me back into the helicopter, then reaching across my chest to slam the door shut. He pushed the handle of the door down a notch, locking it. I hoped.

Nevertheless I wound my arms tightly through the shoulder harness that Fitch had thought to put on, and from that woven thread hung above the earth, which was located still over my right shoulder, irregular patches of green and brown swinging back and forth. A moment later the horizon slid back into view, then rose halfway into the sky. We leaned forward in this direction, like divers set to jump off the edge of the world, and, poised just so, sailed on over the countryside. As soon as I could manage it, I lay curled up like a dead spider in a cranny behind Fitch's seat, clinging still to the webbing of his seat belt, meanwhile listening to the throb of the engines and to the pilot's full-throated rendition of "Anchors Aweigh." Over this din Fitch reported to me, at last, the doings of Colonel Oleg Penkovsky, known familiarly in spy circles as PENK, and that person's tenuous but singular relationship with Lieutenant Sidney Konigsberg.

Oleg Penkovsky was a hard worker and a sharp guy, according to Fitch. And a good Communist, too, until he got passed over for an assignment he wanted. Either that or he got blackmailed by a broad, or maybe a guy. Or maybe he started worrying about civil rights in the Soviet Union, or something. Fitch didn't know all the details, he admitted. Anyway, about a year and a half ago, Penkovsky comes over to our side. At first he gives us garbage, low-grade technical stuff we could pick up just as well from an engineering manual. But one particular day, at a meeting in honor of the East-West Growing Camaraderie for Cultural Exchange, or something, he sidles up to one of our military attachés and hands him, very casual, microfilm that he says in a low voice, covering his mouth with his hand, is a map of all missile emplacements along the northern tier of Eastern Europe. Plus, he is including targeting. The attaché swallows his martini olive without chewing, but has the presence of mind to hold out his hand. Turns out this stuff is accurate, including a couple missiles we didn't know about. Since then PENK brings in Russian troop deployments, all the way from India to the Urals, specifications on their new tank, designs for a new machine gun —mostly military stuff, which is what you'd expect; the guy is in army intelligence, after all. Then, like most guys who are screwing the company, he gets promoted. He begins to sit in regularly on KGB briefings for the Central Committee. So we start getting contingency planning, high-level strategy, also intelligence and counterintelligence. For instance, we hear stuff about NATO that even the guys in NATO don't know. We pick up a French major who's been supplying this information and turn him around. Now, for the first time, we're really sure about Penkovsky. Nobody gives up an agent in place just to establish credentials for somebody else. All warmed up, Penkovsky starts delivering stuff a suitcaseful at a time, about every other day. Unbelievable. We're following their submarines from base to base, reading about maintenance problems with their strategic bombers. A test pilot crashes, we hear about it. If Joe Blow gets transferred to Vladivostok because of a buildup in North Korea, we hear about it. We pick up one of our defectors before they can pick him up. We make friends with Tito a little, by dropping a hint that the Russians are going to leave him alone for a while. Also, we give China a couple months' notice the Russians are moving a new division into Mongolia. Who knows, maybe someday we can make friends with them too. If you've been reading the newspapers recently, you might think that we discovered missiles in Cuba by using very-high-altitude airplane flights. Wrong. Mostly wrong, anyway. You can look at those pictures from now till next year without seeing anything. First Penkovsky told us, *then* we looked at the pictures.

All this is terrific, of course, so, of course, there's a problem. PENK, who is in a position to know, maybe, doesn't trust ordinary tradecraft. He has no regular control. Wants no cutout. Uses no regular drop. He's willing to hand over microfilm at a cocktail party, in front of everybody—that's when he's in the mood—but he thinks set routine is dangerous. So we get stuff in the mail, in the laundry. Once he telephones the ambassador at home. We can't tell if he's very smart or very stupid. Maybe he's smart, because so far no one's caught him. Trouble is, back three or four months all of a sudden we don't hear from him. We know now the Cuban thing was brewing. Khrushchev must've thought he'd have the missiles in place before we ever got around to noticing. By then, it would be too late. We can't stop them; and God knows what they do next. But it had to happen quick and in secret, or it wasn't going to happen at all. So the KGB start following everyone around, just to make sure there isn't a leak. The funny thing is, they don't follow Penkovsky, they follow us. The Americans. Anyone connected with the embassy and, it turns out, everybody else PENK happens to know. He knows all about the missiles, of course, but he's not about to lay this on the first American tourist he sees. Luckily somebody figured something like this ahead of time. PENK takes a little ride for himself out to the country and looks in this hollow tree —they got a lot of hollow trees in Russia they keep just for spies —and he digs out a small transmitter already tuned to a wavelength where somebody is listening twenty-four hours a day. Supposedly. But, of course, nobody is listening, since the guy who is supposed to be listening got bored a long time before. Except Konigsberg. Konigsberg is listening on the Big Ear about a thousand miles away. By coincidence. He tells his boss, Collins, and maybe some other people too, unfortunately; and the word gets back to Washington. The problem is PENK broadcasts in the clear—Morse code and Russian, with a code word here and there; and we have to think the Russians picked it up too. Penkovsky didn't sign his name, exactly, but they must be wondering who's broadcasting from the woods outside of Moscow. Even if they didn't hear all this—those guys get bored listening just like we do—they still have to be sort of suspicious about how come Kennedy finds out about the missiles just at the wrong time. Anyway, they stop following us around and start following each other. PENK doesn't like this. It means he's forced to use a dead drop after all, like hiding things behind the radiator in the Moscow Library. There's no choice. Khrushchev is deciding whether or not he wants to have a war, and where and when, and PENK is sitting at the other end of the table listening.

"Maybe he's the most important spy there ever was." Fitch stopped for a moment to contemplate this thought.

Meanwhile our little ship hurried along, entering after a time into fog, or a low-flying cloud. The sudden dimness seemed to affect the pilot's mood. He left off his rollicking tune and began a melancholy and off-key rendition of "The Whiffenpoof Song."

"Which brings us back to Konigsberg. If PENK is the biggest spy that ever was, why Konigsberg wrote the guy's name on a laundry ticket is the biggest puzzle. Since World War Two anyway," Fitch said, eschewing hyperbole.

"Now, you might have noticed security at Waldheim is not everything it could be," he went on, "which is what you would expect when the head of security himself is a fag. Back a couple of weeks, only Konigsberg and Collins heard about PENK; by now, who knows? If that kid Biddle knows, everybody knows."

"Too much cloud," said the pilot. "I'm taking her down."

Immediately we dropped off the edge of an invisible cliff. A second later we bounced. In particular, I bounced, first off a metal rib on the roof of the cabin, then off Fitch, then off the windshield, if that's what it was, then off Fitch again.

"I told you, quit the horsing around!" Fitch said, shoving me away.

I grabbed tighter hold to Fitch's harness, which had slipped from my grasp, but kept bouncing as the helicopter itself rocked from side to side and rose and fell abruptly and repeatedly. We were flying below the cloud now, through a patch of rain. Very low. So low I could look *up* every once in a while into the mist and see a tree. The sudden elevator movements came at the end of every field as we cleared hedges or stone fences.

"This is called hedgehopping," the pilot explained unnecessarily. "Wheee."

"Now what maybe everyone doesn't know," Fitch went on, "there's a secret inside this secret."

Fitch lit up a cigar and immediately filled our small vessel with a cloud denser than the one we had flown through. I let myself sink closer to the floor, where there was still some fresh air.

"See, nobody runs into Penkovsky face-to-face anymore, what with his being followed around all the time and using a dead drop. For all we know, it's some other guy leaving these messages for us to pick up. A plant. Except for one thing. Buried in each message is a code signature. A letter sequence, but also spaces between letters. Half and quarter spaces. That's in print. Over the air it's a hesitation. Not the sort of thing we expect the Russians or anybody else is likely to pick up just listening in— except Konigsberg, who must have some kind of ear. Konigsberg knows the code signature."

Besides rushing forward and rising and falling intermittently, the helicopter was now swinging like a pendulum to avoid trees that loomed up first on one side then on the other. The horizon also danced before me in a lazy arc.

"So it adds up to this: Besides all the other reasons we don't want Konigsberg going over to the Russians—dragged off to them or bought off, or whatever—we got this big reason. We don't want him giving them that signature. Or do they got it already? What then?" This was a sobering thought. Fitch paused and made a snuffling, phlegm-sucking noise. For a brief, awful moment, I thought he was going to spit on me.

"See, it's a matter of who knows what. Do we know what they're going to do, or do we know just what they want us to know? Are we going to do what they want us to do because they're telling us to do it, and we don't even know, or the right thing, the smart thing, which depends on what they do, or at least on what they're planning on doing. And also on what they know, for that matter. Now how much do they know about what we know about from PENK, and what we heard? And when did they know it? If they know we know something, it's like we don't know it at all, for all the good it does us. Except for the missiles, where it's too late to do anything already. For them, I mean. But if they're putting one over on us—if they let us figure we've figured them out on the basis of some fake intelligence by their guy posing as our guy—then they know what we think we know. What then? Should we pretend? Even if Konigsberg turns up dead, we're going to have to figure that out. If they know what we figure we know, even if we don't know it, they're going to be doing something we didn't think they'd do; and in this business there's no room for miscalculation. Just suppose we suppose they suppose we're going to back off in Cuba because we think they think we think they're going to back off; and we don't and they don't? Then what? We got to know if they really know what's going on. Anyway, that's why we got to find Konigsberg right away.

"Are you following this, Redden?"

"I think I'm going to throw up," I told him.

"*NOT ON MY SHOES!*" he replied.

"And they said I couldn't hack it anymore!" said the pilot, who was flying the helicopter upside down. "Look at that, fingertip control. *Fin-ger-tip control!*"

Sure enough, the pilot was guiding our craft with the fingers on one hand, I noticed with a certain alarm, as I bounced around like a marble in a cup.

"We're coming in now," the pilot announced a moment later. "Fast, like you wanted."

The outside world was still oscillating when we abruptly came up against it, hard enough to bounce me completely over Fitch and onto the pilot's lap. The helicopter teetered, then, ever so slowly, fell over on its side, propped up just a little by a propeller that made an oddly nonmetallic sound as it crumpled, sort of like someone stepping into snow.

"Whoops," said the pilot.

"You asshole," said Fitch, addressing himself to the pilot (I immediately felt better knowing I wasn't alone in Fitch's pantheon of assholes), ". . . you could have taken another minute or two!"

"No smoke pots," explained the pilot, a remark that may have made sense, but not to me.

A few minutes later we were back in Kraven's office. The sergeant and I were listening while Fitch issued orders, first over the telephone to someone who had called asking for Captain Redden, then to us. Most of the time he read off a strip of paper that kept curling up whenever he let go of it.

"I want to talk to all those guys," Fitch told Kraven, "whoever rooms near him, works with him. His friends. Find some excuse.

I'm taking care of Konigsberg's depression, tell them, so I got to get background information on what's making him depressed, or something."

"He didn't have many friends. Spent a lot of time in his room. Sergeant Bell, maybe."

"Yeah, we met already. Have him in here about twelve hundred hours. I can sort of accidentally run into him. In the meantime I'll want to look through Konigsberg's room again. This time for real."

"The place is loaded with clues," I explained to Kraven.

"Since you're here, Redden," Fitch said, "and got nothing better to do, I want you to look over Konigsberg's medical record. In fact, his personal file is locked up here somewhere along with all his military records. Get a hold of that and see if you can figure what was going on with him. Was he prone to getting depressed, or did something happen, or what? Maybe he got some kind of disease that makes you go over to the enemy first chance you get."

"Aha! A joke," I exclaimed. "Fuchs was right, Fitch. You got some sense of humor."

"A couple other things about Konigsberg need figuring out," Fitch went on, talking now to Kraven, "like the stuff we got from Muncie, which is not much, but what there is is peculiar. First of all, according to his doctor, he never had any depression before, not as of two or three years ago, anyway, which is when he saw him last. He was a shy kid, a little sensitive, or maybe nervous, especially after his brother was killed; but that's it. Right about then is the first peculiar thing. This shy, sensitive kid, who is about thirteen or fourteen at the time, gets picked up in a street demonstration run according to the local cops by some kind of radical subversive organization."

"In Muncie, Indiana?" I asked. "I thought the only radical group they had out there was the 4-H club."

"Yeah, maybe," Fitch agreed. "I don't have the details. Remember, though, this was just after the McCarthy era. Doing anything political would have seemed peculiar, especially for a kid. Must have took guts. Or stupidity. From there he took up a half-dozen other things: civil rights, the ADA, a Zionist group—which is another hard thing to understand. According to his rabbi, who he never saw, the kid was an atheist from the time he was eleven or twelve. Then he got into some kind of antiwar thing, even though there was no war at the time. Also he started a local chapter of the American Labor party, until they learned back in New York he was sixteen and took away his charter. Mostly left-wing stuff, but, funny thing is, he did belong to the 4-H club, and the YMCA too. He used to run picnics with them for kids in a local reformatory. Then, when he turns seventeen, all of a sudden he quits everything. 'No more politics. That's for kids,' he tells a friend. No more groups at all. Instead he starts studying a little harder. Languages mostly. His marks go up from A to A plus. Probably he could have gotten into any college, but he goes locally, apparently to be near home. It seems his mother is lonely. And depressed. If depression runs in families, that's where Konigsberg got it. From his mother, who is in a blue funk ever since her favorite son got knocked off. Then, when Konigsberg is a sophomore and headed, it looks like, into an academic career, suddenly he quits college, leaves his depressed mother, and goes and joins the army. Also, this kid, who has never even been out of Indiana, except for one summer in Israel, decides to go to Germany of all places." Fitch stuck out a couple of fingers and picked up a large ant that was striding confidently across Kraven's desk. He put it in the ashtray.

"One possibility is maybe Konigsberg is still left-wing after all. Maybe by now he's a Communist. Maybe he volunteered for this post to get access to the Big Ear. Or maybe to signal out on one of the transmitters. Konigsberg had access to the transmitters, didn't he?"

"He wasn't supposed to," Kraven replied, "but I'll check."

"If he could send a message using a transmitter, why would he have to disappear?" I asked.

"I don't know," Fitch said. "Maybe the message was too important. Maybe he wanted to make sure the wrong guys didn't hear it. If we can just find out what Konigsberg did, we won't have to find out why he did it.

"By the way, there's a second town of Königsberg, spelled the right way, KON . . . Actually, it's a city. That's where Konigsberg's family started off a couple of hundred years ago. In East Prussia. Russia now. Within reach of the transmitter."

"The birthplace of Immanuel Kant," Kraven remarked unexpectedly, "the philosopher. He lived there all his life—it was just a small town then—yet his influence spread all over the world."

Fitch stared at Kraven down the barrel of his cigar.

The door behind me opened quietly and Colonel Collins came into the room. He was dressed very neatly, as he had been when I first saw him; but he was shaven now. Whatever effect the death of his daughter had had on him, it was not apparent. Kraven and I stood up.

"As you were, Sergeant," Collins said, taking a seat by the door. He nodded at me, then at Fitch. "Please go on. I don't want to interrupt."

"Uh . . . you know, we're trying to figure out what happened to your lieutenant," Fitch said.

"Of course."

"Do you have any ideas?"

"No, I don't think so."

"You don't think he could have just wandered off for a while to be by himself, maybe?"

"No."

Fitch studied the colonel dispassionately, his expression opaque. He went on finally:

"I got this report from Berlin and Munich. Konigsberg cashed a couple of traveler's checks here and there, but nothing unusual. Restaurants. A couple of hotels. Nothing you wouldn't expect for a tourist. The address he wrote on that timetable was the address of one of the hotels. A waitress remembers him in a place called, believe it or not, the Berlin Jewish Center, where all fourteen Jews left in Berlin can get together over chicken soup along with about a thousand tourists."

This was another joke, I thought; but I couldn't be sure.

"She remembered him because he was wearing a bright green jacket that looked like it didn't fit. He was sitting with a man she didn't remember too well. A German, she thought. He had light brown hair, very curly. That's it from Berlin and Munich. Except one thing. The large money deposits and then withdrawals from American Express started the week after he came back." Fitch turned over his strip of paper and unrolled it again.

"Also nothing new from around here," he said. "The German police can't find Konigsberg. The military police can't find him.

One thing, though—a couple of my people say they got the feeling the Jews from the local synagogue are holding something back. Maybe you can help there, Redden."

"Me? How?"

"Check them out. Ask about Konigsberg if you can."

"Why me?"

"Because you're Jewish. They'll trust you."

"I'm not Jewish."

"You're not Jewish?"

"No."

"You look Jewish. I thought, uh . . . you know, your name is . . ."

"I'm not Jewish."

"Well, dammit, you look Jewish. That's what counts. Pretend you're Jewish. If they ask you to pray in Hebrew, move your lips. Now, one other thing . . ." Fitch tilted back in his chair. "His fiancée. A seventeen-year-old. German national. Spends all day smoking marijuana and talking with her girl friends. At night she drinks. An all-around ninny, according to her teachers. It looks like she doesn't know where Konigsberg is either. In fact, she thinks he's in the hospital, like we told her. But I had Fuchs bug her telephone just in case. If he calls, the polizei will takes notes. She lives with her father, by the way, an ex-SS general who chewed up Norway among other things, but managed to wiggle out of denazification."

"He was a professional soldier, nothing more," Colonel Collins interjected in measured tones. "Also, his daughter is not a ninny. She is young, of course, and sometimes foolish, as the young are inclined to be, but she is lively, and quite charming. I know them both, although not very well. We live a few houses away from each other in Waldheim."

"So you knew about their relationship, Konigsberg and, uh . . . Helga . . ." Fitch was looking for the right place on his strip of paper. "Helga Gutman."

"Yes."

"You approved?"

Before replying, Collins studied Fitch carefully, as if he thought there might be some meaning hidden in this silly question.

"I have enough to do without approving or disapproving the

various social relationships my men enter into," he said finally. "Technically, an officer under my command cannot marry without my permission, but if he were willing to wait two or three months, he would have no trouble marrying whatever I said. I would never exercise such authority anyway, except when a soldier is very young or immature."

"You didn't know Konigsberg very long, I know," Fitch went on, "but it was your impression he was mature?"

"Yes."

"He didn't seem . . . unstable?"

"Scarcely. I would have described him as a young man of great . . . determination," the colonel replied, having found the word he was looking for. "Of course, he came to me, as you know, about a week ago, saying he was depressed, and then a few days later saying he was so depressed he was thinking of killing himself. He didn't explain why. But, frankly, I wasn't sure I believed him. It seemed out of character. He was always contained, self-assured. You had the feeling talking to him that there was another person inside of him standing guard. Or, perhaps, sitting in judgment. Not that he wasn't always polite. He knew how to behave like a proper soldier."

"Did you like him?" I asked.

"Well, Doctor, I didn't really have much of a relationship with him. We only met a few times. I have larger responsibilities than just this base, and I don't undertake to make friends with the junior officers in my command."

"You said you didn't believe Konigsberg was really depressed," Fitch said, stamping out his cigar on top of the ant. "What other reason could he have for asking to see a psychiatrist?"

"I didn't say I didn't believe him, Mr. Fitch. I said I wasn't sure I believed him. I thought there was a possibility . . ." For a moment Collins hesitated. He looked uncomfortable. "Ordinarily I don't like doing this, you know," he said, "repeating stray thoughts that may have crossed my mind for one reason or another, perhaps for no good reason. But I suppose under these circumstances . . . well, I thought he might be using his so-called depression as a device for getting off base. That was one of the reasons I had Sergeant Kraven accompany him, although someone had to be present anyway, since Konigsberg hadn't been debriefed."

"He was depressed, all right," I commented. "Besides, I have the feeling if someone wants to get off this base, he wouldn't have that much trouble."

"I hope that's not true. What would you say, Sergeant?"

Kraven shifted uneasily in his chair. "Well, sir, it isn't. Not exactly. But . . . uh, I think security wasn't everything it should have been while Johnson was in charge. I'm looking into all security procedures now. One thing I found, there was a Major Ryan, a tank commander from 3rd Division, who was seen on base a number of times without ever signing in. I found somebody who thinks he saw him talking to Konigsberg."

Fitch grunted and marked down the major's name on his curvy piece of paper. "Since you're here, Colonel," he commented, looking up, "I've been meaning to ask you a question. You called Sergeant Kraven at the hospital. Just at the wrong moment. If Kraven hadn't stepped into the sergeant major's office, Konigsberg wouldn't have disappeared—not just then, anyway. What did you talk about?"

"I had been trying to reach Kraven for about a half hour. I wanted to make sure he remained with Konigsberg if the lieutenant was admitted into the hospital. I had just heard about the missile crisis blowing up publicly, and it was obvious that Konigsberg's information made him extremely important."

"News of the crisis came through the previous evening," Fitch said.

"Yes? I didn't know. You see . . . my daughter. I had only just then realized she was missing, and I was preoccupied with finding her. I didn't listen to the radio until the following day.

"Dr. Redden," Collins said, turning to me, "I understand you managed to see Lieutenant Konigsberg alone for a few minutes. Did he say anything . . . did he give any reason for wanting to see you? Other than being depressed."

"He hinted there was something in particular he wanted to talk about, but there wasn't time."

A sudden breeze blew a cascade of leaves past the window, reminding me of the inexorable passage of time, the loneliness of winter, and other regrettable things.

"I heard that someone has been shooting at you," Collins said to me.

"Not since yesterday."

"There can only be one explanation for someone wanting to kill you. Konigsberg told you something, or someone thinks Konigsberg told you something. Something obviously that had to do with his work here in military intelligence. Do you have any idea of what that might be?"

"He had something he wanted to say to me, all right," I agreed, "but I assumed it was personal. I can't imagine any other reason why. . . ."

"We've been through all of this," Fitch said impatiently. "Redden doesn't know anything about anything. We can't figure out what Konigsberg would have said if he said it."

"Two things," Collins said, stopping Fitch, who had stood up to leave. "First of all, this man with curly hair. In Berlin. I think I saw such a man here in the town of Waldheim. He was dressed in civilian clothes, and he was talking to Konigsberg. I remember because I thought they stepped back into a doorway when they caught sight of me, as if they were trying to avoid being seen. I wondered at the time whether Konigsberg was away from post without leave. When I checked later on, though, it turned out he had a pass. I forgot about the incident until now."

"Maybe that guy was Ryan," Kraven commented. "He has sort of curly hair."

"No," replied Collins quickly. "I've met Major Ryan. Besides, this fellow was definitely not American. He was German, I think. You know, you can tell that sort of thing when you live in a country a number of years. By the way someone dresses, or combs his hair. Even by the way he carries himself when he walks."

"Maybe a guy named Beck?" said Fitch. "You don't happen to know him, too, do you? Somebody who called himself Beck tried to reach Konigsberg at the hospital yesterday."

"No," said Collins. "But I can describe this other man. He was quite tall, about six feet three inches, I would say. Slender. A tendency to hunch over. A thin nose too. Pinched. Eyes set closely together. Freckles."

"Freckles?" Fitch repeated, looking up from the paper on which he had been taking notes.

"Yes. A great many freckles. And, of course, the hair. He had a remarkable mass of light-brown curly hair. A halo, almost."

"No kidding," said Fitch, making a wry face. "I guess you must have got a pretty good look at him after all. Before he stepped back into that doorway. All right," he added, getting up a second time, "we'll start looking right away for a tall guy with freckles and a halo of curly hair."

"One more thing, Mr. Fitch, before you leave," Collins said, still sitting. "Remember, please, that you and Dr. Redden have a responsibility to Lieutenant Baker. I visited him this morning, and he's obviously in a bad way. I want him properly cared for, whatever else is going on."

"Sir, I couldn't agree with you more," I said, leaning forward in my chair. "We have to help those we can help," which was a remark, I realized, that meant less than I wanted it to.

"Yeah, right," replied Fitch, looking at his watch. "I'm planning on that right afterwards." He left the room without explaining after what was afterwards.

"I have a question too, Colonel," I said, "if you don't mind."

"Yes?"

"You needed a psychiatrist here, I know, for Lieutenant Baker, but why did you ask for me in particular?"

"I heard Dr. Wormley give a lecture once."

"Oh, I see."

A few minutes later Sergeant Kraven led me through a door marked DO NOT ENTER into a small windowless room. Then he drew out Konigsberg's personnel file from a steel cabinet so secure it needed three keys to open. Ordinarily, according to Kraven, each key was kept separately by the commanding officer, the exec, and by him. Since the executive officer was still in the dark about Konigsberg, the keys were expropriated by Collins and lent to Kraven. One more violation of procedures, the sergeant pointed out before leaving to attend to Fitch's other urgent business. He closed the door securely behind him.

I sat down at a steel desk lit by a gooseneck lamp and began searching through Konigsberg's records for some clue from the past that would tell me where he was in the present. Not where he was as a human being—in a way a psychiatrist might be expected to figure that out somehow—but where he was geographically. If there was such evidence, I didn't find it. There was so little of Sidney Konigsberg in his military records, I began to think Fitch had set me at this task just to keep me out of his hair while he rifled the lieutenant's apartment.

The FBI check made prior to Konigsberg's appointment consisted of only a few lines and made no mention of his period of *Sturm und Drang* political activities. He was a "bright, clean-cut American youth," according to their account. "Uncomplicated," they added, making the only possible observation about him I knew for certain was wrong. Since security clearances are not just handed out to anyone, I was not surprised to find letters of recommendation from various people in his hometown. These turned out, however, to be the banal sort that get sent off to college. "Nice guy." "A hard worker." "A very good student." "The best student I have ever had," his German teacher had said. That was more than an ordinary tribute, perhaps. For some reason, his college academic transcript had been included in his file. Konigsberg's marks in general were good, and once again excellent in languages, this time Russian in addition to German.

That was it. There was nothing else. But then, I thought, he had only been in the service a few months. My own file, no doubt, conveyed as little about me. Neither one of us had been court-martialed. Yet.

I had glanced at his medical record previously in my office; but I took a closer look now. He had seen a physician about two weeks ago, complaining of sleeplessness, and had been given a small dose of barbiturates. The physician, I was startled to note, was Captain Robert Schulz, who had neglected to mention to me during our conversation the previous night that he knew Konigsberg. I wondered how Schulz, who didn't seem to me the sort of person likely to have been awarded a security clearance, could have gotten on base; but then I saw the stamp of a 3rd Division aid station hidden in the margin. That must have been the closest medical facility. According to the very brief medical note, Konigsberg's condition was within normal limits. He was probably already depressed, I guessed, and was having trouble sleeping for that reason. A few days later he saw a different doctor for what was diagnosed as a URI. He had a runny nose and a sore throat, in other words, a cold. He was treated, of course, with aspirin. All in all, though, he seemed to be a healthy guy, I judged, collecting his records and returning them to the filing cabinet.

Before shutting the filing cabinet, I took out three other larger records, curious to see what sort of information the army usually considered worth accumulating. And just plain curious. I took these back to the desk and began reading them.

Sergeant Richard Kraven was an "exemplerary soldier," according to the piece of paper in front of me, "attentitive to his duties, reliable, brave. He has leadership potential." He was being recommended, therefore, for the "Distinguished Flying Cross." That couldn't be right, I realized, looking more closely at the smudged typewriting. The man was only a corporal in the infantry at the time. I was evidently reading the last of the obligatory eight carbons of whatever. Leafing further through the chart, I came across similar words of commendation written by his various commanders over the previous fifteen years. Most commonly he was described as "responsible." He had seen combat only briefly during the end of the Korean War, but had acquitted himself well and was awarded the Bronze Star. The security check performed when he transferred to army intelligence was no more revealing than Konigsberg's. He grew up in Milwaukee, had an indifferent school record, except in sports, at which he was "fair plus," and was said to be a "good kid," which is somewhere northeast of being "uncomplicated." He enlisted in the army at the age of seventeen, got married along the way, divorced, and married again. Currently he was separated from his wife and children, who were living in England. He was, at the age of thirty-four, one of that relatively small group of competent soldiers, the senior NCO's, who do the job of running the army while the officers make decisions and the enlisted men run around in a circle.

But there was not much I could make out about Kraven, riffling through these pages. His virtues, besides being "responsible," and "a good kid," were that he was "punctual" and a "hard worker." His sole vice, if I could judge by an occasional oblique reference, was also unremarkable. On occasion he drank.

I read nothing that would explain his knowing that a man named Immanuel Kant had been born and spent his entire life in a town called Königsberg.

Sergeant Albert Bell, Konigsberg's next-door neighbor, was not such a good kid, his records suggested. Before getting drafted he went around throwing rocks through windows, including school windows. In addition he had a bad temper and snarled a lot, according to one of his teachers. Also, he got into fights. When he was a teen-ager, he single-handedly held off a gang of guys who were picking on a kid, then later on was arrested for beating up the kid. Years later while he was serving as a machine gunner during the invasion of Normandy, he was party to a strangely similar incident. Pinned down on the beach with the rest of his company, he suddenly stood up in the line of fire and, *contrary to the express orders of his commanding officer,* ran for the enemy, throwing grenades here and there, jumping up and down, and in general making an ass of himself. Luckily, or maybe skillfully, he made his way up the fortified embankment without sustaining injury, along the way wiping out a machine-gun nest. Manning the gun himself, he laid down such a ferocious and indiscriminate volley of fire, he wounded two of the men in his own unit who were advancing behind him. As a result of this action he was awarded a medal and reduced in rank. The citation stated that he was "brave and belligerent." For some reason he was assigned thereafter to military intelligence. He seemed to have served satisfactorily, getting promoted from time to time, only to lose rank again as the result of brawling. He was court-martialed once during the Korean War for operating a black market in drugs, but was found innocent. He was pushing papers now while he waited for the last two years of his enlistment to elapse so he could retire. According to his previous CO, he was "always by himself. No family. No friends. A loner." Also he had no hobbies, no interests, and no politics. Those were his good qualities. On the down side, he was still "nasty and belligerent." Also he snarled a lot, which shows you how persistent certain quirks of personality tend to be.

According to his medical records, he had been treated for gonorrhea a number of times over the years, which suggested that he wasn't always by himself after all.

The last records I looked at were those of Colonel James Collins. His military career started, it seemed, before he was born. His father was a distinguished soldier, as had been his father before him. He had ancestors who had fought on both sides during the Civil War. James himself attended military school from the age of eight. He had an unexceptional academic record, but partly owing to his distinguished forebears he was accepted at West Point, where, by dint of what his teachers considered "unusual application," he was able to finish in the top half of his class. He spent the early years of World War Two acting as adjutant in a training facility, until finally his persistent requests for active duty were honored and he was given command of a company of soldiers in the South Pacific. These troops were charged with "mopping up" after the Marines, who were in the process of repossessing one island after another from the Japanese. The unit under Collins was cited repeatedly for bravery and became known respectfully as the "Jungle Jims." But it was dangerous work. Of those who served under him initially, only one out of five survived.

There were two incidents during this period of his military career that stood out in the record. The action for which he won the Silver Star took place one Sunday morning during religious services. A Japanese sniper had found his way into a slot in the tin roof of the communications shack and from that vantage rapidly picked off the chaplain and a half-dozen other men. Collins immediately drew fire to himself by running across open ground to the rear of the shack. Although wounded in the thigh, and unarmed except for a Bowie knife, he made his way into the building and out a rear window from where he proceeded with minimal cover, and in danger of being struck by the return fire of his own men, up the crumbling outer wall of the building to the roof. Somehow he killed the Japanese soldier.

The second incident, even more dramatic than the first, perhaps, took place almost exactly one year later. The only account of it I could find in Collins's records, however, was the report of a board of enquiry, which chose obviously to omit certain relevant details. The Jungle Jims were on another island by then, providing security for a company of Seabees who were trying to clear away enough jungle to lay out a landing strip. Although, once again an occasional sniper found his way past the defense perimeter, the posting was considered safe for the most part. For that reason Collins was a little slow checking after an overdue patrol. When he found them finally, they were all dead. Their bodies had been mutilated. Collins, then a major, went after the perpetrators along with a small number of volunteers in an act that was characterized subsequently as "unprofessional." What happened exactly was not recorded. The men returned to camp after an absence of nine days, "a prolonged abandonment of his primary command responsibility," according to the board of enquiry. He had with him the bodies of fifteen Japanese soldiers. There was reason to believe he had given orders to his troops to take no prisoners, an illegal command that was against army policy and in violation of the Geneva convention. He was reprimanded and transferred to the States. Not long after, he was assigned, at his request, to military intelligence. He performed in all the years since then in a manner that was described as "excellent." Yet, considering his capabilities, and his background, he had not really advanced to a very senior rank. That small action he had instigated a long time ago, a long way away, had blocked his career. Odd. During my brief tour of duty, I had learned enough about the military to know that the Geneva convention was not usually at the focus of everyone's attention. I wouldn't have expected anyone to get very excited in wartime by finding a pile of the enemy dumped on his front stoop.

On a hunch I glanced through the colonel's old medical charts, and, sure enough, there was a brief note from a psychiatrist dated around that time—too brief to mean anything though. "Dx: no mental illness," the doctor had written. Nothing else. No reason for the referral. No explanation of his findings.

Because dependents were marked down here and there, I knew Collins was married at some point, became a father, and a number of years later was divorced. Seven or eight years after that, after arriving in Germany, he was married again to someone named Hildegard, a German, I presumed. They had a son, and he was divorced again almost at once. Life on a military base was evidently not conducive to stable marriages. The son was only about a year and a half, almost two years old, now, I figured. His daughter was, or would have been, almost eighteen.

I gathered up all these records, and returned them to their proper place, annoyed meanwhile by a random thought. Maybe, as people say, we are all the same deep down, I reflected, but you sure couldn't prove it by these guys. Or maybe I would have to look deeper.

I wandered through the woods and emerged five or ten minutes later in front of the BOQ. I opened the door to Konigsberg's apartment expecting to find Fitch, but there was no one there. Not just empty, the place seemed hollow, silent, musty a little—uninhabited—as if Konigsberg's presence, having faded only a little bit at a time, was gone now forever.

I walked about aimlessly for a few minutes, looking again at the books crowding the shelves, looking out the windows at the somber gray of the woods. What I didn't look at was the pile of papers on the desk. I had begun to think of Konigsberg as dead, I realized, and these few scraps of poetry and notes written to himself seemed to me no longer any of my business. Even so I felt like an intruder—an idea made explicit a moment later when Fitch, after rattling a key in the door, burst in.

"How'd you get in?" he barked at me.

"I walked in."

"This door was supposed to be locked."

"Yeah?"

"What do you mean, 'yeah'? You were there when I locked it. You got a key? I was supposed to have the only key."

"No, I don't have a key. The door was unlocked when I got here a few minutes ago. I thought you were here first."

"I been interviewing these guys, like I told you. Ah, shit," he added, coming all the way into the room and closing the door behind him, "nothing around this place is locked up like it's supposed to be. I don't suppose you checked, maybe Konigsberg snuck in and is napping in the bedroom?"

I hadn't checked, so we went together into the bedroom. Konigsberg was not there or in the bathroom. The pile of laundry was there, though, just as I had left it, along with the Russian novel, the jar of mustard, and everything else. I watched quietly while Fitch went around the bedroom taking inventory, or whatever. After a time I commented idly that Konigsberg's personnel and health records had not suggested to me any cause for his disappearance or clues to his current whereabouts, a bit of news that seemed neither to surprise Fitch nor interest him. He took a quick look at the green jacket I had described to him the previous day and a quicker look at the bathroom, although stopping for some reason to peer into the water tank behind the toilet. Then he returned to the other room, where he spent the next fifteen or twenty minutes reading letters, notes, and poetry; also, I noticed, methodically crumpling each sheet after he finished with it into a ball. I sat in an armchair and watched him throw each of these one after the other to the floor.

"Say . . . uh, are you going to tell me what those guys said?" I asked finally.

Fitch looked up at me. "Huh?" he replied, frowning.

"You know, those guys you just interviewed, the ones who wouldn't trust you being you, so you pretended to be me to get their confidence."

"What, Bell and those other guys?"

"I don't know. Yeah, I suppose Bell. Who did you just talk to?"

"Bell and a couple of other guys."

"Fine. Terrific. So maybe you'll tell me what they said?" This guy was not going to catch any master spies, I thought to myself.

"What for?" Fitch said.

"Listen, I thought you wanted me to help figure out what was going on with Konigsberg. You know, why he was depressed, why he was talking about killing himself."

"I don't give a damn why he was depressed."

"Wait a second," I said, getting excited, "what are you talking about? You asked me about this guy maybe a hundred times. Why was he depressed, why was he coming to see me. Aren't you the same guy who told me a couple of days ago you had to know everything there was to know about Konigsberg?"

"That was before I found out he was traipsing all over the countryside, meeting guys in one city when he's supposed to be in a different city, and at the same time each time putting away five or ten grand. And that was before I found out—which I just now did—he got caught once or twice working the transmitter."

"The transmitter?"

"That's what they tell me. Of course, he said he was just looking at it. Because he has an interest in electronics equipment, he said. All I know is the transmitter points east."

"I see. So you made up your mind. He's been selling secrets to the Russians. Except instead of handing secrets to any of the couple hundred Communist spies in the neighborhood, for some reason he broadcasts them so everyone can listen in. Then he gets this particularly big secret and disappears. Someone buys him off with a big bundle of money, except for some reason he leaves all the rest of his money back here. Or maybe this secret is so big, his control hits him over the head, then drags him out of a busy hospital without anybody noticing. Except first the lieutenant says, excuse me just a minute, and he writes out a little secret message on a laundry ticket. For some strange reason. For a big spy, he sounds a little confused to me."

"I don't care if he's confused, or depressed, or just plain fed up, like I am."

"It might help if we could figure out why," I remarked mildly.

"Why what?"

"Look, Fitch, this stuff we're getting on Konigsberg doesn't add up. Not to me, anyway. Some of it is consistent maybe with his being a Russian spy—I suppose anything is consistent with being a Russian spy—but what about . . . what about his coming to see me, for instance? Spies don't go to visit psychiatrists even if they do get depressed, right? And they don't call attention to themselves by getting engaged to the daughter of a Nazi general. And once they're in place, they don't suddenly take off, not in the middle of the biggest crisis since the war."

"So?" said Fitch, who was studying the wet end of his cigar.

"So, before you can find out where Konigsberg is, I think you're going to have to find out how he got there. I mean, you're going to have to find out what kind of person he really is. What does he really want? Why did he meet a girl and right away get engaged? Why did he make best friends with a guy like Bell? They don't have anything in common. And, for that matter, why did he get depressed? Why a lot of things."

"Yeah," he muttered. "Well, for your interest, according to one of those guys I talked to, I forget who, he heard Konigsberg had girl trouble. Maybe a Nazi general doesn't like somebody Jewish for a son-in-law. Or maybe it was something else. With women you never know. Anyway, maybe that's why he got depressed. That's the usual reason, isn't it? Women." Fitch sounded bitter.

"There's nothing in this crap," Fitch said, sweeping a pile of papers to the floor with a sudden ferocious gesture, "and nobody else around here is going to tell me anything either, looks like. What I'm going to do is—"

I didn't immediately find out what Fitch intended to do, because the telephone rang. I reached over and picked it up.

"Hello," I said.

". . . is that you?" someone asked. It was a man's voice, obscured by static as usual.

"What?" I said. I was distracted by Fitch, who was spitting pieces of a new cigar all over the floor.

". . . in the hospital. I'm glad . . . we were wondering if you would be able to . . . our arrangement . . ."

I interrupted. "No, this isn't Lieutenant Konigsberg. To whom am I speaking, please?"

There was a brief silence, except for the static, then the sound of someone hanging up. I looked up at Fitch, who was staring at me. Then I put the receiver down.

"You handled that beautifully," Fitch said sarcastically. "He hung up, right? Some imagination you got. If the guy takes you for Konigsberg, why don't you go along?"

Just then the telephone rang again. Fitch started for it, but I got there first.

"Hello," I said, "this is Lieutenant Konigsberg."

"Who? Sid? Is that you, Sid?"

"Yes, it's me. Uh huh."

"No kidding. That's great."

"Right," I said enthusiastically.

"But . . . uh, how are you?"

"Fine, fine. How are things with you?"

"With me? Things are great. But you . . . I mean, what's doing with you?"

"Oh, the usual stuff. Ah . . . uh, what's doing with you?"

"I mean, how are you feeling?"

"I'm feeling fine." I chuckled a little to add verisimilitude.

"Uh, but I thought . . . shouldn't you be in the hospital?"

"Oh, that. Well, I'm much better now. Much." I sort of smiled into the telephone, meanwhile trying to think of some casual way of working Russian spies into the conversation. "Say, uh . . ." I went on, a light beginning to dawn slowly. "How come if you thought I was in the hospital you called me here?"

"I didn't call you; I called Captain Redden. Isn't he there?"

"Hey, who is this?"

"Me? It's Randy Biddle. Who'd you think it was?"

"All right, Corporal, I'm Captain Redden. What do you want?"

"What do you mean, you're Captain Redden? I thought you were Lieutenant Konigsberg."

"Just a little joke. Now, what do you want?"

"The colonel wants Captain Redden, and you don't sound like him. In fact . . . you sound like that Corporal Vigliotti."

"You're right. I made a mistake. Hang on." I handed the telephone to Fitch.

I paced restlessly about the room while Fitch spoke laconically into the telephone and stared at me. When he hung up, he looked at the pile of papers on the floor, then at me.

"I'm going to interview this psycho lieutenant in ten minutes," he said, "then Ryan, as soon as I can get a hold of him—he's off hiding somewhere with his tank—then you can go back to being psychiatrist Captain Redden, M.D. I'm finished with being subtle. . . ."

"Subtle?" I repeated incredulously. "You're right, Fitch," I went on after catching my breath, "subtle isn't your long suit."

"Oh yeah, so maybe I can't pass myself off as Sigmund Freud. What about you? Take a look at yourself, you don't even make a convincing civilian."

That was unfair, I thought. I had an unobstructed view of myself in the mirror, and except for my ripped shirt and jacket that was beat up a little—both the result of caroming around inside the helicopter—I looked fine. Maybe just a little disheveled, that's all.

"I'm starting back at the hospital," Fitch said, "and I'm interviewing everyone, staff, patients, visitors, I don't give a damn . . . and I don't care how many men it takes. I'll strip Munich

and Berlin if I have to. You're right: if Konigsberg walked out of
a busy hospital, or was carried out, maybe somebody noticed.
Then I'm searching the woods, every inch from here to the border. Third Division can handle that; they're wandering all
around here anyway. If somebody got tired of having Konigsberg around, maybe they parked him under a tree. That was a
favorite trick of the German gentry during the days before the
Nazis declared a monopoly on making people disappear. Meantime I'm restricting everyone here to base until I find out who's
been into this room, and why—that's probably thirty-eight guys
right there—and until there's some kind of proper security set
up. At least there's a fence. I'm putting a cork in the bottle so no
one else disappears. Or pops up suddenly. Guys with curly hair,"
Fitch muttered to himself, getting up and walking to the door.
"C'mon," he added on the way out, "and lock the Goddamn door
behind you." He exited so abruptly, an uncrumpled piece of
paper slid across the floor in his wake.

I took a deep breath and followed after, but before closing the
door I looked back into the room. Something was different, but I
couldn't put my finger on what it was. Of course, there was a
hell of a mess on the floor that wasn't there before, but I thought
it was something else. But what? Finally I turned away. I
fiddled with the lock on the door, slammed it, then tried it. It
was locked securely. Just like last time.

Fitch was standing in the hallway in front of a bulletin board
on which was displayed prominently the celebrated reward
poster. This notice, which I read with a professional interest,
proclaimed in large block letters the invidious aspects of homosexuality, particularly with regard to matters of security, morale,
and general health, not failing to mention various venereal disorders. There were certain veiled comments about a homosexual
problem on this particular base (veiled in respect, at least, of
making no reference to a "nest"). The appropriate army regulations were listed. Finally, a promise was made to redeem any
homosexual anyone might have lying about with $250 cash, or
the equivalent in deutschemarks, such transaction to be kept in
strict confidence. Fitch had neglected to print a picture or give
an identifying description, I noticed with regret. He did sign his
name prominently, however, along with his rank, telephone

number, etc. Someone else had written on this document in a
sloppy hand a few words of poetry, to wit:

> There was a policeman named Fitch
> Who developed a sexual itch.
> He wanted a fairy
> All naked and hairy,
> And tried to buy the cute son of a bitch.

"Shit," commented Fitch with feeling.

"You're right," I said, "it doesn't even scan."

"I'm talking about this." Fitch ripped a piece of paper off the
bulletin board and held it under my nose. It was a notice for a
baseball game to be held on the field outside the northwest hole
in the fence.

"Now, what would the American fighting man be without
baseball," I remarked amiably.

"Holes! The Goddamn fence got holes. You know, Redden,"
he snarled at me as if I had put the holes in the fence, "maybe
the only thing that's going to work—the only way I'm going to
catch anyone—is by standing you up in plain sight and grabbing
hold of whoever shoots you first. Unless maybe I lose control
and blow your head off myself."

"Hahaha. Omigosh, another joke," I said, patting Fitch on the
shoulder. "You horse's ass."

IX

AS WE WALKED THROUGH THE WOODS, Fitch carefully explained to me his reasons for not wanting me present while he examined Lieutenant Baker.

"Because I said so, that's why," he said, slashing at some branches with his forearm. "Because I want to ask the guy a couple of questions without you butting in, and also because you annoy me."

"Listen, Fitch—"

"No, you listen. I'm not going to ruin your patient. I'm just going to talk to him. Just for a few minutes. I don't have any more time to waste around here. Anyway, I fixed it so you can watch. That way you see what's going on, you make whatever decisions you want. You tell me, I'll tell Biddle, or whatever. That's the way we're going to work it."

"How am I going to see what's going on if I'm not going to be there?"

"After the war this place was a screening center for POW's; and they still got a one-way mirror over in the ops building which they used for interrogation. We can use that room. I got it all set up. I'll interview Baker while you sit behind the mirror and watch. Biddle will be with me in case Baker gets loose. . . ."

"What do you mean, in case Baker—"

"I'm going to move expeditiously," Fitch said in a rising voice, also walking faster, "I am not going to investigate his sex drive for his mother, so forget that. If the guy's crazy, he's crazy, right?"

"Listen, Fitch—"

"No, you listen. I'm not going to waste any time. I'll squeeze what I can out of Baker—a guy can be crazy and still be pretty sharp, you know. Maybe he spotted something. Maybe he's on to something. Who knows? But if he starts to cry or act up, forget it. He gets the hypo—"

"Listen, Fitch," I yelled at him again. "You're not giving this guy any medication. Also, I don't want you badgering him. He's upset to begin with. . . ."

"Hey, what do you take me for?" said Fitch, stopping suddenly and spreading his arms in a gesture of innocence, at the same time letting a branch snap back at me. "You got an upset guy, I don't want to badger him. Hell, no. Forget the missile crisis. First things first, right?"

"You're damn right. . . ."

Fitch waved me away. "Don't worry," he said, stepping out of the jungle, "I'm just going to talk to him. That's all. Very sympathetic. Soothing. Congenial. If you think I'm doing something wrong, just tap on the mirror. Just make sure you tap *discreet,* would you?"

The room on the other side of the one-way mirror must have been a closet at one time. Two strides carried me from one end to the other. It was only half as wide. Across one wall, extending from the level of my waist to above my head, there was what seemed to be a double-glazed window, the outer sheet of glass tilted at a slight angle. But one of the panes was silvered, somehow, I knew. As long as there was light on the other side of the window and dark on my side, I could look out. Anyone looking the other way would see only his own reflection, although dimmed just slightly by that fraction of light transmitted through the glass. I was alone in the closet. I sat on a stool, the only furniture. The air, cold and damp, smelled of the earth. Waiting there in the silence, and in the dark, I imagined I was underground in a coffin, separated once and for all from everything and everyone.

Suddenly the room beyond lit up, and life sprang back into the world. In the form of Fitch. He stood inside the doorway of a room not much larger than my closet. Opposite the door was a small window, curtained over. There was a small table bearing a lamp and an ashtray. On the far side of the desk was a straight-backed chair, so uncomfortable-looking, I was reminded of Wormley's office. Hanging down conspicuously from the light fixture in the center of the room was a microphone. It was a dismal room, suitable perhaps for a police interrogation, but not for a psychiatric interview.

Fitch, chewing a toothpick for a change, instead of a cigar, looked about the room critically, then came over to the mirror. Right up to it. Directly opposite me. He squinted and peered within, so that I thought he was actually looking at me, which is sometimes possible if too much light filters across. I smiled back and gave a little wave; whereupon he opened his mouth and began picking his crooked teeth, which were stained too, I could see from this uncommon vantage. I drew back and held my breath, as if the essence of Fitch were strong enough to seep through the glass.

I heard a scratching noise from a loudspeaker somewhere over my shoulder, then the sound of voices. Fitch and I left off the contemplation of his mouth and turned to consider Lieutenant Baker, who had entered the interrogation room in the company of Corporal Randy Biddle. For just a second I had trouble recognizing Baker, who had been more or less unconscious the last time I saw him and devoid of expression. Also, Baker was dressed now—in a camisole, I realized with a start. I hadn't ordered a straitjacket. This was Fitch's doing. For a moment I thought of going next door to complain, but then decided it was too late. At least he wasn't wrapped up, his arms tied around his chest, as patients often are, in that peculiar pose of a man hugging himself, as if he were so full of rage or some other passion, he would otherwise burst.

Baker seemed quiet enough. He sat with both arms resting—no, tied—I could see, to the arms of the wheelchair on which Biddle had propelled him into the room. Occasionally he pulled absentmindedly on these restraints and at the same time looked about anxiously, his glance coming to rest finally on Fitch.

"Sir," he said in an urgent whisper, which crackled a little over the speaker, "are you . . . could you be *the messenger?*"

Fitch didn't say anything right away. He sat down at the desk and stared at Baker with fish eyes. Then, abruptly, he smiled. It wasn't just his crooked teeth hanging down like fangs that made his smile peculiar; it had a pasted-on, drawn-back look, which I recognized suddenly as risus sardonicus, the twisted, involuntary grimace caused by tetanus and seen also sometimes in rigor mortis. It was a very off-putting expression, witness the survival of the opossum, which affects risus sardonicus as part of its dead act.

The effect on Baker was not cheering. "Oh, no," he said in dismay, "you're the other one, aren't you?"

"I'm Captain Abraham Redden," Fitch said slowly and distinctly, as if he were speaking to a deaf person, at the same time pointing to his name tag—my name tag, that is. "I'm a doctor, a psychiatrist. I have come to help you with your emotional problems. And your mental. I know you have . . . uh, worries. Everybody's got worries. And that's why you talk to the toilet seat. I'm very sympathetic to that sort of problem. So that's why I'm here. To help you."

"Who are you . . . who are you, really?" Baker said, frowning.

"What do you mean, who am I?" Fitch snapped back. "I just told you who I am. You got some reason to think I'm not who I am?"

"Oh, he's really him," said Biddle, who had been standing off to one side, but paying close attention. "That's Dr. Redden. He's a psychiatrist. Yes sir." He nodded his head vigorously. "I've known him for years," he added, evidently in proof.

"Underneath," Baker said. "Are you God's messenger underneath? Or are you the messenger of the Devil?"

"What was that?" said Fitch.

"The messenger," Baker repeated urgently. "God's messenger is coming. I know because of what they said. The voices. I was in the dark when they began. In the beginning I didn't see anything to notice. Especially the way everyone is around here. Secretive. Because of the danger. God's way is courage; but He doesn't have it all His own way. Destruction is rife in the world. That's what the world is made up of. The contention of forces. A conspiracy of evil. Communism and the Mafia on one side. Sneaking in. Infiltrating. On the other side the forces of good play Frisbee and watch the helicopters come and go. Like that broken helicopter outside. Listening on the Big Ear. The Small Ear. God's ear. The ear of the Devil. The year of the Devil. Anyway, it'll be my fault. I was responsible. We're all responsible for the human race. Commitment to each other. That's the only important thing. God was signaling to me. I could tell you . . . It's a secret though. An end-of-the-world secret. The end of everything." Baker tried to reach up a hand to his face, but was stopped short by the linen cord tied around his wrist.

"Uh . . . right," said Fitch thoughtfully. "Communism. I think you said something about Communism. A conspiracy . . ."

"It makes me feel bad to think about it," Baker said.

"Right, right," said Fitch. "Tell me about the Communist conspiracy. Maybe . . . uh." Fitch leaned closer and lowered his voice just a little. "Maybe you've noticed something going on?"

I began to knock on the mirror. Discreetly.

"I have," said Baker lowering his voice too. "It began just a couple of weeks ago, but it's a secret."

"A secret? You're talking about something on the base here?"
"Yes."

"Does this have to do with . . . any of the people here?"
"Yes."

"What?"

"How do I know I can trust you?" Baker said. "It's the biggest secret probably since World War Two. It's the . . ."

Biddle leaned forward at this point and started to maneuver Baker's wheelchair closer to the desk. "Speak just a little louder. There you go," he said.

"Go ahead," said Fitch, tendering Biddle an evil glance, which went unnoticed by the corporal. Biddle busied himself an additional moment or two fiddling with the microphone, stimulating an earsplitting shriek from the loudspeaker behind me. I knew he had been told I was watching behind the mirror "for teaching purposes"; and evidently he thought I wasn't hearing well enough. Actually I could hear only too well.

"You can trust the captain," he said to Baker, angling the microphone in his direction. "This is all very confidential. You know, professional confidence."

"Uh . . . thank you, Corporal," Fitch said, his smile dwindling to the proportions of a twitch. "The lieutenant and I are getting along swell. Why don't you just pull up a chair and sit down. Over there." He pointed off somewhere in the distance.

But, except for the one Fitch occupied, there was no chair.

Biddle looked around the room a couple of times to make sure. "Right," he said enthusiastically, "I'll have to go get one."

"Good," said Fitch.

"They usually keep a couple of extra chairs in the storeroom," Biddle commented, pointing over his shoulder. "That's for Colonel Collins. He likes to give a party every once in a while, usually a tea party. The chairs are for people to sit on. Most of the time it's not much of a party, really, kind of sedate. But, you know, that's okay; it's the only chance usually to see a girl on base. Well, not really on the base proper. Collins is very strict about that kind of thing. Usually the picnic is on the picnic grounds—we call it the picnic grounds—off in the field behind the north hole in the fence. The chairs and stuff, I got to check that out. . . ."

"Good. Why don't you check that out right away."

"Check what out?"

"Whatever the hell you got to check out."

"I mean, when Colonel Collins gives a tea party, I got to check out all the stuff, chairs, tablecloths. I don't know why a medical corpsman should have to do that. Just because I don't speak Russian or Morse code or . . ."

Fitch didn't say anything. He was working the toothpick around in his mouth so fast, I thought he might do himself an injury.

"Anyway, I'll go now and get a chair, right?"

"Okay," said Fitch.

Biddle left, then leaned in again a couple of seconds later. "Anything I can get you guys? A Coke? I'd offer you some tea, but there's not much demand for tea around here except when Colonel Collins . . ."

Fitch looked wildly about the surface of the desk. Finding nothing but the ashtray, he picked it up; and I wondered for a moment whether he was going to throw it.

"I'll get Cokes, all right?" the corporal concluded cheerily.

Fitch nodded, evidently not trusting himself to speak. Then, a moment later, after Biddle had vanished again, he turned back to Baker.

"Go right ahead," he said in a mellow voice, the grin back in place.

"Where?" said Baker.

"What you were saying."

"What?" said Baker.

"You know, about the secret. The biggest secret since the war. About the Communists infiltrating the base."

"When?"

"What do you mean, 'when'?" Exit the grin. "How am I supposed to know when? You were telling me, weren't you? All about messengers and secrets. Something to do with one of the guys on base, right?"

Baker squinted at Fitch, as if an impenetrable fog had suddenly settled between them. "Who?" he asked finally.

Fitch stubbed out his toothpick in the ashtray and lit up a cigar. "Listen . . . fella," he began again. "You're probably sitting opposite the only guy in the world who's going to take you seriously. There *is* something funny going on on this base. Something important, could be. Just possibly somebody around here has been feeding intelligence to the Russians. The Russians, in case you haven't heard, have been threatening the U.S. the last couple of days with missiles. Atomic warheads. From Cuba. If they get away with that, we can forget about being a world power. We're going to have trouble defending Miami Beach, let alone West Germany. So whoever is supplying this information to the Russians, and we think maybe there's more than one guy, well . . . they're endangering all of us. The whole country. Maybe the whole world. So, when you talk about a conspiracy, I know where you're coming from. So that's why you got to tell me, because if we move fast enough, we can still head them off."

"What?" said Baker.

"*I just told you what,*" Fitch explained. "The *big secret!* The Communists infiltrating the post! The conspiracy!"

I began knocking on the mirror again, a little louder.

Baker's eyes narrowed. "Why?" he asked Fitch suspiciously.

"*Why what? I just told you why* . . ." Fitch was screaming now, and his hands were trembling.

"Cream sodas," announced Biddle ebulliently, coming back into the room, "with the creamy taste. For the noble psychiatrist and the troubled patient. And don't forget the faithful medical corpsman," he added with a chuckle, placing a trio of bottles he had brought with him onto the desk. Hanging on his other arm was a folding chair and a linen napkin. He reminded me of the host at an outdoor barbecue.

"No Cokes left," he said, popping the tops of the bottles with an opener he had with him. "But this stuff is terrific. Made locally. The Germans have a way with cream soda. Also beer. The hops, I think. They've been breeding their own hops for centuries. Every day they deliver the stuff—the beer and soda, I mean—to the northwest hole in the fence. A truck with a horse in front. Heh." Biddle was having trouble setting up his folding chair. He kept bouncing it against the floor and banging it. The noise, amplified through the loudspeaker in my closet, sounded like loose pieces of furniture being dropped down a flight of stairs. Finally, his chair shaken loose and dusted off with the napkin, he sat down at the far side of the desk and looked with interest back and forth at Baker and Fitch, rather in the manner of someone prepared to view an athletic contest.

"Whoops, excuse me," said Biddle, realizing that the bottles of soda were out of reach of Baker's bound arms. He leaned forward and handed one to him. The lieutenant, who had remained silent throughout all of this, stared at the cream soda as if he were searching for the hops.

Fitch was also sitting very still. His expression was entirely blank. He looked like Lon Chaney without makeup, trying to make up his mind whether he was going to become the phantom of the Opera or the hunchback of Notre Dame. He was staring at Baker and giving off a low-pitched keening sound. Or it might have been the loudspeaker again.

"It was in the evening," Baker remarked obliquely, coming back to life a little, "after all day on the Big Ear. I was just listening to the sounds of the wind. Voices. The wind was talking through the leaves. Poetry, it was. Rhyming voices. Mysterious. I knew something funny had been going on by the way people were acting. Making little gestures. Talking to each other, and when I walked in, they'd look up and stop talking. Somebody was always laughing. Even on the Big Ear. I heard laughing. And other things . . . things."

"Yeah? Yeah?" said Fitch impatiently. "What things?"

"Troop movements. You could see they were building up to something. The Baltic states in ferment. Tanks. But there was something underneath. A code. God's message to us. About love, right? A message for spies. But no one pays attention. Everyone maneuvers around. Fool the other side. Trick them. Sneak up on them. The Devil's message. I could hear that, too. In whispers. My God, no one pays attention. . . ."

Fitch seemed to want to say something, but Baker, having been prodded finally into speech, was lost now in a confused, discordant, but unstoppable reverie. He went on about God, love, the peculiar voices that came out of the walls, and the Devil's sneaky ways.

". . . I am waiting for the messenger of God to tell me how we can stop these evil men pushing us into war. . . ."

"Who?" said Fitch, interrupting at last.

"*Who what?*" exclaimed Baker.

I stood up and started rapping on the mirror. This routine Fitch was running on Baker was giving me a headache; and Baker wasn't getting much out of it either. He had started to cry.

"Who, what?" Baker muttered. "The Communists, that's who where when why. I'm thirsty," he added, calming down abruptly. He tried to bring the bottle of soda he was holding in one hand to his lips, but was held back by the restraint. He lowered his head and tried to pour the soda into his mouth, but ended up spilling most of it all over himself. Biddle, who had been watching very attentively, almost rapt, jumped up and wiped off the lieutenant's chin with his napkin.

"There we go," he said carefully, as if he were talking to an infant who was dribbling cereal, "all clean now."

Fitch, I was surprised to see, was made uneasy by Baker's yelling at him. He backed his chair away just a little, as if he wanted to make sure he was out of reach.

"The world is coming to an end," Baker said, sounding kind of discouraged. "All we can do is wait for God's messenger. Oh, Jesus," he called out suddenly. "Oh, God, where are you?"

"Listen, fella," Fitch said, hunching over and muttering, opting evidently for the hunchback role, "I know how you feel; but for the last time, I got to know this one thing . . ."

"God has deserted me!" Baker yelled.

"I'm sympathetic to that, sincerely sympathetic," Fitch said, "but for the last time, I got to know . . ."

You could just tell Fitch was sincerely sympathetic by the way he said, "fella." What he wanted to know, of course, was whether or not Baker, who was an acute, if not astute, observer of the passing scene, had ever observed Konigsberg passing secrets to the enemy. He assumed, naturally, that they hung out together, what with their both being mentally ill. He did a little rambling of his own, hemming and hawing about surreptitious behavior, secret rendezvous, and guys with curly hair.

Baker looked puzzled, which didn't surprise me. Even knowing what Fitch was talking about, I didn't know what he was talking about.

I began rapping louder on the mirror. If Fitch heard me, he gave no sign of it.

"Pay attention, Lieutenant," said Corporal Biddle, who had noticed that Baker was carefully pouring a slow stream of cream soda onto his shoes. "The doctor's trying to get to the bottom of your problem."

"What do you know about it?" the lieutenant snapped back vehemently, showing the sudden, unpredictable change of feeling that is another sign of schizophrenia. "I am in God's service, and I await God's messenger.

"You . . . which are you?" he asked in a rising voice, addressing himself now to Fitch. "I have to know. Are you the agent of God or the Devil?"

"Uh . . . yeah," replied Fitch, looking at his watch.

At this point I was rapping on the mirror loud enough to hear an echo come back through the speaker. Biddle evidently could hear me. He looked all around, at the ceiling, then under his chair, as if he thought a small animal with a good sense of rhythm had gotten into the room somehow.

Baker also heard me. "I hear a knocking," he said, struggling to get out of the wheelchair. "It is a sign! The voice of the turtle is heard throughout the land! God's kingdom is unfolding! His word—"

"Jesus," said Fitch, put off by this latest outburst. He drew back and shielded his face, just in case Baker began to give off sparks. "How tight is he tied into that thing?" He asked Biddle. "One more minute and he looks like he's going to break out in a rash."

"Of course, I should have thought of that," Biddle replied inexplicably. He got up and started to loosen the straitjacket.

"What are you doing?" Fitch cried out excitedly. "He's getting worse! You got that hypo I told you?"

I banged on the mirror loud enough to make sure I was heard over Biddle's maundering, Fitch's ranting, and Baker's announcement of the millennium. And to make sure this time somebody was going to pay attention to me.

"All right, all right," Fitch yelled, I thought to me.

"Calm down, will you, for Christ's sake!" he added, speaking this time, I thought, to Baker, who was pounding his fists against the arms of his wheelchair. "I got one question. Just one last question, that's all. Then you can go back to your . . . uh, religious stuff, or whatever. Easy! That's it, just take it easy. This don't have anything to do with spies or Konigsberg. Forget that. Or even . . . God. This got nothing to do with that either. All I want to know is one thing."

Having seized Baker's attention one last time, Fitch leaned forward, affecting for one last time his sickly smile.

"Tell me," he said, "have you noticed any fags around here?"

The glass must have been cracked already. Glass is especially sensitive to all kinds of stress, just like metal fatigue in airplanes. As everyone knows, even a singer can break glass just by striking the right note. There are many cases on record. Nevertheless, I suppose it's true, if I hadn't banged against the mirror quite so sharply it would not have shattered. As it was, though, jagged sheets of glass came sliding down out of their frame, smashing against other pieces of glass, then against the floor in the closet. First the inner surface went, then the outer mirrored pane. The clatter, magnified through the speaker system, was enormous, a brass band throwing their instruments through a window.

After the echoes died down, I was able to look directly at the actors in this little drama, and they at me. Biddle was frozen into place, his mouth jutting open, a syringe in one hand, a bottle of cream soda in the other. Fitch was chewing on his cigar and staring at me disdainfully, as if my making an entrance through the wall was just about what he expected from me. Only Baker retained the power of speech.

"Aieee! There he is," he screamed triumphantly, waving his

arms and standing up somehow with the wheelchair on his back
like the shell of a turtle, "God's messenger at last!"

"Excuse me," I said.

Fifteen minutes later, Fitch had discovered that he had a lot
to say to me. We were in Kraven's office at the time. I was leaning against a corner of the desk and listening. Kraven sat quietly
off to one side.

We weren't working well together, Fitch pointed out. This
was due in large part, in his opinion, to my having my
"fuckin' head" up my "fuckin' ass." He objected in particular to
my "fuckin' impudence," my "fuckin' interference," and my
"fuckin' sarcasm." In sum, I was "a fuckin' idiot," as a consequence of which he was "fuckin' fed up."

"Hey, listen, I didn't volunteer for this assignment," I reminded him. "I got drafted. You don't like working with me,
that's fine. Give me back my name tag."

He took off the small strip of plastic and slammed it onto the
desk. The clasp was bent, I noticed, picking it up.

"And you can take back your patient too," he added. "He can
teach you to talk to the angels, and you can show him how to
walk through walls."

"You know, Fitch," I told him calmly, "you are not only a dis-
agreeable person and a particularly lousy imitation psychiatrist,
I think maybe you're not such a good detective."

"Oh yeah?"

"That's right. First off, with your friendly interviewing tech-
nique it's no wonder nobody has been telling you anything. Second place, I don't think you've been talking to the right people
anyway. What about Konigsberg's fiancée? She's got to know
something about why he's depressed, even if she doesn't know
where he went. In the third place, if you're such a good detective, how come Konigsberg isn't sitting over there right now next
to Sergeant Kraven?"

"Listen to me, shithead," Fitch snarled, putting his nose about
an inch away from mine, evidently taking exception to my
remarks, "from now on you stay out of my way or I'll have your
ass in a sling."

"Shithead! Shithead! I'm a shithead!" I exclaimed after him.

"What happened to asshole? I liked it better when I was an asshole. . . ."

Fitch left without saying good-bye.

Kraven sighed. "A difficult man to work with," he opined, a judgment I was not inclined to dispute.

"All those guys Fitch was talking to—anything come of it?" I asked.

"I don't know. He doesn't confide in me. I don't think so, though. You're right, he gets down to the nitty-gritty a little too fast for anyone to trust him. He says hello, then right off he asks whether Konigsberg—who he's supposed to be interested in for medical reasons—has been associating with foreigners. You know, we live in the middle of a foreign country. I can't go out to lunch without associating with foreigners. The next minute, he asks if maybe this person noticed Konigsberg doing something funny in bed, or if not, maybe this person himself does something funny in bed. I don't know, maybe there's no time to go about it any other way."

"What about Bell?"

"Nothing, I guess."

"What about that major—the tank commander with curly hair? Or all those other guys with curly hair?"

Kraven shrugged. "I don't know. All I know is we had a couple of hundred people looking for Konigsberg before, and now we got a couple of thousand. Or more. Meanwhile Penkovsky hasn't said a thing for the last twenty-four hours, so we don't know if he's alive or dead. Or if we do, no one's letting me in on it. Meanwhile, Fitch is throwing his weight around. He closed the base so no one can get in or out, except maybe the colonel. Ah, none of that makes any difference," Kraven added, coming over to his desk and sitting down. "This paper work, that's what counts. It doesn't matter if Konigsberg turns up dead or alive, or if the Russians bomb the U.S. or vice versa, I still got to do this paper work."

"This is giving me a headache," I said.

The aspirin was kept safe inside a locked metal cabinet, along with a wide variety of other medicines, including, I noticed, morphine and codeine, penicillin, digitalis, nose drops, and a bottle of something labeled JOCK ITCH.

"We got to lock all this stuff up," Biddle said, giving me a bottle of quinine to hold while he reached into the back of a shelf. "We got so much boredom here, every once in a while somebody tries to get high on foot powder.

"What are you staring at that for?" he asked. "That's quinine. You know quinine. It's used for malaria. We're equipped to treat anything here."

"Yeah, I know. I was just thinking . . . I was just thinking, it's funny to find something around here that's supposed to be locked up actually locked up. Tell me, if nobody from outside is ever allowed on this base, who prescribes all this stuff?"

"Well, sometimes somebody can come on base if he's got a top-secret clearance. It could be a doctor, somebody like Captain Redden, if he's completing a priority mission, like saving a man's sanity or well-being, for example an emergency like Lieutenant Baker, who you can tell is very nervous. Even worse than Lieutenant Konigsberg. Boy, is this work tough on lieutenants. Most of the time, though, a doctor from an aid station calls in a prescription, and I dish it out. I'm responsible for all the medication," Biddle said again with a certain not unreasonable pride. "Even if I can't type," he added.

It turned out we had to dish out some medication to Lieutenant Baker, who was still agitated. I sat down with him first, and tried talking to him, but after his encounter with Fitch, no amount of talking was likely to help. Not right away, anyway. It was an hour later before he was calm enough, even on Thorazine, to be left safely in Biddle's care.

Ten minutes after that I was back again in the doorway to Kraven's office. I wanted his permission to make some telephone calls. I thought I heard his muffled voice, along with a great many others, coming from Collins's office next door; but I thought they would not want me to intrude upon them. Instead I closed Kraven's door behind me, picked up the telephone, and asked for an outside line. I told the operator I was Sergeant Kraven, and since I was calling from his office, I must have sounded convincing. In any case, a couple of minutes later I was talking to Corporal Vigliotti, the real one.

I explained about Baker, that he would be arriving at the hospital sometime that evening, and that he would require special attention. I dictated orders for the nursing staff. Somebody was going to have to sit up with him that night. Because we had no formal psychiatric facilities as such, probably we would have to transfer him farther back eventually to Frankfurt; but maybe not.

Then, of course, we had other business, Vigliotti and I, to conduct—more of the routine business of dealing with sick people, which is what my business happens to be. Even in the army I had patients who depended on me. Among them was Sergeant Lingeman, who was not doing well, Vigliotti reported. They had spent the morning together looking at helicopters. The sergeant had studied them very carefully, watching them land and take off, first from the hospital helipad, then from the airport, inspecting them up close, running his hands over the rivets, slamming the doors, kicking the tires; but he refused absolutely to climb into a helicopter, let alone fly in one. Maybe as a result he had begun feeling uneasy again about heights in general.

"Maybe he's just not cut out for the army," Vigliotti remarked.

"That's not it, Vito. I'm not cut out for the army either, but I can still get into a helicopter if I have to." Although not, I was prepared to admit, with the same careless abandon that had been my way prior to that morning.

"Also, Beck called. You remember, that guy for Lieutenant Konigsberg? He left a number this time."

"Yeah?"

"Yeah. I called the CID. They had somebody down there in a couple of minutes—it's a *Gasthaus* in Fürth—but there was nobody there named Beck. Funny, huh?"

"Yeah. Listen, Vito. I'm stuck out here near Waldheim, that place we were talking about. In fact, I'm up here on the mountain. Konigsberg's base. We were looking for . . ." What the hell were we looking for? I had forgotten. "Anyway, it looks like Fitch took off without me. I'm stuck. How about climbing into my Volkswagen and driving up here. There's an extra key in my—"

"I don't think it would be a good idea for me to drive your car."

"Why not?"

"Well, it's sort of beat up."

"So what? You only drive fancy cars?"

"It's not that. It's just . . . Well, you shouldn't have parked up

against the hospital like that. You know, with the back end sticking out . . ."

"Vigliotti . . ." I said, getting a sick feeling again.

". . . right in front of the mess hall."

"What happened to the car?"

"Well, it got clipped a little by a truck. No big deal. The truck
was carrying frozen turkeys for Thanksgiving."

". . . Turkeys?"

"Right. And other things. Anyhow, it dented your right rear
fender. That was the one that wasn't dented before."

"Look, I don't care about that. Just get in the car and
drive. . . ."

"Also, the car got pushed kind of at an angle. . . . You know,
the back end of the car?"

There was a silence.

"Captain? . . ."

"I'm listening."

"Well, they called an alert here this afternoon. Because of the
Cuba crisis. Everyone's got to be on their toes. Everyone rushing
around. Everybody excited. It was very dark, I think, for two
o'clock in the afternoon. You know the ways the storms come up
around here. Black clouds. Wind. It was probably the clouds. All
I could think of at the time was that line, you know, about
the lights going out all over the world. Like in World War
Two . . ."

"Vito . . ."

"Right, right. Well, to make a long story short, there were all
these vehicles moving by. Half-ton trucks, armored vehicles.
And don't ask me why, a couple of tanks. And . . . well . . ."

"I see. What you're telling me is that it wouldn't be a good
idea to drive my car because there isn't any more car. Is that
right?"

"One of the tanks kind of pushed it into one of the other
tanks. It got all scrunched up. The radio still works, though,
would you believe it. Fate plays a funny hand."

"I was just getting the hang of it too."

"Say again, Captain?"

"Vito," I said, "call up the motor pool. Borrow a car. I don't
care. Just pick me up here. . . ."

"No can do. Sorry. I got strict orders from Major Wormley. I got to stay here all day and count the urinations. You see—"

"Stop! I don't want to hear about it. Goddamn it . . . ask Herr Bromberg."

"What?"

"Ask Herr Bromberg if he'll pick me up in the Messerschmitt. I'm in Waldheim. That's about a hundred clicks east of Nuremberg. I'll have to give him directions."

"Hang on, I'll talk to him."

There was a silence, a relative silence. I could hear muttering from across the hall. Also I could just barely make out a faraway voice on the telephone mumbling in a foreign language, in Russian, probably. I was probably eavesdropping on a Russian who was eavesdropping on our supersecret team of eavesdroppers. Or we were eavesdropping on him. Or something even more complicated.

"He knows the place," Vigliotti said, coming back on the line. "He says he's sorry, though. He says he'd like to help, but there's a top-secret base there at the top of the hill, and he doesn't want to get involved."

This was probably the least secret base in the history of secret bases, it occurred to me, putting the receiver down. I wondered what Konigsberg could have had to say to me that wasn't already public knowledge. Also, I wondered how I was going to get home. I grabbed hold of a Nuremberg-Fürth telephone directory I saw lying in a corner along with some others, and a minute later I was speaking to the librarian at the local school for U.S. Army dependents. Everyone else had left the school for the day. She had been working there since September, she said, and she had never heard of anyone called Krista Brandt. Which didn't surprise me. The librarian was able to give me the telephone numbers of the high school and the various satellite schools spread over northern Bavaria. It turned out nobody at any of these places knew a teacher by that name. Finally, I unfolded the piece of paper Krista had handed to me and tried the number she had written on it. She picked up after the first ring, as if she had been sitting there waiting for me to call. She remembered me.

"You think I forgot already?" she said, laughing. "It was only last night."

"It seems a long time ago to me."

We talked back and forth politely for a moment or so about my amusing companion, the captain, and about her charming and cheerful friend. She enquired after my health, which was satisfactory; and we spoke briefly about the weather. For once, I brought up the subject. I was not good making small talk over the telephone; and I felt under a particular strain on this occasion.

"Am I interrupting anything?" I asked finally. "Are you with a student?"

"No, I am free."

"All through with classes for the day? So early? No homework to do?"

"All finished."

"Oh. Well, look. This problem I told you about. Were you serious about wanting to help?"

"Yes, of course. It sounds like that man is in trouble. If I can help, I would be glad to. Also, it might be . . . interesting doing this with you."

"In that case, you can start by picking me up. . . ."

And so it was arranged. I gave Krista directions—she seemed to know the area pretty well—and we agreed to meet by the west hole in the fence, i.e. the front gate. I would be the fellow who was not chewing on the piece of straw, I told her, in case she had trouble recognizing me in daylight.

The door to Konigsberg's room was still locked. The next room over belonged to Sergeant Bell, according to a small scribbled card tacked onto the door. I knocked. A few indistinct but angry words came back to me. I recognized Bell's Southern twang. I knocked again. A moment later the door opened, and the sergeant stood before me. He was wearing dirty Jockey underwear, a T-shirt, and a terry-cloth bathrobe that hung open. He was unshaven, and his hair was uncombed.

"I'm sorry, did I wake you up?" I asked politely.

"What do you want?" said Bell, another man not given evidently to small talk.

"You remember me? Vigliotti?"

Apparently he did. He snickered, regarding me with a jaundiced expression that suggested he thought he knew me only too well.

"I tried Konigsberg's door, but it's locked," I said.

"Yeah?" he replied without interest.

"Yeah. I thought maybe you could open it for me."

"Is that right? How come?"

"I thought you might have a key."

"Is that right?"

I waited while Bell reached into a pocket of his bathrobe, took out a crumpled pack of cigarettes, and went through the business of lighting up.

"I thought you got into his room a couple of times already," he said, "you and that guy . . . uh, Redden. Right? And if you're going to be in and out of his room all the time, how come you don't get Konigsberg's key? You see him every day, don't you?"

"That's a good idea," I agreed. "In the meantime . . ."

"Listen, I don't know what kind of routine you guys are working, but I don't like it. You and that friend of yours. I ran into him in Kraven's office a little while ago, and he had a whole lot of funny questions to ask for a psychiatrist, like how much money was Konigsberg sending home, and did he sneak off sometimes to be alone with the transmitter, and did he ever introduce me to guys with curly hair."

Bell came a step forward, filling the doorway. He rested one arm against the top of the door and looked down at me. I was at armpit level. Suddenly I remembered why I never wanted to play football.

"I don't believe that guy is a psychiatrist, and I don't believe your name is Vigliotti, unless you got two corporals named Vigliotti in that unit. I just spoke to the other one a minute ago over the telephone. I wanted to talk to Konigsberg, but, of course, he was 'too sick.'" Bell stuck a finger in my shirt and pulled me even closer to him. The lit end of his cigarette wavered in front of my eyes like the brake light of a swerving car. "You want to let me in on what's going on? Is it a secret? You can whisper in my ear."

"I'd rather stand a little farther back, if you don't mind," I said to him, pressing my knuckle against his xiphoid process. The xiphoid process is that little bone at the end of the sternum. It hurts a lot when you press on it, I discovered even before I went to medical school, when a horse fell on me. The horse made me uncomfortable all over, but mostly around the xiphoid process, where a little rock was lodged under my chest.

Bell didn't like the feeling either. He let go of my shirt and took a halfhearted swipe at me, slapping the doorjamb with the back of his hand when I moved out of the way.

"Better not, I'm an officer," I said, wagging my finger at him.

"Yeah? You told me you were a corporal," Bell replied. "I can hit a corporal."

"I'm an officer," I repeated quickly. "CID," I added, flashing my YMCA card. "So watch it."

"Ah, I knew it," Bell said in disgust, rubbing his wrist and turning back into the room. "I can recognize you types a mile away. So?" he remarked irritably, after inserting himself into an overstuffed chair.

I didn't bother to reply, but followed him into the room, closing the door behind me.

Even on this privileged post there was still a difference between officers' quarters and those of an NCO. Although next door to Konigsberg's apartment, Bell had only one room, and a small one at that. There were, however, no bookcases to take up space, and no books. At one end of the room was an unmade bed, at the other an open closet, spilling out clothes, and an open bathroom. In between there was a fireplace full of cigarette butts. It was graced by another ornate mantel, bearing, however, no elaborate porcelain figurine or, indeed, anything except a windup alarm clock, which had wound down. On the adjacent wall there was hung crookedly an autographed picture of Jack Dempsey. Just below was a framed newspaper clipping, yellowed but showing still a recognizable photograph of a younger, and leaner, Sergeant Bell in a boxing stance. A small card table, its legs entwined, stood on one edge up against a wall. Propped up against the table in turn was a folding chair. That day's issue of *Stars and Stripes* was strewn about on the floor in front of me, reminding me in bold headlines of the Cuban missile crisis and the imminence of war. Two particular aspects of the room's clutter were interesting. First, there were articles of dripping underwear hung like decorations everywhere, from the bedposts, from a lamp, and, like mistletoe, from a light that hung down into the center of the room.

"Very festive," I said, moving to one side of this last object, "but you got to walk carefully, looks like. How come you don't use Herman's Chinese Laundry?"

Bell took a drag on his cigarette. "Wrong day," he said finally. "Besides, I don't like starch in my T-shirts."

The second thing was the row of beer bottles. Starting below the window, spaced at regular intervals about an inch apart and extending in a graceful curve past the radiator, past a small telephone table, past the card table with the folding chair leaning against it, past the upholstered chair in which Bell was ensconced, and disappearing finally into the bathroom, there was a row of beer bottles, of which approximately the first third were empty, the others full, except for one in between, which was half full and surrounded by a wet spot on the floor. I imagined Bell lying on the floor and starting at the window, methodically and with foresight, drinking his way into the bathroom. It seemed a singularly mindless yet determined way of spending an afternoon and probably said a lot about his character, if I could figure out what.

"A-workin' in the woods, a-sweatin' and a-haulin', brings a mighty thirst on a man," I remarked conversationally, meanwhile trying to clear a space on a footlocker so I could sit down. The trunk was serving, incredibly, as a platform for a goldfish bowl. Two goldfish swam dispiritedly through murky waters.

Bell stood up and grabbed the folding chair. "Here, why don't you sit down here," he said, strangely solicitous all of a sudden. He even went so far as to offer me a beer.

"Look," he said when we were sitting opposite each other, "I don't know what Konigsberg was doing; but I didn't have any part of it."

"What makes you think he was doing anything?"

"C'mon, you take me for a jerk? What are you guys dressed up like doctors for if he didn't do anything?"

"Well, he really was depressed, wasn't he?"

"Huh?" Bell was absentmindedly rubbing his wrist against his xiphoid process, soothing them both.

"Before he went to the hospital. Something was bothering him?"

"Aaa." Bell waved away the idea. "He was always worrying about something or somebody. This thing or that."

"Something in particular, maybe, the last couple of weeks?"

Bell finished the bottle he was holding and stared into space thoughtfully, or maybe he was just dazed.

"Aaa, I don't know," he said finally. "Yeah, maybe. Come to think of it, he was kind of moping around. Walked by himself a lot in the woods. Skipped a couple of meals."

"Girl trouble, you think?"

"Nope. No girl trouble," Bell said, reaching for another beer. He seemed uneasy a little. He had selected a bottle from the wrong end of the row. "I can be very definite about that," he went on, opening the bottle with a practiced swipe of a church key he dug out of the recesses of his chair. "He was engaged to a cute little kid who was all over him. They were as happy as two peas in a pod."

"Maybe they had a fight. Even peas bump into each other every once in a while, I imagine."

"Negative."

"How come you're so sure?"

"We hung out together. I would of knowed. He was a sensitive kid, that's all."

"I bet all the guys you hang out with are sensitive, right?"

"Huh? Listen, you . . ." Bill said, leaning forward, "what the hell is your name, anyway?"

"Fitch," I said. "Henry Fitch."

"Oh. Yeah. You're the guy who's looking for fags." Bell pulled the flaps of his bathrobe together, as if he expected me to leap forward and inspect his genitals for signs of latent homosexuality. "Well, listen, Fitch, if you're telling me that Sid really is in the hospital, I'd like to know a couple of things. First, why is he being held communicado, and second"—this in a louder voice—"why are you guys pretending to be doctors?"

"Threats."

"What threats?"

"Threats against Konigsberg's life. They've been coming into the hospital the last couple of days. From Munich. From Berlin. Guys with German accents. He got a postcard with a death's head drawn on it. It was signed 'Curley.' You know what that's all about?"

Bell sat back again. "Are you shittin' me?" he asked.

"Would I shit you?" I replied.

"Why would anyone threaten Sid?"

"Secrets. That's what we think. The guy knew a lot of secrets. You wouldn't believe."

"So what do you want from me?"

"I told you before. I want to get into Konigsberg's room. So give me the key."

"What are you asking me for? I don't got any key."

"Come on." My turn to get annoyed. I stood up. "Yesterday you barged in on us doing your loudmouth routine, *after* I locked the door. Either you know some kind of magic I never heard of, or you got a key."

Bell stared at me. "Aaa," he said under his breath.

A moment later I had the key.

"Listen," he said as I was leaving, "the only curly guy I know here is a major in the tank corps, used to get on base somehow and hang around. Seems to me I saw him talking a couple of times to Konigsberg."

"Yeah, thanks. I heard about him already."

"I don't think you're going to find much in there," Bell said, watching me open Konigsberg's door.

It turned out he was right. The porcelain Diana was still absent from the mantelpiece. I had sort of noticed when I looked into the mirror earlier that day, without really noticing, that the figurine was gone. Nor was it present anywhere else in the apartment. And something else was missing, too—the bright green jacket that stood out so conspicuously from the rest of Konigsberg's wardrobe. Without these few cheerful things, his rooms seemed even more desolate, and he seemed farther away.

X

I COULD HEAR KRISTA COMING before I could see her. A soft thrumming, muted by the trees but perceptible nevertheless in the otherwise silent forest, grew very quickly to the rumble of an automobile engine, rising and falling in pitch as the car accelerated past the hairpin turns leading to the base. She arrived in a spray of pebbles a moment later. She was driving a small red convertible, which I took note with some perverse satisfaction had a bashed-in fender. I was not the only imperfect driver in the world. If she had any other imperfection, however, it was not obvious. As she stopped short her golden hair swirled about her face, becoming entangled, a few strands, in her smile, making her laugh. She laughed at me also with her eyes. She was sparkling, animated by some secret amusement. Beautiful now in the sunset, even more beautiful than the previous night, she seemed to me still out of her time. She reminded me of a sunrise, merry and all aglow.

I waved good-bye to the sentry, who was still in his cornpone disguise, although chewing a cigarette now instead of the piece of straw.

"Now, yo' all stay out of trouble, hear?" he called out to me as I climbed into the car.

"Sho' will," I replied.

"An' I'm takin' you up on that invite one of these days," he said, holding up the piece of paper on which I had written my address, my real address, back home.

"Anytime after 1964," I yelled back.

"You made friends with that soldier?" Krista asked as we

wended our way down the hill. "I didn't keep you waiting very long, did I?"

"A man can get a-mighty lonely in the woods mighty fast a-waiting all by hisself," I remarked idiotically. Sitting so close to this woman was making me nervous. "Besides," I added, "he had a pocket chess set. We were playing speed chess."

"Did you win?"

"Of course. But I cheated."

"I didn't know it was possible to cheat at chess."

"It is always possible to cheat. Deception. The key is deception. You see, first I hide the king. I slip it under the table or up my sleeve when my opponent isn't looking, so he doesn't know exactly where to attack."

"But what about when he does look at the board? Doesn't he become suspicious?"

"I distract him. I roll my eyes, or I make choking sounds. Or I chuckle knowingly. Sometimes I fall to the floor and pretend to have an epileptic fit. If it occurs to him nevertheless to look for the king, I pretend the queen is the king. Or maybe the bishop; and I enter quickly into a discussion of church-state relations. Maybe, for no reason, I sacrifice a pawn, which always confuses the enemy, like sacrificing your own soldier. Or spy. Then, slowly, very slowly, I reach around the board, meanwhile whistling, and slip the queen onto a back file where I pretend for the time being that the queen is a pawn. Then I start sliding the horse around like it's a rook, and jumping the bishop around like it's a horse, all the time moving very fast. And I look innocent, which is very important."

"The way you play," Krista commented thoughtfully, "I suppose it's a good idea if your opponent is mostly blind."

"Very true," I said. "Extremely true. Of course, if he seems to be winning nevertheless, I take out a gun and shoot him."

"Well, I suppose that's all right," Krista replied, making the turn smoothly back onto the main road, "as long as you're a good sport."

We were going to Waldheim, I informed Krista, where we had something important to do. I pointed out the town, which was visible once again on the other side of the valley, looking

just a little less pastoral, less *gemütlich*, than when I first saw it
—some trick of the lengthening shadows, or more likely my
darkening mood. I brought Krista up-to-date as we drove.
Konigsberg had left plenty of tracks, I explained, from Munich
to Berlin, most of them going in circles, but if he had left any
real trails, they went through Waldheim. I told her what I knew,
taking care, however, to make no mention of Colonel Oleg
Penkovsky. "There's something funny going on around here," I
concluded feebly as we came into the valley. "Maybe dangerous."

As if in support of that idea, there was a line of tanks moving
ponderously, but quickly, in front of us in the direction of
Waldheim. The M-60 is a medium tank only, but from up close
it looked bigger, and sterner, all abristle with the demeanor of
war, three machine guns that I could see and that cannon up
front. We passed the tanks one after the other.

"Everything sounds very sinister, almost," Krista commented
after we had driven on in silence for a few minutes.

I grunted. Since Wormley's lesson in etymology, all the word
sinister suggested to me were visions of the left bank and left-
handed Romans.

"I notice you don't seem very frightened," I said. "I mean,
considering somebody has been shooting at me, and here we are
driving around in an open car."

"Oh. It didn't occur to me," she replied, although sounding no
more frightened now that it had occurred to her. "I think it is
safe. All these trees, and we are traveling so fast. Are you
worried? After all, it is you they are shooting at." She turned and
smiled radiantly at me.

"Nah," I said bravely. "We soldiers are used to getting shot at.
It's our job. Besides, whoever's doing it is a lousy shot." We
passed a *Gasthaus* and a row of houses set closely together. We
were entering Waldheim. "Either that or he's an awfully good
shot," I added a moment later.

There was nothing to set Waldheim apart from all the other
villages in Bavaria, no suggestion of impending war and no spies
—none that I could see, anyway. There was nothing . . . sinister. In fact, from up close the place was calm, sleepy even.

There was little traffic. A series of curving lanes intersected with a main street that ran to the center of town under an old, probably centuries old, stone arch and to a church. On the other side of the arch was a village square and a squat, but formal, building—no doubt the town hall. Surprisingly, across its facade a glockenspiel was making its stately but merry way. A painted soldier marched out of the wall, its metal arms banging on a drum, followed by a bear playing a wind instrument and bowing to the soldier. A unicorn pranced forward. He reared every so often when a violinist sneaking up behind him struck at his tail with his bow. And all to the tune of a sprightly march. I asked Krista to stop for a moment so we could watch.

"We soldiers are a sentimental lot," I explained, indeed, feeling strangely moved.

We sat in the car quietly and watched while these figures gestured and danced, then slowed abruptly as a bell began to toll, and then trembled altogether to a halt, taking up that dreaming pose of the windup toy whose time is over. The bell signaled the time, which was six o'clock, or eighteen hundred hours, as we soldiers like to say.

We turned at a street marked Kesselstrasse, except that the *s*'s were written like small *f*'s, which the Germans were wont to do, and which was one reason I tended to drive into things. Krista stopped the car a few blocks down, and we got out. I leaned against the car and petted a mongrel dog who had expressed an interest in my shoes. Meanwhile Krista made some enquiries of a housewife who was busy tending snails in her backyard, collecting them for dinner, or more probably for sale. She stooped every few moments to snatch up and bag another one of these creatures, who I imagined were fleeing desperately at a snail's pace. In between times, she gave directions to Krista, nodding vigorously and pointing first one way then another, then upward, suggesting, it seemed, that General Gutman, who was the gentleman we had come to see, and whose address we knew only approximately, lived in a tree house. Actually, he lived around the corner and up a small hill, Krista explained to me a moment later. I shook my leg, which the dog had urinated on—although I think he was aiming for the wheel of the car—and got back into the car. The woman's directions turned out to be correct.

I would not have described the general's residence as a mansion, but it was considerably larger than any of the homes nearby and was finished with an attention to detail that I knew was expensive. A slate walk, unusual in Germany, was bordered neatly by carefully tended rosebushes still in bloom. An enclosed porch in the front of the building extended around the side, seeming to merge with a greenhouse. The front door was oak, carved elaborately, and so were the shutters—hand-carved, I thought. I remembered my father telling me exactly how many thousands of dollars similar ornamentation on our own house had cost when the building had been put up some forty years before. My father always had a good memory for such things.

Krista knocked on the door, and we were confronted almost at once by a large dog, a German shepherd, of course, and by a buxom and blowsy woman. The dog growled, a sound like old plumbing. The woman, who held the dog back on a short leash, studied us suspiciously while Krista explained who we were—I assumed that's what she was doing. She signaled emphatically with her hands and repeated my name from time to time, each time a little louder. The dog left off growling and began to bark. The woman, for her part, kept shaking her head from side to side and at one point would have closed the door in our faces, except that Krista, who seemed more forceful than I might have guessed, leaned against it. Soon a quarrel was in progress, full of sibilants and guttural fricatives, hisses and growls. German is a language made for arguing. It always sounds to me like somebody is getting ready to spit. Meanwhile, the dog, who I thought might be a little cross-eyed, was staring at me as if I had taken on the aspect of a lamb chop. In another moment this spat had sputtered out. Both women were left glaring at each other speechlessly, both still holding on to the door. Then, for no apparent reason, Krista chuckled softly. She took a step forward and, after looking about to make sure she wasn't being overheard, started whispering to the old woman. A new conversation ensued, conducted at a mumble. Krista's remarks must have been startling, however, because I was the subject now of a wide-eyed, although I thought no less skeptical, scrutiny. Finally, Krista turned back to me.

"Listen," she said under her breath, barely moving her lips, "this woman is mad. She says you can't be a doctor, that you don't look like a doctor, and besides, they didn't call any doctor. You should have worn your uniform. A German will believe any-one who wears a uniform. But with this one, maybe not; she is very stubborn. I tried to explain that you are Lieutenant Sidney Konigsberg's doctor, but she says she never heard of Lieutenant Sidney Konigsberg, or any other lieutenant. Instead, she thinks we are from the butcher, and so we should go around to the ser-vants' entrance. Also, if we are from the butcher, where is the ham?"

"Oh, for God's sake, so let's go in the back way. . . ."

"Shhh. Quiet. She thinks now you are a German . . ." Krista had grabbed hold of my shirt and was pulling on it. ". . . and take it from me, when you are dealing with an SS general, you don't approach him by coming through the servants' entrance. And what are you going to do if he asks you for the ham?"

"She thinks I'm a German?" I asked in a whisper, this strange idea just sinking in.

"I had to tell her something," Krista whispered, her face com-pletely immobile. She could have been a ventriloquist. "You want to get in, don't you?"

"How can she think I'm German?" I looked down at my chino pants. "No one has ever taken me for a German."

"Listen, this lady thought you were a butcher. Has anybody ever thought you were a butcher before? She doesn't believe you're an army doctor, so I told her that was just a pose, because you're traveling incognito. Really you're a comrade of the gen-eral from the old days in the panzer division, one *Hauptmann* Menzel."

"What? Wait a second . . ."

"Don't argue. Once we are talking to the general, we can ex-plain. Either that or we punch this woman unconscious and step over her body, in which case we have to fight then with the dog."

The woman in question was staring at me sullenly, but warily. Evidently I was entitled to more respect as an officer in the Ger-man army, defeated though it may have been, than I was hold-ing the same rank in the American army.

"You don't think she's getting some funny ideas," I said, "all this mumbling on her front stoop?"

"I told her you're shy and distrustful. You need to be coaxed."

"A shy SS captain?"

"Well, you look shy. You're always backing away if I move close to you."

That much was true. We had retreated from the door and were standing about ten feet down the walk, off the walk, as a matter of fact. Krista had me pinned against the rosebushes.

"Besides," she went on, "it is only natural, believe me, for an ex-SS officer to be distrustful. Especially when it comes to the secret password."

"Wait just one second . . ."

"Shh. We can't wait. You're right, that lady isn't going to stand in that doorway forever. Look, she's closing the door. Come on." Krista grabbed hold of my sleeve and started prodding me back to the house. "All the old Nazis had passwords, so they know each other. Like . . . uh, what you call an old-boys' network. But they got so many old boys, they got about seventy-three passwords, which they forget all the time. Just say anything at all. I can explain when we get to the general."

We came back into the rapidly shrinking rectangle of light shed by the open door. Krista was in time to push back again before the door closed entirely. Immediately she began another conversation with the housekeeper, who was visible to me now mostly as a frizzy silhouette. Evening had descended around us.

"Say something," Krista whispered, nudging me with her elbow.

"Now is the time for all good men to . . ."

"In German, you idiot," Krista whispered, pressing her foot on top of mine.

I would have liked to explain that I didn't know any German, but I saw that another tug of war had begun with the door.

"*Ich bin ein blauer Zwerg*," I announced firmly.

The housekeeper drew back. I thought I heard a gasp. The German shepherd looked nonplussed. Even Krista gave out a small strangled sound.

This revelation precipitated another burst of animated conversation, after which the door was closed with us still on the wrong side—but not entirely closed.

"That was very good," Krista said, smiling up at me, "to make up something peculiar like that without even thinking. She believed you."

"I am at my best when I'm not thinking," I commented immodestly.

A moment later the housekeeper appeared again without the dog and gestured for us to follow her.

We walked through rooms and hallways bright with gilt mirrors and long polished tables. Small straight-backed chairs with plush cushions—antiques, I supposed—stood at intervals against the wall. In a niche in one wall, sitting on an elaborate mahogany pedestal, was a small porcelain cup. There were also paintings. I stopped for a moment to look at a small line-drawing of a nude. It was a Picasso, an original, too, not the sort of thing I'd expect an upright German general to appreciate. But then again, what did I know about German generals?

We were ushered into a small paneled library that smelled of leather and whiskey. An Oriental rug, on which we walked soundlessly, covered the entire floor. There were books and more paintings, one of them a Corot, more in keeping with the pastoral flavor of Bavaria. And, by God, transporting me in a rush back to my father's library, there were guns. These were hung on brackets in a glass case and were of more recent vintage than my father's collection. The man who was sitting facing us also reminded me of my father, perhaps because he was holding a drink. His other hand rested comfortably on a book. He was a tall man, I judged, dressed conservatively in a suit and tie. His long gray hair was combed back neatly. His features were thin and sharp. He wore slight rimless glasses, small half-moons, over which he was staring at me with some amusement. Unamused still was the German shepherd, who sat at his master's side, trembling with anticipation and aimed in my direction.

Krista began at once to discourse in German, an apology or an explanation, I imagined; but she was cut short by the general.

"You are tall for a dwarf," he said to me in almost unaccented English, "and you do not in this light appear to be colored blue at all." He was smiling, but there was an edge to his voice.

"Ah, you talk English," said Krista. "That makes it easy. We were worried that—"

"Also, you should know," the general went on, continuing to speak directly to me, "that the former soldiers of Germany do not associate in some sort of fraternal order with secret passwords. You have taken advantage of my *Putzfrau,* my . . . woman, who is very suggestible, unfortunately."

"Hardly suggestible," I said. "My friend tried to point out a number of times, I think, that I am a psychiatrist; but we were unable to convince her. I am treating Lieutenant Sidney Konigsberg, who I had been told was known to you, but is not known apparently to your housekeeper. She never heard of him, she said. Also she seemed to confuse me with your butcher."

"*Ach, du Lieber* . . . forgive me," the general replied, making a wry face and putting his drink down on the table beside him. He stood up and shook my hand, then Krista's.

"Please sit down," he said, indicating a couch. "Can I offer you a drink, perhaps?"

We declined the drink, but sat down, I on the near end of the couch, Krista on the far end. She rested her hands primly on her lap and looked askance at the general, plainly annoyed, perhaps because he was addressing himself exclusively to me. I thought it likely that such a beautiful woman was not used to being ignored. But, then again, what did I know about beautiful women?

"That woman—the housekeeper—has been with my household for many years," the general went on, "but she is not so good anymore. Her memory is failing. Of course she knows the lieutenant very well. Also in a way I think she is suggestible. If you told her you were indeed the butcher and told her you had a leg of venison hidden under your shirt, I think she would have believed you; but if you tell her something she doesn't expect . . . well, you know. Some people, it is possible to be very suspicious and very gullible at the same time. As a psychiatrist, don't you think that can be true?"

"I suppose."

"So, then you understand. Now, tell me, how is Sidney doing?" The general had sat down again and was idly stroking his dog. Both dog and master were staring at me fixedly.

"Well, I suppose as well as can be expected. He's depressed, you know."

"So I have been told."

"In fact, that's why I'm here. I was hoping that your daughter —or maybe you—could tell us a little about the lieutenant. Something to help us understand his condition."

"You come this far to talk with his friends? How unusual. A psychiatrist who makes house calls."

"I do it all the time," I told him, truthfully.

"Yes. Well, I don't know what I can say. Sidney is engaged to my daughter, you see; but we—he and I—did not have much occasion to talk. He has only been stationed in Bavaria about five or six weeks."

I nodded. "Still," I said, "that was long enough to get engaged. You didn't object? I mean, that your daughter should marry someone on such short acquaintance?"

"I don't think that really matters so much. Besides," the general added, reaching for his glass and sighing inaudibly, "my daughter is of a modern generation, Dr. Redden. Women today, they don't always ask for approval." His glance strayed briefly to Krista. "Nowadays they go anywhere with anyone they like."

"Excuse me for asking, General, but Konigsberg is Jewish. That also doesn't matter? You don't object to your daughter marrying someone who is Jewish?"

The general kept on smiling. "People don't usually call me 'general' anymore," he remarked. "That was a long time ago, eighteen years ago. Before the German army disappeared. Before even my daughter was born." He looked away into an empty fireplace. "Before my wife was killed. That was in the last days of the war, and she made the mistake of tending patients in a hospital when the Russians decided the Germans had no further need of hospitals. Or maybe it was the Americans. Bombs or artillery shells. I don't know. There was no way I could find out even that much. After that, I didn't care a lot about rank; and no one else did either. Also no one cared anymore about Jewish or not Jewish. If you ask Sidney, he will tell you we get along. He called me Gustav—as you are welcome to do, if you wish."

This remark struck me as disingenuous. The imposing, tightly wound man in front of me was not the kind of person who would ordinarily allow himself to be addressed casually.

"So there is no longer any anti-Semitism in Germany?" I asked. Perhaps the wrong tone crept into my voice. The dog began to growl, a locomotive sound, faraway but coming closer. The general stilled this noise with a touch of his hand.

"I suppose coming from America, the land of the free, you have never encountered anti-Semitism?" the general commented coldly.

I started to reply, but he interrupted.

"Never mind. It doesn't matter, I think. It's true I grew up to be a man in a place very different from what you know, very far away and a very long time ago. It is easy, natural, perhaps, for you to judge somebody by your standards anyway. I must seem very strange to you. I was a general willing to fight for his country, even when it was run by a madman."

"Not strange. I was thinking just a minute ago that you remind me of my father."

"So, then you understand."

"Also, I try not to judge people," I told him. "I don't know what I would have done in your place, although . . ."

"Probably there is anti-Semitism in Germany," the general said, sounding bored suddenly, "but I am a businessman now, not a soldier. I am not interested in politics, and I no longer have to concern myself with such things."

"Yes. Konigsberg mentioned to me just yesterday that you were a successful businessman." Judging from the surroundings, that was plainly the case. Either that or retired SS generals got more of a pension than I would have thought. I made this remark more or less innocently. I wanted only to establish that I was in fact in contact with the lieutenant—that he was in the hospital as he was supposed to be—but something flickered momentarily to life behind the general's otherwise impassive expression, then just as quickly died.

"Yes?" he said.

"Yeah, uh . . . look, we don't want to take up your time unnecessarily. I just thought maybe you or your daughter could tell me what has been going on in Konigsberg's life recently that would explain his getting depressed."

"I'm afraid I don't know. Besides, surely he himself could tell you better than anyone."

"He's too upset to talk about these things comfortably."

"Yet he is calm enough to gossip about my business affairs?"

"No. I wouldn't have put it just that way . . ."

At this point the dog jumped me. Having studied me carefully for the last quarter hour, he evidently found me wanting, or maybe the idea that I represented a threat to the herd of sheep he was guarding in the kitchen had percolated to the surface of his tiny mind and seized irresistible hold of him. In any case, the creature was all over me—and I mean all over me. Instinctively

I had drawn up my feet and was trying to squeeze between the cushions of the sofa when this deranged animal, weighing about as much as the horse that had once fallen on top of me, landed similarly on top of me, two feet on my stomach, one foot in my right ear and the other foot on my xiphoid process. Adolf—I gathered, listening to his master speak reprovingly to him, that the dog was named Adolf—began to walk heavily over my chest. Rather than ripping my throat out, however, he was facing the other way. Snarling and snuffling, he began to savage my pants leg. But it was my shoe he was really interested in, I realized when he bit into it—the same shoe visited recently by the mongrel dog.

A second-degree uproar ensued. There were screams, mine, I think, and much vituperation in German. Krista was hitting Adolf on the head with a book, and even the general seemed put out, although not as much as I would have liked.

"I'm very sorry," the general said after dragging a still irate Adolf into an adjoining room, out of which from then on there issued occasional dispirited barking and doggie-type moans.

"'The enmity of a dog is a sign of respect,'" I said, pretending to quote somebody. My shoe had developed a flap over the distal end, like a mouth, and I was able to examine my toes directly without having to take the shoe off first. Adolf had bitten through the leather, torn my sock and disarranged the bandage underneath; but my foot itself seemed to be intact, except for the laceration I had incurred earlier when I was kicking my broken windowpane around. It was kind of red, and I began to wonder whether it was infected.

"Are you all right?" Krista remarked dryly, for some reason looking at me with disapproval.

"You know, dog bites can be dangerous," I pointed out defensively.

"Listen," Krista said to the general, obviously growing impatient, "naturally your daughter knows more about Lieutenant Konigsberg than you do. Maybe it is possible for us to speak to her?"

"I'm sure she does, but I'm afraid she isn't in now," the general replied, moving to the door. Evidently he was also growing tired of our conversation.

We got up to leave, but before the general could open the

door, a young woman, a very young woman, opened it from the other side and came into the room. She had curly brown hair that hung down in ringlets, a pert face, a lively expression, and nice even white teeth, which I could see because she was chewing gum with her mouth open. She wore a loose sweater over a skirt that seemed to be falling down on one side. She was all over, top to bottom, cute. But she really was awfully young. I would have guessed she was fifteen years old, if I didn't know for a fact that she was three years older.

"It seems my daughter is at home after all," the general said, not looking particularly pleased to see her. He introduced her to us nevertheless.

"Hello, hello," said the young woman, who was called Hellie by her father. She pumped my hand enthusiastically, then Krista's. "Happy to meet you," she added, then immediately lapsed into German.

It was interesting to me as a psychiatrist to discover that I was able to make some sense out of the following discussion even though it took place entirely in a language foreign to me. Maybe for just that reason it made more sense. There was a subtle interplay between father and daughter, who sat next to each other, evident in intonation and gesture and in an occasional unguarded expression. This dumb show came after a while to include Krista as well. The general began, obviously, by explaining to his daughter who we were, or who I was, at least. Krista's presence was justified, or dismissed, by a vague wave of the hand. Hellie smiled, but stared quizzically at her father, and seemed for a moment not to understand. He smiled back at her insipidly and took up her hand, squeezing it, I noticed, as if to emphasize the importance of what he was saying. Then, carefully, he said whatever it was he was saying a second time. She nodded slowly. Her ebullient expression had melted away, and she had left off chewing, although her mouth was still open, an oyster bearing a pink pearl, a small wad of chewing gum glued to her teeth. Then she repeated Konigsberg's name, as if to make sure she knew exactly who we were talking about. Finally Krista began questioning the girl. She began calmly and sympathetically, repeating, I was sure, those enquiries I had made of the general and of everyone else who knew the lieutenant. Hellie's responses were always carefully considered. First she frowned, as if adding up a long string of figures in her head, then she answered briefly, keeping a wary eye on her father, who was studying her in turn, an expression of distaste unmistakable under his frozen smile. Sometimes she simply shrugged. As this nervous colloquy proceeded, the general became increasingly brusque. He interrupted impatiently. A couple of times, when his daughter hesitated too long in response to a question, he answered for her. She seemed used to this sort of prompting and nodded agreeably most of the time, while her hands strayed restlessly over the fabric of her chair. Sometimes she erupted unpredictably in a giggle. Krista, sympathetic at first, was also growing impatient. Obviously exasperated by Hellie's grudging answers and by the general's repeated interruptions, she began waving her arms around, and her voice rose steadily.

"I'm sorry," the general said to me abruptly, "it is unfortunate that you don't speak German. But perhaps it doesn't matter; my daughter, I'm afraid, is not able to tell you very much."

"Nothing," Krista put in. "She doesn't know when the lieutenant got depressed, or why. She didn't notice. They had a really good relationship, which she is unable, however, to describe at all. Also she doesn't know the names of any of his friends or what he did when he wasn't with her. They were supposed to be married, by the way, this coming spring."

"I'm sorry my daughter, perhaps, gives answers that do not satisfy you," the general commented acidly. "Perhaps she is not used to being interrogated in her own home by strangers."

I tried without much success to interrupt Krista, who had begun to reply loudly in German. I apologized just as loudly and grabbed hold of Krista's arm—I would have sat on her if I could —but she went on angrily. It was the girl who stopped her finally.

"Sidney okay? Sidney . . . is okay now?" Hellie asked me, hesitating between each word.

"Uh . . . yes. Well, not entirely," I replied tentatively. I wouldn't have known what to say to her even if I knew how to speak her language.

"Ferry goot," she said back to me, smiling broadly.

The general made a show of looking at his watch; but I ventured a last question. Krista translated:

"Lieutenant Konigsberg has been in the hospital two days already. You haven't gone to see him, or spoken to him either, I think. How come?"

Hellie looked fleetingly at her father, then proceeded to answer, hesitantly at first, then in a rush, until the general stilled her with just a touch of his hand. I had applied an armlock to Krista a few minutes before with much less effect.

"She says she has been ill up to now, but she is planning on visiting him this weekend," Krista explained to me. "But she says also you are misinformed. She has been speaking to Sidney every day by the telephone. If you ask him if this is so, he will tell you. Also," Krista went on, looking at me oddly, "she says the lieutenant is very pleased by the care he is getting at the hospital."

Something must have shown on my face, for the general firmly ended our interview at that point. We said good-bye to each other at the entrance to the library—inaudibly, for Adolf, sensing our departure, had begun howling and throwing himself against the door that contained him, and intermittently, in moments of particular furor, making a weird grating noise that came, I realized, from his trying to bite off the doorknob.

Krista and I got back into her car. She just sat there, her hands on the wheel, staring straight ahead, while I stared at her. She was frowning.

"I noticed you and the general didn't seem to hit it off," I commented.

"Oh, did you notice that?" she replied archly.

"Yes, I did," I said, ignoring the sarcastic tone. "How come?"

"Because he is an insufferable, an arrogant—how do you say it —he is a prig. That kind of man, so sure of himself, so full of explanation, contemptuous of everyone. I know the type, I'm telling you. Did you see how he acts to his daughter? She has to ask her father first before she knows what to think. Even, she doesn't know how she feels about her boyfriend without looking first at her father. Also he is anti-Semitic."

"How can you tell?"

"His attitude. He looks down at women. He is patronizing to you—maybe you noticed that too. Of course he is anti-Semitic. When a man like that looks down at people, he looks down at Jews first of all. Besides, he was an SS general, you remember.

Or maybe you believe, like he says, that, comes the end of the war, all that is forgotten. Bullshit, that's what I say. Bullshit." She said it again for emphasis.

"He didn't seem to like you very much either," I mused.

"Because he couldn't bully me. You, on the other hand, if you are too respectful, he thinks you are frightened of him. Maybe you are. Maybe that's why the dog attacks you. They can smell anyone who is afraid."

"I thought it was a different smell," I mumbled.

"What?"

"Never mind."

"He is a prig, a liar, an anti-Semite, and a . . . a jerk," Krista concluded.

"Well, he is at least a liar. So is she. I don't believe anything they said about Konigsberg. Nobody seems to know much about the kid—his best friend, his commanding officer—but his fiancée, judging from her own account, seems to know less than anybody else. They're hiding something. I had the feeling her father was telling her what to say, prompting her. The funny things is—that last stupid lie the girl told about talking every day to Konigsberg—she expects Konigsberg to cover for her."

Krista, who was still mumbling indignantly, started the car and with a screech pulled away from the curb. We drove quickly through darkened streets. It was night. The sky was black, clouded over. Suddenly it began raining again, and we had to stop briefly to put up the canvas roof of the convertible. Then we drove on silently.

"I'll tell you what I think," I volunteered, although it hadn't occurred to Krista to ask me, "I don't think Konigsberg is really engaged to that girl. Love creeps into pretty funny places, but not this time. The lieutenant was mixed up, all right. Depressed. But he was filled with some kind of . . . some kind of *purpose.* He wasn't about to stop off to marry this kid, who doesn't even seem to have noticed that he hasn't been coming around lately. On the other hand," I added a moment later, "something was going on between them."

We were halfway to the Autobahn when I asked Krista to turn back. "Why?" she asked.

"I want to talk to Colonel Collins. He's probably home by now."

"What about?"

"Nothing . . . very much. I just wanted to ask him a couple of questions about Konigsberg and . . . well, also I'd just like to take a look around."

"I'm hungry."

"Yeah. I'll take you to dinner . . . I mean, if you'd like me to. This'll just take a minute, I think."

Krista made a U-turn without slowing down, and in just a few minutes we were back in the general's neighborhood. The night was opaque and starless. Krista seemed to know her way about, though. We had no trouble finding the Collins home.

Officers of field-grade rank were entitled to a housing allowance if they wanted to live on the economy. Or they could, if they preferred, live in base housing—apartment buildings, usually, put up within throwing distance of each other. There were advantages to living in these U.S. Army enclaves besides central heating and bathrooms large enough to walk around in. You were surrounded by people all of whom were just like you, all Americans, with similar tastes and habits. Children ran up and down stairs all day, yelling and tripping over each other, full of life. Neighbors gossiped—in English, about their in-laws, or the prices in the PX, or the latest movie to come to the base theater. They were, in short, a community, marked by shared interests and concerns. Wormley, for instance, who resided in such a facility, took a serious interest in the children who lived in his entryway. Because he himself had no children—and was objective, therefore, he explained to me—he was able to point out to a number of parents serious deficiencies in their child-rearing practices. His advice was not always taken in the spirit with which it was offered, he admitted to me with some regret. In fact, there were a few who, together, had written to him to tell him to go fuck himself. It was the first time I had seen language like that used in a petition.

Of course, there were disadvantages also, in the eyes of some people, to living on base. You were surrounded by people all of whom were just like you, all Americans, with similar tastes and habits. Children ran up and down stairs all day, yelling and tripping over each other. . . . Neighbors gossiped. . . . And so on. There were some who had come to Germany to live among the Germans. Perhaps Colonel Collins was one of these. Or maybe he preferred to live privately, or even, being a spy, secretly. In any case, his home was off by itself at the end of a street, although only a block away and across a small field from the Gutman residence. More modest, it may have been a farmhouse at one time.

I stopped Krista as she was getting out of the car. "Uh . . . look," I said, "if you don't mind, I'd just as soon talk to the colonel alone."

"Why?" Krista replied, looking cross. "I thought you wanted me to help."

"Mostly to translate. Colonel Collins made himself understood pretty well in English, last time we spoke. Also, the guy's sort of had a hard time lately. What happens if you take a dislike to him? I mean, in a quiet way, he's just as arrogant as the general. I don't want you biting his head off."

"Is that what you think of me? I can't tell the difference between a Nazi general and a man whose daughter has just been murdered?"

"No, of course I don't mean that. The truth is," I said, deciding to tell her the truth, some of it, anyway, "I want to ask Collins about a couple of things he's likely to consider secret. I don't think he's going to want to talk in front of you. Look, this'll just take a second. I'll be right back."

Krista looked at me somberly; but I got out of the car before she could object further.

I turned up the collar of my jacket and hurried up the unpaved driveway, already muddy in spots from the rain. My torn shoe slapped against the ground, making an odd sound, like an awning flapping in the wind. I stepped up to the front door, rapped, leaned against a doorbell, which didn't seem to work, and a moment later rapped again. The entire bottom floor of the house was lit up, although dimly, the faint incandescence scarcely penetrating the fog and rain. I could hear someone moving about inside, but all I could see through an adjacent window was an indistinct, and very short, shadow outlined against a curtain. The curtain moved slowly to one side, uncovering an eye. I and the eye studied each other for a moment, then the curtain very slowly moved back the other way. Then nothing. When it became obvious to me that no one was coming to the door, I began to pound on it. I heard muttering, and off somewhere in the back of the house, a child began to cry, but it was still another full minute before the door opened, and then only a crack. The eye was once again in evidence, along with an ear and a thatch of dirty brown hair, all at belt-buckle height. The door remained on the latch, the chain dangling down.

"I would like to speak to Colonel Collins, please," I said.

"You woke up the kid," came the reply in a scratchy voice. I was talking to a kid, I realized, about twelve years old, judging from the occasional glimpse I got of him. He was still hiding behind the door.

"I'm sorry. I'd like to speak to Colonel Collins," I said again.

"Who are you?" said the kid.

"I'm Captain Redden."

"A soldier? You don't look like a soldier."

"Oh, for God's sake, open the door." I couldn't believe it. It seemed to me I'd been standing outside one door or another all day long, trying to talk my way in. I didn't feel like running through another reprise in the rain. "I'm a doctor," I said. "In the army. I don't have to wear my uniform all the time. Colonel Collins knows all about it."

"You don't look like a doctor."

"Let me in!" I said, giving the door a shove, harder than I intended. The wood splintered and the door, chain still attached, flew open. The kid had stepped away in time and stood off now to one side, looking at me wide-eyed. It turned out he had two eyes, dirty brown, the color of his hair and his shirt too. His pants, and the rest of him, were sort of yellow, spotted yellow pants, a sallow complexion.

"Say, I'm sorry," I said, trying to reassure the kid, who was in a crouch. "I didn't mean to do that."

"You broke in! That's what you did," the kid replied, his voice cracking.

"I'm really sorry. Don't get frightened. I just pushed a little too hard. I meant to—"

"Boy, just like that you broke in. A puny-looking guy like you. I never would have believed it."

"Listen, tell Colonel Collins I'm here. Captain Redden."

"Captain Redden, Captain Redden," the kid said in a singsong voice, mocking me. "Who do you think you're kidding. You're no doctor-captain. You're a private eye."

"What?"

"Admit it."

"Listen, kid . . ."

"George-George."

"What?"

"My name is George-George. Stop calling me kid."

"George-George? They call you George-George?" The president had a son called John-John, but he was a couple of years old.

"That's my last name."

"Your last name is George-George?" I repeated dimly, trying to keep track of the conversation before it slipped away from me altogether.

"You know, you're not too sharp for a private eye," George-George said, looking at me with dissatisfaction. "My first name is George, and my last name is George." He gave this account patiently and a little wearily. I had the feeling he had made the same explanation a number of times before. I wondered what kind of simpleton parents would saddle a kid with a bifid name.

"My father is a professor," the kid said, reading my mind. "Very traditional. Very British. You know the type. He teaches English somewhere around here. A public school. We live a couple of doors away, so I baby-sit here. His father's name was George George," George George added, plainly regretting the whole business.

"Listen, George . . ." I said, feeling suddenly very tired.

"You gave it a karate chop, didn't you?" George George said, closing the door. It was beginning to rain in. "That's how come you did it, right?"

"Did what?" I muttered, not paying much attention. It had occurred to me belatedly that Collins might not be home, which would explain the loony kid.

"A puny guy, and you just crashed the door anyway. You picked up a black belt along the way, right? Comes in handy, I bet. You're casing a joint, maybe for the feds, or a private job, tracing a dame who's skipped out on her rich daddy. Into drugs, whoring around, the whole ugly scene. Suddenly a hood pops up from behind the bar, waving a rod and kind of breathing heavy, but quick you drop him with a kick to the groin. Just like that. He lies there chewing carpet and moaning, his eyes like little red marbles . . ."

"What time does Colonel Collins come home usually?" I asked.

"Depends. You're here to snoop, why don't you admit it? Like to know, wouldn't you, about how come the girl died, right?" George George looked at me slyly, silently. The baby, wherever he was, had stopped crying and except for the rain, there was quiet.

"That's . . . well, that's not entirely true," I said, perhaps not convincingly. It wasn't entirely wrong, either.

George threw himself down on an easy chair, his legs folded under him. He folded his arms behind his head. "Too bad," he said. "A guy like me, hangs out a lot, he gets to see more than people think. But I don't spill my guts to guys pretending to be what they ain't."

I took a long look at George George, who stared smugly back at me. I had trouble believing the kid had a father who taught English, especially the British variety. Then again, if his father was really a gunrunner for the mob, they were a long way from home.

"All right, George, you made me," I said, twitching a little about the mouth. "I shoulda knowed I couldn't con a wise guy."

"I knew it! I can spot a shamus a mile away."

"So tell me, George. What else do you know?"

"Ask me a question?"

"A question. Okay. So how come in your opinion the girl died?"

"Wrong question."

"What do you mean, wrong question? You just said—"

"Wrong question. You want the right answers, you got to ask the right questions."

"All right. Before Sandra Collins died, was she behaving strangely in any way, especially maybe over the last few weeks, as if something was bothering her?"

"Wrong question."

"What time does Colonel Collins come home?"

"First you should ask about money. What kind of detective

are you? 'Who stands to gain?' Right? That's why you're here, right? The money."

I stared at the kid, who was back to one eye. He was winking the other, or maybe just twitching.

"Sandra's mother, she sent you here, right?" he asked, raising his brows expressively. "To check up on the trust fund before the colonel can grab hold of it. Well . . ." At this point George looked about surreptitiously, as if he thought someone had snuck up behind him. "The bankbook is in the top drawer of the bureau next to the handkerchiefs. Now you got the motive, you got the criminal."

I muttered something suitable, on the order of, "Uhaaamm . . . ?"

"Money or passion. You should know that," George said, leaning back in his chair. "It's the old story. And in this case it isn't passion, because that old buzzard never felt anything about anyone. Not in his whole life. Unless it was the U.S. Army, maybe."

"Hey, are we talking about Colonel James Collins? And his daughter Sandra?"

"Don't play dumb, shamus."

"Wait a second. You're telling me the colonel wanted his daughter's money, so he . . . he . . ."

"Right. He knocked her off. Fifty grand is a lot of cash for a bird colonel."

"You think that's enough motive to kill your own daughter?"

"For him? Sure. One time, out in the Pacific, he got annoyed a little at a bunch of POW's, so he cut their throats from ear to ear. He did such a neat job, it even made the army a little nervous."

"Is that right?"

"Sure. Sandra told me. And he wouldn't hesitate to bump her off either."

"I see. That's interesting. I take it you don't think Collins had much affection for his daughter."

"You catch on real fast, like a turtle going uphill."

"I spoke to him once about her, and I got a different feeling."

"Yeah? Well, I'm around here all the time, and I know better. First of all, he was hardly ever home. He had lots of work. That's what he used to say. All evening, all night, sometimes. If everyone in the U.S. Army worked as hard as he does, the Russians would have given up a long time ago. When he was home, he never talked to Sandra much, never asked her how she was feeling or what she was doing. Or who she was doing it with. I know. Sandra used to tell me. We were friends." George was looking at the floor. His voice had dropped and for the first time picked up a vaguely British intonation. He sounded less like a gangster, and more real, a skinny and nervous kid.

"She hung out with the wrong crowd?" I asked tentatively.

"She was lonely," George snapped, jutting out a lip petulantly, "so she went out whenever she could. Just like anybody would. All day long she took care of her brother—and that's no fun— and at night, every once in a while anyway, as a big treat she got to talk to her father, who is about as warm as a witch's tit. I couldn't help much. I'm only fourteen, you know," he added plaintively.

I thought of telling him he was a little puny for a fourteen-year-old, but I changed my mind.

"So she went out a lot. Sometimes with the wrong guys. You know, a kid that age needs a lot of supervision."

"Was she going out with anyone special?"

"Still the wrong question."

"All right, George, tell me . . . tell me whatever you want to tell me."

"I already did tell you," George retorted. "Her father killed her for the money. Or maybe she knew too much. That might have been it. Military secrets. If he had to kill her to protect the U.S. Army, he wouldn't hesitate. Maybe she listened too close to the wrong conversation. You know, just living here you get to meet a lot of visiting spies. Or maybe she just stood up to him finally. He's not the kind of guy to put up with that. So he pushed her off the cliff."

"Whaaat? Pushed her off a cliff? Listen, George George, you haven't been asking all the right questions yourself."

"Huh? She didn't go off a cliff? My mother told me she fell off a cliff. I assumed naturally that her father pushed her."

"Naturally."

Mrs. George, I imagined, found it easier to tell her son that Sandra had fallen off a cliff than to explain how she really had died.

I got up to leave. Collins evidently wasn't at home, and

George, if he really did know anything about Sandra Collins, did not seem inclined to tell me. But then, figuring what the hell, I tried one more time. "Did Sandra know a lieutenant called Sidney Konigsberg?" I asked.

"*Wrong question!*" George cried out, almost in tears. There was an answering cry from the back of the house. "Now you woke up Junior again," George said, jumping up from the chair.

"So long, kid, I gotta go case a couple joints, or something."

"You might as well wait around. Collins called about a half hour back to say he was coming home. He ought to be here any minute. Besides," he said, grabbing hold of my sleeve and pulling, "you wanted to know who Sandra spent all her time with; I'll show you. Junior, that's who. That's why Collins kept her around instead of sending her back to the States to live with her mother. Not because he loved her so much. He never even talked to her. He needed someone to take care of Junior. I get paid by the hour, you know."

I pulled my arm away, but there was something in the boy's face that held me. Finally, against my better judgment, I let him lead me into the recesses of the house.

It was a small and unremarkable home, low, slanting ceilings, dull green walls. I recognized a desk and bureau that were standard U.S. Army issue. Faded photographs of soldiers in formation were hung here and there along a hallway, carelessly, among pictures of snow-covered mountains. These cheerier scenes, which might have come from a calendar, struck me paradoxically as depressing, painted landscapes empty of people. As we walked along, I caught a glimpse of a flowery bedspread in one of the rooms, Sandra's, I imagined; but that small flicker of color did little to lighten the shadows. It was a dreary house, made grimmer by the drumming of rain on the roof and the child's insistent cry.

"Don't hurt Junior's feelings," George warned me. "He's a sensitive kid."

"I have this rule. I try not to hurt people's feelings, especially kids'."

"I have this rule, I try not to hurt people's feelings . . ." George repeated after me in a whiny voice, mimicking me again. "Well, try extra hard this time. And make sure you smile. I know all about you hard-boiled detectives. You think you got tight control. You've been everywhere, seen everything. Nothing touches you, except inside you're all mush. A girl in trouble. A lonely old man. It shows all over your face. Identification with the underdog, yeah. Well, you're about to see the world's number-one underdog."

A moment later I understood what he meant. I caught my breath and smiled, as I was told to, but it wasn't easy.

Junior, who was about twenty months old, I knew, was standing naked in a crib and crying when we walked into the room. He saw us and immediately threw himself down, and laughed. He waved at us with his feet, calling "George, George, George, George," as if he thought George's name was not sufficiently redundant as it was. He was waving with his feet because he had no arms, just flippers, on his right side about four or five inches long, four webbed fingers growing out of his shoulder. On his left there may have been an abbreviated arm—I thought I saw an elbow—and again the flipper hand, useless fingers that flopped against the bed sheet.

"Junior, you took your pants off again, you rotten kid," George said, peering into the crib between the slats, and smiling.

"Not rotten kid," said Junior emphatically.

"Then put your pajamas back on. You're not supposed to be running around nude like a baby."

"Not a baby," said Junior. He looked cross, but then suddenly broke into a laugh. Still lying on his back, the child picked up his pajama bottom with his toes, juggled them somehow, then slithered into them like a snake. Then, with his toes, he pulled the drawstring tight. It was like watching a magic trick, a visitor from another planet doing sleight of hand.

"You're a smart kid, Junior," George said.

"A smart kid," Junior echoed, smiling broadly around an uneven but gleaming set of teeth.

"This is the shamus," George said, stabbing a thumb in my direction.

"Hi buddy, buddy, buddy," Junior said.

"Hiya, fella," I replied.

"Hiya, fella," he said again, in a high-pitched echo.

"He's trained and everything," George told me proudly, "but you got to watch what you say. He's like a tape recorder. Repeats everything."

"Not repeat everything," Junior objected, looking offended again. Suddenly he rolled on a side, twisted and leaped to his feet. Not just a juggler, a gymnast too.

"Hold me, buddy," Junior commanded me, holding out an appendage.

I took careful purchase on the child and lifted him up. "Boy, you're a big kid," I said, pretending to exert myself. He laughed. "You want to see a trick?" I asked. Tricks were on my mind. I did a little sleight of hand of my own and produced a box of jujubes from a pocket.

"Jujube!" Junior exclaimed gleefully.

"This is what she did," George said quietly.

"Who?"

"Sandra. All day long she played with Junior. That was her job. She graduated high school last spring and since then she was a cheap baby-sitter. . . ."

"I let her out from time to time," came a tired voice from behind me. It was Collins. He stood leaning against the doorway, one arm akimbo. He looked at me without surprise, perhaps even without interest.

"Daddy, Daddy, Daddy!" said Junior in a crescendo, leaning in the direction of his father, who came over and took him from me. A moment later, after a hug and a brief, uncomfortable smile, he put the child back in the crib. I put the box of jujubes into the crib next to him.

"The fact is," Collins went on, starting to dress his son, who was admiring a purple jujube he held between his toes, "Sandra liked taking care of her brother." The colonel reached out and took small articles of clothing from George, without looking up, as a surgeon might take an instrument. "Which was lucky. The neighbors, with the exception of George here, are unwilling to mind the child. His appearance makes them uneasy. 'The Devil's child,' they call him. The Germans, sophisticated in so many ways, are superstitious. It was a drug, you know. My wife took a drug . . ."

"Thalidomide," I said.

"Yes."

"It must have been difficult for Sandra. I mean, emotionally."

"I didn't think so, but I suppose it might have been. She was alone most of the time."

I looked over at George, who was leaning against a bureau and staring at different parts of the wall. He was affecting a bored expression, or skeptical.

"Maybe she was upset enough to want to see a psychiatrist," I ventured. "That would explain why she seemed to know who I was."

"I don't think so . . ." Collins began, but was interrupted by George.

"A psychiatrist," he said, clapping his hand to his forehead. "You're the psychiatrist! Why didn't you . . . He told me he was a private detective."

"I did not!" I responded heatedly. "I said I was a doctor. That's what I said. I said it twice. You wouldn't listen. I tried to tell him," I explained to Collins, who had finished dressing Junior except for socks and shoes. He put the child down on the floor and turned to me.

"What is it you want, Dr. Redden?" he asked.

"Sir, I didn't mean to intrude. I know it's only been a few days since Sandra died. I just wanted . . . there were just a couple of questions I wanted to ask. About Konigsberg. And about the base."

Collins stared at me. He took a breath, then let it out slowly. It was as close as I could imagine him coming to a sigh. Meanwhile, Junior was rubbing against his father's leg, trying to climb up, but having no arms to climb—and talking, not always sentences, but words in a blur, all the exuberance of childhood condensed into perfervid conversation and laughter.

"George, please take care of Junior for a few minutes, would you?" Collins said. "In the other room."

"Sure," George replied, sounding disgruntled. "Sure, I'll take him off your hands." He bent down and grabbed Junior, or tried to grab him. The child slipped out of his grasp, then ducked behind his father.

"No, no, no, no. Want Daddy," he cried out, contriving to wrap his feet around his father's ankles.

"C'mon, Junior," said George, seizing him at last, and yanking him free. "They're going to have a grown-up talk. All about the cold war and messages with invisible ink. They don't want us here."

Junior began yowling, a din, dampened only a little by a

series of slamming doors as George withdrew with him to the other end of the house. Colonel Collins, who hadn't moved since he spoke last, sat down slowly on a round, gaily colored toy chest. When it rolled unexpectedly, he reached out shakily to the crib to steady himself, as if he were getting into a rowboat.

"Are you all right, sir?" I asked.

"Yes," he replied in a grim tone that discouraged further enquiry. He leaned back a little and watched me patiently—not so patiently—and waited.

"First of all," I began quickly. "I don't want you to think I talked my way in here by making up some stupid story about being a detective. I told George I was a doctor. He *insisted* I was a private eye, so I agreed. I thought we were playing some kind of game."

"You don't have to explain. I know George. He has an active imagination."

"If he had told me you weren't home, when I asked him, I wouldn't have come in in the first place."

"But as it was, you broke in."

"Uh . . . right. The door. I'm sorry. I didn't mean to push on it that hard."

"You had some questions," the colonel reminded me.

"Yes. Colonel, I know your responsibility extends to other bases in addition to Waldheim. There are a lot of men under your command. You couldn't be expected . . . no one could be expected to keep track of everyone all the time. It wouldn't be your fault if . . ."

"Get to the point."

"Yes. I was wondering if you might have had reason to think that Lieutenant Konigsberg was engaged in some kind of criminal activity?"

The colonel stared at me somberly, a judge posed gravely and incongruously on a toy chest.

"What makes you ask that?" he said finally.

"Well, according to a policeman I spoke to a couple of days ago, there's a considerable amount of smuggling East to West. All kinds of things. He called it a 'garage sale.'"

"Yes? What about it? There's smuggling across any border. The Germans specialize in smuggling people, but that's been going on ever since the Wall went up. Konigsberg has only been here a month and a half. I don't see how he could have involved himself in any of that. He's only been off base once, I think."

"Uh . . . you mean that three-day pass."

"That's right."

"I know. But I thought . . . Well, this town isn't very far from the border. The base is even closer. What with the holes in the fence and other . . . uh, deficiencies in . . ."

"Security."

"Yeah. I thought maybe Konigsberg got around more than people realized. After all, he managed to get himself engaged."

"And in his spare time—whatever spare time he had left over —you think he was smuggling. Why?"

"I don't really think anything, sir. I'm just asking. I know for a fact that there is, or was, a smuggling ring operating out of the town of Waldheim. I'm trying to find out more about it. What makes me wonder if Konigsberg was involved is, first, of course, the large, otherwise unexplained transfers of money through his bank account."

"You don't like Fitch's theory that the money is a payoff from the Russians?"

I shrugged. "Jees, I don't know. I wouldn't have thought a spy would be that obvious somehow. Then again, our side doesn't seem so clever, and I don't suppose they're any better than we are. But there's something else. When I was in Konigsberg's room, I noticed a porcelain statue. It was an elaborate piece. It may have been Meissen, the so-called Dresden china. If so, it would be valuable. Konigsberg's family came from that area, now in East Germany, of course. He may have some relatives still left alive. If they managed to smuggle some of this stuff over to him, he would be able to sell it for quite a lot of money."

"Did you tell Fitch about all this?"

"No. I didn't really stop to think about the porcelain until I noticed it was missing. That was today."

"I see. So your theory, then, is that Konigsberg was part of a smuggling ring. Presumably there was some kind of falling-out among them, as happens often enough, and for whatever reason Konigsberg was abducted and by now probably killed."

"That's going too fast. I don't have any theory. I was just won-dering what you thought. Maybe you know something that would fit in with all of this."

"What about the other . . . uh, circumstances surrounding his disappearance?" Collins said, proceeding at his own pace.

"Guys with curly hair? I suppose they could be in on it."

"I was thinking of someone shooting at you. It seems to me, still, that makes sense only one way. You know—or someone thinks you know—something dangerous."

"Konigsberg didn't tell me anything. There wasn't time. But it makes just as much sense to shoot me for not knowing about his smuggling as not knowing about his spying . . . if you follow me. Besides, whoever was shooting at me stopped. All of a sudden."

The colonel grabbed the edge of the crib and pulled himself to his feet. The crib, also on wheels, slid one way while the toy chest moved in another. I reached out for him, but with an angry gesture he shoved me to one side.

"I'm sorry," he said at once, embarrassed. "I'm . . . all right. It's just . . . well, I'm tired. Between looking for Sandra that night, then . . . finding her. Then, afterwards, looking for Konigsberg . . . I'm just tired, that's all."

Collins reached into the crib and pried loose a teddy bear that was stuck between the slats. He turned it over in his hand and seemed to study it, pulling tentatively on an arm. "Now that you mention it," he said at length, "there have been reports of smuggling at the base. Nothing important, PX goods and cameras. We court-martialed an NCO a couple of years back for exporting Swiss watches across the border. Maybe you're onto something, Doctor. After all, Konigsberg requested assignment in this area. He must have had something in mind."

The colonel began pacing in front of me, still carrying the stuffed bear. Now that he thought about it, he went on to say there were other things: the long-distance telephone calls Konigsberg had received, those clandestine meetings, the evasions the lies. All of a sudden Collins began to wax more enthusiastic about my "theory" than I felt myself. He recalled all sorts of discrepancies in Konigsberg's behavior. Misleading remarks about his whereabouts, sly questions about the rates of currency exchange or the peculiarities of local geography, an interest in timetables and such, and also a tendency to secretiveness. None of these clues—he referred to them as "clues"—added much to what I already knew; and at one point I had the disquieting thought that Collins was making most of it up as he went along.

"Make sure you tell Fitch," he concluded finally. "Smuggling is never a one-man operation. For one thing, if the stuff is coming East to West, he would need a dealer, a fence. The CID collaborates on such things with local police and with Interpol. By the way, some of the local racketeers have a bad reputation."

"Is that so?" I said, wondering why a racketeer would have a bad reputation.

"Yes. If Konigsberg ran afoul of those guys, we'll never find him. There are a couple of hundred miles of woods around here. If you plant something underground, like a human being, it's lost for the next thousand years."

A moment later I was at the front door, still listening to the colonel, who plainly preferred thinking of Konigsberg as a criminal rather than as a Russian spy, perhaps for obvious reasons. George was back in his chair again, restraining Junior by a shirttail, not without effort though. The child was attempting to pull George, along with the chair, over to the door. George, I noticed, had contorted his face into a peculiar expression. He was mouthing words at me silently, rolling his eyes and winking. In between, he jerked his head back spasmodically. He looked like he was having some kind of seizure.

With some difficulty, I turned my attention from this Grand Guignol back to Colonel Collins. There was still something I wanted to know.

"That first time we met, Colonel," I began, then hesitated a moment as I tried to find a way to remind him of that morning without hurting him; but I could think of none. "You asked me if your daughter had said anything to me before she died. I had the feeling you were concerned about her saying some particular thing. Was I right? Did she know . . . is it possible, maybe just by living here with you, that she learned something, some . . . military secret, or something?"

"Do you mean, do I leave military secrets lying around on the kitchen table?"

"No, of course not, but . . ."

"No, Doctor. Sandra did not have knowledge of any military intelligence or any other classified information. I never spoke to her about such things, and I don't bring my work home. She wouldn't have been interested anyway. She was barely out of high school. To describe her as politically naive would have been charitable. I'm not sure she knew who the President was . . ."

I could see George over the colonel's shoulder. He was crossing his eyes and chewing on his upper lip.

". . . She was a sensitive, innocent young girl, responsible about domestic matters. Caring for my son. She was perhaps more a mother than a sister. I don't know what I would have . . . what I'm going to do now, without her. But in every other way, she was immature and, to put it bluntly, ignorant."

"Still, when she visited you on base, she might have . . ."

"She did *not* visit me on base. Neither she nor anyone else visits that base, as you know. Frankly, I wouldn't have allowed her to visit even if it were an ordinary army installation. Soldiers are not proper companions for young girls, or, for that matter, older women. And the soldiers themselves are better off left alone. We teach them how to fight wars, not how to make good husbands. I've had a couple of disastrous marriages myself—my second wife just disappeared—and I wasn't about to let Sandra get into any similar entanglement."

In the background George was grimacing, as if in pain, and with his free hand pretending to strangle himself. With the other he still had hold of Junior's shirt.

"I see," I muttered. "There's no chance then, I suppose," I said, smiling feebly at Collins, who was not smiling, "that Sandra knew Konigsberg?"

"No."

"Somehow I thought . . . well, the coincidence, I suppose, of seeing the two of them so soon after each other, both of them connected to Waldheim in some way. It turns out he was engaged to a girl who lives only a couple of blocks away."

"Sandra never met him. She would have mentioned it to me. As for my wanting to know what Sandra said to you before she died, it was not out of concern that she might have breached some military secret. I was a father enquiring about his daughter's last words. That's all there was to it."

"I see."

George was silently in his death throes. He had slipped half-way to the floor and was hanging upside down, his mouth working convulsively, his eyes squeezed shut. Also, he was shaking a fist at me.

"Thank you," I said to the colonel. "Uh . . . so long, George," I called out, waving to the kid, who was immediately back in place, smiling benevolently. "See you around."

"I hope so," George replied unexpectedly.

I waved good-bye to Junior also, who was still squirming in place and chattering.

"Bye, bye, buddy, bye, buddy, buddy, bye, buddy."

"Good-bye, sir. I'm sorry about the door," I said again, running my hand over the broken wood and picking up a splinter. I put my collar up again and went out into the rain.

"Psychiatrists are okay too," George yelled out to me reassuringly, if ambiguously.

Krista was in a bad mood, at least she drove as if she was in a bad mood, smoothly and silently and too fast.

"That took a long time for just a few questions," she said finally.

"You're right," I replied, trying to pry the splinter out with a fingernail, "but he was lying. It always takes longer when someone lies."

"Who was lying? The colonel?"

I looked up to see a car approaching, a pair of bright, white eyes blurred by the rain on the windshield, but opening wider and wider. The car came at us head on, only to swerve at the last moment, sending a shaft of light along a desolate street.

"Ayaagh! Jesus Christ!" I exclaimed.

"What happened? Did you hurt yourself again?" Krista enquired calmly, steering serenely into the night.

"Turn around. Quick!"

Krista looked over to me to make sure I was serious, then, putting both hands on the wheel—for a change—she swung the car over to the right, running it halfway across a sidewalk. Without taking a deep breath, and without slowing down, she twisted the wheel sharply the other way. We spun across the narrow road, just missing a truck, hurtled into the curb and up onto the opposite sidewalk, speeding now in the opposite direction. We passed someone wearing a rain slicker and a surprised expression, then with a jolt slipped back into the roadway.

"Not this quick!" I yelled.

"I thought you wanted to follow that car."

"Turn here."

It was more an alley than a street, a space between two houses that faced away from each other and were too unfriendly to touch. Into this tiny avenue jutted the sign I had caught sight of a moment before in the glare of headlights.

"My God, I don't believe it," I said after we had stopped. "There really is a Herman's Chinese Laundry." I got out of the car and made my way around a puddle to the storefront. There was a second sign printed in large black letters on the window. Sloppy black arrows were drawn all around the periphery of the window pointing out this sign, just in case a casual stroller might otherwise wander by without taking notice.

The sign said, in English:

HERMAN'S CHINESE HAND LAUNDRY
FAST SHIRTS AND SHEETS
GET A CHEAP CLEANING

I peered into the darkened store. There was a cash register on a counter, a few bare shelves, and, toward the back, machinery —strange, shadowy machines, which loomed over each other like monsters, a mangle that looked like a giant in a crouch, an openmouthed press, and, farther into the darkness, an elephant, or, more likely, a boiler with a long handle. I knocked against a door, then against the window itself, but, of course, there was no answer, except for a faint and mysterious echo and the soft sounds of the rain. I made a shelf of my fingers to keep off the rain and stared again, more closely, into the window. I could make out row after row of disembodied shirts hanging from racks. The place was peculiar in some way, I thought, eerie almost. Lonely, uncomfortable, it had some quality I couldn't quite put my finger on, some indescribable, undefinable . . .

"Looks empty," said Krista, who had come over to see what was going on.

"Yeah, empty. Right," I agreed. "Just the word I was looking for."

XI

"I'M HUNGRY," Krista reminded me.

"I know. This will just take a minute. I had to transfer a psychotic patient in from Waldheim today, and I want to make sure he's settled down."

"At this hour? There is no one else to do that?"

"Not really."

"You want me to sit in the car again."

"No, come on along. I'll give you a tour of the hospital. You'll love it. We have some very exciting diseases here."

Krista turned into the hospital grounds, ignoring the malignant stare of the Nazi eagle graven into the stone entranceway. The swastika on which the eagle had been posed, easier to reach than those on the face of the hospital itself, had been obliterated, leaving the bird to sit imperiously on an empty circle, a naught. The grounds, too, were empty. The only people I could see were a couple of soldiers huddled against the rain in the doorway of the emergency room. There were no especially hardy enlisted men fornicating in the bushes; at least no one leaped naked to his feet as we drove by. My car, I realized with a start, was within view, lying to one side of the road next to bags of garbage. They had thrown my automobile away in the garbage. I turned around to look at it as we went past. A misshapen clot of metal and glass, dangling tendrils of chrome off in different directions, it more closely resembled a spider, a dead and desiccated spider, than the beetle after which it was named. Its bright red color, so cheery, I thought, when I first saw it, was all that made it recognizable to me. I felt disheartened.

The front hall of the hospital was deserted also, but so it was usually. Most medical business came in through the clinic and emergency entrances. We walked to the sergeant major's office across a flagstone floor, our footfalls making the only sound. The report of Krista's definite step echoed and intermingled with the slap of my torn shoe. I flicked the lights on in the waiting room of the sergeant's office and went over to the sign-in book.

"Let me take care of this," I told Krista, "then I'll call nursing and we'll see where they filed the lieutenant away."

"Take your time. I have to call someone too."

"Here," I said, shoving the telephone on the sergeant's desk over to her.

"No, no. You make your call. I'll use the pay telephone outside."

"What for? Here, there's another phone inside in the office. I can use that."

"No, no. That's all right." She waved at me as if she didn't want to put me out in some way. Then she walked out to the pay phones across the hall. I watched her go. When she reached the telephones, she turned back to me and smiled, and waved.

She was a remarkable woman, bright, spirited and, of course, beautiful. And charming. And unpredictable. And altogether wonderful. Too bad she was a spy, I thought. Then again, if she wasn't a spy, I would never have met her.

Lieutenant Baker had arrived by helicopter about an hour before, at which time, according to nursing, he communicated readily and was cooperative. He had an enjoyable trip, he told them. Now he was bedded down for the night on one of the medical wards, sleeping quietly.

I explained to Krista I wanted to check on him myself. The last time someone had told me Baker was sleeping comfortably, he was in a coma. I invited her along, naturally. Women are often impressed, I knew, even hard-to-impress women, by the medical savant making rounds. I knew this from watching television. In fact, Krista seemed to be in a better mood already. I assumed her control—or whomever she had just spoken to on the telephone—had instructed her to be more agreeable. She laughed at a couple of feeble jokes I made; and when we walked through a darkened hallway, she took hold of my arm.

Krista went over big on the ward, of course. A few men who only a moment before seemed moribund sprang back to life. They were sitting on the edges of their beds, bantering with her, inviting her under the covers for a moment or two, and, in general, somehow striking the right note to make her giggle.

It turned out Baker was sleeping after all. I woke him up and asked a number of penetrating questions—what day is it, who was President of the United States, how much is seventeen and eighteen—all of which he answered more or less correctly. I asked him if he knew who I was. This was not an attempt to gauge my reputation in the community, but rather a test of memory, which can be disturbed by excessive amounts of medication and other pathological processes.

"You're the man who lives in the wall," he said, which I figured was close enough.

"Did that guy say you were off the wall, Captain? Is that what he said?" remarked Vigliotti, who had appeared suddenly next to me. "A guy like that, he should talk. Before, when he first came in, I caught him trying to make a long-distance phone call to God."

"To God?"

"He wanted to resign his commission."

"If that works, I'll give it a shot myself. What are you doing here, Vito? And why are you carrying around all that rope and . . . what is that, rubber tubing?"

"I'm checking on this lieutenant, like you asked me to do. The rope is for the bed wetters. And the tubing. Major Wormley has this idea—"

"No. Stop! I don't want to hear."

"Who is this man, Abe?" Krista asked, interrupting. She fingered the rubber tubing Vigliotti had wound around his shoulder. "A plumber?"

Vito introduced himself and immediately offered Krista a chocolate bar, which made a big hit—which usually made a big hit in Germany, come to think of it, ever since postwar days. In just a minute or two they were on intimate terms, trading recipes for schnitzel.

Baker looked calm enough, considering what he had been through that day. I spoke to him a while longer, explaining what he was likely to expect from treatment in the hospital, and trying to reassure him; but he was still suspicious. He kept asking why, if I was really Dr. Redden, had they told him that other man was Dr. Redden; and why did they tell him my name was Vigliotti when Vigliotti was really the man down at the foot of the bed talking to that lady. And, of course, I had no sensible answer.

I waited for Krista to say good-bye to the patients on the ward, shaking hands with each one, then I walked with her down the hall to my office. I wanted to pick up my messages and also show her my spittoon. Vito, who suddenly seemed much less busy, tagged along. In the guise of describing to me Sergeant Lingeman's difficulties climbing into a helicopter, he expanded to Krista on the varying challenge the army represented to a medical corpsman—during the day, the dread acrophobia; at night, enuresis.

"I don't know what to do about Lingeman," I said. "But whatever it is, we'll have to do it tomorrow. We're running out of time."

I turned in to the office waiting room and flipped the light switch. Krista, who had come in behind me, gasped. I turned away from the desk and looked to see what had startled her. It was a man. A soldier. He was sitting immobile in a chair—he had been sitting in the dark—his body rigidly upright, his hands on his knees. He was staring in front of him, at nothing.

Krista took a step forward, then turned back to me. "Is he . . . dead?" she whispered.

He was not. I walked over to where he was sitting and stood in front of him. He took no notice of me, stared through me; but he was breathing.

"Holy smokes," Vito said, shaking his head vaguely. "Is he still here? They weren't supposed to leave him overnight. They were supposed to spruce him up there."

"What? Who? Where?" I exclaimed, realizing I was sounding like Baker during Fitch's cross-examination.

"It's a strange story," said Vito.

The story: The private sitting in front of me had been drafted three months before and was noted to have a quiet disposition; that is to say, he didn't talk to anyone. Not ever. However, he did dress himself, eat, go to sleep from time to time, and obey orders. On balance he was considered a good soldier and, had he been able to talk, he might have been considered for promotion to corporal. At the end of basic training, he shipped overseas to Bremen. The trip was uneventful, except that he was no longer so quick to obey orders. It was so stated in a reprimand someone had placed on his chart. Also he ate and dressed himself more slowly. By the time he disembarked his movements had slowed further and continued to slow until his posture had congealed into an unusual plastic state. He tended to stay in one position until someone moved his limbs, whereupon he kept in that new position. Also he had given up the use of public facilities. He relieved himself wherever he happened to be, whenever the urge struck him, or when he could contain the urge no longer. At this point some officer began to suspect—it wasn't clear why—that there might be something the matter with him. Special transport was laid on to convey the private south, directly to his post somewhere in Bavaria and from there directly to the 20th Station Hospital, where he arrived that afternoon. Major Wormley, unfortunately, had a pressing commitment to speak to a women's group that afternoon on "War as an Emotional Trauma," and so left the private for me to deal with the following day.

"But they were supposed to take him back to base first to spruce him up," Vito said again.

By now the soldier had frozen into complete immobility, his hands clenched tightly against his knees, his face a mask. He didn't respond to me, not even to Krista, although she touched his hand and talked to him quietly. He just sat there. He had withdrawn into a hard shell. He was, in short, catatonic.

Vito, who could move quickly when he had reason to, located Colonel S. Poole in a hotel steam room, where he was hiding out. I spoke to him on the telephone, then in quick succession to medevac, nursing, the head of the psych unit at Frankfurt, the private's commanding officer, and finally the patient's family, off in Iowa someplace. A half hour later the guy was on a helicopter, bundled up tight in case he suddenly entered into an excitement and became violent, which happens sometimes. Still frozen into a sitting position, he made a peculiar oblong package. An hour later he would be in Frankfurt and by tomorrow back in the States. His tour of duty in Europe would be less than thirty-six hours, close to a record, I imagined. Even measured out in seconds, it sounded short.

While I listened to the helicopter buzz off into the night, I checked my schedule for the next day.

"Well, he left safely," said Krista a moment later. She had accompanied the soldier downstairs and was back now. "So we can go eat finally, yes?"

"Uh . . . yeah. Let me make just one phone call," I said. "Wait a second! Hey . . . calm down, will you? This'll just take a second. Fitch. I want to talk to Fitch, the policeman. You can listen, okay?"

Krista subsided into a chair, still glowering at me, though. For someone as thin as she was, she was hungry a lot of the time; but she was curious, too, as I had expected, prepared to take a moment or two out to eavesdrop. When you're a spy, spying comes first. Come to think of it, though, I had met a number of spies the last few days, and spying itself didn't seem to preoccupy them very much.

I waited on the order of an additional thousand seconds while Vigliotti pursued Fitch across the trackless wastes of Bavaria with only the telephone to guide him. We discovered him finally on some outpost along the border.

"What do you want?" the policeman snarled at me by way of greeting.

"I think we may be approaching this problem from the wrong direction, Fitch."

"Yeah? Oh, yeah? Is that right?"

"Yeah, listen. I talked to Konigsberg's fiancée, that German girl; and I think there's something funny going on there. It doesn't feel right, and . . ."

"Feel right? Feel right . . ." The rest of Fitch's reaction was lost in a burst of static.

"All right, forget that. There's something else. I don't know if you noticed, but there was a porcelain figurine in Konigsberg's room a couple of days ago. Today it was gone. Despite the locked door."

A silence—an encouraging silence—from the other end of the telephone.

"I thought maybe Konigsberg was into some kind of smuggling racket," I went on. "Not just me. Colonel Collins has the same idea now. It would explain—well, you know, a lot, the money, the . . ."

"It might fit in," Fitch said grudgingly. "You remember that . . . uh, Major Ryan, the tank commander . . ."

"One of the curly-haired guys."

"Yeah. I think he knew Konigsberg. We're looking for him. He seems to be missing, too, the last couple of hours. Also he has a little trick with the border, maybe I'll tell you about some day. Smuggling is not impossible. Maybe after you see those Jews tomorrow, we'll talk."

"What Jews?"

"That bunch in Nuremberg."

"Oh, that's right. Listen, tomorrow's not a good day. I got a busy schedule . . ."

A small explosion. Rattles, screams. I thought war had broken out. "The whole fuckin' world's going up in smoke, and you're worried about your schedule? You hear about something going on in Cuba recently? Those Goddamn boats are closing in on each other. We gotta find out what happened to Konigsberg."

"Well, I thought if the problem turned out to be smuggling, we don't have to worry about Russia, or you know who from you know where."

"Bullshit. It's just one more angle. And don't go making any references. This phone isn't secure."

"Somebody is going to figure out 'you know who from you know where'?"

"Somebody who already knows more than he should is going to have no trouble figuring out the rest. Especially if some asshole like you is going to run off at the mouth. I got directives on this. We're supposed to be talking *in code,* for Chrissakes, and with the radio going in the background."

"OwaboutHay igPay atinLay," I suggested.

He hung up.

"You'll spoil your appetite if you eat all that chocolate," I said, getting back into the car. Vigliotti had given her another candy bar from his inexhaustible supply.

"So what? It's too late to have dinner."

"Why? It's only . . . only—" I looked at my watch. It was only ten thirty in a town that shut down at ten.

"Listen to me . . ." Krista said. "I don't know why I should do this, but if you want, I can cook for us dinner. Maybe."

"That would be terrific. In your . . . uh, apartment?"

"That's where the stove is."

"Swell. Just drop me off first at the BOQ for a few minutes . . ."

"What? Are you crazy? You want me to wait for you again?"

"Just a second. I want to change my shoes and wash my face."

"Your shoes?"

"Look at my shoe. My toes are freezing, and I got a cut there. You want it to get infected?"

A few minutes later Krista left me at the door to the BOQ and drove away without saying good-bye, which I don't think she would have done if she'd known how serious infections of the foot can be.

About thirty seconds after that I was knocking on Schulz's door. There were subdued sounds from within and a moment later Schulz's urbane and measured tones. "Yes? Who is that rapping at my door?"

"The raven," I replied in a raspy voice. "Now, open up."

A key turned, and Schulz stood revealed in front of me, enrobed resplendently once again in his silken dressing gown, but with hair mussed a little and a faintly dazed look in his eyes. He had an empty glass in his hand.

"Why, it's not the raven at all, it's my special buddy. What can I do for you, old special buddy?"

"We have business to talk about, remember?"

"Uh . . . right. Business. But this isn't exactly a good time. What about tomorrow, right after coffee break?" He smiled at me benevolently.

"Sorry," I said, walking past him into the room. "For a five-thousand-dollar investment, I figure I get to set the office hours."

The room was as I had seen it last, except for the presence of a mostly empty bottle of vodka on the desk, along with an ice bucket and another glass, also empty. I wondered where in the world Schulz had been able to find ice. There was no kitchen of any kind in the BOQ. But then he was a resourceful man, I had come to realize, able to get ahold of things when he wanted them. Certainly he had hold of five thousand dollars of mine. There was one other change in the room. Missing from immediate view was the silver-framed photograph of Schulz and the girl in the fur coat, although I caught a glimpse of it a moment later. It was lying facedown on the desk covered by a book.

"Where is she?" I asked.

"She? Who?"

"The girl you got in here someplace. Or is it 'them'? Two of them again? I only see one extra glass."

Schulz, less lofty, smiled at me again. "Hilda, Hilda," he sang out, *"Kommen Sie herein."*

Hilda, Krista's chubby friend, giggling, emerged from the closet. She was fully dressed.

"I wasn't hiding her from you, old buddy; but when you knocked on the door, I didn't know it was my old buddy, I thought it might be the cruddy, fuddy-duddy MP who hangs out . . . Hey, that rhymes. Jesus. Buddy, cruddy, fuddy . . ."

"Listen, Bob, I really would like to talk to you alone." I smiled at Hilda. "I hope you understand."

"No, she doesn't understand, Abe. Not a word." He turned to the girl, who was still standing demurely by the closet door. "Hilda," he said carefully, "Up your hole with a ten-foot pole." Hilda smiled graciously.

"See," Schulz said to me, shuffling unsteadily over to the desk, where he poured what was left in the vodka bottle into his glass. *"No comprende.* Zilch. Not a single Goddamn word of English. Not even curse words."

Probably she was acting, I figured. Since she showed up in Krista's company, I assumed she was a spy also.

"How did you invite her over, if she doesn't speak English."

"I shpreken a little Deutsch. And I didn't invite her over. She called me about an hour ago."

"A whole hour? And she still has all her clothes on?"

No reaction from Hilda. Not even a giggle.

"She only showed up about fifteen minutes ago."

Schulz removed another bottle of vodka from a cabinet and another glass. He poured out a round of drinks. For a moment or two he fished for ice from the bucket with silver tongs, but the delicate operation proved beyond him. He grabbed a couple of ice cubes finally with his hand. I decided that if I ever needed emergency surgery, I would prefer Schulz high on marijuana to drunk. He handed me a drink, and another to Hilda, then sat down heavily on a couch, pulling the girl by the hand down beside him. She landed partly on top of him, which set her to laughing again musically.

"That's it, you fat turkey," Schulz remarked gaily, "make believe I'm a pillow."

"I want to talk to our partner," I said, getting to the point. I decided to ignore Hilda, who might or might not understand what I was saying, but was not likely to be interested anyway.

"Our partner is about halfway to Berlin by now, going lickety-splickety, your check squeezed ever so tightly in his hot little hand."

"What do you mean?"

"I mean he's not here where you can talk to him. He's someplace else. But don't worry, the guy's a pro; and he knows what he's doing."

"What do you mean he has my check with him?"

"What do you mean, what do I mean?"

"He has the check itself? With my signature on it? I can't believe it. You gave him the check. You were supposed to cash it. What the hell good is the check going to do him? And what happens to *me* if they catch him sneaking across the border with a load of hot jewelry and my check?"

". . . When you're a pro, you know what you're doing," Schulz said for the third time, having said it twice before while I was talking to him. "Take me. I was resting here early this afternoon on that very bed. The one you're sitting on. Except maybe up a little higher, nearer the pillow. Right. That's where I was. Suddenly, from out of the blue, so to speak, comes a ringing on the telephone, which I pick up and speak into. 'Who,' I ask, 'is that ring, ring, ringing on my telephone?' 'The raven,' comes the stark reply. No, wait. I'm getting mixed up. You're the raven. I remember now. It was Colonel Bosely, or Bassly. Wait a second! I got it now! It was Colonel Beasely. He called to tell me there was an accident, right there on the hospital grounds. The medical detachment, it seems, having nothing medical to do, was ordered to clean the storeroom inside and out. The inside was easy, but you could only get to the outside through a set of bars. Either that or you had to walk all the way down the hall, out the door, and all the way around the back, which was a lot of trouble. So in order to clean the outside of the window, this guy sticks his head through the bars . . ."

"Schulz . . ."

"Of course the sergeant in charge of the detail orders him to remove his head forthwith, since he is blocking the mop. When the aforesaid soldier fails forthwithly to retract the offending organ, the sergeant, according to Beastley, grabs hold of his legs and pulls. Naturally, on the way out he gets his neck torn. The jugular is gone and the carotid is a colored fountain. Also maybe the guy is hurt seriously because he's unconscious and doesn't seem to be moving from the neck down. At this point I say unto Beastley, 'Wherefore do you call me, a general surgeon, when you need a head and neck surgeon, a neurosurgeon, a vascular surgeon, and probably an orthopedic surgeon?' You will not be surprised, Abe, ole buddy, when I tell you that there is nobody here at the 20th Station Hospital who is a head and neck surgeon—unless you count that specialist in sinusitis—no neurosurgeon at all, no vascular surgeon, and the two orthopedic surgeons are off somewhere wife-swapping. Since this unfortunate soldier is not likely to survive the next minute and a half, they are not planning to evacuate him to Frankfurt. Now, can I refuse to operate? A man's life at stake. The human drama . . ."

"Schulz, I don't want to . . ."

"Of course, under the circumstances, I say okay. A minute and a quarter after that, and we're in the OR. The unfortunate soldier, having swallowed up eight or nine pints of blood—maybe quarts, who knows—is still bleeding, but still alive. About four and a half hours later, you know what? He's still alive, and it looks like maybe he might stay alive, sutured, treponemed—the guy had a subdural along with everything—casted and bandaged. If he's lucky, who knows, maybe he gets to walk again someday.

"Now, *liebchen*, my baby walrus." A chuck to Hilda's chin, a tickle to the tummy. Some mutual laughter. "How come I can do on short notice an arterial reanastomosis and a decompression, and top it off with a plastic repair of a neck wound? I'll tell you how come, you cute li'l hippapotamatumus. Because I'm a pro. A professional. A guy who knows what to expect. A guy who's ready." Suddenly Schulz got to his feet, one foot anyway, teetered, then sprawled back on top of Hilda, who gave out a sound like a whoopee cushion. The young woman, in implacable good humor, laughed. Schulz, muttering under his breath, pulled himself upright again, grabbing a handhold variously on Hilda's dress or person. Then he traced a curvy path over to the desk, where he poured himself another drink.

"We're dealing here with a professional crook," I commented, "so I should relax. Right? That's what you're saying."

"Right. Bennie . . . uh, that's my friend, I shouldn't have told you—but he knows his shtuff," Schulz replied confidently. "Take it from me."

"Why should I? So you're a versatile surgeon. What do you know about smuggling?"

Schulz smiled cunningly. He shuffled closer to me, winked, then put a finger to his lips. He was, I gathered, about to deliver up a secret. "Well, as . . . it . . . just . . . so . . . happens," he said in a pungent whisper, "I've done a little smuggling of my own."

"Is that so?"

"Yes, it is so. I had a regular run. Used to bring in drugs from Mexico."

"You're kidding. What? Marijuana?"

"Marijuana. Some coke. Mostly heroin."

"Heroin! Come off it, will you."

"A couple of years. Until I got picked up in New Mexico once. Scared the shit out of me. They're down on that kind of thing out there. It would have meant my medical license. They had me lined up and mugged before I skipped out an open window. Funny, come to think of it. A storeroom that's guarding a lot of toilet paper has got bars, and a jail has got nothing but a screen to keep out flies." Schulz chuckled. "Anyway, I gave them a phony name so I figure I'm safe now unless I get my picture in the papers for operating on the President."

"Heroin?" I said again. "I don't believe it."

"Hey, listen," Schulz said, sensing some element of disapproval in my response. "Judge not lest ye be judged. Right? Some of us didn't have the advantage of a rich daddy. I had to work my way through medical school. Anyway, I cut that out a long time ago. I shouldn't have told you, but I figured . . . ah, what the hell, you're my ol' buddy. I just wanted you to relax a little. Loosen up."

"That was not a reassuring story."

Hilda, ignored during this exchange, was shifting about uneasily on the couch, still smiling bravely, though. Schulz turned to her suddenly and held out his arms, as if he had just discovered her on a train platform. "Hilda, Hilda," he cried out enthusiastically, along with some other words of endearment, which I couldn't make out, since they were in German. He sat down beside her and began feeling her up.

"Hey, wait a second, would you," I complained, putting my drink down on the desk. "For God's sake, bad enough you're a smuggler. At least you can observe a couple of the amenities." I got up. "You know, I just now ditched the most beautiful woman I've ever seen just so I could talk to you; so I'd appreciate it if maybe you could hold up with that stuff for another couple of minutes. Okay?"

"All right, all right," Schulz said, resting his head against the back of the couch, staring at the ceiling. "What do you want to talk about?"

"First of all," I said, speaking slowly for emphasis, "I want you to ask this professional crook . . . uh, Bennie, who the local fence is around here. Also mention . . . mention General Gutman. I want to know if he's hooked up somehow in anything criminal. Second, I want to know if he ever heard of smuggling out of Waldheim itself. In case you haven't figured it out yet, that's why I joined this outfit, to find out what the hell was going on around Waldheim. Thank goodness I have a rich daddy, and I don't have to make a living dealing in heroin or whatever."

"Holier than thou."

"I want to know especially if he ever heard of Sidney Konigsberg, and if maybe Konigsberg was doing some smuggling."

"You still looking for that guy?"

"So far he hasn't turned up. I don't think he will."

"So you think he was smuggling, eh?" Schulz mused. "The guy's a spy. If he wanted to go into business for himself, he'd have a hell of a head start. Connections across the border. Communications. Ah, phooey." He shook his head. "Around here, everybody and his brother is smuggling. In medical school, at least there wasn't any competition."

"Are you paying attention, Schulz?" I asked. His head was resting again against the back of the couch, and he was pretending to snore. At the same time, moving just a few fingers at a time, he was edging a hand across Hilda's thigh. She slapped his hand playfully.

"Right," said Schulz. "Bennie will be crossing tomorrow at Checkpoint Charlie. He'll call at the last minute just in case. I'll ask him then. I don't like it, though. All these extraneous questions. Even a professional gets nervous."

"I got one last question before I leave. Why is this professional crook carrying around my uncashed check?"

"Well, it's kind of insurance. Suppose you're working for the police. If you turn him in, first of all, he never cashed the check, so it doesn't mean anything. In your case the check is as good as the money itself. You got a good credit rating, kid. Besides, they've got ways on the other side of cashing checks on foreign banks. Probably they'll just hold on to it. It's just a piece of paper, kind of . . . well, kind of a statement of trust. You know, to make sure you're going to cooperate, and we're all going to cooperate in the future."

"I see."

"And, after all, it's easier if you're searched to hide a check than to hide five thousand dollars in cash."

"You don't think there's some potential danger to me in this arrangement? And how come if the check is just a piece of paper, you don't give him one of your own instead of mine?"

"The way I see it, there's no real danger." Schulz leaned back and yawned. "But better you than me." He began working his hand back in Hilda's direction.

"Just one last question . . ."

"No fair! No fair!" Schulz called out, jumping to his feet. "You said the last question was the last question."

"This is a bonus question. You were stationed near Waldheim. Did you ever run into Konigsberg . . . or, for that matter, the Collins girl? Sandra Collins."

"The girl who died on the table?"

"Yes."

"I was with 3rd Division. They were on the move most of the time. I went where they went. Here and there." Schulz went to the desk and poured himself still another drink. Despite all that he had been drinking, he seemed somehow less drunk. Some people are like that. They can turn it on and off.

"But sometimes around Waldheim."

"Sure. Also around a lot of other places."

"Well, did you know them or not?"

"Certainly I didn't *know* them," Schulz said, holding the newly opened bottle to the light as if he thought something might have crawled inside since he opened it. "If you mean did I run into Konigsberg on sick call, I don't know. I saw a lot of guys on sick call out there in the boondocks. Sore throats and hemorrhoids. I specialized in the treatment of dandruff. Unless somebody had a really malignant case of dandruff, I wasn't likely to remember him." Schulz grabbed hold of my elbow and prodded me in the direction of the door. "If I remember something crucial, like whether they came in together one day with a bad case of crabs, I'll give you a ring. And listen, don't slam the door on your way out. My nerves aren't as good as they used to be."

I turned back at the doorway. Schulz was facing away from me, hunched over, legs apart. Suddenly he pulled his robe open and held the flaps out to the side, like great wings. I caught a glimpse of Hilda staring at him wide-eyed.

"Hee, hee, hee," he cried out maniacally, waving his arms as if he were about to take flight. "I am Count Dracula, my little blue whale, and I am going to bite you on the blubber. Here I come!" He swooped down on her amidst squeals and laughter. When I closed the door, he was perched on Hilda's lap like a great bird, nuzzling her about the neck and making slurping sounds—and looking pretty relaxed for a guy whose nerves were in bad shape.

Cardboard had been taped over my broken window, but the rain had soaked it through. The room was cold and damp, and dreary beyond any physical explanation. Coming back every day to this lonely place, I was reminded, every day, of my failure to find someplace else to be—or someone to be with. That night in particular, listening to the muted sounds of gaiety from the next room, I didn't want to be alone. Especially I didn't want to sleep on the floor.

Krista picked up the telephone on the second ring. I called to apologize, I explained to her. She had been very helpful, not just translating, but in other ways, for example, in her kindness to the catatonic soldier we ran into in the hospital; and if I had kept her waiting . . ."

". . . *if* you kept me waiting?" she commented.

"Yes, *when* I kept you waiting, I didn't mean to be rude." I went on in this vein for a few minutes, sincerely for the most part. We talked back and forth about General Gutman, and about Collins and his daughter. I told her about the Colonel's son.

"Listen, did you . . . you ate dinner someplace?" she asked me finally.

"No, that's all right, though. I had something to eat yesterday," I said, trying to sound forlorn, which required no special effort.

"Maybe, if you want, you can come over still," Krista said hesitantly, "I have dinner prepared just now. But if you don't want to, that's all right. It's late. I understand. Maybe you would like to get some sleep instead."

"Hey, I'll be right over."

"Right now?"

"Just as soon as I call a taxi. I'm just going to wash my face and change my clothes first."

"Forget it," she said. "That means you'll be coming in time for breakfast maybe." But she said it laughing.

It was only ten minutes later, but already past midnight, when I set out for Krista's apartment building. Nuremberg was a small town, and if you knew where you were going, which I did not usually, you could travel from one place to any other in a matter of minutes. The taxicab picked me up outside the BOQ, which was located in a kind of rural suburbia, and carried me quickly in an arc across the modern city.

All of Nuremberg was visible from the balcony that ringed Krista's apartment building. I admired the view while I waited for her to answer my knock.

"Oh, my God. For a moment I didn't recognize you," Krista said, after I turned to face her.

"Well, you did say to me that German women were impressed by a man in uniform."

"You dressed up to please me? How thoughtful. Come in, please."

As I walked by, she grabbed hold of me long enough to straighten my tie and put down my collar. I did not construe this as an affectionate gesture. There is something about me, something sickly, I think, or insipid, that invites these indignities from everyone, up to the rank of one-star general at least. My encounter with the general took place in an airport terminal. He stepped away from a conclave of field-grade officers in order to call me to attention and fiddle with my uniform, all the time muttering to himself.

"Besides," I said to Krista, "these are the only clean clothes I have."

"You American soldiers tend to make a lot of dirty clothes. I remember from when I was married to one. I expect you are probably especially bad."

"I expect you're probably right." My mind turned to Konigsberg, who had also accumulated a lot of dirty clothes.

Krista's apartment was small—small rooms, low ceilings in the German style. The furniture itself seemed not quite to American scale. There were a few chairs placed carefully about an inlaid coffee table, and a small room-divider with a few books and an aquarium. Mostly there were plants, green, but purple-leaved, too, and red, accents of color against pastel walls. Krista herself wore a light green sweater, loose and furry, and a matching skirt. The only yellow anywhere was the gold of her hair repeated endlessly in two large opposing mirrors. She looked terrific. I saw reflections of myself standing beside her, a line of slouching soldiers all set to march off in different directions.

In a corner of the living room there was a small table set for two with crystal goblets and a vase of flowers. And candles. For the next half hour I sat at one end of the table drinking wine and eating something, some kind of bouillabaisse, which looked and tasted as if it had taken much more than a half hour or so to prepare, and listening to an acerbic account of Krista's marriage. After a while, I began telling her about myself, not wanting to really, having particular reason not to, I thought, yet melting in the warmth of the comfortable room and in Krista's glow.

I found myself telling her, of all things, about Suzanne, the woman whose name my housekeeper had given Fitch as a reference. She was supposed to attest to my heterosexuality, on which she was supposed to be an authority by virtue of claiming at the age of fifteen that I had raped her.

I was about sixteen at the time. Suzanne showed up one day during dinner, and I listened dumbfounded part of the time and screeching indignantly the remainder while she explained tearfully how it happened. She had come to my room at my request, she said, innocently, to witness my latest biological experiment, an attempt to make dead animals move realistically by a system of pulleys and weights. She found me lying quietly on my bed reading an issue of *Whiz Comics*. Suddenly I threw the comic book to one side, grabbed and then tossed her on the bed. When she resisted, I knocked her on the head with a bust of Schopenhauer I took from a shelf. She struggled against me nevertheless, until she slipped into a brain daze, her mind drifting away from her body. When she woke up, there were bite marks all over her. I laughed at her when she regained consciousness and stared at her with a mean look, so that she ran out of the room, bumping her elbow against the door. Not wanting to create a fuss, she refrained from mentioning the incident to anyone; but when she discovered four months later she was pregnant, she felt she simply had to say something. "What to do! What to do!" she wailed, sticking out her belly.

"It cannot be true," remarked my mother, who had been listening soberly. "I will not believe my son reads comic books"—which shows you all she knew. The comic book was the only part of the story that was true. Suzanne had enlivened my existence in succeeding years by telling similar stories to my friends.

Between my mother, who was not all there all the time, and my father, who was there all too much of the time, I was sort of an unhappy kid. I ventured to say something of the sort to Krista—and felt silly as soon as I said it. I was more used to other people talking to me about their childhoods than complaining about my own. Besides, I had learned a long time ago that if you were rich, really rich, nobody was going to sympathize with your domestic problems, or your other problems, for that matter. Still, Krista didn't seem to think I was ridiculous. For a while we talked to each other as if we were friends and not as if I were just someone with a secret and she an enemy agent.

Later on, when we were sitting on the couch, she asked about Konigsberg, idle gossip about his job, how did he spend his day, who were the people he ran into, what sort of machinery did he have access to, why did he need to be a linguist, and so on. I hemmed and hawed and conversed pleasantly about the interesting design on the drapes. She persisted. Finally, in order not to seem too obviously evasive, I kissed her. I felt some misgivings taking advantage of the situation, but it was the patriotic thing to do. Probably she had similar motives. She kissed me back.

After a while we moseyed over to the bedroom. There were two beds.

"You have a roommate?" I asked.

"Yes."

"Oh. She's out late tonight? Or is it . . . are you attached to . . ."

"I'm not attached to anybody. My roommate is Hilda. You remember her. But she is not going to be here tonight because her aunt is sick, and she went to visit."

"She's visiting her *aunt*?"

"Yes. Her aunt has a heart condition. She is very tired all the time, and weak."

"That's too bad," I said, not very sympathetically. Hilda's aunt looked pretty lively the last time I saw him.

We progressed in due course from the doorway of the bedroom to the bed itself, one of them, then to that narrow but warm space beneath the covers. If I was clumsy within those narrow confines, as I was everywhere else, Krista was kind enough not to say so. She did comment later on that she had looked forward to being bitten here and there, à la Suzanne; but it seemed to me she was joking.

"I have a question to ask you, Abe, if it would not offend you," she said to me still later, tentatively, interrupting a silence that had taken on a texture and character of its own, a soft, comfortable presence that separated us from everyone else in the world. "Why do you wear your pajamas underneath your pants?"

I sighed. I was hoping she hadn't noticed. "It's not really . . ."
My voice cracked. "I use the pajamas . . . you see, I'm allergic
to wool. It makes my skin itchy. So I have to line the pants with
something soft. It's not . . . well, I don't think of them as pajamas anymore. They used to be pajamas. But now . . . well, I
had to line the pants with *something*. I've been this way all my
life. You know . . . uh, unless I want to go around scratching all
the time and . . ."

"Oh."

In the middle of the night Krista turned over and woke up
suddenly. "Abe," she said, propping herself up to look at me,
and smiling, "your eyes are open. What are you looking at? Do
you sleep with your eyes open usually?"

"Not usually."

She put her head down on my shoulder and an arm across my
chest. I took hold of her hand.

"You are thinking about something all this time?" she asked.
"Is it me?"

"Yes," I replied.

I couldn't tell her the truth. Not without hurting her feelings.
For a while I had been thinking about her, along with everything else; but what was keeping me up was a different thought.
I was wondering how in the world the treatment of enuresis was
tied up in Wormley's mind with wearing a full field uniform.

XII

"YOU PUT YOUR UNDERWEAR ON," Krista said, peeking at me over a coverlet.

"True," I replied. I reached for my pants, which lay on the floor somewhere.

"Why? It's only . . . My God," she said, looking at her wristwatch, "it's only six o'clock in the morning. We just went to sleep. Why are you getting up now?"

"Time and tide waits for no man," I reminded her, struggling into my pants. The pajama lining had been pulled halfway out. "A bird in the hand is worth two in the bush."

"I know just what you mean," she said, reaching for me.

"Hey! Watch it! That's not very ladylike."

"It is too!" She made another grab.

I tottered to my feet, my pants down to knee level.

"You weren't so shy a few hours ago," Krista complained. Then she laughed. "You look . . . cute, bouncing around like that. Mmmm. Not as cute as last night, of course. But very cute. Oh . . . I don't believe it. You're blushing. Even in this light, I can see you're blushing all over. Your belly, even."

"I'm not blushing. It's a vasomotor instability. Runs in the family. You should see my father after he's been drinking, like anytime between eleven A.M. and midnight. He turns the color of a red rose—you know, when the petals are beginning to fray a little around the edges and fall off . . ."

"You're blushing!"

"I'm not blushing. It's the heat."

"The heat? It's freezing in here!" She reached over and toppled me back into the bed. Between one thing and another, it was a while before I could disentangle myself.

"Why do you have to leave now?" Krista said. She was standing by the bed, naked except for her wristwatch, which made her seem more naked still. She dressed without hurrying by the dawn light that came through the unshaded window, without self-consciousness, gracefully, as if her movements were choreographed.

"I'm supposed to interview somebody," I said, getting dressed myself. "You remember, Fitch, that guy from CID, wants me to talk to someone from the Jewish community in Nuremberg. About Konigsberg. I don't know who I'm supposed to talk to exactly, or where, but I figure it better be now. I got a busy day. Besides, I think they have some kind of morning prayers."

"Well, I better cook you breakfast. That will make three days in a row you ate something."

Krista busied herself in the kitchen while I washed and shaved, then trimmed the pajama lining coming out of my pants leg. I had torn it hopping up and down, and a fragment of colored flannel was hanging down over one shoe. By the time I had finished, breakfast was ready.

Krista watched me while I ate. She smiled from time to time for no particular reason and pushed condiments in my direction, but didn't say very much. I felt uncomfortable under her scrutiny. In fact, I was beginning to feel uncomfortable in her presence. Guilty, somehow.

"Hilda stayed out all night," I commented. "I guess her aunt took a turn for the worse."

"Isn't that fortunate?" Krista smiled broadly. She was resting her chin on both hands, so she could more effectively study the way I chewed toast.

"You will call me this afternoon?" she asked a moment later, pouring me a second cup of coffee. "I would like to know how things are going."

"At school?"

"No. You can reach me here if you call after three or four o'clock. Or, if you want me to help in some way, I think I can get off early."

"Is that right?" I stopped feeling guilty and began feeling angry. Then I looked at her, her uncombed hair falling naturally into waves, her luminous eyes, her blithe, ingenuous expression —how did she manage that, I wondered—and a jumble of conflicting feelings rose up inside of me. And suddenly I wanted to stop pretending.

"Hey, listen," I said. "I know you're a Russian spy."

"A Russian spy?"

"Well, whatever. Spy, agent. I don't know what you call it. You're working for the other side."

"Yes?" said Krista. She leaned forward again and smiled brightly, unperturbed, or pretending to be unperturbed. The sun was edging up over the horizon, lighting up the room.

I got up from the table. I wanted to make sure I said this just right, and her closeness was distracting me. "I knew from the beginning," I said, pacing in front of the opposing mirrors, "that night in the restaurant. The most important spy in Europe disappears practically straight from my office, and the next night, by coincidence, the most beautiful girl in Europe tries to pick me up. . . ."

"I didn't think I was being that obvious," Krista commented amiably.

"Well, I had been eating in restaurants around here for the last three months, and nobody tried to pick me up before. Maybe if you had made a play for Schulz at first, I could have believed it. He sort of has a way with women. . . ."

"Wait a second. I want to make sure I understand. Partly you figured out I was a spy because I was more attracted to you than to your friend, Captain Schulz. Is that it? I got it right? Yes?"

"It was obvious you intended to give that impression."

"Your friend is a boor. Also he is a loudmouth and a pig."

"He has a kind of animal charm."

Krista made a rude noise with her mouth. "Anyway, I have the idea, now," she said. "A pretty woman is interested in you, so naturally she is a spy."

"Second of all, another funny coincidence. As soon as I meet you, whoever is shooting at me stops."

"I was wondering about that myself, Abe. Are you sure . . . I mean, did you actually see a bullet ever?"

"What? Yes, I did see a bullet!" I retorted indignantly. "You thought I was imagining someone shooting at me?"

"I thought it was possible. That kind of thing, someone could make a mistake like that. Besides, I noticed you do worry a lot. Like a cut on your toe."

"The obvious explanation for someone shooting at me," I said in a loud voice, ignoring this last remark, "is that someone thought I had special information that he wanted to make sure I didn't tell anyone; and the obvious reason for not shooting at me anymore is because he found out from someone close to me that I don't have any such information."

"Or because your information is no longer important, maybe," Krista commented thoughtfully, "or because maybe if you knew something important, he thinks you must have told somebody already. Or maybe a dozen other reasons," she added irritably, beginning to clear the breakfast dishes. "Maybe he thinks you are too hard to kill. You are a very slippery person in some ways. Maybe he lost track of where you are. On the other hand, maybe he is following you around to see if you lead him to the lieutenant. Maybe he ran out of bullets. And maybe . . . maybe he didn't stop shooting at you. Maybe he is just taking a rest."

"The third reason," I announced, moving ahead stubbornly, "is your lying to me. You told me you worked in the local school, but when I called there yesterday, they never heard of you. And you lied to me about Hilda visiting her aunt, and God knows what else."

I heard a noise from the kitchen, and a moment later Krista stood in the doorway, frowning, her agreeable mood having evaporated between one moment and the next.

"Abe," she said, "I'm beginning to get the bad feeling that you are not joking."

I said nothing.

"I do work in the local school system, but in special education. I teach in the children's homes. Reading problems, mostly. I don't go to the school itself much. I'm surprised anyway you talked to somebody there who never heard of me. Maybe it's someone new. Classes just started a few weeks ago. About Hilda, you're right. I called her up from the hospital, when I was with you; and I asked her to go someplace for the evening if she could. Do I have to explain why to you?"

"Well, what about . . ." I could feel myself flushing again. "What about pumping me all the time, asking those questions about Konigsberg and . . ."

"I thought I was helping you, you idiot! I thought I was on your side! I thought . . ." Suddenly she was yelling at me in German.

"Listen, don't get excited . . ."

"I shouldn't get excited?" she exclaimed, getting more excited.

"I just wanted . . . I brought it up because . . . well, you know, I like you a lot; and I thought maybe . . . maybe I could get you, well, sort of, to move over to our side."

"You . . . You . . ." What I was was evidently not translatable. Krista lapsed back into German. Meanwhile, she rolled up my uniform jacket, which she had taken off the back of a chair, and shoved it at me. She was so upset, her hands were shaking.

"Listen," I said, "if I made a mistake, I'm sorry, but . . ."

"Get out," she said, opening the door to her apartment and pointing the way.

"I didn't mean to upset you," I said lamely.

"You made love to me last night because you thought I am a spy!" she cried out.

"Hey, no! I made love to you *despite* thinking you were a spy."

"Get out! Get out!" She put both hands on my chest and shoved me out onto the terrace.

"Krista, please, listen . . ." I said, holding the door so she couldn't slam it.

"No, I don't want to listen."

"Aw, come on."

"No! No!"

"All right, I'm going. Just . . . one thing."

"What?"

"You got my hat."

Krista glared at me, then turned back into the room. A moment later my hat sailed out. I made a grab for it; but it flew past me, over the railing, and out into space, soaring at first like a bird, then tumbling end over end. The door slammed behind me, and simultaneously my hat landed six stories down in a muddy patch of ground next to a bench. I hurried to the elevator in hopes that I could retrieve it before it ended up, like my

Volkswagen, in the trash. Riding down in the elevator, I wondered how my interview with Krista would have gone if I hadn't taken care to handle it just right.

Sitting primly on the bench when I arrived was a round, carefully suited woman wearing the small, dainty fedora that seemed to be the current style. I smiled at her while I dusted my muddy hat off on my pants, but she tilted her head back and looked away. It was going to be one of those days, I was afraid. A mushroom cloud appearing suddenly over the old city would not have surprised me.

I hailed a cab and showed the driver the piece of paper on which Fitch had marked the address of the Nuremberg synagogue. He gave me a strange look, which I understood a moment later when he made a U-turn and parked directly across the street. I could see the door to Krista's apartment from where I sat. I offered to pay the cabbie for his trouble, of course; but he laughed and waved my money away.

The temple, or synagogue, was, in reality, a second-floor apartment above an empty store. Moreover, it was only a single large room, as far as I could see from the back, furnished starkly with a half-dozen benches.

At the far end was the ark, an inlaid, brightly varnished wooden structure, lit up from the inside. It bore a large scroll covered in dark purple velvet, elaborately embroidered in gold thread. Hung on top this gaudy slip was a large medallion and other glittering bits of gold and silver. A second scroll was lying partially unrolled on a dais. There was no other decoration in the room. There was nothing, in fact, in the structure of the room itself or in its contents to suggest to me I was in a place of worship, not on the basis, anyway, of my limited childhood experience.

But there were people praying. Three people. They were standing apart from each other near windows. Each was wearing a skullcap and a long, striped shawl, tasseled on both ends. Also, each had wound about one arm a long, thin leather strap. They looked up as I came into the room, then turned away again, bending from the waist over and over as they chanted in what I took to be Hebrew. I stood also, feeling out of place and conspicuous.

I took off my hat and put on a skullcap, a pile of which lay on a table near the door, along with a number of worn clothbound books, one of which I also took up. It was written in Hebrew after all. I stared uncomprehendingly at the pages, which were numbered in reverse order; and I waited for the service to come to an end. I wondered what I was going to say to these men, probably none of whom spoke English.

It turned out, of course, that they all spoke English, well enough at least to say hello and welcome me. Two of the men, both elderly, and neither very vigorous, left suddenly after shaking my hand but not before speaking to me effusively, both of them simultaneously, about Americans and Jewishness and the city of Nuremberg, the whole thing going by too fast for me to comprehend exactly. After they left, the third man, whose name was Bender, sat down heavily next to me on a bench, as if he were already tired, although it was still very early in the morning.

"It is very good seeing another face here," he said. "We are so few." He waved his hand about at the empty room. Suddenly a shaft of sunlight came through a small window, making the room seem paradoxically drabber and more dismal.

I nodded. "How many?" I asked.

"Excuse me?"

"How many actually are there in the congregation?"

"Now?" He took a breath. "Fourteen. Fourteen Jews left in Nuremberg out of I don't know how many when I was a boy. Thousands. Not enough now, except on the High Holidays, even for a *minyan*. Like today. I hope God forgives us we address him only three men at a time. And old, we are all old now, Captain Redden."

He was not so old in years, perhaps forty-five or fifty. His hair, thinning a little, was still black. The line of his mouth was still firm. But his eyes, gray, faded eyes focused on the past, on the memory of the Holocaust, made him seem ancient, timeworn, yet timeless too. To have been present at that extraordinary moment in the history of the world when human beings attempted for the first time to destroy systematically a whole race of other human beings, even children—to survive that terrible time—was to exist out of time itself. He himself was the icon that made that dim apartment a religious place.

I nodded again. "Yes . . . but at least some people . . . at least there were a few then who survived."

"Very few."

"Someday . . . that number will grow again. The Jewish people have always survived. They are the spirit of civilization. Spinoza. Men like that. Einstein, Freud. Jesus Christ. They can never be killed altogether."

"Yes, I know," Bender replied impatiently. "We are wonderful people. The conscience of the world. Always telling everyone how to live. That's why they kill us, because of what we stand for. It is very little consolation. But everyone needs a conscience, no matter how unpleasant; so there will always be a few of us left. Also not so much consolation. Let me tell you, young man . . ." He reached forward and grabbed my arm. "There will be . . . there are Jewish communities. In your country. In Israel. Yes. But no longer in Nuremberg. Not anywhere else in Germany either. What for? Only a few idiots like me came back. Too old to get used to living in a kibbutz. Too tired. Also . . . I am ashamed to say it . . ." He held an arm out and shrugged. "I missed Germany. The streets. Even the music. *Ach.*" He got up suddenly, seemingly disgusted with himself.

"Maybe it will turn out you're wrong. I hope so. People forget. People change. Even the Germans."

"Don't hold your breath." Bender carefully folded his prayer shawl into a small square and tucked it into a soft velvet pouch, along with the leather philacteries. "You are just now stationed in Nuremberg?" he asked, looking up at me.

"Well, a few months."

"A few months, and you come here now for the first time. You should be ashamed. We are only a dozen people maybe, but we are friendly. No daughters, of course." He smiled. "No young people at all," he said a moment later, the smile fading, "as I told you before. But still, you will come now to my house, and I give you breakfast. Yes?"

"That's very kind of you, but I don't think . . ."

"Too busy, huh? Come on, you don't fool me. I notice you didn't come here to pray. The same as all you American soldiers. You want some good Jewish cooking, right?"

"No, sir. Actually I came to ask about another American soldier. A man named Sidney Konigsberg."

Bender looked up at me for a moment. Then he picked up a long scarf from one of the benches and started winding it about his neck. "This year it is getting cold early," he said. "Usually the Gulf Stream makes our weather, you know. That's right. Here in the middle of Europe. Makes it warm. I used to live for a while in New Hampshire, U.S.A., which is the same latitude, but much colder."

Bender sat down again and smiled at me. "You know Sidney?" he asked.

"I met him."

"Oh?"

"He came to me for help."

"You are a doctor, I see," he said, looking at my insignia. "He was . . . he is sick?"

"I'm a psychiatrist. Yes, he was depressed. I was hoping someone who knew him might be able to tell me about him. Something that would help . . . understand him."

"A very smart young man. Speaks absolutely perfect German. Also nice. You know, you can tell that sort of thing. Polite. Very serious. A nice, you know, friendly smile. But I don't think this is helping you very much. I don't know why he should be depressed or whatever is going on in his mind. He has not been in Germany very long, you know, and he is stationed someplace inconvenient, so he only came to one, maybe two, *shabbis* services. Also, I don't think he is very religious. Like most American Jews. They eat lox and bagels, which is about it. Well, I don't have to tell you . . ."

"Why would he come to services at all if he wasn't religious?"

Bender fiddled with his scarf, which had tassels on the ends, like the prayer shawls.

"Who knows?" he said finally. "Loneliness, maybe. Jews, all Jews, know from loneliness. And, of course, like I said before, maybe looking for good Jewish food. Which brings us back, young man, to the subject of breakfast. If you want some lox and bagels, too, maybe I can fix you up."

I had the feeling that Bender knew more about Konigsberg than he was telling me—but that was nothing new. Everyone, I thought, knew more about the lieutenant than they were willing to say. The only person who really wanted to talk to me about Konigsberg was Konigsberg; and he didn't get the chance. What

I was supposed to do now, I realized, was go home with Bender and try to ingratiate myself, then wheedle information out of him. But I was tired of pretending to be someone else.

"I'm not Jewish," I said.

"Oh . . . I see," he said. "You just came about Konigsberg. Of course." He looked at me closely. "It's funny," he added, shaking his head a little, "I would have bet . . ."

"I know."

"Captain Redden, you have come a long way to ask me about this man. How come? What is the matter?"

"Konigsberg is missing. When he came to see me, he was depressed, all right; but what I think now is he really wanted help with some particular problem. Something was going wrong. I never had a chance to help him. I never even found out just what was bothering him. After he spoke to me—almost immediately after—he disappeared. A lot of people, and I really mean an awful lot of people, are looking for him. He had some kind of job in army security; and they're afraid . . . Well, you can imagine what they're afraid of. As far as the police are concerned, they're telling everyone he's tucked away safely in the hospital; but if he doesn't turn up pretty soon, they're going to—"

"Now that you mention it," Bender said, "I did hear something about he was in the hospital sick. Are you sure he's not sick, maybe in another hospital?"

"I'm sure. Army CID is working with the local police. They checked all the hospitals, the jails, even the morgue. This guy Fitch, who is running the investigation, is some kind of maniac. He's looking up everyone Konigsberg ever said hello to. If he doesn't find the guy soon, I think he's going to start giving everyone the third degree."

"I see. You think he will question us even? That would be unpleasant. Some of us have had bad times before with the police."

"He sent me here. Sooner or later he'll get around to coming here himself, unless I can put him off somehow. Or unless Konigsberg turns up first, which, I'm afraid, doesn't seem likely anymore."

"I am very sorry to hear this. Sidney was . . . well, like I said, a nice kid. Listen, let me talk to somebody. Maybe somebody knows something about something. In the meantime," Bender said, putting his arm around my shoulder as we walked to the door, "maybe you want to come home with me anyway for some lox and bagels?"

"You know, I really would like to do that," I told him; but, of course, I went off in the opposite direction.

The taxicab drew up to the hospital while the flag was being raised. I shielded my eyes. No use upsetting myself further. I ran into Colonel Beasely near the elevator and picked up the latest war news, to wit:

Things were looking better. There was a report of Russian ships veering off from an encounter with the American blockading force. On the other hand, not so encouraging, one ship tried to slip through and was boarded and searched. On the plus side, Castro had made no provocative threats during the last twenty-four hours, although, on the not-so-good side, the Cubans were known to be speeding completion of the missile sites. In Europe, on the other hand, the Warsaw Pact nations had halted all troop movements along the frontier. Good news. Still, on the down side, the East Germans were squeezing truck traffic on the road to Berlin. On the other hand, coming through diplomatic channels were a number of conciliatory messages, which weren't, on the other hand, all that conciliatory. At least things were becoming clearer, he told me. He was personally optimistic. If we got through the next twenty-four hours without nuclear war, probably we'd be okay. On the other hand . . .

"I'm glad to hear that," I said, taking leave of him. "I think." I ran off, literally, to check on Lieutenant Baker. But he was still asleep and required nothing. Not at the moment. I could have taken my time.

Vigliotti, sitting at his desk, was idly staring out the window. He was counting seconds. I could see his lips move.

"I talked to the officer in charge of raising the flag," he said, turning to me. "Also lowering the flag in the afternoon. It's a heavy responsibility. In between he folds the flag and has it cleaned sometimes. According to his account, he raises the flag upside down because it's an upside-down flag. Heh. He said it twice and laughed, so maybe he was joking." Vigliotti informed me also that I was late for Major Wormley's special, urgent, hypercritical emergency departmental meeting, which was being held early that morning as it usually was on Thursdays. When I entered Wormley's office, he was speaking with great intensity about the growing danger of war and its psychological effects, already in evidence, unfortunately, on the military community, primarily repression, unconscious reaction-formation, and ennui. I thought naturally he had started the conference without me, although I began to have doubts when I noticed he was addressing himself to the brain model that sat on his desk and was otherwise alone.

"Rehearsing my talk to the wives' club," he explained. He picked up a small dumbbell and flexed his arm a couple of times. It was the dumbbell that kept him in fighting shape when he was too busy to hang like a bat from The Monkeybars.

A few minutes later all the members of our little department had reassembled and were evidencing that esprit de corps for which I will always remember them. Wormley was at his desk, frowning, his chin in hand, his lips drawn into a line. It was a fierce, focused expression, but no more indicative of rational thought, I knew, than the look on a turtle. Herr Bromberg was off in a corner out of harm's way. His pen was poised to catch the very first syllable. Vigliotti was at the other end of the room, slumped in a chair. His eyes were open, but I was sure he wasn't looking at anything. I could sleep standing up, but Vigliotti could sleep—I had taken note of it before—with his eyes open. In the meantime I sat down next to the door. If I lost control of myself, I could run that way instead of jumping out the window.

"Things are boiling to a head," Wormley began. "This Cuban business. The next few hours may well bring total victory or annihilation. And the way I see it, the stakes are even higher here in West Germany. We're on the frontier, the bastion. Which is how come World War One and Two were fought here. It's not just a matter of saving face, like who's got the most missiles. Historically many nations have been destroyed by their vital interests, which were ignored. The Greeks lost the Punic Wars because of their preoccupation with physical beauty. So keep on your toes. Germany is the gateway to the Balkans on one side and on the other side, France. Germany has got the manpower.

A cunning, resourceful people, Churchill called them. And he was part American, so he didn't have any prejudices; although on his father's side he went back to the Duke of Marlborough. Of course, in those days they never even heard of Cuba. Psychologically they were very unsophisticated.

"Any questions so far?" Wormley asked.

"Ed," I said, "according to your schedule you had an appointment this morning to see Konigsberg, you know, the guy who disappeared. I know you never did see him, but I was wondering if you heard ahead of time, maybe, what it was all about. Did he call? Did someone else call?"

Wormley stared at me disapprovingly. "Does this have anything to do with what I was just talking about?" he asked.

"I don't know. What were you talking about?"

"If you were listening, Abe, you would know what I was talking about. A good psychiatrist knows how to listen. I was talking about the Cuban missile crisis."

"Oh. Well, actually this may have to do with that."

"What? What does?"

"Konigsberg's disappearance," I said, gritting my teeth. "The missile crisis."

"I don't usually accept calls on patients I haven't seen yet," Wormley reminded me.

"I know. I thought maybe . . ."

"Seems to me now that you mention it, someone did call about something," Wormley said, scratching the part in his hair, an irregular crack in a bright copper pot. "Some lieutenant. Maybe it was Konigsberg, maybe not. I don't remember. He was in a very big rush, but he didn't say what about. Some administrative matter, although I'm not sure. I told him he was going to have to wait on line like everybody else."

"Wait a second. You say Konigsberg might have called you, or he might not, about something that may or may not have been administrative. He wasn't talking about depression or suicide?"

"I don't think suicide," Wormley said slowly, struggling to think back an entire week. "But I'm not sure."

"Ed, I hope you don't mind," I said, getting up, "but I got a lot of things—"

"Forget it!" Wormley screeched. "You're staying right here.

We have important business to discuss, and for once we're going
to discuss it. My God, man, let's try to keep a perspective. The
world's a tinderbox."

"*C'est la vie*," commented Vigliotti, who was still asleep as far
as I could judge.

I subsided into my chair.

"Speaking of which," Wormley added, "have you finished
designing your presentation to the troops?"

"The presentation," I repeated after him. ". . . Oh, right. My
presentation on the emotional problems of atomic war. Not quite
finished. Almost. It's coming along terrifically, though. On the
verge of completion. Right. Almost exactly on the very verge,
you could say."

"Good. Good. We have other fish to fry, remember."

Wormley swiveled his chair and his attention to Vigliotti,
whose head was slowly dropping to his chest, eyes still open.
"Which brings us to our little bed-wetting project. How are
things going, Vito?"

"Yes sir!" said Vigliotti, startled, and speaking so loudly
Wormley himself jumped a little. "I appreciate that!"

Evidently Vigliotti was hallucinating, driven mad by Wormley
after only ten or twelve million seconds. How much longer could
I last?

The major was puffing like a little red fire engine, and grunting. "Uhghch, uhghch, tsk, tsk," he said, making a wry face.
"'Bed-wetting project' doesn't sound quite right, does it?
Clumsy. You don't get the feeling of any significance. What we
really need," he said, tilting his chair back and staring at the
ceiling, "is a code name."

"What about 'Operation Overlord'?" I suggested.

"Didn't they use that in World War Two?"

"Sure, but that was a long time ago."

"Still . . . someone might remember," Wormley said, mulling
it over. "No. Too confusing. Besides, it's not very descriptive."

"I got it," Vigliotti said, definitely awake now, "'The Yellow
Peril.' Or . . .'" he said, holding up, then biting into, a pretzel he
had conjured. "Shomething shimple." He was spraying bits of
pretzel around. "'Dry shleets,' 'Operation Dry Shleets.'" Vigliotti
turned to me proudly. "I used to write shong lyrics," he explained.

"*Drei Schlessen?*" queried Herr Bromberg, who was marking down all this drivel. "That means three bolts or pins. Did you mean . . . ?"

"I was thinking maybe 'Behavior Modification Control of Enuresis,' said Wormley. "The BMC of E project."

"Very catchy," I agreed.

"Well, I don't suppose it matters," Wormley admitted. "How's it coming, anyway?"

"I would say . . . good," Vigliotti replied judiciously. "There is still some bad feeling. One guy tried to hit me . . ."

"Displacement," Wormley explained. "Also catharsis."

"Catharsis?" repeated Vigliotti. "Uh . . . I thought that was a laxative."

"That's 'cathartic,' " I pointed out.

"Yeah? I thought that was some kind of sniffles," said Vigliotti.

"Sniffles? That's 'catarrh,' " said I.

"Nah, that's a musical instrument."

"Guitar," I said.

"Or sitar," added Wormley.

"No kidding?" said Vigliotti. "I thought that was a city someplace in Africa."

"That's Dakar." I could hear a despairing tone creep into my voice.

Herr Bromberg suddenly erupted into a laugh. "I thought that was when you turned out the lights. Ha. You know, it gets 'Dakar.' "

There was a silence during which the secretary smiled feebly at each of us. "*Entschuldigen Sie mich, bitte,*" he mumbled, turning his attention back to his notebook.

"Another problem," said Vigliotti, who was not only awake, but was blinking from time to time. "There's a guy with a limp. He says the bed-wetting is tied in with the limp, and he complains a lot."

"Nature favors the healthy," commented Wormley. "That's why there are more children than dwarfs."

". . . otherwise things are developing nicely. Some of the men have banded together during the evening hours for a sing. I didn't have to use the hose or the bells. They're getting used to the bathroom, what with all the tea and lemonade . . ."

"They're American toilets," Wormley remarked, turning to me.

Unable to think of an adequate response, I remained silent.

"You've seen the German toilets, I imagine?" Wormley went on.

"What do you mean?" I asked suspiciously.

"The toilets they use over here in Germany."

"I've been stationed here three months," I pointed out. "Now and then during that period I've had to go to the bathroom."

"I know. But sometimes I think you don't pay attention to things."

"Well," I said expansively, "it's true I'm not really *into* toilets. You might say I'm not a *student* of toilets; but I do think it's fair to say I've *seen* quite a few toilets since coming to Europe."

"Well, you probably noticed, then, they have a platform inside. Instead of a puddle—a deep puddle, like we have in our toilets back in the States—they have a little elevated platform to defecate on. All dry, so the stool kind of just sits there. Before you flush the toilet, I mean. Well, putting two and two together, it seems to me there might be, there just might be, a relationship between that simple everyday sanitary device, which every German is exposed to every day of his or her life, and the development of the German character. This is my hypothesis: The German child, he or she, is confronted by the unmistakable presence of his own or her own bowel movement, the stark presence—the smell, the look of it—which causes an emotional reaction. They have a word for it, *Angst*, I think. Right? *Angst?* or *Angts?*"

"*Angts* is a lot of little things crawling on your picnic lunch," I commented.

"I think it's *Angst*," repeated Wormley, ignoring me. "As the result of the angst, through a process of reaction formation and denial and overcompensation, the German man, or woman, becomes excessively clean and tidy and, of course, constipated. From there, it's one step to the development of the full-blown obsessive-compulsive character with an overly rigid superego, and authoritarian government and Hitler. What do you think, Abe?"

"Remarkable. I really would like to know how you get these ideas."

"It takes a certain kind of mind," Wormley suggested modestly.

I turned to our secretary. "What do you think, Herr Bromberg?" I asked him.

"I don't have political opinions," he replied.

"Well, go ahead, Vito," Wormley said, swiveling around, "what do the statistics look like so far?"

"It's hard to keep track. One guy had a wet bed, but he says somebody else came into the bed when he wasn't looking and wet it."

"I doubt that, Vito," said Wormley. "I don't see that happening." He thought about it a moment longer. "No motive," he pointed out.

"One guy I'm sure didn't wet his bed. He didn't even sleep in his bed. Didn't want to take any chances. He slept on the floor."

"I don't think we can count that as a success," Wormley said, shaking his head.

I was shaking all over. "I don't want to hear any more of this. This . . ." I started to stammer. "This . . . crazy stuff. You think you can treat these guys as if . . . as if they got a plumbing problem?"

"Just the sort of skeptical remark I would expect from a Freudian."

"I'm not a Freudian! All I am is just tired of listening to this shit! That's what I am!"

"Now wait just a second . . ." Wormley was turning bright red again.

"I'll tell you . . . I'll tell you, why don't you just tie them down in the Goddamn bed and hook them up with wires. You know, wrap an electric wire around their pricks and plug it into a wall socket. Then, if they wet themselves, you zap 'em!"

I could see the muscles working in Wormley's jaw. He was breathing hard. "You know, Abe," he said, scowling at me, his eyes narrowed. "That . . . just . . . might . . . work."

I began to scream. I was rocking back and forth in my seat and holding on to it with both hands so I wouldn't throw it, or throw myself, on Wormley.

"My God, man, get ahold of yourself!" Wormley instructed me, then waited patiently until I stopped gibbering. "I don't think you're getting enough sleep," he said finally. "Sleep is very important. . . . Well, I don't have to tell you. I need you in top shape," he added, leaning over to pat me on the knee. "You're an important part of the team. You know, I have plans for this outfit. I don't expect to spend the rest of my life filling out forms or making administrative decisions any clerk could handle. I got better things to do with my time than figure out if someone is mature enough to get married, or sane enough to make out a will, or if it's okay for someone to go on leave, or go to the stockade, or get transferred to the Marine Corps, or whatever. Those things are important, sure, but I have bigger dreams. I want to understand the mind of man. . . . Why are you looking at me like that?"

"I was listening to you. Something you said."

"Is that the way you look when you listen to me? You look funny."

"Huh?"

"Maybe not electric wires," Vigliotti interjected, "but let's think of something besides field uniforms."

"What do you mean?" asked Wormley.

"Well, I got them wearing battle dress, like you said, but it's hard to sleep in, and they're all complaining."

"Battle dress? What are you talking about?"

"You said . . . you told me you wanted to see how they were going to do in battle dress. . . . You remember?"

"Battle dress? Battle stress, that's what I said. I wanted to see how they were going to do in the stress of battle, that's what I said. You dressed them all up in combat uniforms?"

"Jesus. Yeah, I did."

Wormley stared enigmatically at Vigliotti, who fidgeted and looked back sheepishly. I stared vacantly at both of them.

"Well?" said Wormley after a pause.

"Well, what?"

"Did the combat uniforms help?"

I started screaming again. When I wouldn't stop, Wormley ordered Vigliotti and Herr Bromberg from the room. Then he paced back and forth in front of me.

"You never liked me, did you?" he said finally. "I'm going to overlook all that foul language you were yelling just now, Abe, because I like you; but I know you never liked me. I can tell."

"Ed, that's not it really," I said, my voice cracking. "It's true I don't like you, but what's upsetting me is the death of that

Collins girl. And that lieutenant. He's still missing. He must be dead now too. I want to find out what happened. I think I know now, but I want to find out for sure. It's not going to take very long; but I have to get away. Just for a while."

"You asked me, Abe, and I'm going to tell you." Wormley went over to the window and looked out. "No. I'm sorry, Abe, I just don't think I can do that."

"Listen, there is a whole web of people out there, connected somehow. But all the strands are coming loose. A young girl is dead already. A man is missing. There's a baby, a little deformed child with flipper arms. You know, one of the thalidomide kids. Now there isn't going to be anyone to take care of him. I want to . . ."

"Abe," Wormley said, still looking out into the sky. "Abe," he said again, "have you ever wondered how come birds can fly and make doo at the same time?"

"Herr Bromberg! Herr Bromberg!" I yelled, bursting out of Wormley's office. "Come with me, please. Right away. Please!"

I hurried into my own office and sat down behind the desk. A moment later Herr Bromberg, pad and pencil in hand, was seated opposite me.

"I want you to type up a letter for me, please," I began, "to the Secretary of the Army. Copies to the Surgeon General's office, the Supreme Commander of NATO, Headquarters USAREUR, my congressman, senator, and my local draft board. I think you have those addresses already.

" 'Dear Sir, I am instructed by the executive officer of the 20th Station Hospital, to which I am assigned currently, that following my tour of active duty, I remain vulnerable'—no, make that 'subject'—'I remain subject to recall to active duty unless I expressly resign from the active reserve. I wish to do so now . . .' Why aren't you getting this down, Herr Bromberg?"

"Well, sir," he replied, shifting about uneasily, "I thought, if you wanted, I would simply send a copy of the last letter you wrote. The wording seems similar. . . ."

"The wording is going to be a hell of a lot stronger this time! Last time I didn't get any response, did I? I'm entitled to a response, and this time I'm going to get it."

"But . . ." Herr Bromberg had an unhappy look on his face.

"According to Major Wormley, USAREUR is getting angry receiving all these letters. They say you are not allowed to resign from the reserves until two years from now, when you have finished your tour. . . ."

"Bullshit! If I wait to the last minute, they'll screw it up; then I'll be stuck here forever, a billion, billion seconds. Do you know . . ." I tried to keep my voice down. "Do you know, I have this recurrent nightmare, that I'm drafted into the army. Isn't that weird? I mean, I already have been drafted . . ."

The telephone buzzed. There was a Mr. Beck on the line asking for me, Vigliotti informed me. He reminded me also that this was the same man who had called the day before about Konigsberg. I heard some clicking on the line as the connection was made, then a gravelly voice.

"Are you Dr. Abraham Redden?" The German accent was very slight. The word *doctor* was accented on the last syllable.

"Yes."

"You are the same Dr. Redden who visited somewhere this morning?"

"Uh . . . yes. A synagogue."

"Good. You were asking about a person this morning. Perhaps I can help. But I want to speak only to you. Is there, perhaps, someone else on the telephone listening?"

"Vito, are you there?" I asked.

"Yes sir," came the prompt reply.

"Please hang up."

I heard the receiver drop into its cradle. Then I asked Herr Bromberg, who was sitting quietly and very attentively as usual, if he would not mind stepping into the waiting room for just a moment. He left, gratefully I thought. He was a man of peace, as he told me every so often, and found it painful, I knew, to type up and initial documents he considered inflammatory.

"Sir," I said into the telephone. "There is no one listening to us now."

"Good. I have only a moment. If we are to talk, we should meet, perhaps at two o'clock this afternoon, if that is convenient to you. Please mark down this address."

I did as he asked. The address was a street corner in Waldheim.

"Dr. Redden," the man went on, "our mutual friend whom you met this morning thinks you are an honest man. I am inclined usually to trust his judgment, so I am prepared to meet you, which is possibly reckless. The last time I called your hospital, the police came looking for me a few minutes later."

"I'll come alone, but how will I recognize you, Mr. . . . uh."

"Beck. You may call me Beck. I would rather recognize you, Doctor. Perhaps you have some distinctive clothing to wear, or if you . . ."

"What about a bright green jacket?" I had suddenly remembered the oversize, and out of place, jacket in Konigsberg's closet.

There was a pause. "That would be fine," Beck said finally.

"No. Come to think of it, the jacket I had in mind is missing."

"Well, you can wear something else; or you can carry something, a book or . . ."

"I have a copy of Fodor's guide to Germany right here on my desk. Would that be okay?" It was the book I had taken from Konigsberg's room.

Another pause. "Why, yes, Doctor," Beck said, laughing for some reason. "That would be just fine. If you hold the book in your left hand, I will find you. Good-bye." And he hung up.

I buzzed Herr Bromberg and asked him to come back into my office, and to bring Vigliotti with him.

"Listen," I said, when they were in place. "This Konigsberg thing is beginning to come together; but I'd like to get hold of all the pieces before that crazy policeman does. Fitch is shrewd, yet stupid somehow at the same time. I think he's dangerous. He's like some kind of out-of-control locomotive. He's going to get wherever the hell he's going no matter who gets in his way; and someone is going to get hurt. I can see it coming. I need your help. Both of you know your way around, kind of, in a way I don't.

"Herr Bromberg . . . relax, would you. You can forget about that resignation letter for a while. I'd like you to find out a couple of things. You live about halfway between here and Waldheim. Ask somebody—maybe your wife could help—ask around and see if you can find out who would do an abortion in this area if somebody needed one."

"You want . . ." The secretary looked up at me nervously. "You want my wife to ask the neighbors how she can find an abortionist?"

"No one will think it's for her. There is always a doctor who is willing to do an illegal abortion for respectable people, or for someone with money. I am looking for someone else. I am interested in learning what person an adolescent would go to, for example, a girl who is afraid to tell her parents that she is pregnant and who has very little money. There is some particular person around here—at least one person, according to the police chief—who does illegal abortions like that. A woman. Last time I heard, they were looking for her. I want to talk to her too.

"Also, there is a General Gutman who lives in Waldheim, an ex-general, SS. I would like you to check on him."

"I know a little about him already," Herr Bromberg said. "Unfriendly. Not a nice man."

"Well, I need to know about him in more detail than that. Actually, there seems to be a difference of opinion about him. Colonel Collins, for instance, regards him as a professional soldier, no more, no less. I would like to know, in particular, how he makes his living. While you're at it, he has a daughter whom Konigsberg was supposed to have been engaged to, and who looks at first glance like she's not too bright, not the kind of girl I would have expected him to marry. See if you can find out what's going on with her.

"Vito, there are a couple of people I'd like you to get hold of for me on the telephone, without going by way of Chicago, if that's possible. Before that, though, would you send . . . send flowers or something to Krista Brandt. Maybe candy, if you think she'd like candy. Her address is listed in the telephone book. Write something on a note, something clever . . . write, uh . . . 'I'm sorry.' Write that."

"You're sorry," Vigliotti repeated after me. "Got it. Is she going to think that's clever?"

"Never mind. Just put down 'I'm sorry.' I don't think anything I say is going to make any difference anyway. Lay out the money, would you?"

"You still owe me for a pizza."

"Don't worry. I got a good credit rating. Somebody just told me. Especially in East Germany.

"Okay, then I want you to look up a kid named George George. First name George, last name George. Don't ask me to explain that. You'll have to find his father first, of course. I don't know his first name. He lives somewhere in Waldheim near this address," I said, handing Vigliotti the piece of paper with Collins's address written on it. "If he's not listed in the directory, try calling up the local schools. He's a teacher. Then get Corporal Randy Biddle. He's posted on that base at Waldheim. While you're at it, I want to talk to the sergeant major. That's Kraven. After that, finally, call up Major Sedgewick of the medical examiner's office in Frankfurt. There's a test I want him to do for me on those blood samples I sent him. Now listen, Vito, it's important we move quickly . . ."

The door to my office opened and Fitch stood before me. He was doing Edward G. Robinson again. His soft, pasty features were composed as usual into an expression of distaste, although I had the feeling not quite the absolute, unequivocal distaste I was accustomed to.

"You don't bother to knock, Fitch?" I asked.

"There was nobody in the waiting room," he replied, not exactly to the point. "There's some stuff I want to say," he added, holding the door open and waving Vigliotti and Herr Bromberg out. When they looked over toward me, I nodded.

"Wait a second, Vito," I said when he was at the door. "Here. In case I get hung up, call Sedgewick for me. That test—tell him I'm looking for this." I scribbled on a piece of scrap paper, folded it over and handed it to Vigliotti. Fitch stared at me with little pig eyes.

"Yeah, he was smuggling," the detective told me when we were alone. "According to Fuchs there's a ring—probably more than one ring—operating out of Waldheim and Nuremberg. Somebody who answers Konigsberg's description was seen associating with a suspect. Although not for the last week. Also, the porcelain thing makes sense. A lot of old porcelain—very expensive, some of it—has been showing up along with, of course, all kinds of odds and ends. Old lithographs, paintings, stamps, even. Some of these transactions seem to match up in time—also the right amounts—with the deposits Konigsberg made in his account."

"If the police know who this gang is, how come they haven't arrested them?"

"First of all, they don't know everybody in the gang. A smuggling ring is more like a wholesale business than, for instance, a gang of bank robbers. They got a bunch of people buying and selling on one end, and another bunch on the other end. And most of the time nobody knows anybody else. You pick a couple of guys up and so what? So probably Fuchs is following them around to pick up a few guys more than usual. Besides, knowing something and proving it is two different things. Of course, I don't give a shit about any of that," he said, flicking his cigar ash in the direction of my ashtray. "What I care is, if he's willing to sell stolen property, maybe selling state secrets is okay too."

Fitch wandered over to the window and looked out. I wondered if, like Wormley, his scientific curiosity was piqued by the birds flying overhead.

"For your information," he went on, "a signal came in today from outside Moscow someplace. From Penkovsky. Maybe. Whoever it is is doing a good imitation of Penkovsky, complete with recognition signal. Of course, we'd have more confidence in what he's telling us if Konigsberg turned up. If he turned up dead from a smuggling problem, that would be just as good."

"So what did the colonel have to say? May I ask?"

"Sure. If you promise not to tell anybody." A strange-looking fissure opened in Fitch's face. He was smiling again.

"How come you're in such a good mood today?" I enquired.

"First of all, Penkovsky, or whoever, says the Russians have made up their minds to back off Cuba. No more missiles. That's nice, isn't it? Maybe we don't all get killed before the weekend. That's if it really is Penkovsky and they're not trying to fool us. Second of all, Konigsberg was stuck on base too much of the time to be doing smuggling all by himself. So he must have had a confederate. On base, I mean. Or on and off the base. We got a good candidate in Major Ryan, the tank commander. He's been hanging around for months for no special reason. And he's been trading perfume and stuff with one of the Czech border guards. He admits that, for Christ's sake. Third of all, he's been missing for the last twenty-four hours. With his tank. Not answering radio calls. Nothing. According to his CO, he's been acting secretive recently; in fact, he always acts secretive. We went through his stuff at the BOQ—he's not married—and didn't find anything except guess what, a trunk with a fake bottom. Nothing in it. But nobody builds a false bottom into a trunk unless he puts something in it sometimes. I figure whatever he's got, he's got on him; and when we catch up with him, we catch him with it. Konigsberg I don't know about, but this guy we're going to find. It's woodsy around there, but how long can you hide an M-60 tank? We catch him, then we squeeze him. He'll tell us everything we want to know. An officer can get a couple of years in the stockade for smuggling.

"What I want from you now," he said, sitting down in the chair in front of me, "is a description of that porcelain. . . ."

Fitch took notes with a stubby pencil while I described the figurine in as much detail as I could remember. It was a distinctive piece, I pointed out, and probably could not be confused with any other.

We were interrupted after a few minutes by a phone call. It was for Fitch. I listened with some interest to his end of the conversation, which he began with a grunt.

"Rragh?" he said again after a brief pause. "Wha'? . . . the border? Well, head him off! . . . What do you mean there are no more tanks? . . . Bomb him! I don't give a damn. . . . Listen, there's a road there, I know there is. . . . All right, I'm coming myself . . . I got a helicopter. . . . Bullshit. How the hell did he get in there? Besides, I know there's a trail. I was around there yesterday. . . . There's a guy with a car here," Fitch said, looking up at me. "I'll use that."

"You're going to borrow my car?" I asked, amused.

"Get troops around to the other side," Fitch said into the telephone, turning his back to me, "with antitank weapons in case he makes a run for it. . . . I don't give a damn how much a tank costs!" He slammed the receiver down.

"C'mon," he said to me, already halfway out the door.

"Listen, Fitch," I said, following him into the waiting room, grabbing hold of the Fodor's, just in case. "I don't know what you have in mind, but you can't borrow my car. I'm saving it for the insurance adjuster."

"Not that wreck. The two-seater I saw you driving around in a couple of days ago. It's small enough to get through a trail in the woods. Also it's small enough to fit in the helicopter."

"Sorry, it's not mine. . . . Hey, Sergeant, how're you doing?"
Lingeman was sitting off to one side, looking downcast. Somehow I had forgotten my appointment with him.

"*Well, then, who the hell does it belong to?*" Fitch screamed at me.

"Over there," I said. "Herr Bromberg."

"Hey," said Fitch, interrupting Herr Bromberg, who was on the telephone. "We got to borrow your car. Gimme your key."

"Uh . . . excuse me, my car . . . ?"

"Yeah, your car. We're in a rush." Fitch held his hand out.

"But . . . why? It's my car."

"Look, I don't got time to explain!" Fitch's short fuse had burned down. "I need your car because it's skinny. Like a motorcycle. Except I don't have time to look around for a motorcycle."

Herr Bromberg, the phone still pressed to an ear, reached into his pocket and brought forth a ring of keys. "But . . ." he said. "I need the car too. Tonight I . . ."

"We'll bring it right back."

". . . and it's hard to drive unless you're familiar . . ." Bromberg added, holding the keys out tentatively.

"Redden can drive it."

"No." Bromberg snatched the keys back. "It's my car. I don't have to give my car to the army."

"Give me the Goddamn keys! I'm requisitioning your car. You know what that means?" Fitch leaned forward and made a grab for the keys. There was a brief tussle during which the telephone cord got wound around the secretary's neck. The telephone itself came crashing to the floor.

"CID. Official," Fitch said, capturing the key ring at last. "Goddamn Kraut," he muttered, turning away. "Come on," he said to me.

"Why?"

"I need you to hold the car," he replied, a remark I was not to understand until later.

Sergeant Lingeman was standing throughout most of this exchange. I looked at him, and an idea occurred to me.

"You come too, Sergeant," I told him. "This is the opportunity we've been waiting for. We're going riding in a helicopter."

"Doc, it's no good," he said. "I just came back today to tell you that. I tried getting in one yesterday, and I just can't."

"It'll be easier today. No kidding. I'll be there, and besides . . ."

"*I'm waiting!*" Fitch, who had left the room, reappeared briefly in the doorway like a Halloween goblin, then disappeared again.

Meanwhile, Wormley had manifested himself at the other end of the waiting room. "I am trying to hypnotize a young child here in my office and not having a whole lot of success, what with all this noise," he announced, and then he, too, vanished, back into his sanctum.

"Let's go," I said, grabbing Lingeman's elbow.

"No, Doctor," he said, his voice rising. "I'll only embarrass you. You don't need me. If it . . . if it was a bomb or something. All I know about is bombs."

"You know . . ." I said, leading him, pushing him a little, into the hall, "Mr. Fitch, that man making faces over there in front of the stairwell, he did say something about a bomb just now. In fact, your being here at just this minute is fortunate. We might have had to call the bomb squad otherwise."

"I don't know," said Lingeman, shaking his head from side to side, but walking along with me nevertheless.

"You'll be fine. I'm sure," I said, hurrying him along, "and I'm an expert."

In front of the stairs, there was a sign:

STAIRS OUT OF ORDER

USE ELEVATOR

So we followed Fitch over to the bank of elevators.

"Who's this guy," the detective asked when we caught up with him.

"Sergeant Lingeman," I replied. "He's coming along." Lingeman held out his hand, which Fitch looked at briefly.

"Yeah?" Fitch grunted, turning back to face the elevators. "What for?"

"He's going to help me hold on to the car," I explained. "And we need him in case there's a bomb," I added a moment later.

Fitch looked at me out of the corner of his eye, but he didn't say anything.

The three of us stood there silently. Fitch was chewing on his cigar, which was bobbing up and down, beckoning, it seemed, to the elevator. Lingeman was shifting uneasily from one foot to the other. We were all three preoccupied. I was wondering how it was possible for stairs to be out of order. And then I wondered why I seemed to be the only soldier in the United States Army who ever wondered about such things.

XIII

I COULD SEE on Lingeman's face the various calamities he was imagining. If he didn't fall to the floor dead as soon as he stepped on board the helicopter, which he thought was a possibility, he expected to go crazy, or suffer something still worse, vague and unimaginable. I knew he was worried more realistically about the simple prospect of failure, the inability to remain on the helicopter long enough to conquer his fear. So I tried to distract him. I had him push the Messerschmitt over to the helipad, while I pulled on it. I had the keys to the car, but I told him it would be faster to shove it along than to drive it; and since I wasn't sure I could drive it at all, that was probably true. With the help of a passing corpsman, we manhandled the vehicle, closer in size to a scooter than to an ordinary automobile, into the bay of the helicopter. Then we climbed in after it.

"Suppose when this thing gets up in the air, I jump out?" Lingeman asked.

"Do you want to jump out?"

"No, of course not."

"Then you won't."

"How can I be sure?"

"Because I'm sure. And I'm an expert."

Fitch peered in. "Are you guys ready?" he asked.

"Yes," I replied, simultaneous to Lingeman's no.

He was never going to be readier than he was at that moment. He was like a kid who had stared for an hour or so at a high diving board, watching other people dive off, then climbed up and down the ladder himself a half-dozen times. Finally there comes a time for jumping off. No further preparation is possible.

"Here," Fitch said, throwing us a rope. "Lash that vehicle. Tight. We're going to need it on the other end. Besides, I don't want this trip any bumpier than it has to be."

"We're not expecting a rough trip, are we?" Lingeman asked; but Fitch had already gone forward to the cockpit.

"Nah, don't worry," I answered for him. "These guys are professional. They fly in and out of this place all day long. Smooth as silk."

The image of the not-so-smooth pilot of the previous day came disagreeably to mind. I could still hear his trembling voice hitting the high notes of our navy's fight song while my stomach hopped from hedge to hedge. This was not entirely an unpleasant trick of the imagination, I realized, suppressing a scream. The singing was getting louder. It was coming from the bulkhead behind me.

"I really don't think I'm ready," Lingeman muttered, and kept muttering as we wound the rope around the Messerschmitt; but he made no attempt to disembark. The difficult moment came afterwards. The car had been secured with a two-handed surgical tie, a knot that required four hands the way I did it. The door to the helicopter had been pulled shut. There was nothing for us to do, in particular for Lingeman to do, but wait. He sat looking at me—through me. His hands were beginning to shake.

"I have a parrot who's afraid to fly," I said, anxious to strike up a conversation, any sort of conversation, for Lingeman's sake and for my own too. "Back home, I mean. He had a bad experience once at a lawn party. My grandfather, before he died, told me all about it, about this time he gave a lawn party and put the parrot up in a tree. It was one of those trees with a lot of leaves hanging down. You know, what are they called?"

"Uh . . . a lot of leaves hanging down?"

"Yeah."

"I don't know. A willow?"

"Right, a willow. Anyway, this lawn party was a drag, full of old ladies with mauve dresses and an arch manner, and short guys with pencil mustaches. So my grandfather decided to add a touch of color. This parrot is a colorful bird, I'll give him that. Did you ever see these really big parrots, red, yellow, and green, you know?"

"I don't think . . . no. Not up close, anyway."

"Iridescent plumage. Sometimes, so help me, I can see this bird glowing in the dark, and staring at me. Also he's got a colorful personality. The usual obscene language, of course; but also he likes to snuggle. If he thinks you got lice in your hair, he'll sit on your shoulder and pick at you. Once when I was just a little kid, he took a bite out of my ear. Here, you can see . . ."

"Hey, yeah. You got a little nick there."

"I really hate this parrot . . ."

There was a sudden, loud sputter from the helicopter engine; and out of a small window, I could see the rotors start to move. Lingeman tensed and started to come to his feet.

". . . Even back then, before I was born, when the parrot was just a kid, he was persnickety. That's what my grandfather told me. So the old man knew he was taking a chance bringing him to the lawn party. It was sort of an uptight preelection lawn party. Everyone was rooting for Hoover to get reelected, but things weren't looking so good in the country just then. Hoover was running against . . . uh, who was he running against?"

"Huh? Hoover's second term? Wasn't that Roosevelt?"

"Right. That's who it was, Roosevelt, the 'traitor to his class.' So this was a fund-raising lawn party for the GOP. Are you a Republican, Sergeant?"

"I'm sort of an independent."

"Right . . ."

The engine noise had risen to a whine, accented by the throb of the rotor blades.

". . . there are no more Republicans. Not since that lawn party. Although, according to my grandfather, it wasn't all the parrot's fault. Now, you've got to concentrate on this scene. It's a cloudy day, very drab. About a hundred people are at this party, milling about, making extremely small talk. Off to one side are a couple of dalmatians. On a chair resting quietly is a gray cat. On a very long table, next to the willow tree, are a couple of bowls of punch and a bowl of fish soup. What is that called . . . you know, fish soup?"

"Fish soup?" echoed Lingeman. "I don't know . . . I guess it's called 'fish soup.'"

"Right. Something like that. And, like I said, except for one lady with a gaudy hat, all feathers, everything is extremely drab and dull. Standing out from all this drab is this colored parrot peeking out between the strands of the willow tree, attracting not much attention so far except for an occasional admiring glance. But now, the parrot gets an idea. Affected by the general level of dull, or maybe out of an urge to get away from it all—this is a bird, after all, who doesn't like people much, not even Republicans—he starts to climb up the tree, hand over hand . . ."

"Hand over hand?" Lingeman said, scowling at me.

"Well, foot over foot, or whatever. According to my grandfather, he climbed up the tree. Definitely did not fly. Then, when he gets almost to the very top, he sort of falls over and hangs upside down, like a bat." I thought of Wormley, another strange bird who liked to hang upside down.

"Wait a second . . ."

The engines were making so much noise now, I had to raise my voice in order to be heard. The rotors were a blur. Lingeman turned to look out the window.

". . . Now comes the exciting part," I said. "The parrot, attempting to right himself, grabs hold of the branch with his beak, but slips, or lets go, with his fingers. So he's hanging there just by his beak, wings stretched way out for balance or something. By now everybody is looking at the parrot, who is staring back at them all, one eye at a time." I paused just a second for effect. "What happened next isn't exactly clear. My grandfather told me there was an earthquake. . . ."

"An earthquake?" Lingeman stared at me suspiciously.

The whir of the helicopter engine rose still higher in pitch. Was the damn thing never going to take off?

". . . Well, it may have been the crack of thunder. One of those summer storms that come up all of a sudden. The sky gets dark, ominous, like. Suddenly there's a big noise. The tree begins to shake, the very ground seems to tremble . . ."

At last the helicopter tilted forward and began to lift into the air. Lingeman looked about wildly and turned pale. With one hand he grabbed tightly to the rope wound about the Messerschmitt.

". . . the parrot cries out 'shit!' at the top of its lungs, which causes it naturally to lose its grip. Down it comes in a swoop." I was shouting now, and I had my arms stretched out, demonstrating the swoop. "It heads for the lady with the fancy hat.

This bird, who hates people and all other animals, for that matter, is especially down on other birds—which my grandfather figures maybe the parrot figures this hat is. Or maybe the parrot is caught up with the romantic idea that the hat is another parrot, since the last real parrot he saw was twenty years before from the inside of an egg. Anyway, turns out the lady is sensitive to parrots trying to do that kind of thing to her hat. She screams, the parrot gets knocked into the fish soup, which he splashes all over everyone, cursing meanwhile like you wouldn't believe. And then a bolt of lightning hits the tree . . ."

"Hey, listen . . ." Lingeman said in a loud voice.

". . . the spotted dogs, who have been waiting for something like this all afternoon, begin howling and make a dash for the cold cuts, upsetting the punch and waking up the cat. A couple of the guests with pencil mustaches get trampled. There is general screaming and a lot of cursing, not all of it coming from the parrot. Then, just to make things even more ominous, somebody looks up and spots a buzzard flying underneath the clouds in great circles, around and around, like an omen. Then it begins to rain . . ."

"And this is why there are no Republicans alive today, right?" Lingeman remarked calmly, even smiling just a little.

"That's right," I replied. We were flying at a good speed now, and Lingeman looked okay.

"I don't believe that part about the buzzard," he added, a moment later.

I nodded. "It could have been an eagle. Anyway, from that time on, the parrot never flapped a wing, and that was thirty years ago."

"You know, Doc, this is not so bad as I thought it would be," Lingeman said a few minutes later, still looking uncomfortable, however, and still holding tightly to the rope.

"Of course not," I agreed. "What you were really afraid of was your own feelings, the feeling of losing control mostly. The trip itself is easy."

I leaned back casually, and smiled, and tried in general to exude a calm that was not exactly what I felt at the moment. The helicopter had begun rising and falling in a familiar rhythm.

There was no opportunity during the rest of our brief trip for worries of any sort, or reminiscences. The rope I had tied around the Messerschmitt came undone, and as the helicopter swung all around, from side to side in addition to up and down, Lingeman and I occupied ourselves trying to keep the automobile from exiting through a wall. After a while we landed, bouncing and teetering briefly, but intact, in a small field adjacent to woods. The sergeant, who was evidently stupefied, rushed out to congratulate the pilot on the smoothness of the flight.

"And they said I was washed up in Korea," the man replied.

After we unloaded the helicopter, Fitch instructed the pilot to park it about seven miles to the east. There was a road there running along the border; but in case reinforcements were late, the pilot was to "keep an eye out for the tank and stop it, no matter what." That was a plan of last resort, I assumed, in case Fitch and I couldn't surround the tank first with our scooter. The pilot saluted and ducked under the still-spinning rotors back into the cockpit. He had a grim look on his face, which made me nervous. I was sending Lingeman off with him again—in case a bomb turned up, I explained; and now that the sergeant was a little less anxious, I didn't want him getting caught in a shoot-out between an M-60 tank and an unarmed helicopter. Not with him in the unarmed helicopter.

"You know, I never looked out the window," Lingeman said as he climbed back into the aircraft. He was frowning again.

"So what?"

"So suppose I can fly with my eyes closed in a helicopter. What good is that if I got to disarm a bomb someday out on a ledge or someplace where I got to look out?"

"It'll be all right, no kidding," I yelled at him.

He made some response, but it was lost in the swelling clangor of the engines.

The helicopter took off with a series of small explosions and a wind that was strong enough to roll the Messerschmitt down a small incline. It shot off into space and in another moment was gone. I caught up with the car, and we got in, I in front, the Fodor's wedged in securely under my seat, and Fitch behind me. I pulled the plastic canopy down over us.

"Go," said Fitch.

And we did, more or less. Driving a Messerschmitt seemed no

more complicated than driving a Volkswagen. Besides, it was skinnier. I was less likely, I thought, to crash into things, even on this narrow trail down which Fitch directed me.

"You want to explain to me what we're doing?" I asked Fitch as we entered the woods.

"Turn right at that tree," he replied into my ear.

One of our wheels bounced over a tree root, and we traveled momentarily on the other two.

"Drive in the middle of the road, would you?" Fitch complained.

"Road? Are you kidding? This is a footpath."

"Listen, this is a nice and easy trail. It happens I was here yesterday walking around. This is one of the thirty or forty different places Konigsberg—or somebody who looks like Konigsberg—got spotted the last few days. Also I've been here a dozen times before, anyway. The trail leads a couple of miles away to a picnic grounds."

"You go on picnics, Fitch?"

"With my wife and daughter, if that's okay with you."

Jesus Christ. Fitch was married, with a *kid*. And he took them on picnics. It was like trying to imagine the bogey man dressed up as Santa Claus.

"There's a wider path heading over to the grounds from the other side, big enough for a truck. That's where Ryan is. But it's straight as an arrow. If we come after him that way, he'll spot us before we get inside of throwing distance. He's likely to take off. The border is only about fifteen minutes away, the way the tank flies, through the woods."

"Uh . . . Fitch, by 'throwing distance' . . . you're not planning, are you, on attacking this tank with a grenade or . . ."

"All we're going to do is, we're going to stop this tank, talk to this guy Ryan, and see why the hell he's been wandering around the countryside the last thirty-two hours without calling in. Then we're going to look inside the tank and see what we see. If he's carrying contraband, we got a handle on him. If he's connected to Konigsberg, we'll find out. Who knows, maybe we'll find Konigsberg inside the tank. Listen," Fitch added, "pick it up a little, will you? We don't got all day."

The trail we were on might very well have been smooth enough for a 'nice and easy' stroll—in fact, as we hurtled along, we knocked to one side an elderly couple who were carrying a picnic basket and strolling along hand in hand—but as a roadway, it was unsatisfactory. At thirty miles an hour, in a vehicle that weighed only about a hundred pounds, we were propelled into the air by every rock or loose branch we drove across. I tried to steer around these obstacles as they loomed in front of me. Thank God the Germans were not inclined to litter. Luckily, at that speed the engine gurgled and whined, making enough noise to scatter the few pedestrians in our path—the elderly couple must have been slightly deaf. And for a while we careened along in this fashion, rattling around like two peas in a plastic pod.

"We're in a rush, I told you," Fitch groused when I took out time to swerve around a little kid. "Move this thing out."

"Hey, Fitch," I said a couple of minutes later, "an M-60 tank comes with a 105mm cannon up front, and it's got a couple of machine guns. How do you expect we're going to stop it?"

"We got the element of surprise," he said.

"I got a question too," he remarked when we got a little way down the road. "How come when we're taking a ride through the woods, you bring along a guide to Germany?"

"Suppose we get lost?"

"All right, pull up here," Fitch said, poking up on the canopy.

We were approaching a rutted dirt road, probably a service road, very narrow, but unmistakably a real road, as opposed to the path down which we had been traveling. Fitch climbed out of the Messerschmitt, which I had stalled, and made his way through a patch of undergrowth to a place where he could peer up and down the road without being seen himself.

"Goddamn it, start this thing up," he said, getting back in the car. "He got past us. When they spotted him an hour ago, he was all the way west, but he must have seen the plane. He's zipping along now as fast as that thing can move. All I see is dust."

There was dust all right, a moving cloud, which did not quite obscure the massive shape of an M-60 tank about a half mile away. With Fitch urging me on, I wrestled the Messerschmitt into what passed for high gear, and took off after it. At top speed, about forty-five miles an hour, which felt in that vehicle on that road as if we were breaching the sound barrier, we managed slowly to close the distance between us. For a while our pursuit seemed to go unnoticed, but as we came within hailing distance, the turret of the tank slowly, inexorably, revolved, until it faced backward. The cannon descended and aligned itself along our trajectory. I was looking directly up the bore, a gaping mouth all set to make some noisy pronouncement.

"I think we lost the element of surprise," I remarked gloomily.

"Swerve a little," Fitch suggested, useless advice since I swerve naturally when I drive. Besides, any additional swerving and we would end up in one of the ruts—end up.

But Fitch was not without other recourse. At this singular moment, after being subject to the prolonged stress of our unremitting search for Konigsberg, and having suffered, also, no doubt, the anguish of knowing the future of the world rested in his hands—along with a soggy cigar—and in the face of a situation that might very well have been construed as dangerous, he acted, without hesitation and without regard to personal safety. He threw open the canopy of the Messerschmitt, which was still swerving along at about forty-five miles an hour, and stood up.

"Halt!" he called out to the tank through the dirt that swirled about us, and over the roar of the tank engine and the whine and rattle of the Messerschmitt, "Halt that tank!"

"Fitch, you fucking idiot! Get down!" We were doing some kind of circus act, balancing on various combinations of wheels, or, on occasion, wheel.

Suddenly Fitch had a big black pistol in his hand. "Halt!" he said again, pointing the gun at the sky. He fired off a warning shot, which made a huge noise behind my ear, then, piqued, he took a couple of shots at the tank itself.

I slowed down as quickly as I could, which sent us further out of balance. We skated off rapidly in a half-dozen different directions, then ended up abruptly in the ditch. Fitch skidded off by himself down the road, still waving his pistol around. The tank also came to a stop.

No one was hurt. Rolling over a couple of times, I picked up a dusting of light brown grit; and my pants were torn around the knees. The pajama lining was visible now in a couple of places.

But otherwise I was okay. So was Fitch, evidently, although the stub of the cigar he had wedged between his teeth had a splayed and blunted look.

A hatch opened on top of the tank, and a man appeared. He was wearing a pinched hat with field-grade trim, and aviator-style sunglasses, which were almost opaque. He had tightly wound curly hair, only a few strands of which I could see from where I was lying on the ground. Except for a thrusting jaw, his features were sharp and regular. His general expression, as far as I could make it out, was grim. Had he been smoking a corncob pipe, he could have passed for Douglas MacArthur, but, lo and behold, he was smoking a cigar.

"That's what you get," he said in a lilting voice. "Didn't nobody ever tell you guys to get over to the left if you want to pass . . ."

"All right, just don't move a muscle," said Fitch, assuming the stance of a boxer—legs apart, knees flexed. He had both hands on his gun, which he held out in front of him. "Put up your hands."

Slowly the fellow raised his hands. "What is this," he asked. "A stickup?"

A few minutes later Fitch had Major Ryan, for that's who it was, standing on the ground, his arms still elevated. Next to him in a similar pose was a Private Englehardt, a nervous-looking, asthenic young man with watery eyes and a quavery smile. Carefully, Fitch frisked them both. Then he flashed his ID and put up his gun.

"I heard of you, Fitch," Ryan said, taking down his arms and giving the policeman what I thought was a steely look. It was hard to tell because of the sunglasses. "You're the top cop around here, right? Made your mark stumbling over spies and chasing fags. But what the hell were you doing during the war, let me ask you that. . . ."

"Where have you been the last thirty-two hours?" Fitch shouted. Plowing a furrow through the dirt with his ass hadn't improved his disposition any.

"I been driving this thing around, what do you think?"

"It's true. It's really true," said Englehardt, who still looked awfully nervous even though Fitch had pocketed the gun. "It's true, no kidding," he added. "I'm a witness."

"Shut up. I'm not talking to you," said Fitch. "I'm talking to you," he went on, turning to Ryan. "And I want to know what the hell you been doing. There's an alert on, you know."

"I know," said Ryan, lighting up his cigar and shaking the match out, "and that's what I been doing. First I'm heading down to the border because I know somebody on the other side, and if I can get to him before a whole army corps shows up, maybe, just maybe, I can find out what's going on over there. Meantime I'm keeping my eye out for that guy Konigsberg we're supposed to keep an eye out for."

"The somebody you know on the other side are a couple of border guards, is that right?" Fitch asked.

Ryan took a long puff on his cigar and stared, or seemed to be staring, straight ahead.

"You got some kind of racket going," Fitch went on. "You give the guards a couple of frozen chickens you get cheap from the PX, they give you a rare book, or something."

"Not too much rare books," Ryan commented leisurely. "An occasional bottle of schnapps. A few knickknacks."

"And money. Right? You take money too."

"You got something against the free enterprise system, Fitch? What the hell are we fighting for?"

"Happens to be against the law, my friend," Fitch said, smiling his crooked, unfriendly smile. "You can get a couple of years in the stockade, maybe."

"Yeah? Am I supposed to be frightened?" Ryan remarked, sticking out his jaw. "I don't frighten so easy. I was at the Inchon landing. . . ."

"This guy is so friendly with the East Germans, you know what he does?" Fitch commented, looking vaguely in my direction. "He drives his fucking *tank* over to the other side. That's right, he crosses the border back and forth with his *tank*. How's that for détente."

"What the hell is all this, Fitch?" Ryan took a couple of steps forward and stood arms akimbo, face-to-face with the policeman, cigars jousting. "You arresting me for smuggling, or I get a speeding ticket, or what?"

"If you're on alert," said Fitch, "how come you don't answer your call? Division headquarters has been trying to reach you since yesterday."

"The radio is broken. They know the radio is broken, I told them a week ago."

"That's true," put in Englehardt. "I told them too."

"Naturally I called in a couple times. I stopped at a candy store once, and a restaurant; but naturally the phone was busy."

"You got a busy number?" Fitch repeated incredulously. "That's how come you're out here two days?" When Fitch was surprised, his eyes bugged out a little. He looked like Peter Lorre.

"So maybe I got other reasons too. None of your business."

"We didn't do anything wrong. Honest," said Englehardt, sounding like a little kid who got his hand caught in the cookie jar. "You can't do anything wrong in a tank."

"Listen, you," Fitch said to the private. "Stand over there." He pointed somewhere off on the other side of the road. "Back farther. Over there. Back." Englehardt ended up standing forlornly behind a stand of trees.

"So you got business that's none of my business," Fitch said to Ryan. "We'll see. First off, we're going to take a look inside the tank."

"Yeah, what for?"

"Get in the tank."

"You got a search warrant?"

"Get in the Goddamn tank!" Fitch said, whipping out his gun.

Ryan snorted contemptuously, but did as he was told. Fitch clambered up the side of the tank after him and disappeared down the hatch. Then there was quiet. The soft sounds of the forest were set off by the distant drone of an airplane; and except for the tank itself, I could have imagined myself back home, wandering through the woods on a lazy autumn afternoon. After a moment or two there was an additional sound, a metallic clatter from the interior of the tank and occasional bits of muted but plainly angry conversation. Then, while I leaned against this iron behemoth, which seemed dropped into this sylvan setting by some neglectful God of War, there issued from it, out of a small vent about waist high, a half dozen or so papers, folded over, crumpled and made small. I grabbed a few of these before they started to blow away. They were, I was surprised to discover, drawings similar to those Fitch had shown to me at the Waldheim base. Men, naked or near naked, were posed immodestly, staring dreamily off into space, yet giving evidence that their thoughts were of earthly matters. Mixed in with these studies from nature were two or three dog-eared, wallet-sized photographs illustrating a similar theme, but more explicit, as photographs tend to be. One such had two men demonstrating an act that the Supreme Court had recently judged constitutional when entered into by a married couple, of sound mind and sober disposition, in the utter privacy of their home—and so long as neither was charging for his, or her, participation. However, committed by one man upon another, the act was disgusting, immoral and reprehensible, even when accomplished privately under the covers. And there was nothing abashed about the men in this photograph, one of whom I recognized, despite the soft, flattering focus, as Major Ryan. The photograph had appeared before me, I realized, because Ryan recognized it as incriminating and suspected—correctly, no doubt—Fitch's search for contraband would not stop short of an examination of his personal effects.

Fitch discovered nothing inside the tank. On the outside of the tank, however, tied loosely to a couple of metal knobs and bolts, out of our view initially, was a picnic basket. This was searched over Ryan's strenuous objections at gunpoint, and was found to contain a picnic lunch, complete with a bottle of wine and two carefully wrapped wineglasses. Evidently the secret purpose Ryan had for coming this way, in the direction of the picnic grounds, was to have a picnic. Ryan refused to say as much, though. He denied everything. He denied knowledge of the picnic basket. Also, when questioned, he said he had not been a frequent visitor to the Waldheim base as had been reported. He did not know Sidney Konigsberg. If there was a secret drawer in his footlocker, that was news to him. He bought the thing from somebody in the quartermaster corps, and you know how those guys were, always trying to rip off some toothpaste or underwear. "I deny everything," he said.

Failing to catch Ryan in the act of smuggling, Fitch threatened him, something about trading with the enemy; but the tank commander laughed in his face.

"Since the landing at Inchon, I don't intimidate so easy," he said. "Putz."

Something flared to brightness behind Fitch's beady eyes, but he said nothing. He turned to me. I was sitting on the apron of the tank, a sheet of metal that ran over the treads like a fender. "C'mon, this is a wild-goose chase."

"Monkeybar race," I said.

"What?"

"Never mind."

"C'mon, I said. I don't got any more time to waste."

"We're not going anywhere in the Messerschmitt. The key's gone. Listen," I said, trying to forestall any more wrangling. "The key fell out when the car was rolling over. I hunted all over the ground for it, and it's gone. That's it. Don't argue. There's mud all over from the rain. It's under the mud someplace, and I'm not going to spend the rest of the day looking for it. I'll get the damn thing towed."

"I need a lift about a mile down the road," Fitch said, addressing himself again to Ryan.

"Isn't that too bad," Ryan said in his singsong voice. "Just happened the engine broke. That last little bump in the road. You'll have to walk."

This remark seemed to me under the circumstances either courageous or foolhardy. Fitch made no reply, but I could see the muscles of his jaw working. Somewhere in the murky recesses of his mind Ryan's name and address were being filed away. Without further conversation, and without invitation to me to accompany him, without even a glance at me, Fitch set off down the road, trudging through the dirt and occasional puddle, staggering once, but moving on implacably.

"Putz," Ryan said, watching him go.

"Yeah," I agreed. "Oh . . . uh, here," I said, handing him a couple of the sketches I had recovered. "These are yours, I think."

Ryan took them from my hand. He looked up at me quickly, then down at the drawings again for a long moment.

"Uh . . . what is this?" he said finally. "This stuff . . . this isn't mine."

"Oh. They must belong to Fitch, then. When the two of you were inside the tank, he pushed them out of a little window for some reason." I reached out for them. "I'll give them back."

"This don't prove anything," he said, holding the papers away from me.

"Nothing of consequence, maybe. But it does suggest to me that if they belonged to you, you might be homosexual."

"Wha . . . at?" Ryan contrived an incredulous expression. "A *what?*"

"You know, a homosexual. What was that word you used before? A fag."

"Come off it. This doesn't mean . . ."

"And there's this photo. See? Where you're doing this thing to this man . . ."

Ryan grabbed the photograph and ripped it into small pieces.

"A homosexual!" I cried out, clapping my hands merrily. "At last, a real homosexual. Fitch is going to be so pleased!"

"Hey, listen . . . listen to me. I'm not really a . . . I was in the Italian campaign, you know. During World War Two. The whole damn thing. A Bronze Star with two oak-leaf clusters. You had to be tough . . . what's so funny?"

"I don't know," I said. And I didn't know exactly. Something inside of me was beginning to fray.

"All right, all right. Listen, I admit it," Ryan said, taking another tack. "It has to do with this hormone. My mother took this hormone when she was pregnant . . ."

That was too much. I started laughing and fell off the tank.

"I don't see what's so fucking funny," Ryan said. "It's a kind of illness. This hormone. I can't help it. Listen . . . get up, will you. Why the hell are you laughing? You're a doctor . . . aren't you a . . ." Ryan was staring at my insignia, most of which had fallen off when I was thrown from the car. ". . . listen, don't you have any compassion?"

"Oh, right. I'm sorry," I said. With an effort I got up. I tried to fix my uniform, which was a waste of time. "I don't know what's the matter with me. Not enough sleep, I guess. A psychiatrist told me that. He also told me Freud himself was a homosexual, so maybe you shouldn't feel so bad. But it is against army regulations, you know. . . ."

"You can't prove a Goddamn thing!" Ryan snarled at me, shifting gears again.

"Well, not from that picture," I conceded. He was using his boot to grind the tiny shreds he had made of the photograph into the mud. "But did you see the look on Fitch's face just now? All I have to tell him is there was such a picture, and he'll be digging up every guy you talked to over the last ten years. Sooner or later he'll find another picture."

Ryan took a deep breath. "What do you want? Money?" he asked.

"Hey, yeah. I forgot. There's a reward, isn't there? Two hundred and fifty bucks for you, another two hundred and fifty bucks for your friend hiding over there in the woods."

"Him? You bastard! He's innocent. He's . . ."

"Listen, don't give me any more shit," I said, interrupting. If this kept up, I was going to be late for my appointment with Beck. "I don't give a damn who's guilty or innocent or what. Homosexuality isn't a crime in my book. Or an illness. It's a matter of taste. As far as I'm concerned, you're entitled to make love to anyone you want, man, woman, or animal, as long as the other person doesn't object. Live and let live, that's my motto. So you don't have to do any routine about hormones. Also, I don't work for the police. All I want is some information about Konigsberg. I was taking care of him—trying to take care of him—when he disappeared. That's all I'm interested in."

"What . . . what do you want to know?"

"You spent some time on that secret base at Waldheim, is that right?"

"Well, yeah. I knew somebody there."

"Who?"

"Johnson."

"Oh. The security chief. The guy Fitch arrested for . . ."

"Right."

"You knew him?"

"That's what I said."

"I see. Well, did you ever meet Konigsberg?"

"I think I ran into him once or twice maybe. He was nothing to me, and I don't know what the big excitement is now that he's missing."

"Did you smuggle any stuff across the border for him, porcelain, for instance?"

"Hey, come on. I didn't even know the guy. As for smuggling, I don't . . ."

"Don't tell me you don't smuggle, because I know better."

"I was going to say, I don't carry stuff over the border for anybody but me. I got this chancy relationship with this border guard, and I got to handle him just right. Mostly with money."

"You have a relationship with one of the border guards? An East German border guard?"

"Jesus Christ! Not that kind of relationship. What do you think I am? You think I screw everybody? I suppose if I were a teacher, you wouldn't let your son sit in my classroom, right? I might fuck him during rest period. It just happens I have a girl friend too, you know."

"What's the secret drawer in the trunk for?"

"Ah, nothing." Ryan kicked some mud off one of the tank treads. "The pictures. I used to keep stuff like that in there. Sentimental. You think that's funny probably. But it's not always just a sexual thing. I had some feeling for . . . ah, what good is explaining. When they picked up Johnson, I figured I better throw out everything. This . . . I just forgot I had it with me."

"If you met Konigsberg once or twice, what did you talk about?"

"Listen, that base is restricted. Nobody is supposed to get in and out. I wouldn't have been there except I knew Johnson, who was head of security, and then it wasn't so easy. I kept a low profile. Yeah, I ran into Konigsberg, and he asked me about how tight the border was; but I don't go around gossiping."

"I suppose not." I walked with Ryan over to the Messerschmitt, which was lying on its side.

"I thought you lost the key to this thing," he said, helping me pull it upright.

"I just found it in my pocket," I said, climbing into the car. "Hey . . . you know, all you guys smuggling out here ought to form some kind of union. Did you ever run into an Indian, an American Indian who is running some kind of racket?"

"I don't hang out with that crowd."

"Yeah," I said, revving the engine. "By the way, don't get too close to the border. Fitch has a couple of battalions out looking for you with antitank guns; and in the mood he was in when he left, maybe he forgot to tell them it was a false alarm. Also, watch out for helicopters."

I waved good-bye to Englehardt, who was still standing in the shadows of the trees; and I set off down the road. Fitch had gone off to the east. I went the other way.

I arrived back at Waldheim in time to see the glockenspiel go round. It was just 1 P.M. My God, it felt like it was already 1 P.M. of the following day. I found a parking space at the center of town. I couldn't get the car into reverse, so I picked up the front end and wheeled the thing into place. Still, I liked the way the Messerschmitt handled, compared to the Volkswagen. It was sturdy too. Except for a missing fender, it was hardly the worse for wear. I found the street corner to which Beck had directed me. There was a *Gasthaus* on the corner, in front of which hung a large sign for Beck's beer, a funny coincidence.

I took up station under the sign and concentrated fixedly on presenting a casual and inconspicuous appearance. Under the circumstances I was having trouble with casual, which usually came naturally to me, and inconspicuous seemed out of the question. Judging from the glances of passersby, this particular corner was not usually frequented by American soldiers wearing dirty uniforms ripped through at the knees and showing ragged tongues of red and blue pajama flannel projecting out of their trouser legs. Probably the guidebook didn't help. I had forgotten which hand I was supposed to carry it in, so I held it in front of me in both hands, like a loincloth.

I spotted Beck before he came up to me. He was a squat, hunched-over man, in his fifties, perhaps, wearing a heavy cardigan sweater and horn-rimmed glasses. He looked flabby and gone to seed a little, not at all my idea of a spy. I had a fixed idea by now about how a spy should look, something intermediate between Krista Brandt and Jungle Jim Collins. This man seemed to fall along a different axis entirely. He looked vague somehow, and uncertain, and he looked worn out. If I had seen him waiting in a mental hygiene clinic, I would have assumed he was under treatment for an involutional depression. He had curly hair, of course, not quite as closely cropped as the graying curls of Major Ryan, but nowhere near the extravaganza of curls Collins had described on the man he had seen talking with Konigsberg. Still, a person is likely to cut his hair from time to time, or let it grow; and there were such things as wigs. Of course, by now I didn't believe Collins had ever seen such a man anyway.

But I noticed Beck probably because of his curly hair. When I first saw him, he was across the street and about a block away, walking away from me. He turned out of sight a moment later around a corner. He appeared the second time a couple of blocks away on the other side. He turned toward me, ambling, stopping to look in store windows every once in a while. He walked up to me, then, without stopping, without even looking at me, went right by. The third and last time, he came down the street behind me. I didn't see him until he said hello and stuck his hand out at me.

"You're late," I remarked, after we had introduced ourselves.

"Actually, no," he replied. "I was here before you, but I thought I would take time to find out if you were alone. You understand, I am sure. You know," he added, studying me, "if I knew you were going to wear such a distinctive uniform, I would not have asked you to bring the Fodor's."

Beck ushered me quickly into the *Gasthaus*. We took a seat near the back and waited silently until someone came to take our order, a couple of beers. I made mine Beck's. My companion smiled at me; but we sat quietly again until the beer arrived. Beck seemed to have a special capacity for quiet. He was not only silent, he was unmoving. He watched me with a leaden curiosity. His eyes, gray and opaque, and somber, reminded me of someone, Konigsberg, I realized suddenly.

"You know Sidney Konigsberg," I said finally, as always less patient than I should be.

"Yes," he replied laconically.

"How?"

"We were associates."

"Oh. Umm . . ."

Beck continued to examine me.

"How come you were associates?" I asked, after a time.

"We had mutual interests."

"Oh," I commented, nodding my head sagely. "Mutual interests, eh? Listen," I said, leaning forward. "A couple of days ago he came to see me . . ."

"Yes, I know." Beck looked down at the table. Slowly, with

one finger, he obliterated a wet circle his glass had made on the surface, as if even that faint mark was an unwanted trace of himself.

"You know he's missing?" I asked.

He nodded slowly, but made no other response.

"Aw, come on," I said irritably, "are you in a position to tell me something about him or not?"

"Perhaps, Dr. Redden, you could tell me what you know and what you need to know, and I will fill in the gaps."

"I see. You said to me over the telephone that you were going to trust me—but you mean to trust me as little as possible."

"Naturally. There is too much at stake. I'm sure you understand. When other people depend on you, you have an obligation not to put them in danger. Still, I know who you are. You are not a policeman or . . . or anything. Just a doctor. I am inclined to tell you as much of the truth as I can. Anyway, I will not tell you any lies." Beck spoke softly. His English was accurate, but accented—not quite a German accent, although he had conversed easily in German to the waiter.

"All right," I agreed. "I'll tell you what I know, which is remarkably little, and what I think I know. All I am certain of is that Konigsberg came to my office a few days ago. He was depressed and talking about killing himself; but I think he was anxious to see me for some particular reason, beyond his getting treatment, or whatever, for his emotional condition. There was some particular thing he wanted to tell me, but couldn't because there was someone else present from his unit."

"He said nothing?"

"Nothing. No one seems to believe that, but all he communicated to me was a feeling, a sense of urgency, desperation even. And, of course, gloom."

"Go on."

"There's not much else. He disappeared about a half hour later and hasn't been heard from since. The police have been dragging me around looking for him. Also half the army is searching for him. He held a sensitive post, you know. I imagine you know. Everyone else seems to."

"Yes."

"That's all. The rest is conjecture. A lot of people making a lot of wild guesses."

"And you, Dr. Redden? You have some ideas of what happened to Sidney Konigsberg?"

I settled back against the corner of the booth and watched Beck draw parallel lines on the frosted surface of his glass. Evidently he was no more inclined to talk to me than anyone else had been.

"All right," I said, figuring I might as well go along. "I'll tell you what I think. You stop me if I make a mistake. I mean, if you want to stop me—and, of course, if you know whether or not I'm making a mistake.

"I suppose I should start when he was growing up. I'm a psychiatrist, you know. Psychiatrists like to understand people from the time they were born, just in case the obstetrician dropped them on their head. In this case nothing so dramatic, although Konigsberg seems to have been a remarkable kid, politically active for a while, committed, involved with other people, then, the rest of the time, a loner, turned off to politics and to everything else. Or so it seemed. There were other apparent contradictions in his life—a scholar who's capable of getting in trouble with the police, a mother's boy who goes off to the army. People in general are complicated, but usually the contradictions disappear when you come to understand them. Each person is driven by his own particular hopes and ambitions. And fears. But sometimes you come across someone whose life is more focused, who is governed by a single ruling purpose or passion. Such a person becomes a fanatic, a revolutionary or a tycoon. Maybe a poet. Konigsberg did not seem remarkable to me when I met him; but I think now he was one of those people.

"I think it had something to do with his being Jewish." I waited for Beck to say something, but still he was silent. He was looking at me, but somehow past me at the same time. I shrugged.

"Yeah, well that's what I think anyway. He went to Israel for vacation one summer, and when he came back, he was different. Maybe because he lost a father and a brother somewhere along the way, he identified with the Israelis, or with Jews in general who had experienced the still more terrible losses of the Holocaust. Since his family came from Germany originally, maybe some of his own relatives were killed. Out of such a background idealists come. They themselves become their lost heritage. I saw a poem he left in his room, full of grand ideals, all about someone committing himself to his people.

"So, the way I figure it, he came to Germany—he asked to come to Germany—with a particular purpose in mind, something he planned for ever since that vacation. And in order to do whatever he had in mind, he had to be stationed for some reason on that secret base near Waldheim. You know the secret base to which I am referring?" I asked.

"Yes." Beck smiled at me weakly.

"Of course you do. This secret base is about as secret as the recipe for scrambled eggs. As soon as he gets signed in to this secret base, he wangles a pass somehow and sets off on a whirlwind tour, Munich, Nuremberg, Berlin, in order to . . . well, I don't know what for. Last-minute arrangements, maybe. He meets you in Berlin—a waitress remembered seeing the two of you. You didn't know Konigsberg before that, or he wouldn't have had to dress for the occasion. He wore a bright green jacket and took along the Fodor's. I don't know why Berlin. Obviously you could have—you must have—met him here, too, otherwise you would not have identified yourself as Beck when you called the hospital. Unless by some coincidence your name really is Beck?"

"My real name is too hard to pronounce. Go ahead, please."

"I assume you are Israeli. The accent, I think. Also, after all, you come to me through the Nuremberg congregation. Anyway, whatever he was doing as an associate of yours, he was keeping it from the U.S. Army. So it was something illegal. Apparently it was smuggling. Porcelains and stuff like that. He had one in his room. Large sums of money were passing through his hands, we know from his bank account. I find the whole thing hard to understand. If you want to smuggle, you don't go out of your way to be stationed on a secret base first. Probably that would be the last thing you would want to do. Security checks all the time. Movements more restricted certainly than, let's say, if you worked in a PX. Besides, smuggling seems to me out of character for this guy. He's not interested in money. I've seen where he lives. He owns cheap clothes, no jewelry, no expensive things, except for the porcelain. In fact, he seems not to be interested in *things* at all. No radio or television set. Just a lot of dirty laundry all over the place. Smuggling just doesn't fit. . . ."

"The smuggling was a mistake," Beck remarked impatiently. "Go on, please." He was frowning. The ring of curls made him look like an angry cherub.

"So," I said, starting up again. "He came to Waldheim with some other idea in mind. Waldheim is a listening post. Maybe he was supposed to listen to somebody special. Or talk to . . . Well, it doesn't matter. Suddenly, somewhere along the line, something happened. Something, I think, of a . . . personal nature. He wanted the help of a psychiatrist. He was depressed all right, but . . ."

"He's dead."

"What?"

"I have not heard from him in a week. That is, for him—as you would say—out of character. He was, as you describe him, a very serious, responsible young man. He would not leave his post without speaking to me. He . . . he worked with me."

"How? What was he doing?"

Beck made a face. "I might as well tell you. It doesn't matter now, I'm sure. But, Dr. Redden. I would not like you anyway to repeat this to the U.S. Army or to Henry Fitch of the CID or to Herr Emil Fuchs of the police. Yes, I know of them. In my business, you get to know about many people. Fuchs knows who I am, although by a different name, and more or less he knows what I do; but I would still like it better—and he would, too, for that matter—if I am not brought to his attention officially too many times. Also I am telling you this, Dr. Redden, because these last few days I have learned something about you, too. You are somebody who cares about what happens to other people. In that respect you are like Sidney. And, anyway, it seems he wanted to tell you something about himself.

"What I do, Dr. Redden, is, indeed, a kind of smuggling. I smuggle people, Jews, from out of Eastern Europe to freedom. To Israel. And Sidney, as you guessed or figured out, was helping me.

"From what I understand, he didn't suddenly become Jewish on a summer vacation; but you're right, when he was in Israel, something happened to him. Maybe he caught something of the spirit, the sharing, the excitement of making something new in a place which is so old. Maybe it was for him like it was for me years before, a place to come to and belong. Sunshine and bright colors, and family. Maybe he just grew up during that time. I don't know what his psychology was. You're a psychiatrist; but I don't care about that business. A man is whatever he becomes. It doesn't matter why. Sidney became a patriot. A Jew. Still American, he made that clear. Not religious at all. He couldn't even speak Hebrew, this young man who spoke so many languages; but he was a Jew nevertheless.

"There aren't so many Jews left. A few million in New York City, more than in all of Israel. A few here and there also in other places. Some, more than a few, still in Eastern Europe, especially Russia. Konigsberg has an uncle in Russia, from the city of Königsberg, which used to be Prussia and a couple of distant cousins who come from around here, the other Koenigsberg, not so many miles away. He met one in Israel, I think. Sooner or later they will probably all be in Israel. Because it is home. That is my job. I help those Jews who want to go home to Israel. Wherever they are. Even in Russia. Since the Berlin Wall, it is not so easy. Transportation, of course, is most difficult. Crossing borders at night. False papers. Bribes. Hiding in circus caravans, even. Boats. Well, you can imagine. But hardest of all, of course, is the last border from East to West. But, if you are patient, there are ways, even now. Sometimes there is a building going up nearby, where somebody can sneak across, or there is a sympathetic guard. Sometimes some vegetables or other commerce are scheduled to cross, and underneath the vegetables there is room for a small person to hide. These opportunities come up suddenly, and you are either there to take advantage of them, or not. Which brings us to the second biggest problem. Communications. You can't talk about these things over the telephone. Letters work sometimes, but that's complicated. A person in Poland can't get too many letters from the West. And unreliable. I, myself, just got a letter, censored, of course, from an old friend in Russia. It was mailed in June. If he was telling me to pick him up someplace, he would have been waiting a long time. So that's where Sidney comes in. He wanted to help, so he joined the army. Since he is fluent in German and Russian, we half expected that he would get sent to Korea or someplace; but, for a change, the U.S. Army acted sensible, and he is stationed here where he can do them the most good and us too. Now we have somebody who listens all day to all of Eastern Europe. And even more important, he has access every once in a while to—"

"To the transmitter."

"Yes. Now if a chance to cross over from the other side comes up, we can act quickly."

Beck sat back and drank down his beer. "So that's it," he said gloomily, wiping his mouth on the back of his hand. "When Sidney arrived, finally, he had to touch base with me and a couple of others first—as you say, I never met him before—and then . . ."

"He didn't come to Germany before he was actually assigned here? To visit maybe? About two or three months ago?"

"No. He spoke fluent German, but this was his first time actually on German ground."

"Are you sure?"

"That's what he told me. Why would he lie? We met in Berlin, by the way, because I happened to be in Berlin. In this business, you move around a lot. And also because I wanted us to talk without someone from his base seeing us accidentally. Finally, he went to work. And what he did for us, even in just a month or so, was very important. I suppose he is not vital to us. This work will continue somehow as it has for many years before; but his not being there will hurt. We are missing now an important connection between East and West. There will be people lost as a result, I can tell you that. Some people are not going to make it across."

"What about the porcelain?" I asked. "And the money?"

"Ah, my fault. You see, these refugees bring with them whatever they can. Sometimes an antique porcelain or jewelry or some other object is easier to handle and more valuable than currency. Sidney happened to be in a position to deal with a particular outlet, a . . . a fence, as you say, more easily than I could. Just every once in a while, I would give Sidney something to sell. He made the contact himself. But I should not have permitted him. We needed him for more important things. . . ."

"The contact was General Gutman?"

Beck smiled his joyless smile at me. "Yes," he said.

"I see. So Konigsberg's engagement to the general's daughter was just a cover, an excuse for making visits. You didn't object to dealing with a Nazi?"

"That business was over a long time ago. I am interested in helping those Jews who are still alive. I would deal with the Devil. Of course, I myself could not walk into the general's house. Fuchs has Gutman under surveillance off and on now for years. My own situation is too precarious to fool around with suspected criminals."

"The money. How did you transfer . . ."

"When I saw Sidney. That part is always easy. Also I should tell you, he had a confederate on base."

"I know. He borrowed the green jacket from someone. It was too big for him. It disappeared later on, after he disappeared. Also the porcelain in his room was missing. It had to be someone on base. Fitch had sealed the place up tight."

"Sidney got to General Gutman in the first place through this other guy."

"Who was he?"

"Funny thing is, I don't know. Sidney said it was a matter of the man confiding in him. The man is a crook, obviously, but Sidney felt he should be loyal. What could I say? It was his loyalty and sense of honor that made him come to us. If he was committed first to being an American, which for him was most important of all, and second to being a Jew, how could I tell him not to be faithful also to a friend? Besides, I didn't care. Maybe I should have paid more attention."

"You think he got killed by somebody he was tied into in the smuggling thing?"

"Nah. I don't know. Maybe. Maybe he got killed in an accident somewhere. All I know for sure is, if he were in a position to let me know where he is, he would have done that a long time ago already. No, he's gone. He was . . . I didn't know him, I suppose, but he was . . . special, a special kid." Surprisingly, Beck's voice broke. George George would not have been surprised. Spies, he would have known, like private detectives, are sensitive underneath their hard-boiled exteriors. "But all I care now," Beck went on, "is to find somebody who could do for me what he was doing."

"Is it possible he might have been abducted or killed by the other side?" I felt this was a foolish question. I didn't even know who the other side was. "The Russians?" I said. "Maybe the Arabs?"

"Anything is possible," Beck replied politely.

"Nothing you have told me explains why Konigsberg was so upset, and why he came to a psychiatrist for help."

"I told you all I know. There is something I don't know, Dr. Redden, that I was hoping you would tell me. Why exactly are all these people, the army, the police, searching for Sidney? I mean, you and I, we have a special motive. I am looking because of what he was doing for me. And you . . . because of the kind of person you are. But why in the middle of all this trouble in Cuba are they searching so hard for one missing lieutenant?"

"I would like to tell you, Herr Beck," I said, after tasting my beer, which had gone flat and insipid, "but I can't. I was told in confidence. I know you understand. It has to do with the possibility of a nuclear war breaking out between Russia and the United States. But, listen, I can tell you this much. It's not too important, I think."

XIV

HERR BECK LEFT FIRST. At his request I remained behind for ten minutes. Even so, when I left the tavern, I made sure to look around carefully before setting forth. On every corner there was, it seemed, someone lurking suspiciously. A middle-aged man, dressed all in gray, was studying me in the reflection of a plate glass window. Across from him was a street vendor. He had silk scarves on display, but he, too, was staring at me. Meanwhile, slowly, as if she were infirm, an elderly lady with a cane was making her way across an intersection, pretending not to see me, but glancing up from time to time. She looked like a spy to me. I was wary especially of an obese gentleman sneaking slowly in my direction. He was wearing Tyrolean shorts, lederhosen, and a feathered cap, but I could tell from his mincing steps and whistle that he was trying to appear inconspicuous. Before he could reach me, I darted around the corner. After an additional five or ten minutes of slipping down side streets and doubling back, I was satisfied that no more than seven or eight of the people then in view could have been following me.

I looked up to find myself outside Herman's Chinese Laundry. This time there were lights inside and a figure could be seen indistinctly moving about behind the steamy windows. I entered, setting a small bell to jangling. The woman who stood before me was about my height, but much broader about the shoulders. She had large breasts, also, which hung down and puddled on the counter. There was about her, in general, a pendulous look, saggy jowls, droopy eyelids, long yellow hair that fell in dirty strands like a torn curtain in front of her face. Wedged almost invisibly in the corner of her mouth was the stub of a cigarette. I smiled at her and stumbled over a few German words of greeting.

"If I was you, I wouldn't bother," she said in a gravelly voice, looking at my uniform, which was still shedding dust whenever I gestured. "Why don't you just throw it away and buy another."

"No, uh, I didn't come for . . . I want to talk to Herman, if that's possible. I . . ."

"You're looking at him."

"You're Herman?"

She nodded. A wisp of smoke issued lazily from the cigarette.

"That's funny," I said. "You don't look Chinese."

"That's what everybody says."

"Listen, Herman. Do you mind if I call you Herman?"

"Call me Adrienne. I only use 'Herman' for business purposes, a parochial appeal to the locals."

"Yeah? So how come the sign outside is in English? Not so good English, at that."

"Well, I service some of the army guys too. You know, from that secret base up the hill. I used to be army myself. As for the grammar, that was courtesy of my husband, who is a German national and a dummy to boot."

"Yeah? No kidding. Listen, Adrienne, there's this problem with one of the soldiers here. Apparently he's a customer of yours. Something happened . . . it's hard to explain. It looks like he dropped his laundry ticket and . . ."

"I don't care what happened. Like they say in the vernacular, 'no tickee, no washee.'"

"I'm not looking for his laundry, I'm looking for him. He dropped his laundry ticket and that was the last anybody saw of him."

Adrienne found the cigarette butt and squashed it into an ashtray with her thumb. "An interesting switch," she said. "Most of the time we get the soldier in here and the ticket is missing."

"This guy's name is Konigsberg, Sidney Konigsberg. He's a lieutenant. Do you know him?"

"Uh . . . what does he look like?"

"I don't know. Sort of average. Regular features, about average height, medium build. Army haircut. He didn't wear glasses or anything. He had sort of a sad look, but that might have been just when I saw him. He's ordinary-looking, I would say, in appearance."

"Sounds familiar. I imagine he wears a lot of khaki clothes?"

"I imagine he does."

"Yeah. I recognize the type; but no one in particular comes to mind."

"Do the letters P.E.N.K. suggest anything to you?"

"P.E.N.K., you say. Hmmm . . ." While Adrienne was considering this, she stared at a patch of wall so intently, I thought for a moment there was something on the wall itself that had attracted her attention. "Boy," she said, shaking her head, "that's a tough one. P.E.N.K. What is that? Some kind of riddle?"

"What about P.L.M.S.?"

"P.L.M.S.? Holy smoke, that's even worse." She started chewing on her lip. "I'll never get that one."

"Wait a second," I said, the light slowly dawning, "somebody told me you're only open Monday and Thursday. Is that right?"

"Sho' 'nuff. In the morning mostly."

"How come?"

"I got other fish to fry. I'm taking up dance, and in the afternoons we got a Nietzsche study group. Besides, no reason to have those guys straggling in every day with a T-shirt or a pair of shorts. Twice a week is plenty. More efficient that way. They collect a pile, and I do it all at once."

"If you're only open in the morning, what are you doing here now?"

"I'm waiting for the study group. You want to sit in? I think you'd like it. You got a very existential style about you. None of your conversation makes any sense. Is something funny?"

"Not much, except I just figured out the biggest puzzle since World War Two."

"You did? And I didn't even notice." She shook her head in amazement. "Ah, you inscrutable Occidentals."

"Can I use your phone?"

"Be my guest."

Vigliotti was in the middle of something when I got hold of him. "Listen, Captain, I got a guy here you got to help," he whispered to me urgently. "Major Wormley is going to have him court-martialed otherwise."

"Vito, I'm sort of in a rush . . ."

"The guy falls asleep all the time. Even when he's driving his vehicle. He had three accidents in his truck in the last week alone. Major Wormley says it's because he's passive-aggressive, and he's taking out his bad feeling toward the army. He wants to court-martial him to teach him a lesson. Jesus, Captain. I got some bad feeling about the army, too, but I don't show it by driving into a tree at forty miles an hour. This guy says he falls asleep all the time, he can't help it."

"All the time? What about when he's having intercourse?"

"Screwing? You mean, when he's screwing?"

"Right, Vito. That's what I mean."

"Hold on, I'll ask him." There was a pause, terminated by another excited whisper. "You're right! The guy falls asleep in the middle of screwing. In my whole life I never heard anything terrible like—"

"Ask him if he ever wakes up from sleep paralyzed for a few seconds. His whole body."

"Wait . . ." A moment later. "He does! I just asked him. It takes a couple of minutes sometimes until he can move, unless someone touches him first. How did you know . . . ?"

"Ask him if he ever gets so emotionally excited, maybe from laughing, he falls to the ground."

"You're kidding! Wait, I'll ask him . . . you're right again! Wow! Every time he gets upset, plop. He falls down. That's three terrific guesses in a row. . . ."

"All right, Vito. Cut it out. Tell the guy he has narcolepsy. No court-martial. In the meantime, if you don't mind, I've got a couple of questions. . . ."

The German army would not have lost the war if every soldier had been as efficient as Herr Bromberg. Since I had left him a couple of hours before, he had somehow located a man who had served under General Gutman during the last few months of the war. From that interview, and from a telephone conversation he conducted with one of the general's neighbors, a picture of the general emerged that was consistent with what I already knew, although some of the details were interesting. Gutman was, as Collins had described him, a professional soldier, competent, and effective even toward the end of the war after his wife had died. It was a time when the army was executing Hitler's last desperate and sometimes unsavory commands. The general played his part in the destruction of Poland; and units of his command assisted in guarding the concentration camps while their fellows within rushed to fulfill their grisly purpose. There were junior officers under him who were accused and subsequently convicted of war crimes, random brutality for the most part, not centered on Jews, but rather extending to anyone in the neighborhood, reprisals against civilian populations, that sort of thing; but at such times, Gutman himself was usually elsewhere. There were rumors of minor atrocities attributable directly to him, a fatal pistol-whipping of a young man, for instance; but these could not be proved. He was considered an officer of some tactical ability, and he was fair to his troops.

Following the war he began a scrap metal business—of the many shortages in postwar Germany, scrap was not one—and he made a lot of money. His real business, however, was thought to be the black market. When goods became plentiful, he dealt in currency, and later on in anything at all. He was said to be ruthless, "capable of killing a person," the uneasy neighbor had volunteered. The police had some idea about his criminal activities, but he had proved as elusive in peacetime as he had during the war.

Frau Bromberg was able to respond immediately when her husband asked about an abortionist. The local woman who performed such services was notorious, an alcoholic who had probably been responsible over a period of a couple of years for the death of two young women, not counting Sandra Collins, if she was, in fact, to be counted. I would not be able to talk to the woman, however. She was found dead yesterday in the woods, where she had wandered off, dead from exposure, according to the police, the final victim of her own drunkenness and clumsiness.

Vito had discovered the address of Mr. and Mrs. George and their son George, he said to me, proceeding to the next item, but the kid himself wasn't expected home until midafternoon when school let out. George the younger was looking forward to speaking to me again, according to his mother.

Finally, Major Sedgewick had run the test I had requested, and he called back just a few minutes ago to say that it was pos-

itive. There was quinine in Sandra Collins's blood. What did it
mean, the major wanted to know.

"Are you there, Captain?" Vigliotti said. "Did you hear me?"

"Vito . . . give me the number of the Waldheim base."

"Here it is," said Adrienne, who had been listening attentively.
She handed me a clipboard with a bunch of names and telephone numbers. The particular number I wanted was entered
across from the notation "secret base."

I said good-bye to Vigliotti, and called up the base. Collins
wasn't in, but I spoke in turn with Colonel Farber, the executive
officer, then Kraven, then, finally, Randy Biddle. When I hung
up fifteen minutes later, I felt like I had been living at the bottom of a well, and suddenly it had begun to rain.

"It can't be as bad as all that," Adrienne said, studying me
over a lighted match.

"Sure it can," I told her.

Before leaving, I made an additional telephone call, to Police
Chief Emil Fuchs, actually to someone in his office since he
wasn't in. I left a message to the effect that I had reason to think
a check stolen from me was in the hands of a man called Bennie
something, who was going to use it for some illicit purpose.

"I.L.L.E.G.A.L.," I said, when I was asked to spell *illicit*.

This guy Bennie was crossing West to East sometime that day
at Checkpoint Charlie, I explained, and maybe they could grab
him if they hurried.

If it's one thing I can't stand, it's being blackmailed. Not that I
have anything against blackmail in general.

I sat in the Messerschmitt, the motor running, and looked
again at the house of General Gustav Gutman. In the light of afternoon it was more striking still than when I first saw it. White
stuccoed walls all agleam were interrupted by a pattern of
wooden beams crisscrossing. There was a flagstone terrace I
hadn't noticed before, and a large bay window framed by a pat-
terned archway of stone. The sun's reflection off one of the panes
was dazzling. The general had done very well for himself, indeed, in those years of despair and opportunity after the war,
despair for some and opportunity for others. Bestirring myself
finally, I turned off the ignition and extracted myself from the
tiny vehicle, made smaller still since I had been driving it.

On the front walk I encountered a cat, which, as usual, followed after me, intertwining itself with my legs. I have this theory, which defines exactly my appeal, such as it is, to various species of animal, to wit: The higher the order of the animal, the less it likes me. Cats, any cat, will come after me affectionately, humming like a bass fiddle, running after me if I try to get away. Dogs, on the other hand, treat me with disdain; although I must say the ill-treatment I had been getting from them recently was exceptional. Mice and squirrels, and other rodents, inexplicably adore me. Field mice gather at my feet. Gerbils, which don't usually take to anyone, take to me. At the other extreme are monkeys and human beings, with whom, for the most part, I have considerable difficulty ingratiating myself. In any case, I had more difficulty than usual shooing this particular cat away; and it was only the throaty rumble of Adolf's voice as I approached the front door that made it disappear finally behind a rosebush, a last languid wave of its tail beckoning me to follow after. I looked at my watch. This trick I was going to perform had to be timed just right.

I expected the housekeeper. I planned on grabbing her as soon as she opened the door and using her body to bludgeon the dog, clearing the way for a quick dash to the library; but it was the general himself who appeared before me.

"Dr. Redden, I didn't expect to see you again so soon," Gutman said, restraining Adolf, who was already in a slavering rage, growling and grunting, the whites of his eyes showing all around. "Have you been in a fight?" the general added, staring at my clothes.

"Not yet," I responded, smiling agreeably. "General, I came today hoping we could talk for a few minutes again about Sidney Konigsberg."

"I thought after our last conversation there was nothing further to say. I have not heard from Sidney since then."

"I think we were neither of us very frank the last time. You were trying to give me the impression that—"

"Doctor, I'm afraid I don't have time for this," Gutman remarked irritably, interrupting me. "Good-bye."

"Wait a second," I said. By now I didn't expect anyone to let me in anywhere without a fight, so I was ready. I had a hand on the door. Now I leaned forward, a small movement that Adolf took note of by making an angry face and a guttural sound suggestive of a cave-in. "You want to hear what I have to say, General. I just came from the police. I told them a little about you and Sidney. Just a little, but if I don't find out from you exactly what I want to know, I'm going to tell them the whole story."

"What whole story?" Gutman looked at me with distaste.

"I'll be glad to tell it to you. Inside. After you lock up Cerberus here," I added, pointing to the dog—with my chin, since I didn't want to stick my finger out.

A servant, not the housekeeper, but a man of similarly cold demeanor, dragged Adolf, howling, to some nether region of the house while the general led me silently to the library. I sat down again on the couch, next to the telephone. He sat opposite me. This time he did not offer me a drink.

"Sidney Konigsberg, as I think you may have discovered by now, is not in the 20th Station Hospital," I said. "He disappeared shortly after I interviewed him a number of days ago. He's been missing ever since."

Gutman raised a querulous eyebrow in surprise, but the surprise was not convincing. Of course, he, or any other determined person, could have found out easily enough whether someone was on the medical wards. Anyone could walk unchallenged through the hospital building, taking a census if he were so inclined.

"Sorry I lied to you about that last time," I went on. "The German police. That's the way they wanted it. According to them, Konigsberg was engaged in some kind of smuggling scheme they were trying to get a line on, and they didn't want to let on he was out of circulation. Unless, of course, the smugglers themselves were the ones who took him out of circulation."

I noticed that I had captured Gutman's attention. His patient half-smile seemed frozen into place, and he was staring at me.

"Of course, I knew some of that already," I said, "since Konigsberg mentioned it to me."

"Before, you told me that Sidney came to you because he was feeling bad. That was not so?"

"Oh, sure it was. It's also true that he didn't have enough time to explain to me what was really upsetting him. I'm still hoping you can help me out about that. After we establish a climate of mutual trust, which is what I'm trying to do now. What he did tell me," I said, trying to keep a tone of controlled intensity in my voice, "was that he was engaged in smuggling activities. He mentioned your name in that connection, I'm afraid. I don't think he meant to say anything, but, you see, he was so upset, it just . . . sort of, spilled out. Naturally I made plain to him that anything revealed in the psychiatric interview is strictly confidential, as far as I'm concerned. Even if I am in the army." I paused long enough to allow the general the opportunity to protest his innocence, but he remained silent.

"You understand, I make no moral judgments," I said. "My obligation as a doctor is to help my patients, whether they are ill, or emotionally troubled, or whatever. I don't have to decide for them how they should spend their lives. I'm not a policeman. I want you to understand that. All I care about now is finding out what happened to Konigsberg; and if . . . if he's still alive, maybe there's still some way I can help him."

"I don't know what I can tell you, Dr. Redden, that would help you to find Sidney. I would like myself to know where he is. Also, frankly, I can't think of a reason why I should tell you anything."

"I'm going to get to that in a minute. First, as an expression of good faith, I am going to tell you what I know—what Konigsberg told me. I think under the circumstances he would not mind." I said this judiciously, after thinking about it for a moment.

"Since he came to Germany five or six weeks ago, he's been a very busy young man," I continued. "Some of it I don't know exactly. But first chance he got, he contacted some relatives, distant relatives, who live all around here, and maybe some other people too. It turned out a lot of these people had something to sell. Sometimes the things they were selling didn't exactly belong to them. Sometimes these articles, some of which were valuable, came across the border without the proper tariff getting paid, or without a provenance. In either case, the valuable thing would become . . . well, less valuable. Konigsberg needed to find somebody who knew how to get around problems like that. Now, it just happened there was a guy like that on his own base. Luckily, or maybe unluckily, this guy was able to put Konigsberg in touch with a fence—with you, that is, General Gutman. The guy's name was . . . uh, Bell. A Sergeant Bell, as I remember."

This was a guess, of course, but a reasonable guess, I figured. Bell did not seem to me the kind of person Konigsberg would have spent a lot of time with just for fun. I had trouble imagining this dedicated Zionist spy, bookish, a loner, lying on the floor with Bell while the two of them drank a path from one end of the BOQ to the other. Living conveniently next door, he had had the best opportunity to remove the porcelain statue without anyone noticing. And the green jacket I had discovered in Konigsberg's closet, and then discovered missing, seemed a more reasonable fit to Bell than to Konigsberg. The sergeant must have known of Konigsberg's assignation with Beck, and probably he knew about the Fodor's, too, which would account for his being surprised, especially surprised, at my bringing that particular book to the hospital to help Konigsberg wile away the hours until his depression lifted. And, finally, the guy had already been tried once for dealing in the black market, a not dissimilar criminal offense.

The general grunted noncommittally. He got up, poured himself a drink, then sat down again. "Disappointing," he said, speaking more to himself than to me. "A few minutes of conversation with a doctor, and he says all of that. I'm surprised he had the time," he added dryly, but not disbelievingly. "But, of course, he was an amateur. I am the person who should have known better."

"Indeed, we had very little time," I agreed. "He mentioned, almost in passing, that he was engaged to your daughter. I thought maybe he was upset because of something that happened between them. That was before visiting you yesterday. It was obvious, I guess you realize, that maybe your daughter had met Konigsberg a couple of times, but she sure as hell wasn't engaged to him. It took her a couple of seconds to remember who he was. The engagement, I figure, is a cover story. Right? So he could drop in here every once in a while."

Gutman had retreated into a sullen silence.

"Right?" I asked again.

"You said before, Doctor, that there was a reason I might want to help you. What is it?"

"Oh, yeah. Right. Look . . . uh, this is always hard, you know, deciding how much you can tell somebody of something somebody told you confidentially, when he's not around to tell you—

if you follow me. I had the same problem before. I was talking to this policeman, Fuchs. His name is Fuchs. Chief or Inspector or something. I just came from his office earlier today. You know him? . . . Well, anyway, he knows you. I sort of dropped your name inadvertently. We were talking, of course, about Konigsberg's disappearance. I didn't say anything about the smuggling, but he got all excited anyway. They've already picked up this porcelain piece, which they think Konigsberg brought onto base—"

"What are you talking about?" Gutman interrupted sharply.

"Oh, you didn't know? A very nice piece of porcelain, a statue of Diana the Huntress was found today in Sergeant Bell's room. . . ."

Actually it hadn't been found yet—it wouldn't be found for another fifteen minutes yet, if everything went off on schedule—but I was counting on Gutman's not knowing one way or the other. Fitch had sealed the base tight, he said, even the holes in the fence; and Bell, unlike Konigsberg, was a professional. I didn't expect him to call Gutman on the telephone to explain what was going on. ". . . actually, it was the same piece Konigsberg was planning on disposing of through you. I didn't say that, of course, to Fuchs . . ."

"Konigsberg mentioned this to you also?"

"Certainly. How else would I know?"

"So. I see. You did not tell Fuchs of this part of the conversation, but if I don't . . . uh, help you, you will. Is that correct?"

"Pretty much. I don't expect that a secondhand report like that is going to get anyone convicted of anything, but judging from Fuchs's reaction when I just mentioned your name, he would start taking a much livelier interest in your business affairs. Especially if Bell tells a similar story."

"Bell won't say anything to the police."

"Oh, right. Honor among thieves."

Gutman smiled graciously. He was a man, evidently, who took offense only when it served his purposes.

"Or maybe he's afraid of you?" I ventured. "Fuchs sort of intimated you were liable to kill me if I got in your way. He made me promise to call him up before I left, you know, so he could make sure I was still alive. Tell me, you didn't murder Sidney, did you?"

"I had no reason to kill Konigsberg," Gutman pointed out

calmly, sounding like a very reasonable man. "There is rarely any reason to kill anyone. Except in war. That Fuchs is an idiot. He was a military policeman in the war. A sergeant."

Gutman invested the word *sergeant* with a mild contempt. I wondered what Fuchs was going to say about the general, once I actually got around to discussing all of this with him.

"If you don't mind, what exactly, Dr. Redden, did you say already to Fuchs that he expected I might want to kill you here in my library."

"Oh, I think it was more what I didn't say. When he told me about the porcelain, I kind of let on Konigsberg had indicated to me something about selling porcelains, and I mentioned your name. It just came out without my thinking. 'Whoops,' I said. 'Sorry I mentioned General Gutman's name. Maybe he doesn't have anything to do with Konigsberg's disappearance. Besides, that's confidential.' That's what I told him. I explained that I couldn't possibly say any more. Not until I spoke to you first, that is. A matter of courtesy. He was angry, but I was adamant. But I did tell him I'd call back exactly at two thirty so he could make sure I was still alive; and I would tell him everything then. That's about five minutes from now," I added, looking at my watch.

Gutman was staring at me skeptically.

"That's the whole story," I said, waving my hands and trying to affect a frank, if not overtly simpleminded, expression.

"All right, Doctor," Gutman began impatiently. "What I am going to tell you, you may consider also a confidence. Certainly if you repeat anything, I will deny it. If you have the idea that what I reveal to you will somehow make it possible for you to . . . uh, 'bring me to justice,' or even inconvenience me in the slightest, you are wrong. Fuchs, and some other people, who are, perhaps, cleverer even than you, have been trying for a long time without success.

"Sidney Konigsberg was . . . a type," Gutman mused irritably. "Asthenic. Intellectual. Not very active physically, you could tell. Tentative. A man who stops to think about everything three times. I didn't care for him much. But I don't allow my feelings to influence me. We were getting along all right. Certainly I didn't kill him. Why would I? He made money for me. Frankly, I thought he was going to make a lot of money for me. Obviously he had a conduit from the East. A source. He didn't explain what exactly, and naturally I didn't ask. I figured some Jews coming across the border. Of course, business with Konigsberg would not have been that easy anyway." Gutman got up and poured himself another drink. "He seemed to know always how much I would pay. He bargained," the general went on. "But I don't have to tell you."

"What do you mean?"

"It's in the blood, I think. I come from a man two centuries ago who was a soldier and a trader of fine goods. And now I am here doing the same things. Konigsberg . . . well, the Jews have been bargaining cleverly longer than anyone. You . . . you are Jewish also, I think. Are you not?"

Gutman looked up from the drink he was pouring and smiled, condescending graciously to me and to all my clever forebears.

"Yes," I replied after a time. "I am Jewish."

"I thought so."

It was only then, after Gutman had established our respective positions to his satisfaction, that he offered me a drink. He shrugged when I made no move to take it. A moment later he sat down again.

"What you have said so far is accurate," he began. "Bell, who I know from a long time ago, introduced us. Konigsberg was not, of course, engaged to my daughter. Even as a cover story, it was not convincing; but it was his idea. I was glad, since I was dealing with an amateur, that at least he was considering matters of security. His commanding officer, you know, lives nearby; and it was possible they might meet accidentally. I know the fellow a little. He could be a German. Very correct, which is peculiar, considering the U.S. Army."

"I know what you mean," I said.

"If he came across one of his troops smuggling, he would be in a bad mood. And Konigsberg was coming here often."

"Is that right? Why? He could not have had that many porcelains to bring you. Or anything else. Not yet."

"It is true, he had only brought a few things so far. Mostly he came to make plans. Arrangements. As you can imagine, I don't like to talk about matters on the telephone. Every once in a while the police find an excuse to record my conversations."

"Is that so?"

"It is true, I'm afraid. The arrangements Konigsberg wanted to make when he came here were not very important all the time; and I had the feeling he was using his visits as an excuse to go someplace else. A cover for a cover, so to speak. Sometimes he came and left right away. But I don't know where he went. I did notice, since you asked me before, that he was looking preoccupied recently; but when I brought up the subject with him, he said it definitely had nothing to do with our business, which is all I care. If he was depressed, I don't know why. If he got himself killed, and probably he did if he is missing all this time, I don't know why. And I don't care. He has been more trouble than he was worth.

"You were going to call Herr Fuchs right about now, I think," Gutman added, looking at his watch. "I would not like Fuchs using you as an excuse to break down the front door. Adolf gets upset so easily."

I reached for the telephone.

"Don't get up," I said to Gutman. "I have the telephone number." I unfolded a piece of paper and, while Gutman watched me from his chair, dialed the number written on it, the number of the Waldheim base. "Hello," I said as soon as Kraven answered, "this is Captain Redden."

"Right, Doc," the sergeant answered. "I'm putting you through to Bell. He's in his room. Hang on."

"They're putting me right through," I said to Gutman.

"Yeah?" This was Bell's hoarse voice. He sounded sleepy, or drunk, or both.

"This is Captain Redden," I said, speaking loudly. "How are you?"

"You again?" said Bell. "Whatta you want?"

"Good," I said. "I'm calling from General Gutman's house. Everything's okay."

"You're what?"

"I've been talking to the general about that porcelain statue you got. The lady with the bow and arrow."

A stunned silence from the other end of the line, then: ". . . what? You . . . you've been talking to Gutman . . ."

"Yeah, listen. I've been thinking about what Konigsberg said to me. Really there was nothing, now that I come to think of it, that would tie the porcelain to the general in any way. I mean, I want to be fair. I'm sitting here talking to him, and he says he's prepared to speak to the police about the whole thing. . . ."

"Huh? What is this? The police? What the hell is he trying to pull?" Bell was speaking now in a whisper, not so low, however, that I couldn't make out what he was saying, which was audible, too, I hoped, to the police who, I knew, were supposed to be tapping Gutman's line in case Konigsberg called his fiancée, and to Sergeant Kraven, who was listening in just in case. I didn't want to rely on the police. I remembered the CIA agent who went out for a sandwich when Penkovsky was broadcasting his various top-secret messages.

"Yeah, that's right," I said. "He wants to go on record with the police, first of all, that Lieutenant Konigsberg never mentioned anything at all to him about this porcelain statue. If it was brought into the country illegally, it has nothing to do with him. Second, the general knows the statue is in your possession now, but as far as he's concerned, it's your headache. He's certainly not going to take the blame. He's prepared to say all that in a written statement to the police, but he wanted you to know now."

Gutman had settled back in his chair. He was smiling at me faintly, enigmatically, like the Mona Lisa. Meanwhile I heard sputtering mostly from the telephone, then silence.

"Listen, Redden," Bell said finally. "I don't know what you think you're up to, but I don't believe any of this. First of all, Gutman is too smart to try to reach me here. And besides, if he wants to talk to me, how come he doesn't talk to me himself?"

"He was having a drink; but you're right, hang on, and he'll tell you himself.

"Fuchs would like you to tell him yourself," I said to Gutman, covering the receiver. "You know, just tell him you were listening and I was reporting accurately what you had told me. In English, please. So I can understand." I handed Gutman the receiver, still holding the base of the telephone on my lap.

Standing very straight, Gutman spoke into the telephone, forcefully, as a general might speak to a sergeant: "This is Gustav Gutman. What Captain Redden has been telling you is true. We have been talking here and . . . hello? hello?" Gutman looked over to me. "The connection was broken," he said, holding the receiver out to me.

"Really?" I replied. "Usually the telephone system is so reliable."

Actually, I was not surprised. I had broken the connection myself at a moment I thought was propitious. Now I held the telephone just slightly off its cradle. I wanted Bell to have a few minutes to think before he called back.

"Dial Fuchs again," the general said. "I'm not sure he heard what I said. There was someone yelling on the line."

"Oh, I'm sure he got the idea. Besides, he knows where you are. If he wants to speak to you, he'll call you."

I put down the telephone, which immediately began to ring. Instead of picking it up, the general began to usher me to the door.

"Aren't you going to answer it?" I asked.

"The servants will take care of it."

"Uh . . . you don't think I should be here? In case it's Fuchs?"

"That won't be necessary. I'm sure you have work to do, as I have myself. I'm glad, however, we had the opportunity to come to an understanding."

"I am too," I said. "I always thought the differences between the Nazis and the Jews were caused primarily by a lack of communication."

Gutman might have sensed a disingenuous note, for he removed his hand from my shoulder, where it had been resting.

Since I was leaving anyway, I left as quickly as possible. I wanted the general to get back to the telephone. Kraven would be knocking at Bell's door in another few minutes, whether or not the sergeant had had time to call Gutman back. Discovering the porcelain in his possession took precedence over everything else. Still, I had the strong feeling that was Bell calling back just then on the telephone. I was sorry I couldn't be present to hear Gutman speak to him. It was a conversation that promised to be interesting, and incriminating. Most of all, I wanted to see the general's reaction. Could he manage still that inscrutable smile?

I drove through the nearby streets until I found the George residence. George George was sitting on the stoop waiting for me. By that time I knew what he was going to tell me, but that didn't stop me from feeling more depressed anyway by the time I started back to Nuremberg fifteen minutes later.

XV

"COLONEL POOLE wants to see you," Vigliotti said as soon as I opened the door. "Wow," he added, "what happened to you?"

"I was sort of in an accident."

"Please, God!" Herr Bromberg exclaimed, putting a hand to his head. "Not the Messerschmitt!"

"The Messerschmitt is fine," I said, tossing the keys onto the desk. "Just a fender. Also, the canopy is squashed in a little, but you can drive it if you hunch up a little."

"Oh, my God. My God!"

"Relax, will you? It's only an automobile. Who is that?" I said, pointing to a man who was stretched out on a couple of chairs, asleep.

"That's the guy with nar . . . narco . . ." Vigliotti replied. "You know, that disease."

"Oh, yeah."

"Hey, listen. Colonel Poole wants you right away. You and Major Wormley both. The major is down there already. . . ."

"Vito, how's Baker doing?" I asked, walking into Wormley's office.

"Who? Oh, the crazy lieutenant? He looks better, I think. He's still suspicious, frightened about all kinds of things, even noises; but he's not talking peculiar anymore. Seems like a nice guy. A Cleveland Indians fan. Funny the way that goes sometimes."

"The way what goes?"

"Last night he was off the wall, today he's halfway better already."

"Yeah, that's the way it goes sometimes," I agreed, picking out one of Wormley's white coats. "The medication, of course."

Wormley liked to wear long white lab coats, he told me once, because it made him look like a surgeon. Why a psychiatrist would want to look like a surgeon was not clear to me, although it seemed to make sense at the time. Set off against Wormley's nitwitted scientific projects, any minor irrationality went unnoticed. Actually the lab coat made him look like a lab technician, I thought—which was much better than the way I looked just then. So I exchanged my uniform jacket, which still smelled of the woods, for a white coat. It was long enough to cover the ragged holes in my pants.

"Operation Dry Sheets isn't going so well, by the way . . ." Vigliotti said.

"Stop! Don't tell me," I insisted quickly. "I don't want to hear any more about that crazy . . . You know," I added, "I think there's something the matter with Wormley."

"You do?" said Vito, lowering his voice confidentially. "I've always wondered. What do you think it is?"

"I don't know. Look, the right sleeve of this coat is about an inch and a half too long for me. The left sleeve is about an inch and a half too short."

"Hmmm. And the left side is the sinister side, according to the major. Speaking of left, I left orders with a florist to send a rose, a single red rose, to Krista Brandt, with a simple card, just your name."

"You think that's going to work? I tried to call her a few minutes ago, and she hung up on me."

"Maybe I should have left off your name."

"Vito, I want you to get a couple of people for me on the telephone," I said, walking back into the waiting room. "It's very important. . . ."

"Captain, no kidding, the colonel wants to see you. And you got a busy day. I pushed the appointments you missed into evening, like you wanted, and, also, Lingeman is stopping by. He's still worried."

"Get hold of Colonel James Collins first. If he's not on the Waldheim base—he wasn't there a while ago—try him at home. Then . . ."

Lieutenant Colonel Beasely entered the room. "There you are," he said in a singsong voice, as if he had found me hiding coyly under a sheet. "They thed you were thumwhere elth, but I thaid it ain't nethetharilytho."

"Bease, if you want to talk to me, take out the toothpick. I don't have time to hire a translator."

"They said you weren't here," he said again, actually complying with my request. He stared at the toothpick for a moment, as if he was surprised to discover it in his hand. Then he turned to Vigliotti. "Why did you say he wasn't here?"

"He just came in a few minutes—"

"I knew you'd be here, though," Beasely said, tossing an affectionate arm around my shoulder. "You're a tough guy to find, but you're always here." Without the toothpick Beasely had a sort of preppy accent.

"I'm busy now, Bease," I said.

"You bet your sweet patootie you're busy. Poole wants to see you."

"What the hell for?"

"Maybe he wants to celebrate!" Beasely stretched both arms into the air. "Victory in the Caribbean!" he yelled.

This was loud enough to wake up the soldier lying stretched out in the corner. "I always wake up refreshed," the man said, suddenly sitting bolt upright.

"My God! I had that automobile only two years," Herr Bromberg cried out, rocking back and forth a little.

"The Russians surrendered?" I asked. "We've annexed Cuba?"

"They gave up. No more missiles in Cuba. Khrushchev has agreed to negotiate. I still think we should have bombed the shit out of them," he added, frowning.

"After you get Collins, Vito, I want you to try to reach this man in the Nuremberg Synagogue . . ."

"C'mon, Abie baby," Beasely said, dragging me by an arm. "Your commanding officer has commanded your presence, and we better hurry along. The fact is, he wasn't in such a good mood when I left him a couple of minutes ago."

I shook myself free; but I knew it was useless. The United States Army was like a huge tar baby, the more you tried to pull loose, the worse you got stuck.

"All right, I'm coming. Listen, Vito," I said, drawing the cor-

poral to one side, "call up that synagogue—if it has a telephone
number, otherwise, here's the address. I want to give you a message to give to somebody, a guy named Bender, to pass along to
someone else named Beck. You understand?"

"I got it, a message about a message."

"Right. I want Beck to know I got hold of somebody who can
move messages back and forth across the border to Czechoslovakia, and maybe other things too."

"You mean, pierce the Iron Curtain?" Vigliotti made his eyes
round.

"Yeah. The man who can do this for him is . . ." I hesitated. It
just didn't seem . . . right, a psychiatrist blackmailing a homosexual, even for a good cause. Homosexuals were another
oppressed minority. Ah, what the hell, so when I got the chance,
I'd apologize. "Major John Ryan. He's in a tank unit, part of 3rd
Division. If Beck just mentions my name, Ryan will be willing to
help any way he can. Maybe that'll make up a little for Konigsberg . . . Well, you don't have to say anything about that."

Beasely was growing impatient, making sucking noises and
blinking.

"And call Collins. I have to see him right away. Here, if possible. Tell him . . . tell him I know who killed Konigsberg. . . ."

"The lieutenant is dead?" Vigliotti whispered feverishly, his
eyes gaping wide again. He grabbed my elbow. "And you know
who did it? Is it somebody I'd never guess?"

"Sixty-five miles from a gallon," Herr Bromberg cried out, his
face a mask of pain.

This outburst was enough to temporarily waken our visitor,
who had a moment before subsiding again into sleep. "I always
wake up refreshed," he said again.

"What is it this time, Bease?" I asked the colonel as we left the
office. "Did I forget to salute somebody? Or did I invalidate
somebody's bus pass by signing it in the wrong place?"

"The major here has a complaint," Poole said, as soon as I took
a seat. He was pointing at Major Wormley, who was perched a
few feet away on an oversize chair, his feet dangling a few
inches off the floor. Wormley was a freak of nature. Not only
was there a three-inch difference in length between his arms, he
could actually shrink his body—grow smaller physically—in the

presence of senior officers. On one occasion a two-star general stopped by the OPD unexpectedly for removal of a wart. Wormley, who happened to be standing around, dwindled suddenly to such a tiny size, it was a few minutes before they could find him. Had he not been wearing a uniform, the dermatologist told me later, they would have confused him with the wart.

"He has sent me a memorandum," Poole went on, reading off a piece of paper that he held aloft, "475200 slash 2, from Chief, Neuropsychiatry section 20th Station Hospital, Nuremberg, Germany, to Commanding Officer 20th Station Hospital, etc. 'It is my unpleasant duty to call to your attention that problem of which I have spoken directly to you previously about. Despite repeated admonitions I have offered Captain Redden concerning the dress code and the importance of which it is to adhere to, for an officer in particular, he has chosen to ignore.'" Poole stared at the memorandum silently, grimacing. "'. . . chosen to ignore,'" he said again. After a time he took a deep breath and went on, "'In particular, despite repeated admonitions, he neglects to button the top button of his shirt. In addition he wears argyle socks . . .'"

"That is not true," I said. "I have never worn argyle socks in my entire life."

"Uh . . . Sir, that's a typo," Major Wormley piped. "I typed up this memo myself in order for purposes of confidentiality. It should have said 'scarf.'"

"I see," said Poole, who didn't look like he did see. He was squinting at Wormley. "Am I to understand then that Captain Redden has been wearing an argyle scarf?"

"All covered with a paisley pattern. Not maroon. Even in summer."

"Is that true, Captain?" Poole asked me.

"Uh . . . I don't understand the question."

"The scarf of the medical corps is maroon," Poole snapped back irritably. "To be worn only with the winter uniform."

"Sir, I'm pretty busy just now, and if you would excuse . . ."

"You're busy?" Poole bellowed. "What about me? You think I got nothing better to do than check on your socks? Here, just answer these Goddamn questions: Is it true or not that . . . let's see, you've been keeping your collar button unbuttoned, wearing a nonregulation scarf, a lizard-skin belt, a hanging key-chain, a boutonniere, and a vest?"

"True. Probably true. False. Definitely false, and I don't remember."

"Well, from now on . . ."

"By the way, it was cowhide."

"What?"

"The belt. Ordinary cowhide."

"From now on," Poole went on, raising his voice, "you will wear a proper . . . what's that stuff coming out of your pants?"

"Oh, sorry," I said, tucking one foot behind the other, "that's the lining of the pants. You remember, I'm allergic to wool. I tore the lining and . . ."

"You will wear a proper uniform in the proper way!" Poole bellowed again, then turned to Wormley. "And I will hear no more of this nonsense! Do you understand me?"

"Uh . . . yes, sir," replied Wormley, taken aback.

"And another thing," Poole said, turning back to me. "I got a report from someplace that the NCO in your unit has been calling you names."

"Me?" I said. "Vigliotti has been calling me names? That doesn't sound like Vito."

"He called you a prick. You took him on some kind of field trip a couple of days ago, and he called you a prick . . ."

"What? I don't go on field trips; and if I did, I certainly wouldn't take Vigliotti. . . ."

"I don't care if you're a prick or not. All I care is it doesn't get broadcast around so it embarrasses me. Are you hearing me?"

"Yes, sir."

"Good. Now that that's settled," Poole said, putting this memorandum down on his desk next to Wormley's, "and now that I have the two of you here, I want to know something. Which one of you guys do I have to thank for that troop of soldiers upstairs pissing up against the wall?"

"They were not authorized to do that, sir," Wormley replied promptly. "That was on their own initiative. Or out of a spirit of willfulness. There is nothing to be learned from urinating against a wall."

"You don't think so?" Poole leaned forward abruptly, as if he were gripped by this question.

"Of course not, I . . ."

"But urinating, *purposely* urinating on yourself, while you're lying *fully dressed* on the floor of the bathroom, *that*, in your opinion, is an educational experience?"

"Well . . . surely not in the conventional sense, sir; but we're breaking new ground here. You see, the paradigm of the unconscious enuretic, who is libidinally cathected to the process, to the very process itself, of soiling the world, and through secondary reinforcement to the bed itself, as it were. I think Dr. Redden will back me up on this . . ."

"Pooey!" I yelled. "This whole business is a lot of crap."

"I was hoping for a little more support than that, Abe," Wormley replied in hurt tones.

"*God knows*, I don't expect much from psychiatrists," Poole said, "but *this*? Do you happen to know my first name, Major Wormley?"

"Uh . . . Seth. Is that right, sir?"

"Yes. Seth Poole. I leave it to your imagination, Major—you seem to have considerable imagination—to figure out the kind of sarcastic remark I've had to listen to down at Headquarters Nuremberg Post ever since this project of yours got started. Well, no more. As of twenty-four hundred hours tonight, I want all those men back in their units. Do you understand?"

"But, sir, paradoxical intention always takes a few days and . . ."

"No more!" Poole screeched, half rising from his chair. "No one in my hospital is going to be . . . engaged in any of these practices. Everyone is going home. Right away . . . I mean, back to their units. Now! Or . . . I don't care where they go, but they're leaving here. At once. Are you listening to me, Major Wormley? At once! That's it! There isn't going to be no more urinating on my wards! No one . . . no psychoratric . . . psychiatric patient is going to be urinating on my medical wards without my permission. In writing! Do I make myself clear, Major Wormley . . . what . . . what," Poole sputtered in my direction, "what do you want?"

I put down my hand. "I would like to put in an application at this time, sir, on behalf of a patient of mine. A paranoid schizo-

phrenic who we're holding on Three West. He will be wanting
to urinate from time to time."

"Will he be using the bathroom?"

"Yes, sir."

"Permission granted."

"Uh . . . I wonder if you'd mind, sir, putting that in writing?"

I walked quickly with Major Wormley, and silently, along the
hospital corridors. I was silent. He was moaning and bemoaning,
and regretting.

"The chance to advance the reservoir of human knowledge
one small step," he remarked sadly, "it's gone now. If only . . . if
only you'd been a little more positive, Abe, I think we could
have talked him into giving us another couple of days. He was
wavering. I have to tell you, Abe, I'm disappointed. I think I
was entitled to a little more loyalty."

"Why is that?" I yelped. "You just turned me in for leaving my
collar unbuttoned!"

"Abe, you asked me and . . ."

"No, you don't! I take it back. I'm not asking you, and you're
not telling me. I'm not interested."

He told me anyway. "That was for your own good, Abe. I
thought maybe if the colonel, himself, told you . . . You know,
Abe, it's only these little things that are holding you back. If you
played your cards right, you might just be able to carve out a
nice little career for yourself in the army."

I tried to talk. A few strangled sounds came out, but no
words.

There was a second-degree uproar in progress in the psychiatric offices. The soldier with narcolepsy must have had a cat-
aplectic fit. He was lying on the floor, trying to fight off Colonel
Beasely, who was attempting to apply mouth-to-mouth resusci-
tation. A couple of corpsmen, one carrying an IV bottle, were
milling about noisily. Herr Bromberg had evidently left for the
day, but Vigliotti was standing in the doorway, chewing dreamily on an ice-cream pop. He had a stopwatch in his other hand.
Either he was measuring out the remainder of his tour of duty in
hundredths of a second—which would be a very large figure, but
which would diminish very quickly—or he was timing how long

it would take for the uproar to rise to third-degree proportions. Wormley rushed in to make his contribution. I chose to wait with Vigliotti on the sidelines.

"Vito, did you tell somebody I was a prick?" I asked during a lull.

"Me? Did I . . . of course not!" Vigliotti looked wounded. "I don't think of you that way, Captain."

"Well, don't do it again. Also stay away from 'asshole' and 'shithead.' I don't like being called any of that."

The corporal seemed about to protest again, but Wormley beckoned to him urgently. Immediately he went off to join the others.

They dragged the still-struggling soldier across the floor of the waiting room toward my office.

"Is the fellow going to be all right?"

This was Colonel James Collins. He had come down the opposite corridor and was standing beside me. He was wearing a field uniform, green fatigues, muddied and still wet. On one hip was a canteen, on the other a holstered pistol. He carried a helmet. He wore boots, too, but had managed to come up beside me without my hearing him. There was something about him that reminded me of the jungle—other than his name—some quality of lissomeness and strength, and silence. Yet he didn't seem out of place in a hospital. He brought the jungle with him.

"Sure he will," I replied. "As soon as they let him stand up."

A chair crashed to the ground as five or six people tried at the same time to squeeze through the doorway between the waiting room and my inner office.

"I understand you have something you want to say to me, Doctor," Collins remarked quietly.

"Yes. It seems a little noisy here," I commented. "I was hoping we'd be able to speak privately."

"I was going to suggest that."

"I know the place." That late in the afternoon the roof would be empty.

The sun was spreading out along the horizon like melting gold. There were a couple of wispy clouds way up high, but otherwise, for a change, the sky was clear, a dark blue edging off to purple in the east. In the vault of the sky a transparent moon was aglow, faint counterpoint to the setting sun. The flock of birds that had wheeled overhead all day had taken up station south and east of the hospital, so far away they were barely visible, tiny specks. They were over Czechoslovakia, probably, but free, moved by their own inclination and by the wind. It was the same wind that swirled about us now at the edge of the roof, bringing with it from somewhere the smells of cooking and the sounds of music. The music may have been coming from a portable radio carried by a young woman proceeding along a path between the nursing residence and the hospital itself. Besides the music and the sough of the wind, there was another sound, a metallic creaking, a grinding, that I realized was The Monkeybars itself, bending in the wind. Indestructible, the damn thing seemed to be breathing.

"I've heard about this . . . this structure," Collins said, waving a hand at the maze of battered iron and cement. "The Monkeybars, right? People climb up it." He stared at it for a long moment and I wondered if he was thinking, as I was, that his son would never climb, not this thing, or anything. "It's bigger than I thought," Collins went on. "God, what a waste of time and energy. It's a symbol, I guess you could call it, in fact, a regular monument, to the folly of man."

"I think of it more as the folly of dermatologists."

"It reminds me, for some reason, of the cargo cults. Did you ever hear of the cargo plane cults in the South Pacific?"

"Uh, yeah . . . something."

Collins put a foot up against a stone parapet. "They are a very naive people," he said, "the natives who live on those islands, although perhaps no more naive than the rest of us. While I was there, I got to know some of them well. They live close to nature, nature being in this case a jungle, a patch of sand, and the ocean. They were friendly to me, even though I was tearing up their island at the time to lay down a landing strip. What they wanted out of life, as far as I could tell, is what we all want, food, a comfortable place to sleep, and a chance to get ahead. And, to tell the truth, they were interested in material possessions, more than you might think. Trousers, seat cushions, canned goods. Whatever they saw, they wanted. These things, they told me, represented the good life. At the same time they were religious. The missionaries had been around for some time, painting their own picture of the good life and speaking of God, from whom all good things come. For a while the natives listened attentively. After all, the missionaries ate a lot of canned goods, sat on cushions, and so on. So these naive people came to services regularly, religiously, you might say. . . ."

"But no canned peaches materialized on top of the altar."

"Exactly. Now, these natives didn't consider themselves naive. They were sharp enough to see that the priest who recommended that they pray to Christ would, nevertheless, sneak off himself every once in a while to the other end of the island where he would pray into a microphone to the Great Cargo Plane, which descended then out of the sky, bearing gifts, bringing the good life. Naturally, the whole tribe set off forthwith to clear a patch of jungle for their own landing strip. They went to a lot of trouble, like with this thing here. They erected a rickety landing tower. They whittled a microphone out of wood, and taking care to station themselves properly next to the field, as they had seen the priest do, they invoked the Great Cargo Plane. The image it conjures up is amusing, isn't it? All of these natives gathering every dusk to pray to this strange new god."

"Yeah . . . sort of."

"Unfortunately, after a time they became discouraged, depressed, even. I mean, when they realized that praying to the Great Cargo Plane was no better than praying to Christ. One man I had become friendly with killed himself. That's the trouble with life, isn't it. You're all set to laugh, and suddenly things aren't funny." Collins turned to face me. "Not that some people don't laugh anyway. There was an officer on the island, I remember, who thought it was very funny that my friend, the native, should kill himself over—as you put it—over some canned peaches. I didn't bother to explain. But you understand, I think. It wasn't that minor frustration that he couldn't live with. It was being made ridiculous. It was because that missionary was everything, and he was nothing. It was because of an idea. That's why someone kills himself, because of what he believes in. Or can no longer believe in."

"Does that bring up the subject of Sidney Konigsberg?" I asked.

"Does it? By the way, speaking of folly, we caught Bell with that porcelain. How did you know it was in his trunk?"

"I didn't know; but he had this goldfish bowl sitting on top of it, and he just didn't seem the sort of person who would keep a goldfish. Not unless it served a purpose."

"What purpose?"

"To distract. Anyway, the porcelain had to be around someplace. He didn't have time to get rid of it."

"Well, Fitch took it away with him this afternoon in a shopping bag. Also he took Bell. This is the man's second court-martial offense, so he'll probably get a couple of years in the stockade and a bad discharge. He's trying to make it easy on himself by cashing in Gutman. It seems he blames the general for his troubles. I understand we have you to thank for that, somehow. He called up the general and accused him of stealing everything but the Empire State Building. It's all there on tape. Gutman was arrested this afternoon too."

"I'm glad to hear it. I didn't like him."

"He always seemed okay to me. An ordinary officer, like the rest of us."

"You consider yourself an ordinary officer?"

"Of course." Collins seemed surprised that I should ask.

"Listen, Colonel, I wanted to talk to you about Sidney Konigsberg. Before I talk to the police, and before the police talk to you."

"I'm listening, Doctor, but . . . I wonder, can we sit down?" Collins pointed at the platform on the edge of the roof, from where only a few days ago I had watched The Monkeybar races with Lingeman. "It's been a long day. A long week," Collins said, echoing my thoughts, "and I'm tired. Besides . . ." he added, scratching his chin and smiling, "we can have a confidential conversation standing here, but scarcely a private one. Or a safe one. There are a half-dozen places—that building over there, for instance—from where someone could take a shot at you."

"I'm not worried about that anymore."

"Is that right?" Collins extended a leg over the edge of the roof and sat down on the platform. "Good. But suppose someone aimed at you and shot me by mistake?"

This was not going to be simple, I could see. I climbed clumsily onto the platform, shaking it, and sat down. We were, indeed, mostly out of sight now, covered by the overhang of The

Monkeybars and obscured by its limbs, hundreds of intersecting poles and crossbars, welded together, or cemented or plastered or whatever. Looking directly down through the scaffolding, four stories down, I could see a cat—as usual, a cat—staring up at me.

"Colonel, we don't have a lot of time . . ."

"Why is that? The missile crisis seems to be receding. The alert was called off a few hours ago, you know. What you may not know is, Penkovsky is still in place. Definitely. He was spotted at the Moscow ballet by one of our own people, who followed him home—actually to an apartment where he's been holed up apparently with a dancer. That's why we couldn't pick up on him earlier. He hasn't been coming home to his own apartment. Anyway, they followed him around for a day or two; and he's clean. His associates in the KGB have no interest in him, except as a drinking buddy. We were able to corroborate that from another source. So, how come Konigsberg wrote Penkovsky's name on a laundry ticket is not exactly clear."

"It had nothing to do with Penkovsky."

"What?"

"He didn't write PENK. He wrote PLMS, which is just what it looked like. And he wasn't writing a secret message on a laundry ticket, which never made any sense, he was writing a message about his laundry. Pickup Laundry Monday Soonest—that's what those letters stood for."

Collins stared at me.

"He wanted to remind himself that he was running out of clean clothes," I explained. "That's all."

"What makes you think so?"

"Because I could see for myself. I went through his bureau. No clean clothes. And because the damn laundry was only open Monday and Thursday mornings."

"Well . . . if Penkovsky doesn't come into this business anywhere, why was somebody shooting at you? And what were all those clandestine meetings all about? Berlin and Waldheim and . . . The smuggling? You think it's because of the smuggling? Smugglers don't always get along. I suppose somebody could have decided to get rid of Konigsberg, and take you along for good measure, just in case the lieutenant confided . . ."

"Listen, Colonel, like I said, I don't have time for this, or the patience. Konigsberg wasn't killed because he was smuggling, and—"

"What makes you think he was killed at all? When I got your message, Fitch happened to be standing next to me. I asked him, and he didn't seem to know what you were talking about. He—"

"Fitch was there?" I interrupted sharply. "Does he know . . . he didn't follow you here, did he?"

"No. I think he went off to talk to the German police about something. Frankly, he didn't seem interested in any theories you might have. In fact, I had the feeling he was no longer interested at all in finding out what happened to Konigsberg. The lieutenant was only important, you see, because of Penkovsky."

"That's wrong. Konigsberg was important to a hell of a lot of people. He was important to your daughter, wasn't he?"

For a long moment Collins studied me. "I told you, I think, that Sandra did not know Konigsberg," he said finally. "She was very young, and I kept her away from the company of soldiers. As much as I could."

"So you said. But things didn't work out just that way. Certainly she was not as innocent as you thought. She was pregnant when she died."

The sun was halfway over the horizon. Long shadows were stretching out across the landscape, fading the fall colors. Similarly, a darkness had descended over Collins. The western sky lay behind him, and his face was in shadow. But even in silhouette, he was visibly angry. It was a silent, yet fierce, rage, evidenced by no particular movement or posture, but there nevertheless.

"I think," he said, "it would be best now if you come to the point."

"Yes. First let me say, Colonel, that I asked to see you today with a particular purpose in mind. Having failed, first, to help your daughter and then failed again when Konigsberg came to me for help, I would like to be able now, before it's too late, to help you at least, if you will let me. Sidney Konigsberg did know your daughter. They wanted to marry. You had some objection. I don't know what it was. Certainly Sandra was very young. If soldiers in general did not seem to you to make good husbands, Konigsberg, who, after all, was engaged a minute before to someone else—as far as anyone knew—must have seemed particularly undesirable. You said no. You were in a position to say no, not so much because Sandra was a minor—I understand there are ways around that here in Europe—but because Konigsberg was in your command. He needed your permission to marry. That was why he came to see me. The suicidal threat was an excuse, although, God knows, he was upset. Between one thing and another. He wanted to get into medical channels. Circumventing regulations, as everybody knows, is the principal useful function of army psychiatry. Or maybe he just wanted to ask advice. I never got to find out. When you learned that Sandra had died from an abortion, you killed him."

"Is that so?" commented Collins wryly. "I was beginning to get the idea that's what you were building up to. So tell me, what makes you think so? For the moment let's not talk about the fact that I happened to be on the other end of a telephone when Konigsberg disappeared."

"Okay. A couple of things. That they knew each other I heard about from a couple of sources. For one, your baby-sitter, George George."

"Oh, for God's sake. If you talked with George for a few minutes, you should have noticed the kid has a kind of active imagination. . . ."

"He can turn it on and off when he wants to, and I can tell when he wants to. You know, he was a good friend to your daughter, even though he's only a kid; and she confided in him. Besides, he was hanging around the house enough to see for himself."

"Go ahead," Collins snapped.

"They met, Sandra and the lieutenant, at one of the base parties. Randy Biddle saw them together, and so did a couple of other people. Not you, I guess. I think you were off at the time at one of the other bases. And from then on they were discreet. They knew how to be discreet. Sandra had to be. Because of you. George George say it's because you're just naturally a bastard; but I think I know better. Maybe you were trying to do in your spare time what you thought a mother should be doing full time. Or maybe you were just naturally overprotective. And, after all, she was very young. And there had been other men. I think you know that. As for Konigsberg, he had his own reasons to be circumspect. Uh . . . the smuggling, for one thing. In fact, it's remarkable considering . . . what he had on his mind that he allowed himself to fall in love at all. Maybe that's a stupid way of putting it. Love happens sometimes like a bad accident. You can't get out of the way in time.

"They met frequently in the evenings. Konigsberg snuck off base to see General Gutman, then snuck away from Gutman to see your daughter, who lived luckily—unluckily, I suppose—a couple of blocks away. This is all according to George George, who tells me also they got formally engaged a couple of weeks ago in a ceremony he was witness to. Over a cupcake. I don't think the kid could have made up that story, Colonel. Not a cupcake."

Collins didn't say anything; so, after a moment, I went on.

"All of that sounds kind of like they were in a rush, doesn't it? After all, they didn't know each other very long. A matter of no more than five or six weeks, isn't that right?"

"Go ahead, Doctor," Collins said impatiently. "You're telling this story."

"Probably Sandra should have told you right away; but she was afraid of you. I don't think that comes as a surprise to you. You intimated something of the sort, I think, when we first spoke. You have a reputation, Colonel, as a strict and in some ways a stern man—certainly a stern commander. Even Konigsberg seems to have hesitated a few days before asking to see you. He must have been concerned that you would respond simply by transferring him. He had reasons, more than one, to want to remain at Waldheim. Or, maybe, army routine being what it is, it just took a couple of days to get an appointment. But he did see you finally. A couple of weeks ago. You were outraged at first. He said he wanted to marry Sandra, and you began to yell at him. For a minute or two. Then, being a sensible man, you told him you would have to speak to Sandra first before even considering giving your consent to a marriage; and, in any case, they were going to have to wait. They were both too young to get married. And you made Konigsberg promise in the meantime not to mention his relationship to Sandra to anyone else."

"By this account, Konigsberg was evidently not a man to keep his word. Otherwise you would have no way of knowing any of this."

"Well, of course he reported the conversation to Sandra, who mentioned it to George. The kid is trustworthy. Even after she died he kept quiet. He only told me when he found out who I was. He knew this was something Konigsberg intended to tell me, you remember. Come to think of it, maybe that was why the lieutenant came to see me. Maybe he wanted my professional advice on how to deal with you."

"I see. You think I'm a little crazy, is that it, Dr. Redden?"

"We'll get to that in a few minutes."

"Good. So far all I've heard is the fairy-tale account of a fourteen-year-old kid."

"Well, not really. The walls of your office are so thin I thought I'd ask Sergeant Kraven if he heard and remembered anything from your interview with Konigsberg; and, guess what, he did. It seemed so out of character for you to raise your voice, he found himself listening. He's very discreet too. He kept his mouth shut all this time, giving you what he calls the benefit of the doubt; but when it was obvious I knew pretty much about the conversation anyway, he confirmed it.

"In any case, Konigsberg did not wait for your consent. He scheduled an appointment to see Wormley. But waiting even a week was too long. The reason he was in a rush is obvious now, I guess. Sandra was pregnant. There wasn't time for them to grow up, or to convince you they were already grown up. So he told somebody he was suicidal and came in as an emergency to see me. Maybe it was an emergency. He was becoming frantic. Sandra was so worried about him, she tried to call me herself. I didn't get the message until too late."

"Yes, he told me he was suicidal," Collins said. "He came in and said that to my face. I was some sort of maneuver, I knew that. But if any soldier in my command asks to see a doctor, I'll see to it."

"So you sent him along, but with Kraven in tow, so there was never any chance to talk. . . ."

"That was regulations. It had nothing to do with me. I didn't really give a damn what he said. Besides . . . later on that day I found out Sandra was missing. After that I didn't spend a hell of a lot of time worrying about Konigsberg."

"Not until after you found out she was dead. Then there wasn't time for anything else. You didn't even bother . . . You never saw the postmortem report, did you?"

"Huh? No. Why? I knew what she died from. An abortion, right? And from innocence. That's how people die. From trusting other people."

I sat there wondering if there was ever a time that Collins had been trusting and innocent. "So you came to my office that morning," I said, "grieving. That much was plain. You looked numb. But you wanted to know if Sandra had said anything to me before dying. It seemed very important to you. I thought maybe you wanted to know who had made her pregnant. Or who had performed the abortion. Except that you said you weren't interested in that. That was such a reasonable point of view, I believed you. But I've come to know you better since then. You're not a reasonable man, Colonel. Not that way."

"I don't know why I bothered to ask. I didn't need to ask who it was. Not really. I already knew," Collins said, evidently no longer pretending to a total ignorance of what I was talking about.

"How come?"

"Who else could it have been? And besides, he really told me himself, I realized when I thought back on it. He was talking that day a couple of weeks ago about how things happened to young people sometimes; and how it was better to rush into things sometimes than wait too long. I didn't know what the hell he was talking about at the time, although I didn't like the sound of it. Later on it was clear enough."

"Yeah, I guess. But if he knocked her up and wanted to marry her, why would he send her to an abortionist?"

"It doesn't matter if he sent her. Suppose she went on her own, he was still responsible, wasn't he? A person is supposed to be responsible, isn't he, for his actions, and for the consequences of his actions?"

"Yes. The problem is figuring out who's responsible for what."

"But saying he deserved to die," Collins pointed out, "doesn't mean I killed him."

"You must have made up your mind to kill him only then, that morning," I went on, leaning up against a metal cast support. "The way he disappeared, no one could have planned it ahead of time. He could not have planned it himself. But after you left my office, you remembered he had an appointment to see me. So you waited downstairs; and you talked him into walking off with

you. No trick to that, I guess. You ordered him to come, and he
went. . . ."

"I was at the other end of a telephone line," Collins retorted.
"You remember, I was talking to Kraven at the time."

"Yes, I remember. You were at the other end of a telephone
line. That's a terrific alibi. At least that's the way it seemed to
me at first. Actually you weren't really talking to Kraven though,
were you? Not according to the sergeant. You asked to be put
through to him. You wanted to talk to him privately, you said;
but when he came on the line, all you told him was to hang on.
You had something important to say to him. Then . . . you had
nothing to say."

"We were disconnected."

"Kraven says he hung on until he heard coins drop and an operator come on the line asking for more money. You were calling
from a pay phone—a particular pay phone, the one in the hospital lobby opposite the sergeant major's office. You can see right
from the telephone booth straight into the office. I only noticed a
couple of days ago.

"While Kraven was holding onto the telephone in the inner
office, you walked away with Konigsberg. And you killed him.
Probably you didn't even bother to confront him with the abortion, right? Maybe you didn't even mention that Sandra was
dead. You didn't explain, and you didn't ask him to explain. You
just hit him over the head, or slit his throat, whatever it is that
you do; and then you buried him someplace in the forest where,
like you said, nobody would ever find him."

I looked over to Collins, who remained silent and still, a
statue. Suddenly there was a loud cawing as a bird flew near The
Monkeybars, then, catching sight of us, careened away.

"I suppose at some point you stopped to think," I said, leaning
back against the parapet. "It probably occurred to you that the
coincidence of a young lieutenant under your command disappearing the same day your daughter was killed would strike
someone as . . . well, as too much of a coincidence. So you
started taking potshots at me. Shooting me would only make
sense, as you pointed out yourself a couple of times, if someone
was worried about what Konigsberg might have said to me. It
would seem then that Konigsberg had been abducted because of
secret information he possessed. It didn't matter what kind of se-

cret information. The inside story on a smuggling ring would do just as well as Russian troop movements. Actually, you didn't shoot exactly at me, sort of near me. Sometimes very near, since I was a little slow to notice. Too near. Anyone who was a good enough shot to come within inches of me over and over again was good enough to hit me if he really wanted to. Somebody was making a point and kept it up just long enough for me to catch on. Then I remembered, you are a rifle marksman.

"Of course, that Penkovsky business fit in nicely. If the Russians knew what was going on, they might very well have considered kidnapping him. And just to muddy the waters a little more, you invented that guy with the super-curly hair. While they were looking for him, they wouldn't be looking for you. That was going a little too far, I think. In fact, I think that's the problem with you, Colonel. You go a little too far."

"Are you saying all this, Doctor, because someone claims to have seen me when I was . . . uh, carrying Konigsberg off, or . . . disposing of him? The police have discovered his body?"

"No, not yet."

"Well, then I don't see why I should take any of this seriously. You have a lot of peculiar ideas. No witnesses, no evidence. Not even a body. There is no proof that Konigsberg is dead, let alone that I killed him."

"You lied about Konigsberg knowing your daughter. Once I explain that to Fitch, along with all the rest of this, he's going to start tracking your movements that day. Sooner or later he's going to find somebody who did see you with the lieutenant, or maybe saw you shooting at me. And after that, if I read Fitch right, he's going to dig up every inch of forest between here and Waldheim. And in the end he's going to find Konigsberg's body wherever you buried it."

Collins looked out into the gathering dusk. A sudden breeze picked up his collar. From somewhere came the sound of a child crying. Nearer, from one of the rooms below, someone laughed, a raucous noise, not very different from the crow's cawing.

"You haven't said anything about this to Fitch?" he asked.

"Nope. Not yet."

"Don't you think you should be worried a little?" Collins said, turning back to me, smiling faintly. "I have a gun, after all. Suppose I decided Fitch couldn't figure out all of this on his own.

Aren't I likely, you think, to shoot you in order to cover my tracks? Or maybe just push you off this thing. One good shake would do it."

Suddenly, Collins shoved at the masonry behind him, and the whole platform came away from the wall. It moved only a few inches before striking the restraining superstructure of The Monkeybars, but struck hard enough to turn us halfway upside down. I grabbed a bit of plumbing and hung for a moment stretched out across empty space before Collins, chuckling malignly, reached out to me. He held me out there for an extra moment, still laughing, before pulling me back. It was the sound of the jungle again, cruel and unfathomable, and unexpected. I held tightly to the edges of the still-shuddering platform, my breath taken away more by the casual rage of the man sitting next to me, than by the nearness of death. He moved back to the edge of the platform and watched me coldly—the big cat at bay.

"Well," I said at length, "putting aside considerations of your getting caught—the fact that it is known that you came here to see me, the fact that someone might look up and catch you in the act this time, and so on—I don't think you can kill me. I don't mean, of course, that you can't manage it physically. Probably if we started a log-rolling contest up here, you would win. And the gun, I grant you, settles the matter. And certainly I know you're not too squeamish to kill. But you only kill people who have done you an injury. Right? A personal injury. Of course, you're a man who takes things personally, like when a couple of your troops get ambushed by a Japanese patrol. Still, I never did anything to you. In fact, the reason I'm here now, as I just said, is because I want to help you."

"What do you have in mind?"

"Look," I said, drawing closer, "the way Konigsberg got killed is suggestive of . . . well, let me say it this way. You were up all that night looking for your daughter, distraught naturally, more than distraught, half out of your head with worry. Then you found out she was killed, not just killed but butchered by some back-alley abortionist. You didn't even know she was pregnant. A seventeen-year-old girl. Suddenly you put two and two together, and it came to you who was really responsible. Somebody had been seeing her secretly—you had just found out—and was exploiting her obviously. Then you look up, and he's there.

Right in front of you. On the spur of the moment, you make up a strategem to get him alone. Then, when you are alone with him, crazed, in a sudden irresistible impulse, you kill him."

"Doctor . . ."

"Don't you see, if you turn yourself in now, before anyone suspects you, they will believe you. You tell them you didn't know what you were doing. You just now came to your senses."

"Doctor, you were very anxious to help Konigsberg. Why are you anxious now to help somebody who you think is his murderer? You don't think I should be punished?"

"What good would that do? Teach you a lesson? You don't have any more daughters to avenge. Besides, there's some justice in a plea of temporary insanity. That defense was intended for this sort of thing, a crazy and sudden act of violence."

"Is that what you think, Doctor? You think I'm crazy?"

"What difference does it make what I think? God knows, you'll have the sympathy of the jury."

"Somebody—a psychiatrist—is going to have to testify in court that I was crazy. Are you willing to do that?"

"Sure, why not?"

"Sorry," Collins remarked calmly. "I don't see myself spending a couple of years in a mental institution."

"A couple of months on a psychiatric service, that's all. Back home. Remember, we're talking about *temporary* insanity. Besides . . . you'll be safer there."

"Safer? Why? Is someone out to get me?"

The danger I was concerned about was from himself; but I couldn't explain that to him. I was afraid that if I told him the truth, he would throw himself off the roof. Insane or not, he was surely impulsive, a dangerously impulsive man.

"It doesn't matter," Collins said, annoyed suddenly. "My God, you presume to know something about my character, what is possible for me and impossible. Do you think I could cop a plea? Do you think I would do something, then get out of the consequences by lying? By pretending to be crazy? Is that what you think?"

He stared at me, and I at him, astonished.

"Your . . . your son," I stammered. "I was thinking of your son."

I don't know what made me realize that Fitch was present,

some objectional smell, perhaps, among the other smells of afternoon. I looked up, and there he was in the flesh, the cigar, the crooked smile. He was standing on the roof, hands in his pockets, one leg up on an overturned pail.

"How'd you get up here, Fitch?" I asked.

"I walked up the stairs. Wasn't that clever of me? I knew you guys were up here, so I thought I'd join you."

"Were you listening to our conversation, Mr. Fitch?" Collins asked, dusting himself off. He had climbed back to the roof proper. I followed him.

"Yeah. Don't worry though. I didn't hear anything incriminating. Just a lot of theories."

"Then why are you pointing that pistol at me?"

Fitch had withdrawn his big black gun from a pocket and was, indeed, pointing it at the colonel.

"What now, Fitch?" I asked. "I thought that was an antitank weapon."

"I don't like people pointing guns at me," Collins said quietly.

"Isn't that too fucking bad," replied the policeman, as congenial as ever.

"Wait a second . . ." I said.

"Shut up," said Fitch.

"If I'm being arrested . . ."

"You too," said Fitch.

". . . for Konigsberg's murder," the colonel went on, "you better make sure—"

"I told you to shut the fuck up!" Fitch screamed.

Collins stared at Fitch as if he were a small, sharp-toothed animal that had just sprung out of a hole. Then he began walking toward him.

"Wait a second . . ." I said, grabbing his arm before he meandered across the narrow and apparently shrinking limits of Fitch's self-control.

"I suppose you think that's funny," Fitch remarked ambiguously to Collins, who was not laughing, "that I should run around looking for—how did you put it—'a man with a halo of curly hair and freckles.' That's very funny. I don't mind your killing Konigsberg, if that's what you did; but I don't like being played for a sucker. Well, I get the satisfaction of taking you in.

You'll only get ten or twenty years, I figure, but that's something. And sending you a card every Christmas will cheer me up."

"Listen," I whispered to Collins, "it's not too late. You can tell them you confessed to me . . ."

"Shut your mouth, you," Fitch squealed, his voice cracking, "I had enough of you. And this doesn't have anything to do with Konigsberg, so you can forget that. Or maybe Konigsberg does figure in, but not so it matters. I'm arresting you, Collins, for the premeditated murder of Ursula Burgholz."

I looked over to Collins, who was standing motionless, then at Fitch. The detective coughed a baby's cough, feeble and delicate, more like a hiccup.

"Who the hell is Ursula Burgholz?" I asked.

"She's this fat woman, a regular pig, who used to sell buttons in a button store," Fitch said, "and in the back, up on a cot, she'd fix up ladies who got themselves in trouble—maybe *ladies* is not exactly the right word—whores, most of them, like this guy's daughter, who fucked once too often, or carelessly. Used to sell buttons, I said, because a few days ago the colonel here coaxed her out of the button shop and then slit her throat from ear to ear. He was mad at her, you see, because of the abortion. He really gets mad when he gets mad. Probably if he had found the knitting needles she used, he would have broken them up in little pieces."

"The abortionist?" I said. "I thought she died of pneumonia."

"It was a convenient story. Better than telling the German press the polizei were looking for a U.S. colonel who was seen dumping the body of a German national in the woods. Even if she was a pig."

"Is this another theory or . . ." Collins began.

"There was a witness. A young guy was peeking out of a barn a few miles down the road. With binoculars. He was looking for birds, but he saw you—carrying a duffel bag into the woods. Bad luck for you, but then again, you couldn't expect to go around dumping bodies every other day without someone catching a glimpse of you. Of course, it was only a glimpse. You were wearing civilian clothes, mostly German, except for a hooded sweater. Not easy to see your face. So the young man looks closer. He sees U.S. Army shoes. A U.S. Army duffel bag and army shoes are kind of suspicious for someone dressed otherwise like a German. A sloppy mistake. Not what I'd expect from you. But I figure maybe you were upset. I don't know . . ." Fitch said, looking at Collins with dissatisfaction, "do you get upset? Look at this guy, Redden, he doesn't bat an eye. I just told him he's going to go to jail, maybe for a very long time, and he just stands there. His daughter died just a few days ago, but you'd never know from looking at him. Maybe he just doesn't give a shit about any of this. . . ."

"Hey, c'mon, Fitch!" I said hurriedly. "There's no reason . . ."

"I mean, I know he was *offended* by someone chopping up his daughter," Fitch drawled. "I know that just must have set his teeth *on edge*. But he didn't even miss a day of work. I mean, I got a daughter too. I think I might feel *something*, if someone killed her . . ."

"My God, Fitch," I yelled, "you're so full of it—"

". . . but no, as soon as he evened things out—balanced the books, you know—that's all he cared about. Then it's business as usual."

"I think for some reason Mr. Fitch is trying to annoy me," Collins said, trying to smile. His voice was low, but steady.

"Well, I don't know," Fitch remarked, the drawl getting more exaggerated, "seems to me I'm the one who might feel annoyed. Me and the U.S. Army too. Maybe the whole country . . ."

"I think maybe that young man with the binoculars couldn't see well enough to make an identification," Collins said. "I think if there was a very good case against me, Mr. Fitch here wouldn't be trying to goad me into jumping him. Shooting me is less chancy, I guess, than risking a court-martial."

"Oh yeah?" said Fitch, snarling and coughing, and chuckling too.

He was the only guy I knew who could snarl, cough, chuckle, sneer, and smoke a cigar, all at the same time. "I'll tell you how strong the case is. We got this young man who sees well enough to pick your picture out from a dozen other West Point grads. We got the duffel bag from the city garbage, where you dumped it. It got the lady's bloodstains all over and inside a torn little piece of paper from off your hometown newspaper. You must have carried that around in there since World War Two. Also, your car, which I have just removed from in front of the hospital, and which has mud all over the license plate, seems to have a couple of nice bloodstains inside the trunk. No analysis yet, but I suspect this bloodstain is a clue. If it turns out you were just carrying around a juicy side of beef back there, then you got nothing to worry about—on that score. But there are a couple other things. It turns out when we show your picture around, a neighbor of the pig lady can place you at the button store talking to her—to the *live* Frau Burgholz and . . ."

"You've been doing a lot of checking since I saw you a couple of hours ago," Collins remarked.

"Not just a couple of hours. Her body turned up yesterday. And not just me. Which is the trouble. The German police. Nobody had any trouble guessing who did it. You're the only guy in the neighborhood who likes to slice people up from ear to ear. And you had a motive. From then on it was just putting the pieces together. Digging the knife out of the garbage, etc. You could have at least took the time to bury her. You tucked the lieutenant away somewhere, didn't you?"

"A woman like that doesn't deserve burial," said Collins casually. "I'm surprised anyone cares. You know, my daughter . . . she left my daughter in the woods. Bleeding to death. Slowly. In the rain."

"Yeah, so she was a bitch," Fitch agreed brusquely. "So no one will miss her except a couple of whores. What I care is, a messy murder like this committed by an American officer on a German national. Fuchs tells me the Germans are taking jurisdiction under the new status of forces agreement. I get the privilege of arresting you, he gets to try you. What a circus that's going to be," Fitch commented wryly, turning to me. "Can't you see the headlines: 'American slashes elderly German citizen.' Wait'll they get ahold of his war record. The East Germans are going to love that. 'Known American war criminal kills again—an example of brutal occupation.' You're a real credit to the United States Army, Colonel. And all because of some *tramp* who was fucking around when she should have been in school."

"Listen," I said, grabbing Collins's arm, "don't pay any attention to this schmuck. This is the way he is all the time. What I said before is still good. Except it goes double now. . . . Instead of being insane for a couple of hours, you're insane for a couple of days. You have to tell them . . ."

"Sounds like you really do have a pretty good case, Mr. Fitch," Collins said, standing away from me. He was smiling again, no longer the jungle cat though. It was as if under the sudden ferocity there was some element of grace, even graciousness. Suddenly he seemed to me only a middle-aged man dressed up inexplicably in a combat uniform. "But . . . uh," he said, "aren't you afraid I might get desperate and jump you? I have a gun, you know."

"Go ahead," said Fitch, grinning wickedly, "you'll save everybody a lot of trouble and embarrassment. I'll put about three holes in you before you even get that gun out." He laughed, a ratchety sound ending in a cough. "If self-defense doesn't hold up, I can always claim temporary insanity."

"Suppose you missed the first three shots? I can move pretty fast when I want to."

"What do you say we find out? I'm willing to take my chances."

Collins put a hand on my shoulder and shoved me farther away.

"Colonel, for God's sake!" I said. "Can't you see he's doing this purposely! He wants an excuse to shoot you. You might as well commit suicide."

I turned to Fitch. "I don't know why you waited this long," I said. "How come you don't just shoot him down in cold blood."

"Because I'm hoping you're going to step between us, and I can accidentally shoot your head off at the same time!" Fitch snapped back. "You asshole!"

Collins nodded. "Probably it would be a good idea for you to step a little farther away, Dr. Redden," he said. "I'm not sure what this man is capable of."

"I'm not going anywhere . . ." I started to say.

Suddenly Collins grabbed me, on the chest somewhere, or on the shoulder. I tried to ward him off with an arm, but somehow —it happened so fast I couldn't tell just how—I was yanked or tripped into the air. I landed a few feet away on my ass, from which out-of-the-way vantage I was able to follow clearly, but not influence, events.

Slowly, as if in slow motion, smiling sardonically, Colonel Collins reached for his gun.

"You understand, Colonel," Fitch said carefully, the edge gone from his voice, "I'm here to arrest you. That's what I've come for. If you surrender, I'm going to turn you over to Fuchs. Then I'm out of it."

Collins unbuttoned the flap of his gun holster.

"But if you take out that gun," Fitch went on, "I'm going to kill you."

"Colonel, don't!" I yelled.

But methodically, no sudden moves now, Collins took out his weapon and brought it up. Fitch waited longer than I thought he would. It seemed painfully long. Forever. But in the end, he shot him. There were two explosions, and Collins was propelled —he seemed to leap—backward. He dropped his gun and grabbed his stomach. Then, as he staggered back toward the edge of the roof, he grabbed at a parapet. Then, before I could reach him, he toppled over.

He did not fall all the way to the ground. He landed on The Monkeybars, about fifteen feet down, ironically, on a stretcher that was serving as a brace between two towers of gnarled and tangled plumbing. One leg was caught beneath him. His arms were thrown out widely. He looked like a spider, a broken, shriveled spider tangled into the web of The Monkeybars. His shirt was torn and bloody from one side to the other, and the stain was widening.

"Hold on," said Fitch, grabbing the sleeve of my lab coat. "Where do you think you're going?"

"He's still alive. Let go." I slipped out of the coat and got back onto the platform before Fitch pulled me back by the hair. "He's alive, Goddamn it!" I cried out. "Let go of me!"

"Don't bother. I figure he'll last about another minute and a half."

"Let go of me, you bastard!" I was losing my second wrestling match in the last couple of minutes. Fitch had me off balance, and every time I tried to get up he bounced my head off the side of the building.

"Stay put!" Fitch said, grabbing a fresh handful of hair to re-place what had come loose. "You start climbing that thing the way you're coordinated, you'll land on your head."

"You'd like to take care of me yourself, Fitch? With the gun?" I managed to say between grunts. "Like you . . . like you just took care of Collins?"

"Take it easy, kid," Fitch said calmly in my ear. He was trying to relax me by applying a stranglehold. "It's all over now; and it's better this way. I saved everyone a lot of trouble. He understood that. Besides, I didn't have any choice. You saw." Suddenly Fitch let go of me. The platform was rocking so hard, I had to grab a pole with both hands to keep from falling over.

"You might as well stay here," Fitch said. "Somebody else is going after him."

I looked down. There was a crowd gathered at the foot of the Monkeybars. They were watching as two and then three men started to climb. The Colonel, I could see peering down between the slats of the platform, was still bleeding, but still breathing too. In fact, he seemed to be conscious. He was grimacing with pain, and with one clenched hand, he pulled feebly on his shirt.

"They're not going to get to him in time," I said.

"It's better this way. This is the way he wanted it."

"Bullshit. You were bugging him. You wanted him to lose control so you had an excuse to shoot him. And you managed it. Congratulations."

A murmur rose up from the crowd. A soldier—Lingeman, I realized with a shock—was standing on a window ledge of the third floor. At that level, the Monkeybars tilted three or four feet away from the building. He stood there with his arms spread wide, filling the window. He was looking down, thinking God knows what terrible thoughts. Then he looked across at the wounded man lying no more than a dozen feet below him, but beyond a huge knot of broken pipes and twisted girders. Then, without hesitation, this man who was afraid of heights leaped through space to the Monkeybars. By some awful mischance, he missed his hold and fell momentarily, but just momentarily, grabbing the cemented end of a torn metal bed railing. He dangled there briefly before pulling himself across to a thin wooden ledge. From there, carefully, he made his way over to the colonel.

Collins seemed suddenly to come back to life a little. He propped himself up on an elbow and looked down at his abdomen, curiously, as if something interesting could be seen inside those torn and shattered muscles, dispassionately, as if it were someone else's wound he was examining. Before falling back, he peered over the edge of the stretcher. Then he looked up at me.

He smiled. In that moment of despair—what could have been despair—unmistakably, he smiled; and, arms out, he shrugged in a half-amused gesture of embarrassment and apology, and surrender. Then he caught sight of Lingeman, almost within reach of him, in fact, already reaching out to him. Collins seemed to say something to the sergeant. I saw his lips move, and again he smiled. Then abruptly he pushed himself off the stretcher. Falling, he struck his head on a sheet of metal, then, very hard, sickeningly, against a metal crosspiece. Then he was on the ground. The crowd, which had parted when his flailing body came down in their midst, surged back to examine him. He was out of my view; but, of course, he was dead.

"Lose control, did you say?" Fitch commented idly. "That guy didn't do anything in his whole life he didn't intend to do."

Schulz seemed pleased to find me waiting in his room. "Hey, buddy," he said enthusiastically, "just the guy I was looking for. I knocked on your door, but you weren't there—which I can see makes perfect sense since you're here. But how'd you get in? Did I leave the door open? I'm always doing that. Uh oh . . ." he said, going quickly over to a bureau and rummaging around in a drawer. He pulled out a crumpled T-shirt, which he held aloft in triumph. "Aha!" he exclaimed. "Safe. Hee. Hee. Hee," he added in a high-pitched, tremulous voice, caressing the T-shirt like a miser fondling a bag of gold. He unrolled the shirt on the desk, uncovering a number of thin cigarettes, which he counted carefully.

"The stash," he whispered.

"Why were you looking for me?" I asked.

"The orgy. You're invited to the orgy. It's a small intimate affair, six or eight people. Men and women only. Heh, heh. By that I don't mean we're excluding horses. I mean couples only. Heterosexual couples. There was some resistance, I'm afraid, when I mentioned your name. I hate to be the one to tell you, but in only three or four short months around here, you've picked up a sorry reputation. One middle-aged but buxom lady from the blood bank, I think, or maybe dietary, went so far as to nominate you for 'Man of the Year Least Likely to Be Fun at an Orgy.' *Stodgy* is the word. But don't you worry, old buddy," Schulz said reassuringly, punching me lightly on the shoulder to keep my spirits up, "I told them I could see beneath that scabby, scaly exterior you present to the world, all crusted over with stodge and stuffy, to the true Abe Redden underneath. Lust, I told them. Inside you got all this naked lust." He illustrated my lust by hanging his tongue out and panting. "And then I told them about Krista, and that settled it. You're invited to Orgy Venerium Sensualis: Number II, Bavarian style. Only you got to bring her along."

"The last time I spoke to Krista, she was not about to go anywhere with me, least of all an orgy."

"Oh, darn it. Someone like Krista can make all the difference at an orgy. Sorry, buddy, maybe next time." Another encouraging punch to the shoulder. "Hey, what's that?" he said.

I was holding the silver-framed photograph featuring Schulz, his fiancée, and the mink coat.

"I wish you'd stop looking at that," he complained, taking the picture away and putting it back where I had found it, under a pile of books on his desk.

"Why?" I asked curiously. "Does it make you feel guilty?"

"No, it doesn't make me feel guilty," Schulz repeated after me in a whine, annoyed. "It makes me . . ." He made a face. "You have this unpleasant look all the time, like you're . . . like you're thinking. It makes me uneasy. Why aren't you smiling? You're not supposed to . . . *think* all the time, you know."

"Sorry."

"Well, that's all right," Schulz remarked tolerantly. "Listen, I got to change now for the orgy."

Schulz held up a bright yellow T-shirt with the words THIS WAY embroidered on the front along with an arrow that pointed, I could see, in the right direction. "Suave, right?" he said.

"Did you hear what happened at the hospital this afternoon?" I asked.

"Huh? What?"

"Collins. Colonel Collins was killed."

"Oh, yeah . . . I heard something. He fell off The Monkeybars. Or jumped or . . ."

"That's right. Actually, he fell and jumped."

"Is that right? Tricky." Schulz opened up his closet and took out a clean shirt.

"It turned out all that time we were chasing after Konigsberg, he was already dead. Collins killed him for knocking up his daughter, then buried him someplace."

"Yeah, I heard. Sort of a Victorian attitude."

I nodded. "Did you ever run into him—Collins—when you were attached to 3rd Division?"

"No. I heard he was freaky, so I stayed away."

"But you knew his daughter."

Schulz looked up at me. "The lady we were just talking about? With the abortion? I told you, I didn't know her."

"I know, but you were lying. You met her the first time back in August when she showed up on sick call. She had a strep throat. I had Randy Biddle, the medical corpsman at the Waldheim base, pull her records."

"That's possible. I told you, I don't always remember . . ."

"Yeah, I know. You don't remember every patient you see. But this one you would remember. A pretty girl to start off with. You're a connoisseur, right? Or, how did you put it—you're a 'consumer.' Besides, you had her come back three days in a row for follow-up. That's sort of conservative treatment for a strep throat."

"She had big glands. I remember her now. You can't be too safe with a strep throat, you know. If you don't watch it, it turns into rheumatic fever, maybe, or glomerulonephritis."

"Then to play it really safe, I guess, you started showing up at her house—when the colonel was away, of course—and . . ."

"Hey, where'd you get that from? I never went to her house and . . ."

"Listen, Bob. Please don't give me that shit. I've been fencing all day with people, and I'm tired of it." I was tired of everything. Just plain tired. "I had an idea," I said, catching my breath, "you were probably hanging around Sandra Collins when I heard her kid brother going 'buddy, buddy' all the time. You're the only guy I know who is buddying everybody all the time. He must have picked it up from . . ."

"Oh, terrific. That's really airtight evidence you got there," Schulz said sarcastically, waving his T-shirt around.

". . . finally, I got around to talking to George George, the baby-sitter. He saw you there a half-dozen times. I know you told him your name was Smith, but the kid has a nosy streak, and he went through your wallet one day. It seems you left your pants on the kitchen table while you were checking on the girl's swollen glands."

Schulz sat down next to his desk. For a moment he played idly with a few coins. "What is all this, Abe?" he said, looking up at me finally. "Sandra is dead. Konigsberg and now Collins, himself, are dead. What difference does it make whether I knew her or not?"

"It doesn't make any difference to you," I asked, "that Konigsberg was killed because of what you did? He didn't get Sandra Collins pregnant. You did."

"Who says?"

"Well, she was three months pregnant when she died. Konigsberg was only over here about a month and a half. He couldn't have impregnated her. He was back in Indiana at the time. Collins would have realized that—that she was too far along—if he had bothered to check the autopsy report; but he had his mind made up already. The lieutenant was seeing his daughter on the sly; so obviously he was to blame."

"So it wasn't Konigsberg. Why me? Sure I knew her. So did half a dozen other guys. Sure I tried to keep it quiet. Her screwball father didn't approve of her dating soldiers; and he was in a position to make trouble. I was already in trouble, remember, for pissing on the flagpole."

"Jesus Christ. She was seventeen. What are you, twenty-seven, twenty-eight?"

"Oh, for God's sake. You're against fornication. Hey, maybe she was seventeen, but I was not the first guy she ever went to bed with. That's what she did in her spare time."

"No, not the first; but back three months ago, you were the only one."

"How do you know?"

"Because that's what she said. She told a friend of hers. The kid. And she told Konigsberg. It didn't matter to him. All he wanted was to marry her. But there wasn't time."

"Maybe that's what she said, but that doesn't make it true. Shit. She told me the same story, as it happens; but so what. I don't know if she was pregnant by me or not, so you sure as hell don't know."

"You knew. And Jungle Jim Collins would have been convinced, too, if I had told him. . . . Of course, I couldn't tell him anything. He was likely to jump off the roof, I thought, if he found out he killed the wrong man. Turns out, he jumped off the roof anyway. Come to think of it, if he knew the truth, he would have held off for a while, probably. Long enough to take you with him."

Schulz stared at me soberly. "Actually, that thought occurred to me these last couple of days," he said. "Aw, come on, Abe," he complained abruptly. "What are we arguing about? It's all over. It's too late to do anything for those people. They're all dead. Listen, we're stuck here in this man's army for the next couple of years, right? And if we stick together, maybe . . . maybe we can have some good times, for Chrissakes. You and I . . . I think, you know, we're . . . kind of kindred spirits, in a way. At least we got the same point of view. Even if you're not much fun at an orgy. If we don't get along, who the hell is there? Wormley? Beasely? Besides, don't forget, we got a little money-making venture going for us and . . ."

"Forget the venture. Your friend Bennie was picked up at Checkpoint Charlie today by the German police."

"Oh, no . . ."

"Yes. Actually I suggested they keep a lookout for him."

"You're kidding! What did you do that for? He has your check on him, I told you."

"What for? I decided I didn't want to be in the smuggling business. That's what for. The only reason I went along in the first place was I was interested in finding out about Konigsberg. I thought the smuggling might be a lead in. The check itself was no problem. I told the police chief it was stolen."

"Stolen? A signed check?"

"The signature was an obvious forgery, according to the chief. A series of loops. Your friend did mention my name, apparently, when he was arrested; but he described someone who sounded more like you than like me. Maybe, come to think of it, the police chief didn't believe me entirely, but as it happens, I went out of my way earlier today to help him with another smuggling problem, so I think he feels inclined to go along with my account. And, after all, I did turn Bennie in."

"Shit," commented Schulz petulantly.

"You're lucky. They would have picked him up sooner or later anyway. He was wanted on a morals charge. Nice people you know."

"Thousands. With his connections in Prague alone, we could have made thousands."

Schulz got up and began pacing irritably around the room, muttering about the Goddamn police, the Goddamn U.S. Army, and all the Goddamn people who ran Europe and, for that matter, ran the whole Goddamn world, most of the time getting in his way. "Money," he exclaimed bitterly, although vaguely. "Money and opportunity, but you need a base. 'To them that have is given.' Or something."

"Hey, is that it?" I said. "What happened to Sandra Collins? We were talking about Sandra Collins, remember?"

"Take it easy, will you? If it's one thing I can't stand, it's a nervous psychiatrist."

"You know," I said, "I don't think you exactly appreciate what happened here. Three people dead, four, counting that woman who did the abortion. Each of them had something to live for, I guess. Certainly Konigsberg did. He was *twenty years old,* for God's sake. He was in love. He had a job that was worth doing, for a change. People were depending on him. He was important to them. And Sandra. And Collins himself. Who's going to take care of his kid? Maybe you know somebody who wants to adopt a kid with no arms. None of this would have happened except for you. Doesn't that matter to you at all? Nobody would have died except for you."

"What, are you crazy? I'm a murderer because I screwed somebody, or knocked her up, or what? I'm not the first guy that ever happened to, you know. Oh, I get it. For want of a nail, the shoe was lost, and the battle, and the war. I killed everybody because I forgot to use a condom."

"You bastard. This whole thing was your fault, and I know it."

"Why? Why? What should I have done?"

"You should have done the abortion yourself! You're a surgeon, aren't you? Instead of sending her to somebody who sells buttons!"

"Wait a second. I'm a murderer because I *didn't* perform an illegal abortion. Is that what you're telling me?"

I stared at Schulz, speechless for a moment.

"I don't do abortions," Schulz remarked, carefully selecting two of the marijuana cigarettes. "It's against my religious principles."

"I see. But smuggling heroin is okay."

"Hey, what happened to 'Judge not lest ye be judged,' 'Live and let live' and all that crap? Listen, the army's got strict rules about abortions; and Jungle Jim Collins made his own rules. I wasn't about to stick out my neck that far. And who told her to have an abortion anyway? I wasn't around anymore. It must have been Konigsberg."

"Ohmigod, are you a bullshitter. Konigsberg didn't send her for an abortion. He wanted to marry her pregnant, and would have if Collins hadn't gotten in the way. You were the one. She was afraid . . . the two of you were afraid of what would happen when her father found out. And you were there that day. . . ."

"I suppose you got all this from that kid who thinks he's a detective. . . ."

"You sent her for the abortion. You gave her directions how to get there. Don't bother telling me different. You don't have any moral objections to abortion, you just have objections to getting caught. In fact . . ." I waited a moment while Schulz, who had put away the marijuana in a pocket, calmly lit up his pipe, then stared at me through the plume of smoke. "In fact, you were willing to help a little more directly. Back, I think it was six weeks ago, you made a diagnosis of malaria on a guy whose chief complaint was acne and who was never out of the states before coming to Germany. More unconventional medicine. Randy Biddle dispensed enough of the drug from his store on the Waldheim base to cure three or four people of malaria. When the patient came back the next day, though, you told him he didn't have malaria after all. You retrieved the quinine, which, after all, being a severe cytotoxin, you got to keep locked up safely; and you told the guy to stay away from chocolate. Then, later that week, you gave the quinine to Sandra Collins.

"Quinine is not a reliable abortifacient, you know. When I was an interne, I saw a kid once whose mother had tried to abort with quinine. It didn't work, not entirely, anyway, although it sort of half killed him. He was left severely retarded, and in the bargain had spina bifida and a half-dozen other congenital

anomalies. The child Sandra Collins was carrying—your child—
was deformed, too, by the way—would have been deformed, had
it lived. You must have kept giving her the quinine. It showed
up on postmortem. But by that time, I guess, her pregnancy
was too far advanced to wait any longer. So you sent her to the
button lady. She might have survived even that, except for the
quinine. It makes the bleeding worse, like aspirin. Funny, a poi-
sonous drug like quinine acts just like aspirin in a lot of ways.
It affects hearing, for instance.

"It took me longer to put all this together than it should have;
but I knew quinine was not a readily available drug. Not unless
you're a physician."

"I don't think a positive test for quinine means very much,
Abe," Schulz said. "It's too sensitive. Somebody drinks a little
too much quinine water, and it shows up in the blood. Sandra
might have stopped for a gin and tonic before she disappeared
that day."

"Yeah, I know. There's no evidence against you of anything, as
far as I can see. You made sure of that. That's one thing you're
good at. You don't leave a trail."

Schulz nodded. "And let's face it," he said, getting up and
going to a mirror, "there's no one around who cares anymore,
thank God. The whole thing was a mess from beginning to end."

"A mess? Is that all it was? You know, Bob, there's something
wrong with you. Somewhere inside . . . you got something missing somewhere. You're not qualified to be a doctor. You don't
even sound much like a human being to me."

"Is that right?" Schulz replied, staring coldly at me from the
mirror while he put his jacket on. "Another thing I'm damn good
at, it just happens, is surgery. I hope that counts for something.
As for my qualifications to be a doctor, they're the same as
yours," he said, turning to face me. "I got good marks in college."

For just a moment we studied each other across the length of
the room. Kindred spirits.

"Ah, c'mon," Schulz whined, coming over to punch me in the
shoulder again, but stopping short, "I got a lot of good qualities
you don't even know about. Besides being friendly and charming, and really terrific in bed—which I don't suppose matters to
you very much—I'm polite and even punctual, for the most part.

Except like now, unfortunately, when I'm held up by unforeseen events and philosophical discussions about ethical imperatives and the existential intertwining of all living creatures—which, frankly, isn't one of my strong points. So, old buddy, if you don't mind—even if you do mind—I'm going to take off now. You're welcome to hang around as long as you like. The stash is in the underwear. Help yourself. But lock up when you leave, would you? I don't trust everybody around here."

For a few minutes, maybe longer, I sat in that dimly lit room, alone, unmoving—unable to move. Once again it had begun to rain. I heard the drops falling occasionally against the window in a soft and subtle rhythm beyond my making out. Otherwise there was silence. I felt like a wax figure posed foolishly in some musty tableau. But, after a time, I wrenched myself free.

I went over to Schulz's desk and extracted from a cubbyhole a sheet of stationery and an envelope. Also I found again the photograph of Schulz and his fiancée, lying by coincidence alongside an unopened letter she had mailed to him, according to the postmark, three weeks before. She was a pretty girl, although a little chubby and bowlegged. No doubt she deserved better than Schulz. I was going to make her unhappy for a while, I realized, but she'd be better off in the long run. I addressed the envelope to the Attorney General of the State of New Mexico. The letter itself, I wrote as follows:

Dear Sir,

I am an army physician stationed currently at the 20th Station Hospital in Nuremberg, Germany. I have just discovered that a colleague, Captain Robert Schulz, is a fugitive from criminal charges in the state of New Mexico. He admits to me readily that he was apprehended in the act of smuggling heroin across the Mexican border. He escaped almost immediately thereafter, but not prior, I understand, to being photographed by the police. I am sending you a recent photograph of Captain Schulz to facilitate his identification.

I write to you now in the interests of justice.

Sincerely,

I marked my name and APO number, taking care to sign legibly.

I took up the photograph and tore it carefully down the middle, enclosing the picture of Schulz into the envelope, along with the letter, and leaving the picture of the girl on the desk, as a memento. Then I sealed the envelope, stamped it, and took it away with me into the rain to mail.

"Live and let live." Sure. "Judge not lest ye be judged." That's right. But like anything else, you could carry that stuff too far.

CHRISTMAS EVE

The snow was coming down in gusts. A cloud of cottony flakes puffed up against my window, melting quickly into a ring of tiny, glistening drops. They sparkled like a diadem for just a moment before blowing away. But except for the swirling snow, there was nothing to see. Somewhere outside my office window, buried in white, were the hospital grounds and beyond, Nuremberg, and farther off in the distance the rest of the world, all of it, for all I knew, snowed under. I was by myself again. For a little while, anyway. Spending Christmas six thousand miles from home might be expected to make anyone feel lonely, I suppose; but the fact is, I used to feel lonely at home. Watching my mother knit interminably and my father stare sullenly into a cut-crystal cocktail glass was not a social occasion, no more so on Christmas Eve than on any other evening. Each year on the holiday I played the piano briefly for a maiden aunt who enjoyed singing "Deck the Halls with Boughs of Holly" off-key, a raucous but spirited sound, but interrupted invariably by the larger sound of my father's snoring, or belching or simply muttering to himself. Another aunt and a cousin played solitaire at separate tables. By the time the clock tolled the day of our Savior's birth —he was Santa Claus, I used to think when I was small—half of our small number had already subsided imperceptibly into sleep. It was a desolate celebration, not the sort I could remember fondly. Yet, looking out now into the timeless snow, I did feel nostalgia of a sort. I saw not so much the ghosts of my own Christmases past, but other shades, all those many people for whom Christmas really did mean something. Out there, enveloped by the same storm that danced before my eyes, there were families and friends who took pleasure in each other's company, who had good cheer and a spirit of good will. And there were even some who stopped this special evening to consider Christ's advice to us, that we live in service to each other.

Included surely among these few was one George George and family, whose number had grown recently by the addition of an armless child. When the baby was orphaned, they took him in temporarily until his mother could be found. Six weeks later she walked in dressed in short pants and a fur coat. Everyone looked at everyone else and concluded promptly that the boy was better off where he was. A formal adoption was now in progress. I was looking forward to visiting them all with Krista later that evening. They were a happy family, always laughing. George George had given up Humphrey Bogart and was doing Mae West impersonations. His father juggled. And the Collins kid, of course, could make Tiny Tim seem like a misanthrope.

If you were German, it was natural to think of Hitler on Christmas Eve rather than Dickens. During each year of his rule he preceded the holiday visit of the *Kristkind* by a radio address to the people. The two were joined together now in the German mind no less than Jesus and Santa were mingled in mine. It was to obliterate this unpleasant association that Krista, who was usually not religious, had gone to church this evening, leaving me alone to stare distractedly out my window.

"It makes you think of the primordial veil, doesn't it?" Wormley asked, coming up unexpectedly behind me.

"What?" I cried out reflexly before I could stop myself. I drew back to a safe distance.

Wormley, I noted, was wearing a maroon sweat suit, complemented by a bandanna and a beret, also maroon, the color of the medical corps. No doubt they were a uniform of some sort. It might have occurred to some unwary person to ask why he was dressed just so on Christmas Eve, but not to me. I had long since made it a rule never to ask Wormley to explain himself. But I had already gone too far.

"The snow," Wormley replied, pointing. "'Tiny lumps of white' was the way Shelley put it, I think, or was it Omar Khayyám? When snow comes down heavy like this, I always think of the amniotic sac. The membrane that surrounds the fetus is like a primordial veil dividing the child from its mother, and, on a symbolic level, life from death, the conscious from the unconscious, and, of course, the whole birth process. Birth has

not been studied, I'm afraid, as it deserves to be. Some lip service is paid to birth trauma, but the bonding, for instance—in
utero and out—and not just with the mother. The father can get
very attached to a child, especially during the years of development. Personally, I think that's why that colonel . . . uh, Collins
jumped off the roof. You invest libido in a child, she grows up
and has an abortion . . . well, that could happen to anyone—
any woman, I mean—no matter how closely supervised. But
then she wants to marry out of the faith. You know, there's a
natural antagonism between in-laws—witness the endless mother-
in-law jokes—but marrying someone of a different faith naturally compounds the problem, particularly, as in this case, when
the person who is Jewish is already engaged to another young
woman who also just . . . happens . . . to be . . . the daughter
of a notorious smuggler and bon vivant. That's enough to depress
anyone. Where are you going?"

"I have to meet someone," I said, seizing the packages I had
been wrapping. There was no ribbon around George George's
chess set, but I thought I had better take it the way it was before I lost control of myself and distributed the pieces all over
Wormley's beret.

"I thought you were on call."

"No. Tomorrow," I replied, exiting my office.

"Then you're coming, I hope, to our little Christmas shindig
upstairs?" Wormley said, falling into step beside me. "It's a
rollicking affair," he added with a wink and a smothered guffaw.
This was likely to mean that someone had won a jackpot on the
slot machine.

"No, thanks."

"No doubt Lieutenant Konigsberg became a spy as a direct result," Wormley declared, possibly continuing his commentary on
the birth process. "Being multilingual does not justify getting involved in power politics any more than having a loaded pistol
entitles you to play around on the roof. I think you did very well
in that connection, by the way."

I chose not to ask in which connection.

"Which brings us back to the Three Wise Men, presaging as
they do, I think, the Arab-Israeli conflict and its ultimate resolution through the Christ child. It's interesting how the number

three is always taken to represent unity—the Christian trinity, for example—whence our tripartite form of government."

"Whence indeed."

"Even physiologically," Wormley went on without pausing for breath. "The three rings of the cochlea, the three valves of the heart. There's a good research study there, I think. The effect of anatomical structure on the way we conceive the world. Perhaps your friend, that surgeon . . . Schulz would like to collaborate."

"He's not my friend, and he's also not here. You remember, they took him away a couple of weeks ago."

"Oh, right," the major replied, scratching his chin thoughtfully. "Something about drugs. Too bad, he was such a young man. Why are you walking so fast?"

I careened around a corner and made it to the side door of the hospital with Wormley not more than a foot behind me. Before I could open it, he bounced off me, off the door then off me again.

"Well, Ed, I don't want to keep you from the party," I said, pushing him away with a finger. "Merry Christmas," I added, smiling with a superhuman effort, meanwhile getting the door open finally. A cold wind blew a flurry of snowflakes into the corridor.

"I'll walk with you a little ways," Wormley said, coming after me. "I want to tell you about a new project I have in mind. Besides, I want to do a half hour or so on The Monkeybars."

"No you don't . . . What? You're going to exercise in this snowstorm? On Christmas Eve?"

"'A fit body in a fitter mind,'" Wormley admonished me with a waggle of his finger, as if I had taken a stand in favor of an unfit body in an unfitter mind.

"Listen, I got to run," I said, beginning literally to run. I tripped a couple of times in the powdery snow, but came to my feet still running. That was the important thing, I told myself, to keep running. I kept on until Wormley's cries were lost in the sough of the wind.

When I looked back a moment later a strange, magical scene was laid out before my eyes. Set off against the speckled sky and lit from behind by the scattered lights of the hospital was The Monkeybars, covered with snow and looking like nothing so much as a Christmas tree, a gigantic Christmas tree, adorning the silent and sparkling night. Hanging from one of the lower branches was a single ornament, a ruby-colored pendant that took particular shape when I peered at it narrowly through the falling snow. It was Wormley, Major Edward Wormley, doing chin-ups.